Praise for *The Bone*

"A fast-paced narrative with historic
of royal intrigue."
—*The Wall Street Journal*

"With equal parts magic and mystery, Mueller weaves together psychological tension and character-driven plots that will keep readers guessing until the very end."
—*Booklist* (starred review)

"Fresh and ambitious . . . It may be an otherworldly, genre-bending fantasy, but *The Bone Orchard* is still intensely human at its heart."
—*BookPage* (starred review)

"The mystery unravels like an interlocking puzzle, with a satisfying ending even the most well-read of the genre will struggle to guess."
—*Publishers Weekly*

"A brilliant, cautionary tale about the dangers of repressing trauma, disguised as a sweeping fantasy about political machinations and magic."
—*Locus*

"A political thriller set in a magical empire, but more than that, it's a compassionate but unflinching look at trauma."
—*GeeklyInc*

"*The Bone Orchard* is reminiscent of a puzzle where pieces need to be slotted together, of a game of chess where the figures start out as pawns and take the shape of the more complex figures as the game goes on and they move across the board. . . . A very satisfying read."
—*Grimdark Magazine*

THE
BONE
ORCHARD

SARA A. MUELLER

TOR PUBLISHING GROUP

NEW YORK

THE BONE ORCHARD

Copyright © 2022 by Sara A. Mueller

A Tor Book
Published by Tom Doherty Associates/Tor Publishing Group
120 Broadway
New York, NY 10271

www.tor-forge.com

Tor® is a registered trademark of Macmillan Publishing Group, LLC.

The Library of Congress has cataloged the hardcover edition as follows:

Names: Mueller, Sara A., author.
Title: The bone orchard / Sara A. Mueller.
Description: First edition. | New York : Tom Doherty Associates, 2022. |
Identifiers: LCCN 2021059127 (print) | LCCN 2021059128 (ebook) |
ISBN 9781250776945 (hardcover) | ISBN 9781250776952 (ebook)
Subjects: LCGFT: Fantasy fiction. | Novels.
Classification: LCC PS3613.U3756 B66 2022 (print) |
LCC PS3613.U3756 (ebook) | DDC 813/.6—dc23
LC record available at https://lccn.loc.gov/2021059127
LC ebook record available at https://lccn.loc.gov/2021059128

ISBN 978-1-250-77696-9 (trade paperback)

Our books may be purchased in bulk for promotional,
educational, or business use. Please contact your local bookseller
or the Macmillan Corporate and Premium Sales Department
at 1-800-221-7945, extension 5442, or by email at
MacmillanSpecialMarkets@macmillan.com.

First Tor Paperback Edition: 2023

Printed in the United States of America

0 9 8 7 6 5 4 3 2 1

For James and Karl

THE
BONE
ORCHARD

CHAPTER ONE

The night breeze off the sea riffled through the bone orchard, playing softly in the ghastly white fruits, making the solid ones clatter while the long bones chimed and fluted. The trees were as foreign to Borenguard as their owner, Charm. She sat in the solarium with the windows open to the mellow night, going over her books. A soothing rhythm of touch, tally, and check, set to the uneven music of her bones.

During the long interim between empresses four and five, the Emperor of Boren had brought Charm to the capital, implanted a mindlock to enforce obedience, and established her in Orchard House. A triumphant prize, his people believed, from across the sea, taken in the Rebellion of Inshil. People of taste and rank forgot such a trifling detail as Inshil's former independence.

Charm, a creature of neither taste nor rank, had not forgotten. She wore no colors save black, yet she colored her hair every tasteless shade available. There seemed little reason beyond amusement for the Emperor to put up with his conquest's futile rebellions of color and her turning Orchard House into a gentleman's club. There seemed even less reason for his continued interest in private Tuesdays at Orchard House, since Mistress Charm was fully a foot too short and her curves far too pronounced for Borenguard's ideal of beauty. What talents might have sustained the Emperor's notoriously fickle fascination was cause for speculation over card tables and cigars in Borenguard—not excepting those at Orchard House itself, as long as its proprietress was not in the room.

In a city of gray and damp, Charm was a scintillating, illicit legend.

Now, she toyed with a spiral of today's brilliant pink hair and rubbed her fingers over the crystal casing of the mindlock in her right temple.

A boneghost with skin like milk glass and eyes the color of blood slipped into the solarium. Assembled from the bones in the orchard, their soft parts grown in a vat, boneghosts did not age. This one had looked eighteen since she'd risen from the growth vat in the greenhouse. If not for her coloring, she would have been the perfect image of Charm herself. Because the boneghosts had skulls identical to Charm's, they all more or less shared her face.

"Yes, Pain?"

The boneghost laid her colorless cheek down on the gathered black satin of Charm's skirt. "Prince Phelan is here, Mistress."

Charm's pen stopped, hovered in the air above the next column. Too soon. Justice wasn't out of the growth vat yet. He was here too soon, but a son of the Emperor couldn't be refused. It wasn't anything in her mindlock that insisted. This was simply reality. One did not say no to princes if one could possibly help it. One particularly did not say no to Prince Phelan. Charm laid her pen in the carved rest at the top of her writing stand, smoothing her hands down the flawless fit of her black, burlesquely ornate evening gown.

Charm tried to cling to the positive. As long as Phelan remained obsessed with Justice, he wasn't seeing some other child. Justice wasn't awake tonight, but he didn't know that yet. Charm knew, and others must have suspected, that a puckered scar on Phelan's temple marked the Emperor's first attempt at mindlock surgery. The surgery had been a resounding failure. All that remained of Phelan's psychic abilites were fits of uncontrolled rage as famous as his other proclivities. That he lived had been a tragedy second only to the ongoing survival of his eldest brother, Prince Aerleas.

"The lock on his usual room?" It was the only room on the second floor that could not be locked from the inside.

"It works, Mistress."

"Then we'll hope we have no need to depend on it. Send him to the second floor. Send him Shame and complimentary supper as my gift to him for his inconvenience."

"He'll want Justice," Pain said softly.

"Then he shouldn't have scalded her last time. According to the Lady's schedule, she needs another week in the growth vat."

"Yes, Mistress." Pain rose and vanished back toward the public front of the house.

Charm picked up her pen, breathed, and went back to her ledger.

Touch. Tally. Check.

From Uptown, the cathedral bells struck twice and went silent. Orchard House closed its doors to incoming customers at two. In the solarium, Charm breathed in the serenity of the bells and the bones. The night was nearly done. The only traffic in the entry now would be customers going home. She sealed her last note, gathered her correspondence, and stopped in sheer surprise.

A woman stood just outside the gates, examining Orchard House. The Lowtowners who worked at Orchard House or came to ask about work came, naturally, to the back door. This was no Lowtown woman. A deep traveling hat buried her face in blackness as absolute as a grave. The satin of her overskirt gleamed palely. She wore a fur stole and muff against the evening's chill. This was a lady of quality. It was impossible that such a lady would be seen below the Uptown wall, much less at the gates of Orchard House. And yet, she stood just . . . looking.

There was something about the stillness of the woman that raised the hair on the back of Charm's neck. Even as she rose to go investigate, the noblewoman turned away and foggy dark swallowed her. A chill traced Charm's arms. She rubbed them briefly. One of her customers would have a bad night when he got home, probably, and that was neither her problem nor her business. She took her letters to the front hall.

Pride, enthroned at the reception desk, stabilized the house. Charm wasn't sure when she'd become aware of Pride, but was reasonably sure that Pain, Justice, Desire, Pride, and lastly Shame had been the chronological order of the ghosts. Even now that all of them had bodies separate from hers, she found Pride's serene blindness a comfort.

Upright, lovely, with ashen hair and blue eyes that saw nothing, Pride's sightless, judging stare reminded each gentleman of how they were to behave when they went upstairs. To break with gentlemanly behavior, even with the outward trappings of rank discarded, was to be barred from the second floor and to risk being unwelcome altogether. To be unwelcome at Orchard House was to lose the political talk of the cardroom, the impeccable dining, and the prestige of being here in the evenings. The only men immune to those rules were the sons of the Emperor. Prince Phelan was still upstairs. Perhaps they would escape his visitation unscathed.

"Tired yet, Pride?" asked Charm, with a smile that Pride could never see.

"Not particularly . . ."

Pain ran down the stairs. Charm's heart ached in that moment of silence.

"Shame is hurt," said Pain softly.

Charm's breath punched out of her. She snatched up her skirts and bolted up the stairs to the second floor as a door along the hallway slammed. Prince Phelan's cursing and the sound of shattering glass met her halfway up. Even Orchard House's thick walls and doors couldn't muffle the sound of his bellows from this close range.

Shame slid down the outside of Prince Phelan's door, weeping, with the safety key in her hand. Her mousy hair had tumbled out of its pins and one hand held her bleeding face. Her cream-colored dress was stained down the front with cocoa, and down the left side with blood. Something smashed into the closed door and made it shudder, but the stout oak held.

"Oh, Shame . . . Shhh, it's going to be all right. I'm here. I've got you." Charm tried to be comforting for Shame even as she seethed inside. "Hush now, we'll fix it. Let's get you out to the laboratory and see how bad it is." Charm slipped an arm around the boneghost's waist, helping her to her feet and down the back stair.

Four Firedrinkers, Borenguard's elite psychic constabulary, came in the kitchen door as Charm and Shame reached the safety of the bottom landing. Of course. Pain had been in a second-floor room with a Firedrinker. Their comrade heard Prince Phelan's fit, so all of them knew. Borenguard's theory was that the Firedrinkers had enough telepaths in their ranks that they were all linked all the time, but the only person likely to truly know was Pain; and Pain could not be forced to speak. Body armor under their scarlet coats, and helmets with mirrored visors, concealed their identities. Only one wore any distinguishing insignia. Charm was grateful to see Captain Oram's white sash, and hoped it was truly the captain.

Captain Oram's gift was a rare and exalted one. He was a telepath of immense power. He could suppress Prince Phelan's rage and take His Highness to Fortress Isle until the princely fit passed. "Mistress," Captain Oram said. His voice through his helmet visor was identical to every other Firedrinker's, but given his name and height he certainly seemed male. He inclined his head politely. "We'll bring Prince Phelan out this way and through the back gate. It will be quieter."

The words were like stabs. "Of course, Captain. We wouldn't want a fuss." Charm all but snarled it, though they were as helpless in this as Charm. Pain, the only one outside of their barracks allowed to see them without their uniforms, had confirmed that every concealing Firedrinker helmet hid a mindlock similar to Charm's own, and that they had standing orders far more stringent than Charm's.

One of the newer kitchen girls, possibly her name was Sally, darted forward with a towel from the stack of clean ones by the sink. The other two just huddled and watched with wide eyes. Charm nodded thanks to Sally and helped Shame press it against her slashed face. She kept her arm around Shame across the little kitchen garden and through the orchard. The bones showed stark white where the moonlight touched them, clattered and clicked to themselves. The long brick building past the uneven trees had been a hothouse, once. It didn't grow orchids anymore. Now, it sheltered far more tender specimens.

Charm unlocked the Lady's laboratory, stepped inside, and closed the door. She let herself fall back inside her own mind so that the other woman in her head could wake up into the body they shared.

The Lady blinked and leaned on Shame for a moment. The familiar sight of her laboratory steadied her.

Carefully tended coal stoves kept the building a constant

temperature and provided a dim orange glow, just enough light to guide them down the half flight of stairs. Growth tanks of glass and steel were ranged neatly along the back wall. The largest tank held a horse skeleton in the middle stages of growing muscles and organs. A creature so large took a long time to grow. The smallest tanks were hardly larger than gallon jars. Lifeless songbirds floated in two of them. They were further along than the horse, feathers just beginning to come in through new skin. The casket-shaped growth tank for her human boneghosts was a little separate from the others, covered with thick black canvas with chains and pulleys hanging over it. Shelves took up part of the other wall, with neatly labeled baskets of bones and trays of surgical equipment. A large table near the shelves was arrayed with beakers, tubes, vials, and catch basins. Storage crocks stood beneath in an orderly row. In the center of the room was a long, marble coroner's slab.

It was dark outside, the Lady noted. She wondered briefly what time it was, but she knew better than to question her surroundings too closely. It would only make her black out again. One glance at Shame told her why she was awake. It had taken her years to learn to make them, the vessels for the other people in her mind. "Don't worry, sweetheart, I'll fix you."

The Lady helped her injured ghost to a stool. She tied on a full-sleeved rubberized apron, collected clean clothes and a bottle of antiseptic, then peeled the gory towel away from the boneghost's face. Shame gripped the edge of the table as the Lady wiped away the blood. The slash ran from just ahead of Shame's ear to her nose, laying open the length of her cheekbone. Her cheek drooped, showing the white flash of bone and the upper edges of her teeth.

"My fault," Shame slurred. The left half of her mouth did not work properly.

The Lady slid her fingers over the upper edge of the wound. A knife. The image of it, slipping through Shame's face, flashed from her fingertips to her brain. The Lady blinked at tears of futile anger. The knife wouldn't have done more than make a shallow cut on Justice or Desire, easily dealt with by a bit of empathy fluid reduced to gel. It would have left barely a scratch on Pain. Shame, not as resilient as her comrades, didn't cling to the vat-grown body enough to give it resilience.

Behind the Lady, in their shared skull, Charm watched. There was nothing she could do except bill Phelan for the time Shame would be incapacitated. Ask him to pay for the damages as she might ask him to pay for a broken cup. He might pay. Usually he did not.

The Lady wished she could stop these things happening. She didn't like her ghosts to be hurt, but neither did she want them back. They were, and should be, separate from her. "This wound is too deep to repair without some help. But we'll pop you into the tank and everything will be fine," the Lady told Shame. "I'm sorry this had to happen to you."

Charm hovered, ready to draw the Lady aside if Shame faltered.

Shame didn't hesitate. "You're not to blame, Lady."

The Lady nodded, wordless. Naturally it was not her fault, but it was kind of Shame to remind her. She got a bottle of solution, washed the wound, then retrieved her suture kit and carefully stitched Shame's cheek closed. "Let me check how Justice is doing, and once we get her out, we'll get you in." She pulled the cover from the human growth tank.

Lavender empathy fluid supported the body of Justice. Eternally fourteen, she floated above the support rack, too lightweight to sink. The Lady had put her here just a week ago. The Lady removed the glass lid on the tank, breathing in the metallic, faintly salty scent of bodies and birth that came from the empathy fluid. She examined Justice's thighs critically, and found the skin smooth and pink. The scalds had healed almost completely. The Lady lowered the chains, hooked them to the corners of the rack, and winched Justice up out of the tank. The little body sagged against the rack as it came free of the supporting gelatinous fluid. The Lady let the majority of empathy fluid on her drip back into the tank, then swung the rack over the dissection table, and lowered it gently down.

She tipped Justice out of the rack onto her side, making sure Justice's head with her sodden braid hung over the edge. Thick, syrupy fluid strung down from Justice's nose and mouth, draining into a pail on the floor.

"The fluid in the tank is still usable," noted the Lady. "That's fortunate." Empathy fluid was the second-rarest substance in the world, second only to the Rejuv that kept the Imperial family and their chosen few eternally frozen in age. It wouldn't do to waste it. She got the rack back over the tank, fetched warmed blankets from their chimney cupboard to wrap Justice's body and warm her up. The Lady prepped an injection from a blue glass bottle and slid it into the dead boneghost's carotid artery. She suctioned a little more fluid out of Justice's airways while the body's temperature came up. When Justice was warm, she started resuscitation. Chest compressions and then breathing into the little body.

The Lady ejected the part of her that was Justice into the body, struggling for a moment to get the clinging ghost out of their mind. *She isn't me. Her experiences are no part of me. I'm the daughter of the Chancellor, not this girl who has to sit sorting people all day.*

Justice jerked, coughed, and dragged in a breath.

The Lady rolled her onto her side again, rubbing her back soothingly. "There now. I'd have liked to give you more time, but this will do."

Justice looked around the lab, wobbly as a new-hatched chick. She curled up, clutching the blankets, and squeezed her eyes closed. Tears slid across the bridge of her nose.

"Just lie still for a moment. I must get Shame into the tank," the Lady soothed her.

Justice craned her head to see Shame sitting, bloody and disheveled. She shivered and curled tighter.

While Shame undressed herself, the Lady prepared a syringe of oubain and an ether mask. She cranked the support rack over the human tank down so the rack was mostly submerged, but with the head end still clear of the fluid.

Shame's distinction was obvious, once she was nude. From throat to feet she was covered with a swirling birthmark the color of Blood Field wine. She stepped into the tank, lying back against the padded steel bands. The Lady put the ether mask over her mouth and nose and carefully dripped in the ether. Shame's eyelids sagged.

The Lady kissed Shame's forehead gently. "Sleep well," she told her ghost. The Lady took a firm grip on the syringe, but lowered the needle again. Shame slept, her face at peace. It was always hard to make the final strike. It would let the ghost back into her mind, even though the Lady didn't have to see or interact with her.

All animals strove to live, but Shame never had. Perhaps more had gone wrong with Shame than her skin. Shame needed to be kept alive just as much as the Lady's other creations, and with Justice back in the tank so frequently these days, it would take far too long to grow Shame an entirely new body. It would be bad enough to know Shame was with her for this little time. To have her that much longer, and risk reabsorbing Justice as well . . . The Lady steeled herself with the thought. Shame must die instantly if the body was to be salvaged.

The Lady stabbed the needle between Shame's ribs and into her heart. The boneghost arched up for one moment, then collapsed as the Lady pressed the oubain into her heart. Lights danced across the Lady's vision and the world whirled unsteadily as her own heart stuttered in sympathy.

In the confinement of their shared skull, Charm drew Shame's battered consciousness back behind the barriers that preserved the Lady's innocence. She cradled Shame close.

The Lady's dizziness passed. It always made her queasy to kill or animate a boneghost. Animals never troubled her. Only her ghosts were so difficult. She pulled the needle free of Shame's chest. The Lady smoothed the mouse-colored hair gently. "Poor thing, you just don't have enough strength," she murmured.

She lowered the body the rest of the way into the empathy fluid, then pushed the lid onto the tank and covered it with its black cloth so that light wouldn't discolor the healing wound.

Justice got herself up to sitting, and after a moment more got to her feet. The Lady smiled. Justice was so strong. The Lady was always glad she'd made this ghost a body, even if the bones had been too small for an adult, and, because the bones grew separately on a tree instead of naturally in a body, one femur was slightly longer than the other. "How are you?" the Lady asked.

Charm watched through the Lady's eyes. Justice sniffled, getting control, and Charm hated herself viciously for doing this to Justice. Of all of them, Justice. She should've thought of a way to refuse Phelan. Now Justice was going to have to deal with him again. The Firedrinkers would let Phelan out as soon as his immediate rage had passed, and everyone would go on pretending just as they always had.

"I'm f-fine, Lady. Just cold," Justice assured her.

"Put your feet into Shame's shoes, then, and hurry to get a bath to warm yourself up," instructed the Lady. "Not too hot, your thighs will still be tender."

"Yes, Lady." Justice helped herself along the table to where her cane leaned by the stair. She left the shoes, let herself out, and limped away into the dark.

The Lady sat with her hands folded serenely together in her lap, listening to the bones in the orchard as they chimed and clattered in the breeze. At first it had seemed as if with more boneghosts she had fewer blackouts, but she wasn't sure anymore. In Inshil, she had been awake almost all the time. She had never been conscious much in Borenguard, though she had this garden behind a great house, and her trees, and this laboratory where some kind person got her everything she could leave notes about. The world beyond this sanctuary was dangerous. The Lady rose, went to the shelf of baskets, reminding herself what bones were still needed for each partial skeleton, then picked up a pair of secateurs. She was awake, and her immediate duty was done; she would tend the bone trees, and collect any bones that were ready. Invisible and undetected, Charm stalked in the back of the Lady's mind. She wrestled with useless anger, and kept Shame safe.

CHAPTER TWO

Orchard House was closed on Tuesdays. Only one customer was permitted to enter. Come siege, storm, or strife, the Emperor called at Orchard House on Tuesdays. Sometimes, like today, he was late; but in the five decades of Charm's life here he had never before failed to call by noon. Normally, she would have attended to the various tasks of Orchard House while she waited. Checked the pantry, reviewed the menus, ordered supplies for the cook and the second floor. Today she could not make herself focus on these trivialities. Today, Charm paced the parlors and halls in restless, rustling black silk, endless circles punctuated by attempts to settle. Phelan must be dealt with. The Emperor must do something about his sons besides pay the bills for their damages. She glanced at the clock. Five minutes after two.

"Mistress, there are two Firedrinkers at the reception desk."

Pain's voice made Charm jump. She turned on the pallid boneghost in a near snap. "Orchard House is closed on Tuesday." She should not have to remind anyone.

"Forgive me, Mistress, but they say that they have a message from the Empress."

Charm paused. This had never happened before. It clashed, discordant, with the fact that today was Tuesday. "Thank you, Pain."

Charm stood and pressed her hands against the comforting armor of her corset, inhaled, let the breath all out. Calm. She did not run. Ladies of position did not run. It pleased her for poise to counterbalance her hair and her clothes. To ape her betters. The murmur of her skirts was loud in the silent hall.

Two Firedrinkers stood at parade rest before the reception desk, crisp in their bright red coats. Their calling outside business hours heralded nothing good; much less with a message from the Empress.

Pride was absent from her post at the grand curve of the reception desk, enjoying a day spent in her attic private bed with her knitting.

"Good morning." Charm greeted the Firedrinkers with a professional smile.

The Firedrinker on the left stepped forward and held out a slim letter. A crystal carved with the imperial seal sparkled, set into the wax.

"Mistress, for your hand from the Empress." The Firedrinker's voice was distorted into androgynous middle tones by his, or her, helm.

Charm took the letter carefully. The seal was identical to the one in the Emperor's ring. The sight of it made Charm's mindlock tick and whir. Inside were two scant lines in a fine hand.

> *Mistress Charm, these guards will bring you to me. Please come at once. It is important.*
>
> *Ylsbeth, Empress of Boren*

Empresses of Boren came and went at irregular intervals. Had the Emperor tired of Ylsbeth? The first empress, Aerleas and Luther's mother, had died in childbirth. Prince Phelan's mother, the second empress, had been beheaded and set a standard after which Prince Strephon's mother had taken her divorce settlement and retired to a quiet life of disgrace in the country. The fourth empress had died in childbirth. The one who'd come in just after Charm arrived had no child and had been divorced and sent back to her native country after objecting loudly and publicly about the Imperial Tuesdays. The current empress, Ylsbeth, had lasted a shade over six years. She was by far the quietest of the Emperor's choices. The girl rarely said a complete sentence in public.

From the moment the Emperor had woken Charm in Orchard House, she had never left the grounds. Orchard House was her world. What could possibly motivate this little wisp of an empress to send for her husband's mistress after six years of tactfully ignoring the situation? No wife, not one, had ever sent for Charm. Charm fingered one pink curl where it fell over her shoulder.

"I . . . can't go to the palace with pink hair," Charm hedged. "It's entirely inappropriate. Surely the palace calls for royal blue."

The Firedrinker on the right shifted uncomfortably inside their bloodred uniform. "I'm sorry, Mistress, but you will come to the palace."

"Ah. I see." Firedrinkers had their own compulsions and Charm wouldn't make their mindlocks punish them for failing in their duty.

Pain brought her a wrap, gloves, and a little tasseled bag. Charm had no wraps, no gloves, no bags. Pain's things fit, of course, and would serve. Charm gave the Empress's note to Pain, shrugged the wrap around her shoulders, and busied her hands putting on the gloves. She couldn't recall the last time she'd worn gloves, if she ever had. The gentlemen who came to Orchard House had never noticed the scars on her palms, or if they had they had politely kept it to themselves. "Pain, if the Emperor comes, please give him the Empress's message. He will understand." It was, after all, Tuesday.

The Firedrinker helms turned toward one another.

A chill ran icy fingers up Charm's spine.

The carriage waiting in the front garden was an unextraordinary vehicle, with no insignia on the door and heavy curtains over the windows. The horses were mismatched, one chestnut and one bay. Not an Imperial carriage. An anonymous visit. She was to be smuggled in. The Firedrinkers held the door and handed her up into the carriage. Charm settled onto the tucked velvet seat. The horses started with a jerk. She had no desire to open the curtains. The confined interior seemed safer than the broad uncertainty of the city. Her fingers bit into the soft cushion. What did Ylsbeth want? Where was the Emperor?

She must not huddle. Charm sat up, away from the back of the seat. She turned up the lamp in the carriage compartment and searched in Pain's bag until she found the gold compact of powder that Pain used to give her pallid complexion some semblance of normalcy. Charm checked her face, dusted powder over the freckles that had started to show on her nose. Charm herself did not have freckles. The Lady had freckles. She shook off the thought. The Lady was safely concealed, and thinking about her would only complicate things.

Charm examined her brilliant hair with a critical eye. It wouldn't do to arrive mussed. Whatever happened in the world, a woman should face it well groomed. Besides, the situation might not be as bad as all that. Empress Ylsbeth would turn twenty-eight in a few months' time. Maybe the poor girl wanted some advice. It seemed reasonable that sooner or later one of the Emperor's wives would have more brains than an inkpot.

⁓

A grim chamberlain showed Charm from a back door through silent servants' passages and into a warm purple and gold sitting room. The Emperor's wife had pale hair and paler skin untouched by cosmetics. She was so thin she looked fragile inside elegantly restrained jewels and heavy brocade. A harsh contrast to Charm's buxom self. A single Firedrinker stood at parade rest by a gilded connecting door emblazoned with the Imperial crown, the firelight flickering in reflection on his featureless helmet. His white sash stood out against his scarlet coat, the only thing in the room more pale than the Empress—Captain Oram. Something was dangerously wrong. Charm wanted to bolt to the carriage and fling herself back into the safety of Orchard House. She held on to her courage. She would not run like a startled partridge, flapping through the halls.

The Empress put on a faint, brave smile. "Thank you for coming, Mistress Charm" was all she said. She gestured for Charm to follow and opened the connecting door, then slipped inside with Charm trailing obediently after her.

The great man in the silk-draped bed lay unmoving. Only the rasping rise and fall of his chest betrayed that he was still alive. Perfumes and incense couldn't cover the sour smell of his dying. Charm looked down on the Emperor of Boren in shock and pressed a shaking hand over her mouth. She'd never seen him in less than perfect health. Rejuvenation drugs kept his age at a robust fifty-two, just as they kept Charm eternally young.

Watching him struggle to breathe jolted Charm's world. "How long has he been like this?"

"Since this morning. The doctors have done all they could."
Ylsbeth looked to Charm for a long moment. "It was not right
that he leave us without you, of all people, being able to say
good-bye to him," said the young empress in her soft voice.
"My lord? My lord, I've brought Charm to you."

The Emperor's gray eyes opened. His smile was weak.
"Thank you, my dear."

His wife put her slim hand on Charm's shoulder for a moment, the grip far stronger than Charm would have credited
her for, and went out, closing the door.

"It was cruel to use her to send for me," managed Charm,
her voice hoarse.

"I didn't. She called you on her own." His gravelly basso
was syrupy with phlegm.

Borenguard had never grasped what was between Charm
and the Emperor, and that somehow Ylsbeth had recognized
something more instead of assuming bestial pride of possession shot emotion through Charm's heart. She tried to swallow the lump in her throat with no success. "A greathearted
lady, to send for her husband's mistress."

He managed a tiny nod. "I recall telling you, once, that
you underestimated her. I'm glad she sent for you. I don't have
much time, and there is something I need you to do."

"Anything, Majesty," she answered automatically.

"When I am dead, one of my sons will take the throne.
The one who manages it is most likely the man who has actually killed me, because none of them would risk it unless they
could secure the throne for themselves." The Emperor's smile
was almost admiring. "I'll go to my death wondering how and
which one managed to poison me, but in the end it doesn't
matter which one it is. They're all . . . I believe the phrase you
favor is 'stone bastards, every one.'"

Charm flushed, but he had long ago commanded her never

to lie to him. "Few have more cause to know their true colors than my ghosts, Majesty." Aerleas was psychic, unmindlocked and somehow still alive in spite of his insanity. His madness had savaged her native Inshil for fifty years. Luther had been banished to sea for an affair that nobody remembered but Desire. Phelan was the pedophiliac whose mindlock surgery had been botched. And Strephon was a bitter little coward of a man who wanted whatever anyone else had.

"No matter which one it is, the other three will not bend to him. They will bicker and fight. Some other nation will invade, and the Boren Empire will be swallowed into time." His great square fist clenched on his silken sheets.

"You'd allow the man who murders you to take your throne?"

"I haven't sweated and fought, tortured and lied to see my legacy dissolve when I'm gone. The only way to save Boren is to remove my sons from the succession and give the crown to someone deserving. You are a woman and unlikely to be suspected, and you're loyal. You have no other choice, I know, but you will choose a new emperor with care."

"You entrust me with what? Revolution?" Charm laughed a little at the thought, and the sound soured with a desperation that made her heart race. He was giving this responsibility to her? To her, with the captain of the Firedrinkers outside the door? "Let me call Captain Oram to you."

"Stay here." His voice kept her there, as if her legs had frozen up. "I have no more time. No Rejuv can save me from this, and I had not intended to die. Not ever. Not until there was someone to leave my country to. You have a position that allows you to interact naturally with the nobility, you have sway with the common people, my sons trust you . . . and without my command no one can force you to tell what goes on in your mind." He lifted one massive, trembling hand. The Imperial seal flashed upon it as he stroked the flat casing in her temple. "I'm sorry it took this to protect you from the world outside your pretty prison."

"At the time I didn't realize what you meant by it." Inshil's walled gardens, its "pretty prison," had been the Lady's, but the Emperor didn't know that. It was her one secret from him, safe because he'd never imagined he needed to ask the questions that would reveal the Lady. Now her secrets would be safe forever.

The Emperor's chuckle made him gasp for air. He heaved himself onto his side, hacking. Charm leaped to help him, dabbing at his lips with the sheets. The Emperor hawked and spat bloody phlegm onto the intricate silk carpet. "Listen to me. I only have enough effort left for one adjustment. It can't undo all I've done to you, but call it my amends as much as I can make them. No man shall ever bend you to his will without your consent. Nothing my sons say or do to you can force you to betray yourself to them unless you choose of your own free will to do so. They aren't fit to dictate to you. I name traitor any of my sons who would wear my crown, and condemn them to death. Find whomever has killed me, and see they and any of their conspirators die. Past that, I give you your freedom. Do what you will with it." His jaw tensed as he concentrated, and the effort made him struggle, wheezing, for breath.

The mindlock in Charm's temple vibrated as the mechanisms within adjusted too quickly. Her muscles spasmed, taking her to her knees. Deep in Charm's mind, the Lady stirred. Charm clung to the edge of the bed for a few moments until she was sure that the world had stopped rippling. The future stretched out before her, vast, unfettered, terrifying.

The Emperor's face was pale as wax. "Be a good girl, now, go call my wife. You shouldn't be with me when I die."

Blinking back tears, Charm pressed a kiss to the Emperor's damp, burning forehead.

He smiled at her as she stood up. "Good-bye, sweetheart. God forgive me for it, but I do love you."

Charm managed to turn. Managed to leave him. Passing out of the royal bedchamber felt like crossing a chasm. Captain Oram hadn't moved from his post beside the door. The Empress stood looking into the sitting room fire. Charm choked out words in her direction—"He wants you."

There were tears streaking the young empress's face when she turned toward Charm, and her eyes were rimmed with red. Her graceful hands clenched in fists in her heavy skirts. With her husband gone, Ylsbeth would be in the care of one of his sons. Charm held no illusions about their mercy. Her eyes met Charm's.

Creatures of the same cage, thought Charm. Whether it was pity, solidarity, truth, or the mindlock that impelled Charm to speak was a subject that Charm declined to examine. "He always spoke of you with great tenderness, and respect," she managed.

"I have something for you." Ylsbeth gestured to a great jewel case on a side table. "I . . ."

One of the doors opened. A woman in a savagely elegant day gown came in. Ylsbeth fell silent. Pain had once or twice seen the Empress's lady of the wardrobe, and most constant companion, Countess Seabrough. The Countess's middle-aged, haughty beauty was unmistakable. The Countess's lip curled, eyes sharp as obsidian. She whipped forward to stand between Charm and her charge, as if Charm might somehow contaminate the Empress. "How dare you come here, whore? How dare you distress the Empress with your presence!"

Standing in heavy brocade, before a blazing fire, the Empress shivered and then drew herself up. "Do not forget your jewels, Mistress Charm." Head bent, Ylsbeth went in to her husband.

Charm snatched the great jewel case by its handles and bolted as well as her bustled-up skirts allowed. She ran, stumbling along the echoing marble halls.

Pain, Desire, and Justice waited on the steps of Orchard House to help their mistress inside. Charm trembled as if she were palsied. They put her to bed and slid in beside her, holding Charm in their arms as she wept for a man she was going to kill for.

CHAPTER THREE

Pain slipped into the back of the ladies' viewing gallery of the Assembly Hall of Boren. The seats there were packed full of the wives, grown daughters, and sweethearts of assemblymen, all come to see what the future would hold. Pain tucked her tinted spectacles into her pocket. There were only two open seats. On the aisle of the highest row, or in the front row, one in from Countess Seabrough and containing that lady's reticule. An easy choice. Pain sat down in the highest row. The ladies seated in front of her presented a small sea of tasteful hats sloping down to the pierced wooden panels that screened the galleries from the tangle of shouting below.

The death of Charm's emperor in the small hours of Wednesday morning had been publicly put out as death from heart failure. Thanks to Rejuv, the Imperially controlled anti-aging drug, he had reigned for longer than any of his subjects had been alive. For three generations the Emperor had pressed down and down on the Assembly until very few men of intelligence bothered with it. Today there was no possibility of the Emperor in his private screened balcony, and a storm of argument reigned on the floor. The sudden absence of the Emperor's authority made the future unreliable and frightening for more people than Charm. Lord Hanover, the chief assemblyman, hammered his lectern in vain pursuit of decorum. The words Pain could make out most often were "new emperor" and "Firedrinkers."

While the Assembly indulged in a cacophony of uncertainty, a feathered hat in the ladies' viewing gallery tipped to let its owner see who'd just sat down. The motion rippled out and down in the gallery as the ladies examined Pain out of the corners of their eyes and from under the brims of their hats. They added their whispers like a soprano line to the general din.

The lower wards of the city were used to Pain. They saw her every day, coming and going on errands for Mistress Charm. The assemblymen, and every other Uptown man old enough to escape his mother, had seen Pain behind the bar at Orchard House. Uptown ladies had no such familiarity. Pain didn't blame them for staring. People found her lack of coloring worth staring at on first acquaintance, and there was no reason gentlewomen shouldn't share the habit.

Lord Hanover managed, through dint of pounding louder than the assemblymen could shout, to produce a semblance of order. "Mr. Anders, you have the floor if you please," he called, choosing the only assemblyman who sat with his walking stick raised, patiently waiting for recognition.

Philip Anders, notoriously not the brightest man in Borenguard, rose. "Dem me, gentlemen, I don't see what you're making such commotion about. Not as if we have to sit on our hands and let come what may, is it? Ain't we the ones supposed to decide on matters that Imperial law don't cover? This ain't a matter of foreign policy, and the Emperor didn't leave any instructions about an heir. Seems to me I recall my history well enough to remember that the Emperor was originally appointed by the Assembly. Don't see at all why we can't appoint the next one." His faddish language and puzzled indignation struck the hall into silence for two of Pain's heartbeats.

A walking stick stabbed up, and Lord Hanover took advantage of the general startlement. "Count Seabrough."

Count Seabrough was in his late forties, with ginger hair going gray. His wife was the Empress's lady of the wardrobe. Pain knew Seabrough's habits well. He came to Orchard House almost every evening to dine and play cards. On occasion he visited the second floor with Pride, who reported him a thoughtful, unselfish companion. Rare praise from Pride. His voice, when he spoke, carried well without any heat to it. "Gentlemen, it's true that we have the legal right to choose a monarch. Given the other countries who look to Boren and our provinces with such avarice, I submit to you that we must have an emperor. The question is who? Prince Aerleas, without whom our territorial holdings on the continent would collapse? That is what all the shouting is about, isn't it?"

Pain feigned a small cough to hide her sour smile behind her glove. Seabrough's comment was tactful in avoiding their true worry—that Aerleas the Butcher and his insane army would come home to roost. Fear of Aerleas lay like a mist over them all. He hadn't been back to Boren since the invasion of Inshil that had broken his unprotected psychic mind. He'd succeeded in seizing the mindlock technology the Emperor had gone to war for, but only after he'd been too far gone to benefit from it himself. That Aerleas hadn't succumbed to something and died was a national tragedy and an international horror.

Lord Wilcox put up his hand and didn't wait on Lord Hanover's permission to interrupt. "Prince Aerleas will come and take the crown by force," he cried. "He'll warp our minds until we're slaves to his whims!"

"Out. Of. Order!" Lord Hanover hammered his lectern. "You will abide by the rules of order!"

Seabrough nodded thanks to Lord Hanover. "Though out

of order, it is a sensible concern. I remind you all that even Prince Aerleas and his army, should they attempt to return to Borenguard without orders to do so, may be brought to heel by the Firedrinkers. The Fire Drinkers." He emphasized the two words as if to make sure his fellows understood the implications. "They can enforce the peace. Even Prince Aerleas's passions may be suppressed should that be necessary. He is also a bastard by birth, and his father chose not to legitimize him even while he married the Prince's mother. He is, for those reasons and the obvious one of insanity, not fit. Thus, whatever we do, we must inspire Prince Aerleas to remain at his post in Inshil until the inevitable end of his life." Count Seabrough left aside that, thus far, Aerleas had outlived the average psychic by decades. Given his direct access to the Rejuv facility in Inshil, and if his powers did not kill him, Aerleas might well live forever. Seabrough went on, "Shall we have the second son, then? Prince Luther the Traitor?"

"The Emperor commuted the punishment for Luther's treason in the Inshil rebellion," said a voice from the crowd of assemblymen. "And that's old history."

"Out of order," judged Lord Hanover, rapping his lectern. "So help me, gentlemen, I will have the next outburst rewarded with removal from the hall."

Seabrough shook his head, smiling as if in pity. "Shall we see if we can make Luther's reign stick with the Firedrinkers? Armed psychics, who are sworn and required by their mindlocks to uphold the law? Shall we tempt their oaths by appointing a man treasonous to the Empire to rule us and them? You think they will not uphold their orders? Prince Luther was judged guilty and removed from the succession. The Emperor saw fit to return Luther to his duties, but did not pardon him. A father's tenderness toward his son is all well and good," said Seabrough rhetorically, "but shall we tempt the Firedrinkers to begin skating around the controls and commands that guard their sanity? Or perhaps you'd like to choose from amongst ourselves, who have no authority over the Firedrinkers at all."

The assemblymen murmured to one another, and many looked ill. The ladies echoed them. Several looked openly at Pain and whispered behind their fans. Pain was the only one who had ever seen the face of a Firedrinker. Save for the Firedrinkers themselves, no one knew them better than Pain.

A new lady entered the viewing gallery and glided down the aisle to take the last open seat. The new lady, either innocent of who the Countess was, or devoid of any social survival instinct, said in exquisitely cultured accents, "May I sit?" without indicating either seat.

The Countess looked up as if to make a tart remark, and went deathly pale. Wordlessly, she moved her bag and shifted over so the newcomer could sit down.

Pain examined the newcomer more closely. Her gunmetal-gray satin was adorned at the wrists and throat with thick falls of costly scarlet lace that made Pain think of blood froth. Her confectionery hat perched on a massive knot of pale golden hair—silvery gold, the kind of color women wished came out of bottles and didn't. That astonishingly glorious hair was the stranger's only true beauty. Her mouth was a little too wide and her lips too thin, her features too sharp; as if her face was made all of blades. She gave the viewing ladies a momentary new target for their whispers, and her indifference was both splendid and dangerous. Her stillness was complete. As if she did not feel such triviality as the heat. As if she didn't need to breathe the stuffy air. The precision of her was like a stiletto. If she had been a noblewoman of Borenguard, surely Pain would have heard of her in the cardroom at Orchard House; but Pain could not place her.

Down on the floor, Seabrough pressed his advantage and the fear of the Firedrinkers, drawing Pain's attention back. "Even if it were safe, does that do a kindness to the men and women who make up that force? Do we condemn them to the slow madness and agonies that psychics in other countries suffer? Shall we shut them up behind stone walls and iron doors where we can't hear the screaming? Or risk them running mad in the streets? And what do you think the common people, whose children make up the vast majority of that force, would do should we so callously cast the Firedrinkers adrift?"

The lords muttered as they worked through the implications of armed psychics going mad. Pain's lips pressed together even as she admired Count Seabrough's tactic. If the Firedrinkers hadn't gone mad with the death of the Emperor, then they wouldn't do so; but Seabrough was appealing to fear, not logic.

Anders's walking stick went up again. "That leaves only Prince Phelan and Prince Strephon."

All of Boren knew Prince Phelan's disposition, even if no one in society spoke of it openly. His rages they might have overlooked, but Seabrough had just cited insanity as a barring concern as if it were true, and no one seemed to mind. The nobility's resolute blindness about their own behaviors behind closed doors had limits Phelan pressed too often. Beaten wives hid their bruises, and whores' bruises didn't matter. Women, men, gambling, and animals the nobility passed politely by without comment. Anything done out of country could be written off as vicious rumor. A predilection for children, made so clear by his perennial choice of Justice as a companion, was a sticking point that even they could not abide.

A new walking stick went up and was recognized by Lord Hanover. "Lord Fergus."

Lord Fergus, a genial and welcome presence in the cardroom, for all he came only a night or two a week, was blessed with an extravagant dark mustache that seemed to try to make up for his entirely bald pate. "Prince Strephon is too inexperienced in matters of government to be qualified." Fergus's bluntness made several men around him wince.

Sir Lyle raised his walking stick and was recognized. Another of the frequent cardplayers at Orchard House. He had good luck and astute judgment of when to stand, when to bid, and when fold his hand. "Prince Strephon might need a great deal of advice, certainly," he said slowly.

Pain mentally applauded Lyle's play. She also doubted the Assembly would be saddened if Strephon could be made reliant on them.

"No matter our choice, gentlemen, if we hope to retain our authority for future Assemblies, we must make our decision quickly and as a single body," Seabrough said.

"Prince Strephon has repeatedly demonstrated an appalling lack of financial restraint in his private life," argued Fergus. "Gentlemen, think what he'll do with the national finances in his hands."

"Have we a better choice at hand?" asked Seabrough. "We must have a member of the Imperial family to assure the safety of the Empire."

A sigh of moving cloth in the gallery caught Pain's ear and she glanced to see Countess Seabrough rising from her seat down by the screen. She'd been lady of the wardrobe to the last four empresses. She raised the sharp pleats edging her skirt the necessary one and one-half inches and not a fraction more, showing only the toe of her shoe with its jeweled ornament as she climbed the gallery stairs toward the exit. As she passed Pain, Countess Seabrough peered from beneath the tastefully curled plumes on her hat and let her cool gaze linger on the boneghost.

"Someone should speak to the Firedrinkers about letting whores run loose in respectable parts of town," Countess Seabrough murmured, just loudly enough for it to travel in the stuffy air. She sniffed, chin rising as if she were examining something foul, and passed out of the gallery toward the exit of the Assembly Hall in a grand sweep of indignity.

"How uncalled for," the lady across the aisle from Pain said quietly.

"Easy for you to say, Lyra," her neighbor retorted. "Your husband doesn't spend six nights a week dining, gambling, and . . . whatever else, at Orchard House."

So, this was Lady Lyra Fergus. The much-beloved wife of the kind, decent, mustached Lord Fergus.

"Firstly," said Lady Fergus in the acerbic tone of a woman giving a lesson, "anyone is allowed to observe the Assembly of Boren. No one, be they high or low, may be barred. It is one of our freedoms of government. In addition," the lady went on crisply, "if the dear countess spent any time whatsoever attending to her household, perhaps her husband would have less cause to Dine Out."

A general stirring of fans almost hid the smirking of the other ladies. Only the lady in gray and scarlet did not join the general amusement. She looked, if anything, upon Lady Fergus with a sligh, bitter tip at the corner of her dagger-slash lips. Lady Lyra Fergus fixed her eyes resolutely on the vote being taken on the Assembly floor. Pain followed suit.

"Very well, gentlemen. Our deputation to the palace will inform Prince Strephon of our choice. On Monday, we will celebrate the coronation of Strephon the First, Emperor of Boren," announced Lord Hanover. Neither he nor anyone else on the floor looked pleased.

CHAPTER FOUR

Charm swept into the red parlor in a rustle of ebony satin and amethysts. She didn't delight in the gems as she should have. Empress Ylsbeth had returned her jewel box intact, but the glittering stones held no comfort. She meant to wear the jewels, though, just as she wore her trademark black. The amethysts were not the best of the lot, but they were dark and rich, complementary to her gown. She must seem unaffected. Her emperor had depended on Orchard House going on as usual.

She couldn't bring herself to believe Strephon was clever enough to murder his father so successfully, and while she bore the princes every fiber of ill will in her not-inconsiderable possession, she didn't want to try hatching a plan to kill the wrong one. Which left aside entirely the sticky situation of surviving such a killing. The Firedrinkers were bound, quite literally, to be finicky about the matter. Then there was the matter of the woman Pain had seen at the Assembly. Who was she?

Two princes of Boren were in Orchard House tonight. Prince Luther, freshly returned admiral of Boren's navy, and Prince Phelan back again. Prince Strephon, now heir apparent, had found business at the palace. Charm's only regret was that he hadn't found occupation for his brothers. Regardless of her feelings toward them, however, it was too good an opportunity for information to pass their visit by. The prospect of her single remaining command tantalized. She could be free. Charm had no idea what she'd do with such liberty, but she wanted it with the desperation of a caged wild animal.

"Mistress Charm, you have cost me four hundred Imperial marks," announced Prince Phelan as she came into the red parlor. He sat in an armchair before the fire, a snifter of brandy in his hand. Justice sat at his feet and Prince Phelan stroked her head as if she were a favored dog.

Across from him, Prince Luther was dour and long-faced. Luther had come to Inshil as an ambassador, before the so-called rebellion, and been recalled in disgrace. Neither Charm nor any of her boneghosts had seen him since the day he'd left Inshil. He had not been in Boren for more than a day or two at a time, and his brothers said with scorn that his admiralship was exile. On the rare occasions he docked in Boren, Luther hadn't called at Orchard House. He had never been there before tonight. His hair was still the color of wet sand, as untouched by silver as Phelan's leonine mane. The Emperor had provided even exiled Luther with Rejuv. What was he doing at Orchard House? Would he have killed his father just to come back to Borenguard?

"How have I cost you money, Prince Phelan?" Charm asked, returning Prince Phelan's smile as if he'd never done a wrong thing in his life.

"You're still in black, Mistress!" Phelan chided her jovially.

"I am?" Charm looked down at her skirts, gasped and opened her eyes very wide in mock surprise. "Why, so I am!"

"I bet Luther four hundred Imperial marks that you'd have left off mourning when the old lecher died."

Charm looked down at her own ample, displayed cleavage. "I hardly think this would be appropriate for a funeral, Prince

Phelan," she teased. "Besides, I hadn't anything else that went with lavender hair."

Phelan laughed and stood. "Get yourself a room, Luther. Spend your winnings and live a little now that you can. Mistress, send me supper, and hot chocolate. Come on, girl." Phelan gave Justice his hand, and she limped out on his arm.

One crisis at a time, and of all of us Justice can handle him. He almost never rages twice in a month. The "almost" that honesty compelled her to admit didn't soothe her worries. Charm turned to the other prince. "Is there anything Orchard House can supply for you, Prince Luther?" Luther's only companions, now, were a side table and a teapot.

Luther's narrow face was impassive, but his lips tightened as he looked at her. "Only a little more tea, thank you, Mistress."

Tea wouldn't teach them enough about Luther. Who had he become since Inshil? Was his restraint real or feigned for some benefit? "Of course, Prince Luther; though if there is anything else, it's on the house this evening," offered Charm. "Perhaps a bath, or a massage?" *How respectable are you determined to be?*

For a long moment, Luther was quiet. "There was a boneghost who brought the tea cart," he said finally, "the one with the crippled hands."

Charm didn't let her face show any emotion, but her heart raced. Virtually no one chose Desire before they'd learned her name. Her hands put off most customers. Worse, Desire could easily ruin Charm's plan to get information from the princes. And she might tell Luther far too much. "That particular boneghost is not my most talented creation, Prince Luther. Perhaps you would prefer Pride, or possibly Shame?"

"I am not interested in talent. I am interested in the young lady who brought the tea."

And Charm could not refuse without raising suspicions. Even if Desire had a later appointment, she would be expected to cancel it for a prince. "I'll send Desire to the second floor, second door on the left. Please be so good as to take the green tassel off the doorknob as you go in."

"I've noted a curious trend in your boneghosts, Mistress Charm. Desire cannot hold on to anything, Pain is pale, and Pride is blind. It cannot be a coincidence, surely?" Luther's dark eyes mirrored the depths of a grave.

It is coincidence, you ass, that's not how those things work. She'd buried enough of the Lady's failed experiments, after all. The one with the heart fully outside its body. The one whose skin never developed, so it rotted in the tank. The one that animated but only drooled and died in spite of everything Charm could think of to try to help and that turned out to have only had a brain stem and no real brain. Damn Luther to hell. He was cold enough to plan patricide, calm enough to carry it off, and he would certainly not have dirtied his own hands. Why would he kill his father without assuring himself the throne? Or perhaps he'd thought it was assured and that brat Strephon was another a victim in waiting? Or might he, after years away, simply have underestimated Count Seabrough? "Human boneghosts are all flawed, Your Highness. The process for them is not as perfect as for simpler animals. If you'd like to go up, I'll send Desire to you." She curtsied and went out.

Desire was in the kitchen, preparing a supper tray and hot chocolate to go upstairs. Phelan always ordered hot chocolate, and Mrs. Westmore, the cook, went home at midnight.

"Let that chocolate cool a bit before you take it up, please," requested Charm, "Shame is still in the tank."

"Prince Phelan is particular about his food and drink," said Desire.

"It upset everyone to have to treat Justice for scalded privates. Phelan will have to live with merely warm chocolate," Charm replied.

Desire put the silver chocolate pot on a cart in the dumbwaiter.

"Prince Luther asked for you."

Desire stuttered back a step, her twisted hands going to her mouth to cover her delighted surprise.

Charm positively itched to throttle Luther. "Don't look so pleased. For all we know he's the one who murdered his father. He mustn't know who you are. Say nothing to him, do you understand? He's the one that needs to do the talking."

Desire pleaded. "Charm . . ."

"I won't let you endanger us. We can be free, Desire. This is the only thing left I have to do. Just this one thing. And it isn't as if any of them deserve better than what's coming to them. Say nothing," snapped Charm. "He must've been good at bed sports, so at least it'll be pleasant. Swear you won't tell him a thing, or so help me I'll see you in a vat tonight instead of in your lover's bed."

Desire's mouth trembled, and her eyes went glassy with tears. "I swear," she managed hoarsely.

Ever pathetic, thought Charm, biting back the urge to snarl aloud in frustration. With Shame and Desire in the house, the customers who enjoyed pushing meek women around would always go home happy. At the same time, she berated herself. They couldn't help it. It was what they were meant to be. Sweet. Compliant. Broken. They shielded the Lady.

"I swear, I won't tell him anything," Desire whispered.

Charm refused to meet Desire's eyes. She tested the side

of the chocolate pot. "You can take this up now. Luther is second on the left. Mind you use your mouth for things besides talking."

Desire washed her face quickly, pushed the tea cart into the dumbwaiter, and went up the back stairs all but glowing.

Charm choked against a sob, leaned her elbows on the table, and pressed her forehead against the heels of her hands. It was petty to be jealous, but she was. The lack of her emperor at the center of Boren was a gaping hole in her orderly life, jailer though he had been. She wanted him to talk to, and she hated it. He had been her captor, but also her steadiest company for so long. And now he'd put freedom just tantalizingly out of reach. So close she could scrabble at the edges of it. And he had known she would. Until her fingers bled. How could she possibly bring down the Princes of Boren for his murder? If Charm pulled Strephon from the throne, there were three more princes waiting to take his place. How could she kill four of them? How could she kill even one prince and survive it? Aerleas wasn't even in Borenguard.

Who would rule Boren in place of their current royalty? The nobility were as contentious as the princes. Charm couldn't think of any one man that might be able to hold off the others. The former emperor had made sure that the nobility's best interests lay in supporting the throne. If one man became too prominent, his peers rose against him. The new government had to step in smoothly, or Boren's "allies" would take advantage of the confusion to overthrow their oppressive masters. Seabrough, canny cardplayer that he was, had been right about that.

She'd need allies, and not the kind that Boren had. There were plenty of people in Borenguard who hated the princes as much as Charm did, but even more who'd be happy to pocket Imperial banknotes to betray her. Or to blackmail her with the knowledge of her orders. The trick would be choosing those who would hate with enough passion to be faithful. Were men ever faithful? Charm had no personal proof of it. She rose, checked her reflection briefly in the little mirror by the green baize door, and went on into the public part of the house. She went to survey the gentlemen taking their leisure in the cardroom.

There was Count Seabrough, in his favorite chair, where he could see who was coming and going while he won at cards. He never won much, but nearly always left with just a little more than he laid out. He'd put Strephon on her emperor's throne. For all she knew, he'd been Strephon's hands for the poisoning. He was at the palace nearly every day, and in the Emperor's presence frequently. Lord Fergus was so afflicted with morality that he'd never booked a single appointment upstairs. Not even a bath or a massage. Lyle was ambitious enough, but she'd need to find out if he'd been at the palace the day of the poisoning. Lord Hanover, in addition to having married his wife, was wedded to the status quo. He had no reason Charm knew of to throw Boren to Strephon. Anders . . . bless him. He was possessed of ridiculous good humor and a truly amazing tailor. The only bluff he'd ever be able to keep up was for the length of a hand of cards. She knew their habits and characters better than their wives and sweethearts did. Was there even one among them she could trust?

Among all the familiar faces was a novelty. He stood at one end of the bar, chatting with the faddish Mr. Anders with his exquisitely polished boot up on the footrest. He wore the brown uniform of the Imperial army with a cavalry major's insignia, the whole set off to advantage by being displayed on a tall, gracile man. Out of it, he might have been bony. In it, he was superb. His fair golden hair was longer than the current fashion, brushing past his collar and raked aside in the front like the forelock of a palomino horse. How old was he? Seventeen? Sixteen was the minimum for a commissioned officer. It was difficult to tell his age from across a smoke-shrouded room. How damnable for him that someone had bought him a commission. What utterly evil swine would send their young man into Prince Aerleas's army? Someone who wanted to be rid of him.

Charm moved through the cardroom. She paused to admire a hand here, to greet there. To touch a shoulder, give a smile, and drift on. One must not startle a man by walking straight up to him. They weren't used to it. Directness should be held in reserve, as a weapon of discomfiture. She slid behind the bar, and stepped up onto the little walk there that put her and her boneghosts more on a comfortable height with their customers.

"Mr. Anders, may I get you and your young friend anything?" she asked, smiling.

"Two more brandies, if it ain't a bother," said Anders jovially. He was possibly the most jovial man in Borenguard. "Major Nathair, 'tis my vast good fortune to introduce you to Mistress Charm, our gracious hostess."

Charm blinked. "Nathair? Forgive me, Major, I wasn't aware that there were any of the royal family left, aside from the Emperor's direct sons." There were far too many shocks and unknowns running amok these days.

The young major took his boot off the footrail and inclined his head and shoulders to Charm with immense propriety. "There was a duel that angered a past empress. My branch hasn't been spoken of in quite a long time." His voice was a pleasant, light tenor, his accent and enunciation perfectly blue-blooded. He was too young or too fair to need to shave much if at all. He looked still in his teens, but his carriage and air of gravitas was not that of any teenager Charm had ever seen in Orchard House.

Anders clapped Major Nathair on the shoulder. "Tell you what, I'll find us a card game. I'd like to take on Seabrough with you. Dem me if I wouldn't." He meandered off, hailing friends heartily along the way, brandy snifter dangling negligently.

"Is he always that friendly, or is someone setting me up to lose my money?" Nathair asked, smiling a little. A glint of charisma that made it easy to smile back at him. This one was going to be dangerous when he grew up.

"You'll probably lose some money, but he isn't that sort. Mr. Anders may lack reticence, but it's rather nice now and then as a refresher from fashionable detachment."

"He seems a good chap," agreed Nathair. "My family history makes me jump at shadows, perhaps."

"If you can be safe anywhere in Boren, Major, I hope it is at Orchard House." She thought about the young major's face some more as she poured their brandies. There was something about his features that picked at the edges of her memory like a child picking at a scab. "You seem . . . familiar, somehow, Major; and yet I feel sure I would remember you if I had met you before. . . ." The mindlock whirred in her temple, but didn't catch or bite.

He smiled a bit, as if he heard it all the time; though with a face like that, he most certainly did not. "It's probably family resemblance, Mistress. I haven't the old emperor's strong build, sadly, but I share a shadow of the family's features with Prince Luther, and the hair is a pretty faithful marker of Nathairs."

Perhaps. Perhaps. People did say the Emperor had been beautifully blond in his youth. By the time Charm had awakened, he'd been gray. "None of the Emperor's sons inherited his hair. Are they not Nathairs?" teased Charm, testing him.

Major Nathair smiled, nearly grinned. "They are Imperial princes, Mistress. Their father, may he rest at last, married from abroad." The last word, though the tone was mellow, held a snobbish, well-bred clip that made Charm suppress a smile. That scorn of the foreign had kept the Emperor's string of wives from ever fitting into Boren well enough to be in danger of popularity.

Nathair was, though so distant he'd been mislaid for a while, in line behind the princes for the Imperial throne. He was unable to refuse to go into Prince Aerleas's madness when ordered to do so. "I am so sorry that my boneghosts are all busy this evening. It would have been an honor to accommodate you. Are you due to ship out soon?"

"I only just arrived back in town. A health situation required that I retire for a time to the country. The Emperor gave me the honor of assigning me as an Imperial courier before his death." Hardness settled into his eyes, his smile a facial gesture of perfect politeness over a terrible wound. The look passed away as ease rolled in to conceal it, like fog blanketing Lowtown and shielding well-bred eyes from the sight. Nathair's smile was quite handsome. "But then it was my fortune to fall in with Anders, so my evening is made immensely pleasant."

A health situation? So young? That was when it struck her. Nathair was wearing powder. Men hadn't worn powder for decades upon decades, but Charm could just remember when very fashionable men had done so. Nathair's makeup, however, was not to produce elegant fair skin. Quite the opposite. Colored base with powder and rouge, just the slightest brush of it, put a healthy complexion on top of a pallor that bordered on deathly. Even his lips were pale beneath the cosmetic that stained them a normal color. The Emperor had done some dreadful damage to this beautiful young man. Ruined him before he was even in his prime. It hurt. A truth flung into her eyes like lemon juice until she wanted to blink them closed against the burn and sting.

Major Nathair turned politely to Philip Anders as Anders returned. "Cigar, sir?" Nathair invited, taking a gold cigar case from an inner pocket. "If Mistress Charm does not mind."

Sadly amused by a courtesy that no one else in the room would bother with, Charm gestured for him to continue.

"Oh yes, excellent, old dear." Anders accepted with hearty terms of intimacy for his new friend, as if they'd known one another for centuries. "Seabrough'll be ready for us in a few minutes." He turned to Charm. "Have to tell you, Mistress, our major, here, is about the most modest man I ever met. That line of spangles, there, on his bars? Every one of those is a meritorious service for exceptional bravery. And there's matchin' ones down both sides. There ain't even room for any more. Can't get him to tell me what they're about, but you can bet he's seen the thick of it. And that ribbon, there? Imperial courier."

So many service decorations. A lamb to the slaughter, poor child, and now an Imperial courier. Thrown into the briars over and over again. It was a miracle he hadn't killed himself. No doubt that was what Aerleas, and probably the Emperor, and now Strephon, had expected. Throw him to Aerleas and tear him back out to have to see the truth, over and over, let the weight settle in until they found the lad dead—dangling from a rafter or with a bullet in his brain. It wouldn't have been the first time a man expelled from the army had done such a thing. Heaven bless Mr. Anders for giving the young man a friend. Maybe he'd make it. Charm found herself hoping so.

"You must come let Pride make you a booking for next time you call, Major. A massage. On the house as a welcome present," she offered, gesturing toward the entry. Charm came out from behind the bar and tucked her hand into his politely extended arm. "Please excuse us, Mr. Anders? I shall return him to you shortly, entirely intact," she teased.

Anders chuckled. "Better than he left, no doubt, Mistress."

This close, she discovered that Major Nathair wore cologne. A floral scent. Very fashionable men, like Anders, did sometimes wear scents. Lilies and hyacinths, underlaid by musk and something green. It reminded her slightly of funerals, which was odd. She'd never been to one.

They were just out of earshot of the room, and not quite to Pride, when Major Nathair paused. His pale blue eyes bored down into Charm. "Mistress, I need you to do me a favor that is not on your books."

She raised a dry, squelching eyebrow.

His light tenor went quiet, intended not to carry. "Have you any care for Lord Fergus?"

Charm blinked. Fergus came to Orchard House for cards, for contacts, sometimes to dine. Famously among his set, he never went upstairs. Of her customers, he spent the least. He was considerate, polite, paid his bills, and never caused her any problems. Was this question a trap of some kind? "He's a very pleasant man, and I would be sorry to lose his mellowing influence in the card parlor."

Major Nathair ducked his fair head, and the muscle at the corners of his jaw stood out briefly before it smoothed. "He speaks the truth too boldly. That was safe under the previous emperor. It puts him in terrible danger, now. I cannot warn him. He wouldn't listen to me even if I tried. He might listen to you."

"Where did you hear of this danger to him?" she asked.

"From outside a door. I did not stoop to listen at key-holes, Mistress, but I do have ears; and I have no mindlock as a Firedrinker might." His angular face was like stone. "In another place, another time, Lord Fergus would be mightily admired. Here, and now? I can only fear for him." The major moved on, tipping his head back and laughing as if they'd paused while she said something witty. Turning the whole event into a visual bagatelle. A little clever nothing that everyone would dismiss.

Major Nathair would not be dangerous when he grew up. He was dangerous now. And he was either willing to spite Strephon or to try to warn a decent man away from harm. If it were both, there was even more real and unlooked-for potential to him.

"Pride, this amazing young gentleman's appointment for a massage is on the house," Charm instructed. She dimpled prettily when the young man kissed her fingers, and swept back into the card parlor. She would learn a great deal from Major Nathair's choice, but she would be very surprised if he did not book Pride or Shame. He had ample amounts of both.

CHAPTER FIVE

On Friday night, rain spat against the windows of Orchard House, and the last two men in the card parlor sat grimly at their table. A brandy bottle stood half empty between them. Their cards sprawled, abandoned. Now that everyone else had gone home or retired, they'd given up any pretense of play. Pain stood silent behind the bar, washing glasses. She defended many secrets at Orchard House, and defended even more from the days before she'd gained a body. Keeping a shield of silence between her sisters and the world was Pain's purpose, her reason for existing. Neither Seabrough nor Fergus seemed to have any concern that she would speak out now.

"Strephon's mad!" snapped Lord Fergus, outrage quivering his jowls.

"Easy, man," Count Seabrough soothed.

Pain couldn't disagree with Fergus's assessment. Whatever someone else had, Strephon wanted. He'd wanted his stepmother, apparently, and he was about to get her. He'd have had Pain long ago if he hadn't been so afraid of the Firedrinkers. The old emperor had suspected one of his sons had assassinated him to get the crown. Pain believed Strephon would cheerfully commit patricide, but she remained skeptical that he had the capacity to carry off any plan that involved handling of the sensibilities of the nobles. He had proven his tact with his first decree.

"Have you read the list of his would-be policies? Apart from the moral issue of marrying his own stepmother, have you seen the trade concessions to Devarik? He'll cripple our imports from the continent."

Seabrough poured Fergus some more brandy. "If Empress Ylsbeth goes home to Devarik we could be in even worse straits. As long as Aerleas is struggling to keep the provinces pacified we cannot have so much as a hiccup in our relations with Devarik. If Ylsbeth married to the Emperor is what it takes to keep them friendly, then that's what it takes."

"Is Strephon marrying her to keep their goodwill, or buying their goodwill for the marriage with this insane trade concession? Why make the concession if it is not to compensate them so they won't rise up in moral outrage at his gall in marrying his father's wife?" argued Fergus.

Pain polished the bar. Fergus did not object to the sports of his fellows, as long as they were discreet. More than once he'd been the downfall of political aspirants who'd allowed their dirty laundry to become too public. No surprise he'd object to such a blatant display of public immorality.

"Have you thought that perhaps all this was to get Ylsbeth to agree to the marriage?" asked Seabrough. "She isn't agreeing for the fun or position of it."

Fergus waved away the question impatiently. "Your wife waits on her, you'd know Ylsbeth's temperament better than I; but I was ambassador to Saranisima for six years, and they will never stand for this imbalance of tariffs. Every corn of pepper, every leaf of tea, every scrap of silk and cotton that comes to Boren comes through Saranisima's waters."

"Then perhaps it will have to come overland through the

provinces to Croisonnè, in which case Prince Aerleas's control there is even more crucial," Seabrough said, pouring himself another few fingers of brandy, "though the land route would be expensive."

"It is not right!" Fergus cried in frustration.

Seabrough sighed. "I don't say it's right, I say it may be necessary. A new emperor must have allies, and relations with Saranisima are already rocky, so there's little to lose there. Isn't it right that we should tax their ships as we're taxed in their ports?"

"We have a very delicate balance that the former emperor went to great pains to implement. To toss it all aside in the first day of any kind of authority . . . Strephon isn't even crowned yet. What will he be like when he is firm upon his throne? When he has the Firedrinkers at his beck and call?"

"If you say in Assembly what you've said here, it will make no difference. Your protests can only succeed in angering our soon-to-be emperor. Have some common sense, man," Seabrough said.

"If we all stand together, perhaps we can make Strephon see reason," argued Fergus.

Seabrough looked at his brandy. Finally, he spoke. "I'll do everything I can, but I won't destroy myself in a bid for parliamentary control that's doomed to fail. Be patient."

"I will not swallow this."

"Then you will choke on it," said Seabrough softly.

"So be it." Fergus shoved back his chair and stalked out. He left the parlor door open and slammed the front behind him.

Seabrough contemplated the brandy in his glass, swirling it gently around the bowl. "Damn," he announced to himself. He raised his glass in the direction of the front door. "To principles." Seabrough tipped back the liquor in a single long gulp.

He looked across the room at Pain, catching her eyes. He smiled wryly. "How are your principles, Miss Pain?"

"Silent," Pain said with a sad smile. "You will not support Lord Fergus?"

"I won't speak against him. At this moment, that's all I can do."

"Are you concerned for Countess Seabrough's safety if you object to Emperor Strephon?"

Seabrough's dry expression went drier. "You needn't worry for her. This owes to simple practicality. There are no choices save Strephon."

"Pain?" Charm stood at the parlor door. "There's a Firedrinker here for you."

"Go on, Miss Pain," allowed Seabrough, "show the poor fellow a pleasant evening."

Charm brought the decanter of brandy from the bar and sat down with Seabrough. It was nice to get off her feet for a few minutes. "Since you appear to be in a somber mood, Count, I hope you do not mind a blunt question."

"Will it include haranguing me on the subject of taxation?"

Charm dimpled. "No."

"In that case, carry on."

"Why did the blond lady who frightened your wife come to town?"

Seabrough frowned. "Whom do you mean?"

"There was a lady Pain saw in the viewing gallery. One with fantastically golden hair and a sharp face. Your wife moved over to make room for her. I wondered if she were a supporter of our new emperor."

"Ah. Her. No, she would not support Strephon."

Anyone the Count didn't wish to speak of would have been of interest even if Charm didn't suspect her of skulking about the front gates. Charm raised her eyebrows.

Seabrough answered the unspoken question grudgingly. "She is the Duchess of Madderley, Aiglentine Nathair. A second cousin of the former emperor who holds her title in her own right. She was, possibly is, Prince Aerleas's closest confidant. They grew up together. Her husband was an Inshili. He left Boren without her when it became clear war was coming and died in the war. They say she once challenged a man to a duel, and the Emperor sent her to the country as a result." The neutrality in Seabrough's voice had a careful feel to it. "If she was going to support any prince, it would be Aerleas."

An agent of Prince Aerleas, who had grown up with him. She hadn't died of old age. Of course the Emperor would provide a cousin, especially a useful cousin, with Rejuv. And Aerleas would doubtless go on providing it. He had that lever, and it would be stupid not to use it. She sounded, from Pain's description, very much like a woman who could commit, or at least plot, murder. With the old emperor, who had banished her, gone, Duchess Aiglentine could rejoin aristocratic life in the capital.

Major Nathair. It resounded in Charm's mind as suddenly as a warning klaxon. The youth with so many decorations and such old eyes. He'd said there'd been a duel in his family. Was he a relation of this duchess? A son, possibly. Charm dipped her chin slightly so that Seabrough wouldn't see her swallow. If Nathair was the murderer, were he or the Duchess hunting her for Aerleas now that there was no emperor to protect Charm? Or was Seabrough throwing Nathairs at her to avoid suspicion falling on him. She managed to school her face to mere interest and looked back up at Seabrough. "Forgive my curiosity, but she is clearly an extraordinary person . . . has the Duchess been back in Borenguard for very long?"

"No. She arrived the night after the Emperor first fell ill. My wife says she was brought to his presence covered in dust and still in her traveling clothes. He ordered her to have rooms at the palace."

Perhaps plotted, then, instead of committed. Or had Major Nathair do it for her. "Why did the Emperor let her come back . . ." She breathed it aloud, dreading an answer.

"No one knows, Mistress. Not even my wife, who knows everything in the palace."

And that was the woman who'd stood at the gates of Orchard House the night the Emperor had taken ill. Charm wished her evening gown had sleeves to hide the way the hair rose on her arms.

⌒⌒

A porcelain-tiled stove warmed Pain's large second-floor room; a tub with heated water waited behind an ornate screen, with a massage table and a comfortable bed completing the important appointments. It was the same as the other business rooms, but no nobleman of Borenguard had ever entered it. Firedrinkers were Pain's only customers.

The tall Firedrinker, her favorite, took up the whole length of her table.

She eased her oily hands across the tight lumps in the muscle between his shoulder blades. "You're full of knots. You've had a bad time of it since you were here last." His skin held only a residual memory of the sun, hidden too long inside his uniform to retain more than faint color.

"I was standing watch over . . ." A shudder rippled up the Firedrinker's back. ". . . the Emperor."

Pain stroked the heels of her hands along his spine, easing the reaction. "So you haven't slept since . . . ?"

"Tuesday."

Pain bent low. "I won't take it as an insult if you fall asleep," she whispered to him.

He spoke doggedly. "Prince Phelan was . . ." His shoulders tensed under Pain's hands. "He was furious. Strephon and he talked. Phelan will be the foreign minister, first in his post instead of second to . . . Aerleassss." The name hissed out through his teeth as his back spasmed.

"You don't need to tell me anything."

"You know Strephon will marry the Empress?"

"Yes." Maybe it was better to let him talk it out. "Why not just send her home?"

The Firedrinker shivered. The subject must be close to his mindlock, but he seemed to want, or need, to speak in spite of that. "Can't. Devarik is across the border from the eastern provinces. Can't defend them and hold Inshil. No one wants to let the provinces go."

Pain worked on the lumps at the points of his shoulder blades. "They need the provinces or they need to keep Aerleas busy outside of Boren?"

"Yes." The Firedrinker's laugh rasped in his throat. "Prince Aerleas wants to supplement the army with conscripted troops from Boren." His hands clenched on the front edge of the table, and his voice grated over the words. "The old emperor never allowed it."

"You think that's going to change under Strephon." That was how Strephon bought Aerleas. As simply as that.

His laugh was bitter. "The only things that cannot change now are my orders . . ." The Firedrinker's muscles twitched and jumped under his skin from nape to heels.

Pain tsked. Any other hurt she could have relieved him of, but his mindlock held her out. Even with Mistress Charm, Pain couldn't take away the mindlock's punishments. All she could do was deal with the aftermath. "Stop it," she told him, soothing his back with her hands. "You're undoing all my hard work. Close your eyes and sleep."

"Your room is too expensive to sleep in. Even for me."

Pain combed her fingers through his hair. His eyes slid closed in pleasure. She smiled to herself, teasing gentle circles on his scalp. His hair slipped around her fingers, the color of wet sand, silky and smooth. She loved to see him relax. It was a better compliment than anything he could have said.

"What are the odds that you'll actually sleep a full night without being woken up if you go back to your barracks?"

"Slim to none," he admitted.

"You need rest, the way you've been beating yourself up just now. No one else will come tonight. I won't bill you."

"Why not?"

"It's after hours. The room would be empty anyway. I just said that." Pain let a bit of fond exasperation out in her tone.

"I know what you said." His words were a contented mumble. He didn't open his eyes. His neck muscles began to ease under the soft stroking of her thumbs. Gradually he faded into sleep.

She didn't sleep in the second-floor rooms. None of them did. Tonight, though, Pain pulled a chair up beside the massage table, crossed her arms beside his head, laid her own head down, and closed her eyes.

CHAPTER SIX

Heavy rain early on Monday morning washed Cathedral Square until the pale pink marble buildings shone like dawn, and the expanse of paving stones gleamed silvery in the morning sun. People began to gather hours before the royal procession was expected, a steady stream that flowed up from the lower city to fill the square and seethe around the foundations of the buildings. Pain stood in the shadow between the Great Library and the Government Offices, disguised by the simple expedient of hiding her face and colorless hair with a veiled hat.

Pain and Desire were the oldest to have bodies, grown from the first fruits of the Lady's orchard, but only Pain had ever found fascination with the world outside of Orchard House.

It seemed unfair that Borenguard's perpetual, sullen overcast should part for this travesty of a coronation. All the lesser dignitaries had arrived first, and now a massive carriage disgorged Countess Seabrough and the Duchess of Madderley. Both wore severely cut gowns of elegant line. The Duchess's satin for the great celebration was as crimson as if she'd been dipped in gore. A coronet of rubies and diamonds glittered in her stunning hair. The Countess's drabber head was adorned only with diamond combs. Crowns or anything that looked like one were for the royal family only. The Countess held herself stiffly. Did it cut to be outranked by a specter from Boren's bloodiest past?

Pain watched Empress Ylsbeth descend from a carriage with the Imperial seal upon the doors. Even as a widow, she had political worth. Today, "for the good of the country," the new emperor Strephon would take her as his wife. As false as the reason given for the old emperor's death. The Empress dripped with jewels, proclaiming to all how Strephon valued his prize. A high diamond collar and necklace clasped her graceful neck. Solitaires the size of grapes flashed in her ears. The crown on her pale hair was dazzling. Pearls and crystals adorned her vast skirts and flashed on her bodice. How had Strephon persuaded the Empress to go through with this marriage? Bribed her with ostentatious display? Considering her usual restraint in dress it didn't seem likely. Mistress Charm had pitied the girl. Pain wasn't so certain. Her heavy train carried by the two other ladies, head held high, Ylsbeth made her way up the steps to the cathedral.

The crowd, silent, seemed to grow even more so as the Imperial carriage rolled up to the cathedral. Prince Strephon stepped out on the side of the carriage facing the crowd, smiling and waving. Luther and Phelan came out onto the steps to walk him into the church. Luther only nodded to his youngest brother. Phelan greeted Strephon with a hearty smile, clasping him warmly on the shoulder. Aerleas hadn't returned for his youngest brother's coronation.

Pain let out a shaky sigh of relief. He wasn't here. With the Duchess implanted in the Imperial court, perhaps Aerleas didn't feel he needed to come to Borenguard, but Pain had needed to be sure. Pain sometimes wondered if her memories had been real at all, or if birth was always a haze. The Lady had pushed Pain and Desire into unseen life. With those two ghosts to shield her, the Lady could not tell her father, nor could Inshil's finest psychics discover, who her lover had been. She no longer knew. Luther's attentions belonged to Desire alone. Pain, who could not speak, could not move, Pain who had been only an empty space. She took the punishment and could not tell who he was even if she had known. When it was over, Pain and Desire had settled back behind the Lady's personality, huddled with the battered scrap of some other, nameless ghost until they might be needed again. Prince Aerleas had brought Pain into the light again. The same questions. Far more creative methods.

Pain's eyes dwelled on Luther. *How easy it is for Strephon to buy you,* Pain thought bitterly. *All he has to do is let you come home now and then.*

The carriage pulled away, and Strephon straightened his cuffs, grinning at his brothers and saying something.

To Pain's right, someone booed. Like an avalanche, the rest of the crowd picked up the scorn, booing their new monarch. A mud clod hit Strephon's shoulder, and a rotten fruit exploded in a dirty smack on his white satin. Instantly, scarlet coats stepped out of the shadows around Cathedral Square. Strephon touched the stain on his shoulder, snarling at the crowd.

Pressure against Pain's mind heralded the Firedrinkers working, holding down the violence of the crowd. Around the crowd, people staggered. Winced. Paled and went still. The Firedrinkers suppressed their riotous emotions. They couldn't suppress Pain. A creature of Charm's making, she inherited the mindlock's protection.

Pain's jaw clenched behind her veil as the three Princes retreated into the cathedral together. No doubt Phelan would be at Orchard House when the official celebration was over. She wondered if Luther would call on Desire again. She wished she'd thought to bring rotten eggs. No matter how much action the Firedrinkers could hold against, the people would remember this too-open display of power. No one moved toward the cathedral, but ugly murmuring swelled up. The mob's outrage and violence seethed beneath the Firedrinkers' control. Either the Firedrinkers could not suppress the mood, or didn't. It was time to leave.

A human sea stood between Pain and the nearest exit from the square. Head down, she began to work her way through the mob toward it. The press around her stole the air from her lungs. She jostled into a man, flung her hands out to break her fall as she went down. A boot came down on her hand, another connected clumsily with her thigh through her skirts. The world around her began to dissolve into the old nightmare. The Lady's father. Doctors. Straps. Glaring lights. Aerleas. Questions floated above her, more indistinct with every passing agony. Pain could not speak. She couldn't even scream.

A gap opened around her. A scarlet-clad arm took hold of her elbow, drawing her up. The bright color jolted her out of her panic. Boren's soldiers wore brown. Slowly, recognition oozed past the sucking swamp of her memory. Firedrinker. Shaking, she pressed her hand against her bodice, feeling the whalebone stays under it. Women in Inshil didn't wear corsets. Her skirt was dusty, the hem trodden on, but it was perfectly sound. The fabric was thick and real in her grip, but the hands in the nightmare felt real too. The gloved hand on her elbow hadn't moved.

She lifted her eyes slowly up until they reached the white sash that denoted Captain Oram, and there she froze like a rabbit beneath a hawk's eye. Various of the Firedrinkers wore that sash at various times, but as they were all connected mentally by Captain Oram's telepathy it didn't matter. Any of them could function as Captain Oram; but this . . . she had no doubt at all that this was the actual Captain Oram. The nobility loathed the captain for his obedience, but the commoners gave him grudging respect. He might be a ruthless bastard in carrying out the Emperor's will, but he was a fair ruthless bastard. Pain relaxed. She was made not to break. If neither Inshil's psychics nor any other torturer could force the vault of her memory, then Captain Oram would not.

"Allow me," said Oram, in the same androgynous middle tones as any other Firedrinker.

The wrist she laid her gloved hand on was probably masculine, broad and bony. The crowd opened before Oram like earth before a plow. He made no effort to halt when they cleared the crowd, but continued on toward the Uptown gate as if he walked with ladies on his arm every day.

"May I see you as far as the wall, Miss Pain?" he asked in a quiet voice.

"You'll have to tell me how you recognized me, Captain," Pain said as lightly as she could. "Though I thank you for your help."

"All of you born from Mistress Charm's orchard have inherited her shields. Even I cannot read you without skin contact. In a crowd, though, a blind spot is as good as an aura, and you are the only one from Orchard House that walks abroad."

Pain considered that for a moment. She could not be anonymous to him. An important detail.

"Shouldn't you be overseeing security at Cathedral Square?" she asked.

Oram didn't say anything for a moment. "My Firedrinkers have their instructions. My emperor left me with specific orders."

Living with Mistress Charm, Pain was familiar with a pause followed by careful phrasing, and the bells had not yet rung for Strephon's coronation. "I see," she said softly.

"My Firedrinkers have not had the same orders," said Oram, feeling his way through the words like a blind man in a strange room, "and I . . ." He trailed off for a moment and tried again. "They are long-standing orders," he finished.

"I see," repeated Pain. "Do you foresee a time in the future when your orders could change, Captain?"

"No, miss, and rest assured I cannot . . . find a reason to . . . bother Emperor Strephon . . . with such trivia," he managed.

Pain pitied the feared Captain Oram. His mindlock must operate under extremely strict instructions if it made him struggle so much. "Do you call at Orchard House, Captain?" Without their uniforms, Firedrinkers were people like any other, though identifiable by the crystal locks in their temples; but any of the men might have been Captain Oram. None of the Firedrinkers who went upstairs with her ever wore a white sash, and neither did any of them use their names. His disguise might be as simple as a black sash instead of the telltale white.

"I think there are few with the means who have not called there, miss. Even the idealistic Lord Fergus comes there for cards and dinner."

"Indeed he does." Pain waited, curious to see where the conversation was going.

They had almost reached the Uptown wall. Oram paused just out of sight of the sentries.

"Lord Fergus spoke out against the marriage," he said quietly. "He had support among some of the lesser assemblymen."

"I'd heard. He signed the ratification act, though, and I suppose he's in the cathedral now," commented Pain.

"What he said can't be . . ." The sound that emerged from the mirrored visor was an unmistakable choke. Oram's gloved hands clenched into fists and his shoulders pulled forward as he ground out his words. They were ragged with effort.

"People won't forget it, miss. I think . . . that if I were he, I would take my family on a tour; perhaps I would spend a few years abroad in someplace warm. For the sake of the children's health," the captain said in a tense whisper. "Borenguard is really too damp for them."

Pain's blood went as cold as snowmelt.

"You understand?" asked Oram, urgency underlying his tone.

Pain answered softly, "I understand." Oram hadn't betrayed the throne, he had only given his opinion. Pain knew well the effort it had cost him to brush that close to his mindlock. On impulse, she slipped her hand up under the concealing helmet. She could not feel his skin through her glove, but she traced the line of his jaw gently. So many Firedrinkers. Which one was he?

Captain Oram stood utterly still for a moment, then let his head tip just faintly into her caress. Pain wondered if his eyes were closed. His headache flowed into her, and his sigh of relief rewarded her for carrying it.

The bells in the cathedral began to toll. Oram shivered inside his wool coat and body armor. The captain's mirrored helmet turned slowly toward Cathedral Square. The action brought his lips into her hand. "Mistress Charm misnamed you," he whispered against her palm, breath warm through her glove. "She should have called you Mercy."

Pain caught her breath as he kissed her palm. He would need to be in Cathedral Square when the Emperor came out of the cathedral. Pain took her hand away, regretting the necessity as the headache became his once more.

"When you are at Orchard House next, you must allow me to thank you properly for your escort, Captain," she managed.

Oram raised her gloved knuckles briefly toward his visor,

then released her. He turned on his heel and strode back toward Cathedral Square.

⤳❧

A handful of diehard cardplayers were the last downstairs customers. Among them was the object of Charm's attention. Lord Fergus generally came late, after putting his children in bed, and stayed until the last politically important people went home. It helped to mellow his reputation as a hopelessly hidebound family man to be seen keeping such late hours at Orchard House. Pain was washing glasses behind the curving mahogany bar.

Charm paused there. "The Blood Field '76, please, Pain, and two glasses," she said quietly, and earned the first approving nod Pain had offered her in weeks. Charm waited until the players were between hands. She wandered over to the card table with a cheerful expression plastered to her face.

"Can I get you anything, Lord Fergus?" she asked, putting her hand on the nobleman's shoulder.

"A little luck?" Fergus suggested with a smile that animated his mustache. His eyes crinkled at the corners, and relieved the plainness of his face. "Poor Major Nathair would like it if I were having more, I feel sure." He offered a smile of apology at his partner.

"You could get me a jar of your superb caviar for our table," requested Count Seabrough. "Pain said she couldn't serve it without your say-so."

"I'm sorry, Your Lordship, but I'm afraid we've run out of everything except Prince Phelan's personal stock. A dispute over Prince . . . over Emperor Strephon's new tariffs." She shook her head and smiled at her "slip."

"Hittin' us already, is it? Well, damnation, that's a bit hard," Anders complained.

"For me as well, gentlemen. I miss charging you for it." There was a general ripple of laughter, which Anders led. "If your cards are cold, Lord Fergus, why not come have a drink with me and let them warm up," Charm suggested. "I have a wine that I'd like your opinion on."

"Go on, Fergus. We'll deal you in as a dummy and I'll see if I can warm our luck up a bit," said Nathair.

Fergus, who was rather proud of his reputation as a connoisseur of fine wine, obligingly rose from the table and followed her. She had placed the bottle and glasses far enough from the cardplayers that they wouldn't be overheard if they spoke quietly. Charm poured.

"I've heard some rumors that concerned me, Lord Fergus," she told him in low tones, passing him a glass of the dark wine. "You are not one of the new emperor's favorites, I understand."

"Someone has to tell him the truth," answered Fergus with a shrug. "The taxes he's proposed are crippling." He held his wine up to the light. "Color's a bit unusual, rather purpler than most reds, particularly along the rim; and I have to say that the clarity is only fair." He closed his eyes, inhaling as he swirled. "Beautiful bouquet, though," he said appreciatively.

"You spoke against his marriage, too. Did you have a moral dilemma, or don't you like the Empress?" whispered Charm, conscious of Count Seabrough and the other cardplayers behind them.

Fergus opened his eyes and let his breath out in a long, tired sigh. "This is not about wine, is it, Mistress?"

Charm hated the world for a moment. He was a decent man, and she didn't like being the one to have to make him afraid. "I wish that it were about wine, my lord, but I believe your life is in danger," Charm told him softly. "I have heard it twice, now; and I believe it to be true."

His gaze flicked to the crystal in her temple. "And where did you learn this?" he asked.

She picked up her own glass and sipped it to give herself resolve. Besides, hesitation would make him leap to his own conclusions. "I cannot say," she murmured, "but the Firedrinkers have their eyes on you."

"Ah." Fergus thought about that for a bit. "Unfortunately, I couldn't leave just now. I've interests that I cannot abandon. I have a little support in the Assembly. If I run, it will dissolve like sugar in a hot cup of tea. Strephon will ruin Boren if we let him."

"Think of your family," urged Charm. "If a man were particularly vicious, that is where he would strike you."

Fergus tasted the wine. He took another drink, ruffled air over it in his mouth, rolled it around, and smiled, a little sadly, as he swallowed. "This is exquisite."

"It's a very special wine," said Charm, stroking the bowl of her glass. "From the Blood Fields in Inshil. Have you heard of them?" Her voice shook a little.

"The Rebellion of Inshil was before my time."

Despite having brought it up, Charm found herself reluctant to speak about Inshil. It was a little like taking one's clothes off in public. *But after all,* she scolded herself, *they're Pride's clothes and Shame's, not mine. It shouldn't bother me at all.* Charm cleared her throat.

"In Inshil psychics were believed to have been touched by God. The Chancellor was God's representative. He and the Holy Family lived in a grand palace, and psychics in cloistered gardens where only the blessed or the fortunate were permitted to walk. Prince Aerleas smashed the gates of that palace, and one by one he defiled Inshil's protected cloisters. The men who tried to defend the city were marched to the golden hills outside the capital, and variously impaled and crucified. They made the Chancellor and his family watch. Then they executed the Chancellor's wife, then his children, and the Chancellor last. Their blood soaked those hills. The only survivor of that family is one daughter, who'd married out of the country before Boren's army arrived." The last was not true, or perhaps more than true. It wasn't a question that Charm chose to think about.

"That is not what the histories say." It wasn't a question. Fergus's voice had gone hoarse. He set his wineglass on the bar.

Charm didn't dignify the stupidity of the comment by replying to it. "I'm told that Prince Aerleas had the bodies tilled into the ground. My emperor had a vineyard planted over those hillsides, and deeded it to me as a gift. This wine is from those vines."

"What is the point to this story, Mistress, if you don't mind my asking?" Whether Fergus believed her or not, he didn't seem interested in drinking his wine anymore.

"My point," said Charm, a little sharply, "is that where there are no witnesses but murderers, there are no crimes."

Fergus was clearly shaken. "I will consider what you say, Mistress."

Charm risked looking up into his troubled face. "My lord, please do not delay too long."

"If I try to send them away, he'll stop them. It will play directly into his hands. Only the guilty run."

"If you get your family to Orchard House, I will do all I can for them," promised Charm. She had no idea how, but she'd think of something. "When they are safe you only need to say that they have gone to warmer climes for the health of one of your children." She regretted the words even as she spoke them. Where had that come from? *First Ylsbeth and now Lady*

Fergus and her horde of chicks on the word of Major Nathair and Captain Oram. Charm cut off the train of thought. Even a whore could have a heart. It was a worn cliché, but there it was.

Fergus didn't ask how she would manage the escape, which was fortunate, because at this moment Charm hadn't any idea at all. He just nodded, and walked back toward his table. Fergus picked up his coat, smiled and made his excuses, and left. Charm waited until the front door had closed, then went out to see Pride at her post at the desk.

CHAPTER SEVEN

On Tuesday morning Pain rose early and opened the orchard gate for the laundress, Maude. Maude's pushcart baskets were already brimming with soiled linens.

"Morning, Miss Pain," said Maude, counting sheets and shifts from Orchard House's hampers into one of her voluminous baskets.

"Good morning, Maude. How is your husband?"

"Jim's got a nasty sort of cough today and had to stay in. The Wilsons are good sorts, though. I spoke to Mrs. Wilson's housekeeper and she said they'd manage a day withou' him."

"If you can wait a moment there's a bit left in the soup pot on the back of the stove. It might soothe that cough."

"Thankee, miss, that'd be very welcome."

Pain saw the laundress and the soup off, then went to dress. She made her way down the Imperial Way toward the lower end of Middletown. It was her daily errand to fetch croissants for Charm's breakfast tray. The Imperial Way ran in lazy switchbacks from Cathedral Square in Uptown through the first of the interior dividing walls, past Orchard House and down through Middletown. In almost the center of Middletown, it forked and branched as if it had grown tired and sprawled off to the left toward the sails and warehouses of Harborward, right toward Boren's landward gates, and on down the long hillside to the cold, gray stone bastion of the Lowtown gate and then into the chaotic congestion of Lowtown.

This morning there was a crowd at the gate to Lowtown. People milled and murmured restlessly in the street. Many were in servants' clothes. Uptown's servants nearly all lived in back wings of their employers' grand homes, but Middletown depended on day servants who walked up from the lower parts of the city. Maude stood with several other laundrywomen, huddled to one side of the gate with their carts and baskets. They had wide, worried eyes, mouths pinched. A great, stinking wagon of stable waste stood stranded in the shadow of the wall, unable to pass through Lowtown on its way to the fields.

Pain forced her feet into action, joining the trickle of people slowly swelling the pool around the gate. As Pain neared the mass of people, she began to make out individual words.

"Press-gangs." "Emperor Strephon's order." "Conscription." "My son?" "My husband?" "My father?" The words repeated within the crowd. "They're coming." "Can you see anyone yet?"

Maude approached Pain, bobbing a little curtsy and plucking at the lace of Pain's sleeve. "Do you know what's happening, Miss Pain? No one seems to know. My Jim . . ."

"Ladies and gentlemen, please clear the gate." A Firedrinker's voice carried across the echoes.

A double row of arterial red moved through the press toward the gate. Their batons stayed in their belts, their pistols holstered. White sash standing out against the brightness of his coat, Captain Oram walked between his Firedrinkers. "I must ask you to clear the gate, ladies and gentlemen. Please." That last word carried a world of weary resignation even through the distortion of his helmet.

The subtle ripple of his command slid past Pain like a soothing caress on her cheek, and the people fell back from the gate as if in a dream. Unnaturally calm. With so many

Firedrinkers here, reinforcing one another, the crowd's agitation eased. The Firedrinkers stretched out their gloved hands and guided the crowd in opposite directions, opening a path before the gate. Questions washed up against the red coats, pleading with the anonymous for fathers, brothers, sons.

"There will be a check at dockside," Oram explained to the anxious faces. "I am assured by the Emperor that those who can prove employment will be free to return to Lowtown. Those of you who are waiting to return home, we ask that you try to be patient." His voice carried calm like a scent on the air as he and the Firedrinkers with him scanned the crowd. The blank of his visor paused for a moment in Pain's general vicinity. "Those with no other business here, please depart."

Pain put an arm around Maude's shoulder. She had business by association, at least, and Mistress Charm would need to know all she could about what happened here today. Either he hadn't put any psychic effort into the command, or Pain was not the only one who had business by association. No one budged.

The gates opened, and the crowd pressed forward into the arms of the Firedrinkers. The Firedrinkers stood fast.

Maude began to move forward too, but Pain tightened her grip on the laundress gently. "If he's taken, we'll see him from here. If there's trouble, up front is where it will be. You'll need to get a letter from his employers, and you need to be outside of the crowd to do it." She felt Maude's shoulders expand as the woman sucked in a steadying breath.

"Level 'ead, Miss Pain, tha's what you've got. A sound, level 'ead," Maude said, patting Pain's hand on her shoulder firmly.

A mounted officer—a colonel, according to the gold stripes on his brown sleeve—led similarly brown-clad soldiers and a triple column of civilians emerging from the Lowtown gate.

The civilians were roped together by their wrists. For a moment, the sight of the army uniforms made Pain sway, but her arm around Maude kept her upright. The soldiers walked in pairs on each side of their captives, rifles cradled in the crooks of their elbows. In each pair, one watched the captives and one watched the crowd past the Firedrinkers. A woman screamed, then someone else cried out. A gradual tide of sound began to emerge, flowing up toward the tops of the walls.

The colonel halted his horse, scanning the crowd.

Maude shuffled, nervous. Pain drank in the man's pallor, his too-bright eyes, and the way he clutched his reins so tightly that his horse gaped and fretted against its bit with a frothing tongue. She felt his gaze pass over her like a spray of cold needles, piercing her throat, freezing her tongue against the roof of her dry mouth. Not psychic. Psychotic.

Maude shrank slightly against Pain. "What in the name of God is wrong with that man?"

Pain cleared her throat, tried twice before she managed to whisper two words—"He's mad."

All around them, the shock of the colonel's gaze was wearing off. Murmurs ebbed and flowed restlessly through the crowd.

The colonel's horse edged forward until the foam from its bit dripped on Captain Oram's shoulder and the steel-shod hooves clashed on the cobbles only inches from his boots. Oram neither flinched nor moved, a silent statue in his red coat. The horse fidgeted, trying to move left or right of the immobile man before it, but the colonel's legs were tight against the animal's sides. Still, Oram didn't move. The horse's chest met Oram's left shoulder, and the horse stopped moving forward. It stayed where it was, chewing its bit, hide twitching and jumping nervously over its shoulders.

The colonel licked his lips, and bared his teeth not in a smile but in what seemed like frustration. "Captain Oram."

"Colonel Fletcher," Oram answered, the artificial voice flat.

"I did not expect to see you here today." Fletcher didn't look at the Firedrinkers' captain.

Oram did not reply.

"Did the Emperor feel we were incapable of our task?" pressed Colonel Fletcher.

"The Firedrinkers are commanded to keep order in the city. We are commanded to be present whenever a crowd gathers. We are commanded to keep the peace." Oram might have been reciting a school lesson for all the passion he gave the list.

Fletcher cleared his throat in a long, rattling inhale and spat, without seeming to look, on the toe of Captain Oram's shining right boot. Several of the Firedrinkers serving as the crowd barricade tensed. Oram did not.

"Beginning at sunset tomorrow, there will be an army detachment stationed at this gate. Anyone passing through who cannot show proof of employment will be pressed into profitable service to the crown," Fletcher shouted at the crowd. "Men in the army, women to work in support in the warehouses or factories."

"The column has proceeded toward the harbor, Colonel Fletcher. Do you wish an escort?" asked Oram's level, anonymous voice.

Colonel Fletcher sneered. "An escort of Firedrinkers?" He wheeled his horse, and it leaped after the retreating column of impressed men.

Oram turned to face the crowd again, his scarlet coat smeared down the left side with the horse's sweat. Slowly, his visor swept the crowd. As one, the Firedrinkers dropped their arms and turned ninety degrees. Six detached themselves from the lines and went to flank the Lowtown gate three on a side. No one uttered a word, but orders had clearly been given. Oram turned on his heel, and he and the two columns of Firedrinkers moved off up the Imperial Way. Slowly, as if waking from a dream, the crowd around started to drift into motion.

"I didn't see Jim," said Maude, hope quivering in her throat. "I need to get home, Miss Pain. Thankee for waiting with me." The laundress went to her cart, heaved against the handles, and got it moving toward the gate.

Pain didn't move, turning what she had seen over in her mind while the crowd flowed around her and gradually melted back into normal morning traffic. It was clever of Aerleas to send his men to remind people of him; clever again, to send those who were most like him. Colonel Fletcher and his men would inspire Strephon, and Boren, to fear him. And to force the Firedrinkers to act again so soon after the near riot in Cathedral Square.

Clever, also, to force Captain Oram to stand between the anxious crowd and the army taking away their loved ones. Had it been enough for the crowd that he'd made the demonstration with the colonel's horse? Perhaps the people would see the distinction between the Firedrinkers and the greater evil. Aerleas was not done with Borenguard. He was making sure that everyone knew it. The thought prickled along Pain's arms, and she rubbed her hands up and down them to try to lay the hair back down inside her sleeves.

Mechanically, Pain fell back into her routine. It was soothing, easy to simply do what she always did and not to think about things too much. She went to the bakery, but had to wait.

"Sorry, Miss Pain, but the army came in this morning on their way to Lowtown and took every blessed dainty they wanted on vouchers. All I have left is from yesterday. You know I don't do this to my regular customers, Miss Pain, but that Colonel Fletcher . . ." The baker looked at Pain in desperate appeal.

"I understand perfectly. You were very wise to give him what he wanted."

"I've got our second batch of croissants in the oven if you can wait a few minutes?"

She forced a smile. "I can wait. And I'd like my usual order of day-old, please, if you have it to spare."

The stumble in routine kept Pain from the insulation of the familiar. She stepped to one side. Servants of Middletown began to trickle in as the morning's events gave way to business. Pain found herself part of a little cluster of maids, all waiting for fresh dainties to take to their respective employers. Usually, Pain had gone by the time these mortal women arrived. They murmured and tsked with one another like flustered pigeons.

"I don't know, my brother . . ." "Do you think they took men over forty?" "Surely this is a one-time occurrence." "My master says it's necessary." "Lord Fergus says it's shameful." "Did you see it?"

A tug at her sleeve made her realize that the last question had been directed to her. "Did you see it, Miss Pain?"

"Yes," she admitted. Suddenly everyone in the shop was looking at her expectantly. "There was a Colonel Fletcher who led the unit. He must be close to Prince Aerleas. . . ." Pain closed her eyes, trying to ward off the tightening in her throat. "He was frightening." Pain opened her eyes and went on. "Captain Oram and his Firedrinkers stood between the army and the crowd so that no one got hurt."

"Those army soldiers could stand a little hurting, if you ask me," hissed one woman, who had been silent up to that point. Tears rose up in her eyes. "My poor Peter . . ." She burst into tears.

The women gathered around her, clucking and soothing and patting. Pain retreated gratefully back against the counter.

"Here's your order, Miss Pain." The baker passed a flat basket across, the scent of fresh croissants drifting up on wisps of steam, and a bag of loaves. "Don't wrap the cloth over 'em. They'll get soggy if you wrap 'em before they're cooled."

A gaggle of children had gathered outside, and they clustered around her as soon as she was a little away from the bakery. They fidgeted, nervous and quiet today. Pain passed out the day-old bread. "I'm sorry there's not much. Maggie, make sure this gets to the Misses Haggerty, will you? And make sure they're all right?" She pressed a couple of pennies and the last loaf into the hands of the eldest girl. "I don't have time to go today."

"I'll do, miss. You're their angel, they said. Their white angel," reported Maggie, and ran off on her errand.

Pain walked back up toward Orchard House. One thought steadied Pain against the memory of the colonel's eyes. Today was Tuesday. Orchard House was closed on Tuesday.

CHAPTER EIGHT

As the bells tolled ten, the boneghosts filed into Charm's turret room with the breakfast tray. This place was their sanctuary from the world, where even the Emperor did not enter. The boneghosts occupied the overstuffed chairs or sat on the thick carpet before the fire, and, save for Pain, were clad in their shifts with their hair down.

This morning they were short one participant. No one moved to take Shame's cushion at the left side of the hearth. Charm cradled her cup and inhaled the scent of her tea as if it could wash away the last hazy impressions of her nightmares. She hadn't been troubled by those particular dreams since the Lady had grown Shame a body. They were Shame's dreams, not Charm's.

"There were soldiers in Lowtown this morning," Pain announced.

Her companions startled slightly, staring at her in surprise at her breach of etiquette. Charm spoke first. It was simply not done to go before her.

"They were impressing men into the army," Pain told them.

"How awful," said Charm. She stirred her tea briefly. "Did they say why?"

"It may be that they need the troops, or it might have been simply a demonstration of power. No one seemed to know if Strephon had supported the idea or only agreed to it. The officer in charge was a Colonel Fletcher. I didn't know him, but he was looking for trouble, wanting an excuse for violence. He tried to start trouble with the Firedrinkers who were holding back the crowd, but Captain Oram wouldn't rise to it."

"How many men did they take?"

"A hundred, perhaps a hundred and fifty. He said that they'd take anyone who passed through the gate that couldn't prove they had a job. The men will go to the army, the women into the factories or warehouses. I didn't hear much, but the city isn't happy about it."

Charm nodded thoughtfully. "Well, I'm sure we can make hay from that. Desire, tell us about Prince Luther," Charm changed the subject lightly, sipping her tea.

Pain opened her mouth, then closed it and sat back. Beside her, Justice slipped her little hand into Pain's and squeezed gently.

Desire considered how to answer Mistress Charm. "Prince Luther hardly said a word. He . . . stared."

"He only stared?" Pride asked, one of her eyebrows going up. "How disappointing for you."

"He isn't like that," said Desire. Her happiness was underlain with misery. "He watched me at first, as if he was studying me, but he knew me. I didn't say anything," she added defensively. "I didn't say a single word and he knew me anyway."

"How well?" pressed Charm.

Desire turned pink. "Very."

Charm buttered her croissant. Desire would clearly be useless in this entire affair. The whole notion of Luther knowing Desire held their history might well be the boneghost's own wistful thinking. Not that Desire's tendency to fantasize was any more reassuring than Luther's powers of observation.

Charm's emperor had been a low-level, finely focused telekinetic, which was what had allowed him to implant and control the mindlocks. His power was small, and the resulting stress on his brain minor; but Boren hadn't had mindlocks when his first son had turned up a psychic. Prince Aerleas was a leaky projecting empath. Aerleas had led the army to Inshil to seize the mindlock technology as well as its inventor. He'd done well: better than his sanity had been able to stand. An empath without any refuge, he had gone into battle after battle until he went blood-mad. He infected his troops with his sickness. If they left his service and shook off the taint, their memories either faded or seemed for vague reasons to be acceptable. The ones who truly shook off their madness killed themselves. The old emperor had not mindlocked his eldest son, most probably because he couldn't get his hands back on him. Prince Aerleas's sickness had swelled until he had earned the epithet "the Butcher" for his doings in Inshil.

"Pain, did you get the impression that Prince Luther was psychic?" asked Charm. They'd never had a psychic walk in the door that Pain had missed, and if the talent was small enough not to injure him, Luther might have passed unnoted all these years.

Pain clasped her hands around her knee, pursing her lips. "No, I'd say not."

"You'd say not? This is important, Pain."

"Acute perception is not the same thing as being psychic, Mistress, but it can have many of the same rewards," Pain pointed out. "And yes, he had a headache, but that's hardly unique to psychics."

"True." Charm took two capsules of Rejuv from a tiny dish and swallowed them with the dregs of her tea. Eternal youth, as long as the Emperor allowed, and as long as the sensitive drug was not contaminated. The Emperor preferred Charm remain nineteen. He'd always ensured Charm's youth. Would Strephon? "Did Luther say when he was leaving Borenguard?"

"No, Mistress," said Desire. "I don't recall that he said four words in a row."

"I don't expect Prince Luther can leave before the celebrations are over," Justice put in. "Prince Phelan said, very importantly, that he'd be staying at least that long."

"Did Phelan say why he let Strephon's coronation go off unchallenged?"

"Not directly," admitted Justice. "He expects to be the new foreign minister, though. If he's right, he's going to have the entire diplomatic corps under him, instead of playing second seat to Aerleas in the army. He did think it necessary to point out that until Strephon gets a legitimate heir, he, Phelan, is the most likely heir apparent. He doesn't think the Empress is capable of bearing a child."

Charm snuggled back into her pillows with her teacup and smiled. So Phelan was still ambitious. That fitted him very comfortably into Charm's orders about condemning to death any prince who wanted his father's throne. Could he be encouraged to kill Strephon before that? It seemed likely.

"Would you make sure you look in the front desk before you go on the errands this afternoon, Pain?" asked Charm. "There's an invitation for Hyacinth Barker, and the Lady has an order for Bern Ostander."

When breakfast was over and the other boneghosts filed out, Pain remained to help Charm dress. Today Justice lingered too.

"Mistress," Justice said hesitantly, "do you know . . . did the Lady mention . . . is Shame going to be all right? I mean . . . when we cleaned the room we found the knife Phelan used. It was the one he'd used on the blue cheese. Doesn't that kind of cheese have mold cultures in it?"

"It does," admitted Charm, fighting the tightening in her throat. She'd nurtured the hope that the knife had been clean.

Shame was so fragile that any kind of contamination could be disastrous. "The Lady washed the wound, but it's too early to be sure of anything. We'll have to wait until we can uncover the tank to know if she was contaminated."

Justice's expressive blue eyes filled with tears. They all knew that it would be a virtual miracle if Shame survived an infection. It wouldn't have bothered one of the others for more than a day or so, but with Shame there was no knowing if or how long the incident would haunt her.

"He kept talking about it. How he'd cut her and thrown her out because she wasn't me." The tears in Justice's eyes spilled miserably over. Pain gathered Justice up in her arms. The little ghost laid her head on Pain's breast and sobbed, clinging.

Charm seethed silently. "This time he'll pay his bill," Charm told them, and the words, uttered aloud, helped to sharpen her resolve. "I don't know how, yet, but he will pay for this."

 ⸺◯⸺

Borenguard's waterfront seethed with activity at all hours of the day and night. The local saying was that while there was tide and wind Boren's port would always be busy. Today the domestic docks were packed full. Ships of Boren crowded every available inch of domestic dockage, their masts a barren forest with the gray stone of Fortress Isle crouching in the channel behind them. Slips were empty only for the time it took the grunting steam-engine tugs to bring another ship in from anchor. The broad way between the wharves and warehouses was crowded with cargo, handcarts, and laboring men. Bowsprits and cargo cranes hung over them like jungle branches, trailing lines like creepers.

Pain had Mistress Charm's lush figure and sweet soft

mouth, and her lack of coloring did not detract from those charms. Men's eyes followed her appreciatively; but in spite of the chorus of whistles and catcalls that usually marked her progress along the waterfront, she was virtually immune to the more vicious elements of humanity that hunted around the edges of the docks. The bright white hair around her young white face had made her well known to local eyes. It warned away wise predators like the shocking colors on a poisonous frog. Today, though, no one was hunting.

A double rank of army soldiers stood at the landward end of dock twelve. A schooner-rigged steamer lay alongside the dock, a fat wallow of a prison ship. At the end of the dock was a platform with a fence around it and another double rank of soldiers standing guard. A herd of men churned slowly within the pen. One at a time, armed soldiers would bring a man out, stand him in front of a bored sergeant at a table. There was some discussion, and then the man would be taken aboard ship. Pain passed dock twelve by, careful to neither pause nor hurry as she made her way on to the international section of the waterfront.

Normally, to be licensed to work the international docks was something longshoreman strove for and sometimes fought over. Merchants paid well for the unloading, reloading, and warehousing of Boren's precious foreign trade. Today men loitered in the area of the international docks instead of worked. They were subdued, eyes downcast, even their curses quiet. Out at the end of these long, important wharves were only the skeletal T shapes of empty piers. In the last week all the foreign trade ships had slipped away in a steady trickle as the world called their emissaries home and pulled away from Boren in distaste. The quality of Boren's wind, tide, and location didn't seem to be holding up against the new reign.

The object of Pain's first errand was a small, heavily reinforced brick building on the far end of the waterfront, by the short dock that served the ferry to Fortress Isle. A neatly lettered sign above the door proclaimed it to be the business of BERN OSTANDER, OPTICS AND INSTRUMENTATION. The locale and the plainness of the building belied its clientele. If one wanted the finest work in instrumentation, and if one had the means, one came to Bern's understated little workshop. Bern Ostander was the man for whom the old emperor had launched a war. A vivisectionist charged with heresy, rescued and brought to Boren from a prison in Inshil. Bern Ostander was the man who'd invented mindlocks.

The vivisectionist, or ex-vivisectionist, was sitting behind the counter in his front room, working on a bit of metal with a tiny file. He looked up and over the top of his magnifying glasses as Pain slipped in the door. Bern viewed the bone-ghosts as a success in which he had a part. He was the one who had learned, from iterations of the Lady's notes, to make the tanks that were the instruments of the Lady's art. How to construct them in such a way that their metal binding and joins didn't contaminate the all-precious empathy fluid.

"G'd morning, Miss Pain," said Bern. "What can I do for you today?"

"Good morning, Mr. Ostander. The Lady wants a dozen new tanks, please," Pain told him. Bern didn't know the difference between Mistress Charm and the Lady, and it usually pleased Pain to make the private joke. Today it fell flat even in her own mind. Pain passed the neatly written order across the counter and hitched herself up on the customer's stool.

Bern examined the list, taking careful note of the dimensions. "Hmp. Awfully small. What's Mistress Charm growing now, goldfish?"

"I wouldn't spoil the surprise even if I knew," said Pain. She softened it with a teasing smile. Bern was pleasant enough, but he'd offered to help dissect them if their bodies failed. He hadn't been informed about the failures, but he was very interested in the Lady's successes. He had always been a little too eager to know how they functioned. He hoped that it was something he could find in their bodies. Some lingering trace of how it had been done. Pain was not entirely sure he wouldn't have been even more eager if he could investigate their innards while they were still alive.

"Thought ma'be you'd come because of Mistress Charm being ill. How's she doing?" Bern asked. "With the Emperor dead, and her mindlock ... She'd been keeping to herself before the coronation, I understand. She and I ... we've known each other a long time, now. You know I'd do anything I could to help her."

"She is recovered enough to begin planning new projects," said Pain with a reassuring smile.

"Exc'llent. Did you see that lot down on dock twelve? They're supposed to play transport for Aerleas." Bern's lips pressed together for a moment. Aerleas's troops had saved his life, after all. He patted Pain's hand on the counter. "Stay clear of them, Miss Pain. The Firedrinkers set store by you. Wouldn't like to see trouble there."

"Mr. Ostander ... has Emperor Strephon placed orders for mindlocks?" she asked, glancing at the one on his desk.

Bern snorted. "Fat lot of good 'twould do our new Imperial Majesty. He can't set the instructions in them. He'd have to be a telekinetic, and a damn'd finely controlled one at that. Those're rare as hairless cats. Takes too much practice. There might be one in the Firedrinkers, but I don't imagine he'd trust it to a Firedrinker t' do. I'm just finishing this one because it was half done. Give it three or six months, and if the Firedrinkers can't get permission for more locks, Boren'll have budding young psychics accidentally burning down buildings, driving people around them insane, and running mad in the streets themselves. You mark my words," he predicted.

"The Emperor can't do it manually?"

"Can't be done manually," said Bern. "Was no point making them that way, and the old emperor wanted them secure." His eyes met Pain's.

How long before Strephon ordered Bern to make a mindlock that could be manually adjusted? "Can you make them so that they don't have the command aspects?"

"They'd be s'mpler to make that way, actually, but they'd st'll need a fine-work telekinetic to implant them. When does Mistress Charm want this order?"

Pain forced herself to smile. "My lady said she'd like the new tanks by Wednesday next if that is not impossible."

Bern nodded. "Small as these are, I can do't with glass I've already got. I'll bring the bill around with the tanks."

⁓

Charm watched from a turn in the stairs as Pride sat utterly unmoved before Emperor Strephon and his escort of Firedrinkers.

"I'm very sorry, Your Imperial Majesty, but today is Tuesday," Pride explained with absolutely no regret in her voice. "Orchard House is closed on Tuesday."

Strephon's scornful lip curled, his fist tightening dangerously. Enthroned behind the reception desk and unable to see this warning sign, Pride did not flinch.

Charm came down the stairs, black taffeta rustling. She sank into a low curtsy, and rose again. "Your Majesty honors Orchard House. We thought that you would be busy preparing for today's celebrations, or with your lady wife," she said pleasantly.

"Today is Tuesday, Mistress Charm." Strephon's voice was as smooth as a serpent.

Her hand on the balustrade tightened. "Indeed. Orchard House is closed on Tuesday," said Charm softly.

"Except to the Emperor."

Tuesday, thought Charm. Tuesday. He was taking over all the properties of his father. His father's throne, his father's wife, his father's mistress. Strephon's choice up to now had always been Shame, but Charm didn't know how to wake Shame up. And at the same time, some part of her was saying quite rationally that of course the Emperor was here. Today was Tuesday. She wanted desperately to flee into the depths of her mind, to hide there with the Lady. The mindlock ticked a notch tighter in her temple.

Charm floundered, trying to find someplace in between the mindlock and Tuesday. Maybe this was something the Lady could handle? She was, after all, an actual lady. Strephon might listen . . . Charm caught a glimpse of Pride past Strephon's shoulder. Pride lifted her sightless eyes toward Charm, and her gaze brought Charm to her senses. No. The Lady mustn't be here. Strephon stood, enjoying her hesitation, her struggle. If Charm took him to bed, he might let his guard down. If he'd killed his father, maybe she could get him to brag and admit it. And it was Tuesday. She was made for Tuesdays.

"Come," commanded Strephon a little sharply, putting out his hand to his father's mistress. The Imperial seal flashed upon Strephon's hand.

The seal. Strephon would sleep, and there were uses for that ring. For perhaps the space of two more heartbeats, Charm stood frozen. A bit of exercise, a drugged cup of wine, and that seal could do her good. Trembling, her hand lifted and came to rest on Emperor Strephon's wrist.

"Pride, bring some wine to my usual room on the second

floor, please; and be sure to decant it properly. I don't want sediment in the glass." The house code for a sleeping draught in the wine.

Pride inclined her head, a cool smile touching the corners of her mouth. "As you wish, Mistress."

⁂

The fabric shop was on Pain's way back to Orchard House, so she went there last. The morning sunshine streamed through the shopwindows. Hyacinth Barker came out of the back room, closing the door carefully. Miss Barker was a big, broad woman with big, strong hands. She smiled when she saw the boneghost. She didn't care who or what her customers were, as long as they paid. With all the ghosts and Mistress Charm to dress, Orchard House was her best account.

"Good afternoon, Miss Pain. What can I do for you?" Hyacinth asked. "We have some lovely silk gauze just in. Perfect for you in the evening."

"I'm sorry, I'm not here to place an order today, but Mistress Charm asked that you call to discuss some new orders. She'd like you to do the measurements personally." Pain passed the pink letter across the counter.

Hyacinth opened the envelope and read the letter. "Well, I had been going to go over my inventory, but for Mistress Charm I can put it off. She tried to help, you know, when Phelan pressed charges against my sons for trying to keep him from beating a man to death."

Pain blinked in surprise. "No, I didn't know. It seems . . . unlike her."

"'Seems' unlike her. That's the trick to your Mistress, isn't it? All the frippery and all that cynical calm wrapped up around a sensible, decent woman?"

The jingle of the bell on the door cut Hyacinth off, and

she jerked into her more public mode in surprise. "Countess Seabrough, this is unexpected. Are we to have the pleasure of your patronage?" she asked brightly.

Countess Seabrough carried herself very upright. "I am here at the Empress's bidding." She sounded less than pleased with the Empress's command. Countess Seabrough glanced at Pain, her thin nostrils twitching as if she'd smelled a wet dog. Slowly she turned her gaze back to Hyacinth. "If you are not busy?" Her tone held nothing but contempt.

"I am never too busy for the Empress, naturally," said Hyacinth.

Countess Seabrough passed a letter to Hyacinth with only the tips of her fingers. As if she didn't want to touch rubbish. The seamstress opened the rich, creamy vellum and scanned the contents. She glanced briefly at Pain, smiled at Countess Seabrough. "It's my honor. I'll be there."

"Wonderful." Countess Seabrough's flat tone stated that there was nothing whatever wonderful about the situation, and her flicked glance at Pain said openly that she'd sooner have her teeth drawn than ever lay eyes on the boneghost again. "Good day," said Countess Seabrough to Hyacinth. She turned in place and left, her dark blue train swirling around behind her in distaste.

"Brrrrr," opined Hyacinth with an exaggerated shiver. Then she laughed; a bright, broad bray of disrespect. "And she's lady of the wardrobe, can you imagine it? You'd freeze to death undressing with her in the room!"

Impact against Charm's mouth, far up the city at Orchard House, made Pain gasp. A punch to Charm's belly. Pain doubled over, clutching her mouth with one hand, clinging to the counter with the other.

"Hey, hey now, Pain, are you all right?" Hyacinth came around the counter to take Pain's elbow. "Should I call a doctor?"

Pain shook her head, too breathless to form words. The next jolt struck her across the shoulders, driving her to her knees.

"Shall I call you a carriage?" pressed Hyacinth. "For heaven's sake, Pain, say something!"

It wasn't her pain, of course, but that didn't matter. This was what she'd been made for. "I'm all right," wheezed Pain with the last of her voice.

"The hell you are, I'm calling you a cab."

CHAPTER NINE

When Charm arrived in the red parlor that afternoon, Hyacinth stood and eyed her with restrained horror. Charm was wearing white. The dress, borrowed from Shame's wardrobe, fit badly. A shawl didn't quite hide the way the bodice strained across Charm's ample bosom and puckered loose around the waist. Shame had preferred more flattering and less lift than Charm's corsets. The contrast to Charm's usual, wildly elegant black was awful. Charm was well aware of that. Indeed, she could have borrowed a dress that fitted from Pain. Charm had known Hyacinth since Hyacinth had been a fitting girl with ambition and a man's head for numbers, but her stare eroded Charm's confidence. Charm fingered a lock of newly butter-yellow hair.

"The white is fine on you," said Hyacinth at last, her voice thick, "but the fit is ghastly. I'll send someone first thing in the morning to alter it."

The strained support of friendship, or almost-friendship, was harder to bear than stares. Charm tried to smile, but couldn't make the expression firm up. Abruptly she took Hyacinth's hands and tugged the bigger woman down seven inches to her own height. The clothier crouched to exchange cheek-touches with Charm. Her hands held on to Charm's for an extra hard moment.

"How is Pain?" asked Hyacinth.

"Pain will be fine. She always is. You know, I believe you've outdone yourself with that dress," said Charm, throwing off her own discomfort to give the other woman's costume a critical examination.

Hyacinth was splendid in bright blue-and-white-striped satin bustled up to show a shockingly orange underskirt. Fully laden with pleats, bows, and billows, the big woman looked like a clipper ship draped for launch. She clashed exuberantly with the dark red wallpaper, too brash and too alive for the propriety of the parlor.

"Thank you. I wondered what was so urgent, but if that's all you have to wear it's definitely an emergency," Hyacinth added.

Charm managed a real smile at the probing. "Awful, isn't it? As it happens, though, the clothing is not why I originally asked you here tonight. I want you to arrange some shipping matters for me."

"Import or export?" Hyacinth asked with a grin.

Charm's customers enjoyed the titillation of refreshments that were not strictly legal, and, even on legal goods, Charm enjoyed not paying tariffs where she could avoid them. Hyacinth had always been exceptionally resourceful in the procurement of those items unavailable through normal channels of commerce. It was also far more profitable than the fabric that was her front and money-laundering device.

"Both." Charm couldn't think of any tactful way to ease into a discussion of revolution, so she spoke bluntly. "On the import side, I want three separate shipments of a thousand guns."

The grin faded. "That's more dangerous merchandise than usual."

"I'll pay for it," said Charm, lifting her chin a bit.

"I never thought you wouldn't," Hyacinth soothed her

hastily. "I know this place turns a profit for you, but . . ." She hesitated, then forged on in a more familiar tone. "Charm, we're talking about a small fortune and large crates. And guns? What possible use could you have for them?"

"I want to find out who killed the old emperor, and I want the Princes of Boren dead," said Charm, "or at the least, any of them who wants the throne."

"What about the one who's on it?" Hyacinth asked. Her plain, heavy features took on a thoughtful expression.

"Especially him," Charm said coldly.

"You can't kill a prince of Boren," Hyacinth declared. "Killing one will only bring the wrath of the other three down on us. I don't have any great desire to be tortured to death."

Charm smiled. "I don't propose we kill them. I propose to have them kill one another."

The dressmaker looked at Charm. Neither said anything.

"Strephon had the effrontery to call upon me today," said Charm at last.

Hyacinth paled. "So, that's why you put aside your black?" she asked Charm.

Charm turned away, pouring herself a glass from the carafe of wine on the sideboard to cover a flush of embarrassment. She cursed the heat in her cheeks. Shame might have taken some of it, she thought resentfully. She must be hiding behind the Lady somewhere, but at the same time Charm knew that wasn't fair. It wasn't like Shame to sulk. If she'd been able to, she would have helped.

"Yes. He commanded that I wear no more black." Charm sipped her wine to help clear her throat. Strephon did not have the power to shift the mindlock, but Charm didn't care to let him know that. If he thought her independent, she wouldn't survive long. It had been harder than it should have been to lay aside her black for the sake of vengeance. Still. They weren't

Charm's people, and Inshil wasn't Charm's homeland. Charm's first memory was opening her eyes in Orchard House. "Strephon's visit was not one of the more pleasant encounters of my life, but at least I am a practiced whore. Can you imagine what he's doing to poor Ylsbeth?" she demanded, turning back to her guest.

"I thought you didn't care for her," said Hyacinth in surprise.

"I don't care for children, either, but that doesn't mean I enjoy standing by watching when I see one beaten." *There was nothing I could do to prevent Phelan from hurting Shame. There's been nothing I can do to keep him away from Justice without doing more harm elsewhere.*

"What do you want me to do?" asked Hyacinth, interested but still wary.

"I want three shipments of arms smuggled into the city. Use your competition's ships if you like," suggested Charm, "but spread things around so that the blame can't be pinned on any one person. I need to have guns cached in places where they'll be found . . . eventually."

"This is high treason, Charm," Hyacinth reminded her.

"Will that stop you now that you have a chance to pay Phelan for sending your sons to the gallows?" asked Charm, her voice gentle. A low shot, but a sure one.

Hyacinth's lips pressed together in a hard, white line and her big hands balled into fists. It took her a moment to speak. "No," she whispered at last, her voice harsh as a gull's. "No, it won't; but why're you doing this, Charm? What can possibly be in it for you?"

Charm's smile was thin. "I have my order from my emperor. And it can be made to include Phelan." She did want to know if Phelan was guilty of his father's death; but whether he was or wasn't, she still didn't intend him to survive his other crimes.

"That wily old bastard," Hyacinth murmured, half admiringly. "And wily little you. Who would replace Strephon?"

"Did you have a candidate?" asked Charm.

"Not off the top of my head, no; it just seems a little hasty to start off a coup d'état without a candidate for the throne," Hyacinth said with a smile.

"If no other alternative rears its head, I believe we could prop up Ylsbeth. The Emperor always told me that I underestimated her. At the moment, though, I'm simply working on making Strephon incurably insecure and stirring up trouble between the brothers. Quite frankly I don't care who rules Boren as long as it isn't one of them." It was a good excuse, and kept Hyacinth out of the hunt for the murderer. The rest of this was dangerous enough.

"You haven't said what you want exported yet," pointed out Hyacinth.

"Lyra Fergus and her children."

"Lady Fergus? Doesn't she have about a dozen kids by now?"

"Eight, I think."

A knock on the door interrupted them. Pride opened the door a half a beat later. "Lady Lyra Fergus, Mistress," she announced.

"Oh my. This is earlier than I expected her. Show her in, Pride, by all means," instructed Charm.

Lyra Fergus was a middle-aged lady of moderate height and unprepossessing looks. Her gown was simple, her hair drawn back into a plain coiled braid. The clean lines of her toilette showed her strong jaw and rather imperious nose to advantage. She couldn't ever have been pretty, but she might have been handsome on other evenings. Tonight, she was drawn and weary.

"Mistress Charm," she said, "I don't believe we've ever formally met. I'm Lyra Fergus." Her tone was even, gentle and low, the epitome of a cultured woman's address, but she could not seem to bring herself to offer Charm her hand.

"Lady Fergus, welcome to Orchard House," Charm greeted her, also without offering to shake. There was no point in rattling the woman further, though she admitted privately to being tempted. "I didn't expect to see you so soon. I hope your children have been made comfortable?"

"Your . . . creatures have been very kind, to offer their attic beds." Lady Fergus sounded a bit relieved. The thought of putting her children into the more regularly used beds had, apparently, distressed her. "I do hope we are not putting you to . . . well, we are putting you to a great deal of trouble," she amended her own statement with a tired smile, "but we are very grateful. We should not have had any warning if not for you."

"It's quite all right, and I never begrudge trouble spent on a worthwhile cause," Charm assured her. "May I introduce my designer, Miss Hyacinth Barker?"

Lady Fergus eyed Hyacinth and her costume with trepidation as they exchanged polite murmurs of greeting.

"Miss Barker is going to be arranging your traveling accommodations," explained Charm.

"They may be a little primitive," Hyacinth warned, "on such short notice."

"Supper is ready," announced Justice from the doorway. "Mrs. Westmore says please come at once, for the sake of the roast."

"I see that cooks are alike in all houses," quipped Lady

Fergus in a valiant attempt to make conversation, "and my husband has told me wonderful things about yours, Mistress Charm."

"We're very fortunate in Mrs. Westmore," Charm admitted. "If she says that supper shouldn't wait, I feel confident she is correct."

The ladies adjourned to the private dining room, where the damask-clothed table was laid for three, with Justice just stepping back from the third place setting. Tall white candles lit the room, glittering on the cut crystal and gleaming along the curves of the silver. Justice served for them.

"What destination did you have in mind, Lady Fergus?" asked Hyacinth when they had tasted the soup and all agreed that Mrs. Westmore was to be congratulated.

"I fear I need advice in that regard. I wish that I had a ready supply of foreign relatives, but I confess I do not."

"Fortunately, I know someone who can give you shelter," said Charm briskly. "I haven't had contact with her for a long time, but I'm sure she'll help you with my letter of introduction. If you do not mind the connection," she added with a wry smile. "My reputation is not desirable to you, but my . . . acquaintance is quite highly thought of in Saranisima. I am certain she will be discreet."

Saranisima was separated from Boren by the latter's provinces, consisting of Inshil and several less troublesome conquests. It was no secret that Boren coveted the ports and trading routes of Saranisima, nor was it particularly surprising that Saranisima aided, abetted, and funded the difficulties with which Prince Aerleas was currently dealing.

"The lives of my children are at stake. I am not in a position to turn away anyone's hospitality, Mistress," said Lady Fergus with a pleasant, if steely, practicality. "The Firedrinkers cannot be inept forever." Her resolute smile wobbled around the edges and her eyes went glassy with tears. "And Major Nathair cannot save us more than once."

"Major Nathair saved you? The Firedrinkers were inept?" Charm prompted, trying to believe two impossibilities at once and finding it difficult on both counts. For Major Nathair to pass on a warning via Charm was one thing. To act directly . . . well, he had earned the spangles on his decorations.

Justice paused at the sideboard.

"Fergus passed on what you'd told him," said Lyra, "but I didn't think it would come to violence against him so soon. Major Nathair . . . he's stopped at our house a few times to come here with Fergus. He half pounded my kitchen door in just before a squad of Firedrinkers arrived. The major ordered all our servants out of the house, then hustled us upstairs to the nurseries. I don't know how he managed to get out of the house before they started to search it, but I didn't hear any fuss . . . they were making a good deal of noise so I knew where they were, and I heard the order was for them to find the children and myself. The children hid under their beds, behind the dust ruffles, and I hid in the wardrobe with Anna, that's my eldest girl. The Firedrinkers walked around the room we were in . . . I could hear their boots on the floorboards."

Lyra Fergus closed her eyes with a shudder of remembered fear. "I could see the red of a coat through the crack between the wardrobe doors. A Firedrinker stood right in front of it. One of them said something like 'I don't see anyone at home.' They went away without looking under a single bed, or in any of the wardrobes. They let us go." She covered her eyes with one hand, and a sob broke from her. "I think . . . I think they must've told Major Nathair to come warn us. So they wouldn't have to . . . to find us . . ."

Was Major Nathair setting Charm up in some way? But

he had warned her about Lord Fergus being in danger. It was rather pleasant to find out he was willing to take a direct hand instead of leaving it all on Charm. "Have a little more wine," said Charm, pouring Lady Fergus's glass fuller than it ought to have been with dark, purple-red Blood Field wine. Could Nathair have some kind of plan to have fugitives caught at Orchard House?

"I shouldn't," objected Lady Fergus as she wiped her eyes.

"You've earned it," Charm said with a sympathetic smile. There was very little she could do about it now, if Nathair had set her up. "Besides, this is a strengthening wine."

Lady Fergus sipped at her refilled glass, perhaps with some relief at having it urged on her. "Anna wanted to stay behind," she said shakily. "She says she's in love."

"How old is Anna?" asked Hyacinth with a kind smile.

"Seventeen," Lady Fergus told them. "I told her that someone who loves her would want her to be safe, if they cared about her at all. She still wants to stay, of course."

Hyacinth's bray of laughter relieved the tension at the table. "Of course. Her mother was never seventeen, and couldn't possibly understand about love and devotion. You're only one of the most famously happy women in Borenguard. Very seventeen."

Lady Fergus smiled, still teary. "She's just like her father." She blinked hard, drawing a shuddering breath, but did not give way to her emotions again.

"Then best we act quickly, before she can do anything foolish. Hyacinth, can you give me any idea when you will be able to arrange a ship?" Charm asked.

"Not for a day, at least. And I'll need good papers for them. Even with them hidden, the ship's captain is going to need one hell of a pass. Diplomatic papers for the whole ship, or something," Hyacinth said seriously.

"I can supply something." If nothing else, she'd made up a small pile of Imperial seals while Strephon snored in his second-floor bed; but a simple Imperial order was a long gamble.

"You should get some sleep if you can, Lady Fergus, and sleep as long tomorrow as you can," Hyacinth said. "I don't know when I'll have that ship and it might be on a night tide."

Lady Fergus rose, lifting her chin. "Thank you, Miss Barker. We shall never forget your kindness. Nor yours, Mistress Charm. And . . . should you see Major Nathair, please give him my eternal thanks," she added. She glided from the room in the direction of the kitchen and the back stairs.

Charm didn't clench her teeth, because Hyacinth might see it. Could one poison an emperor and still have mercy for women and children? All things considered, it seemed likely one could. Had the Duchess of Madderley committed murder for Aerleas? If she had, was Major Nathair in it with her or not? One thing was clear. To save Lady Fergus, Charm was going to have to see Major Nathair. Perhaps he knew nothing about the assassination, but now Charm must be certain.

CHAPTER TEN

Pain drew her coverlet up over the lap of the Ferguses' eldest daughter, Anna. Pain and Justice would sleep in one of the working rooms tonight. Faded patchwork in the attics was probably not what the daughter of Lord Fergus was used to.

"I know you." Anna Fergus watched Pain with eyes slightly dilated by the night's anxiety.

"I suppose anyone without coloring is bound to stand out." She knew perfectly well that ladies watched her when she was in the upper wards of the city, whispering behind their fans.

"No, I mean you were mentioned to me particularly, pointed out. You're Captain Oram's girl."

Pain blinked. "Beg pardon?"

"You are, aren't you?"

"Captain Oram's girl . . . ?" Pain trailed off in surprise.

"That's what the Firedrinkers say."

"It's odd that they didn't say it to me," Pain said.

Anna Fergus was not blessed with great beauty, but she had glossy mahogany hair and a scattering of golden flecks across her pert nose. Just now her eyes were uncertain, but that gradually resolved into determination worthy of her father's moral certainty. "They keep your book full, though, so that the captain doesn't have to share you except with them," Anna said. "That's what everyone says. He didn't ask them to, but they do."

It was true that they kept her book full, but there were so many of them that it was no surprise Pain was always busy. Still, how in the world could the girl know that?

Anna fidgeted with the edge of the coverlet. A quick breath of wind brought the smell of rain and wet grass in through the window, and made the bones in the orchard clatter. "Is it true that Firedrinkers don't . . . ?" Anna left the question hanging.

Pain all but gaped at the question. "No. They don't," she told Anna shortly. Which was as close to an answer as she was going to give.

A crimson blush was starting to creep up Anna's neck and cheeks, but every mote of her father's unbending stubbornness possessed her eyes. "Nothing? None of them?"

Firedrinkers were not allowed to risk reproduction, though that left them quite a lot of leeway. Pain didn't answer at once. Someone had told Anna about Pain's bookings. Why this insistence on rooting out information that young gentlewomen should have absolutely refused to acknowledge?

"I just want to know . . ."

"I know what you want to know," Pain cut her off. "You're a well-bred, gently reared young lady, Miss Fergus. Your mother would peel me like an orange for speaking of bedroom sports with you, and justly so." Pain paused, relented a little. "This much I can say—they don't visit here because they love me."

"Except for Captain Oram."

This girl had far too romantic a notion of Pain's position. "None of the Firedrinkers has ever come to me wearing a white sash. Even if what you say is true, I have no way to know which one he is."

Anna reached out to take Pain's hand. "I'm sorry. I didn't mean to hurt you."

Pain forced a smile for the consideration, but the solution to Anna's curiosity now seemed obvious. No one worried about hurting Pain unless they themselves were hurting or afraid of being hurt. Anna wasn't hurting physically. Pain would have felt that. "So you are in love with a Firedrinker." Not a question. "You wouldn't be so concerned with their habits if you weren't."

"His name is John Seabrough."

It seemed to be Pain's evening for shocks. "Seabrough? How old would he be?"

"Eighteen. We've known each other all our lives. The way he walks, the gestures he makes when he speaks . . . they couldn't hide those with a coat and visor." Fierce tears rose in Anna's hazel eyes. "Count and Countess Seabrough told everyone that he died. He can't even say his own name!" she hissed.

Pain didn't answer at once. It was hard to think of the positives of the mindlocks. They weren't fair, but at least the psychics lived. It was seductive to think of her own favorite free. Free to kiss her, free to hold her, or free to leave her for someone he loved instead of making do. It made her belly twist, to think of her long-faced, weary Firedrinker going to someone else. Pain was a little surprised by that. Apparently Pride did not have an entire market on her namesake. Anna Fergus waited.

Pain swallowed hard, made herself answer. "It wasn't as if the Seabroughs had another choice. When a psychic manifests they almost always go mad in one way or another. Usually they die or kill themselves. If they're very lucky, they don't take other people with them. The Seabroughs probably thought that it would be better that your John was alive in the Emperor's service, rather than mad or dead."

"What am I going to do, Miss Pain? I can't just leave him." Anna's voice broke, and she caught up the coverlet and pressed it over her mouth to muffle a sob.

Pain took hold of the girl's wrists. "Listen to me, Miss Fergus. If he loves you even a little, he wants you alive."

Anna tossed her head with a frustrated cry. "You sound just like my mother!"

"Then she's an uncommonly sensible lady."

"I can't bear it! I can't bear to leave him. . . ."

Pain forced a smile, and quoted Mistress Charm. "You'll find that what you can bear increases a great deal when you are not offered any other choice."

⤳⟿

Charm saw Hyacinth to the front door. She put a thick leather wallet into the "designer's" gloved hands. "Give what you don't need for the guns to Lady Fergus."

Hyacinth opened the wallet, and froze in surprise. "This . . . Charm, these are Imperial notes of draft! Only the Emperor and the princes can issue these!"

"What do you think the Imperial financier paid me with, buttons? The princes may not pay all their bills, but they do pay some of them. These are all recorded somewhere as issued to Prince Phelan. They're proof that Phelan is planning to overthrow Strephon," said Charm, the thought bringing a smile. "Also, I'm going to send a case of wine with Lady Fergus as a gift for her hostess."

"I didn't want to press in front of Lady Fergus, but I wasn't kidding. I'd need an Imperial writ to get a ship past Croissonè without being searched," said Hyacinth, appalled.

"I have a plan for that, too. Find a ship, and trust me. I'll have them to you by tomorrow night."

Hyacinth bent and planted a firm kiss on Charm's cheek, the salute of a friend. It raised Charm up at the same time that it pulled the Lady down the slippery rungs of society into the companionship of smugglers and pirates. A whore couldn't really be any lower.

"What color do you want your new dresses in?" asked Hyacinth. "I'll send some samples up in the morning with Lillian, and something premade that she can trim if I have anything that might be altered quickly."

"White," Charm said. "I want mourning crepe, but in bone white. Better just make one for day and one for evening."

Hyacinth laughed her broad, coarse laugh. "Good for you."

Charm kissed Hyacinth good night at the door, climbed up to her room in the top of Orchard House's great turret, and went to her desk. She laid a sheet of fine paper on the blotter, picked up her mother-of-pearl pen, and opened the crystal inkpot. First, she wrote a note to Major Nathair, inviting him to call tomorrow.

Charm took out a sheet of white vellum, smoothed it as if she could make it more perfect. The Lady would never have written a letter on pink paper. Charm sat for a long time looking at the blank page. She couldn't think of any good way to begin the letter. How could she say anything without peeling the Lady open like a pomegranate to bleed onto the whiteness before her? Taking her resolution in hand, Charm touched the pen into the ink.

To Mari-Tres Mendacciano of Saranisima. Dearest . . .

She stopped, her pen hovering over the paper. She assumed that Mari-Tres thought the Lady dead. At the least symbolically dead. The only reason Charm was sure that Mari-Tres was still alive was because the news from abroad usually included small mentions of her. Mari-Tres's philanthropy was as famous as the graciousness of the city of Saranisima.

Thoughts of the past made Charm chew on the end of her pen. Shame did not come out of whatever corner of Charm's mind she had hidden in. She could take over, thought Charm resentfully. This was just her sort of letter. A low laugh bubbled in Charm's throat at her own cowardice. She swallowed hard, wiped her eyes on her sleeve, and took a fresh sheet of vellum. Best to let Mari-Tres make mention of a connection if she wished to do it. Charm would not be the one to link the greatest lady in Saranisima to the Emperor of Boren's infamous whore. Charm breathed in, and made herself breathe out. All she had to do was write the letter, and let the Lady surface just enough to write the signature as an automatic reflex.

To Mari-Tres Mendacciano of Saranisima.

After all this time with no contact, it is surely gross impertinence to send Lady Lyra Fergus and her children to you for shelter, but I could not act until now. I hope that what these refugees bring with them will, in a small way, make up for any inconvenience. The wine that arrives with this is a rare vintage I believe you will recognize. I flatter myself you might inspect it immediately. It will not age well in the crate. In future I hope to be able to provide your honor with gifts of more strategic value. I pray that this letter finds you well and happy, and that you continue so. My love is with you always . . .

Charm let the Lady carry on the thought, the pen moving in smooth habit:

. . . don't forget your squirrel.
                                                    With my love, Charmaine

Squirrel? Well, if a childhood detail worked it would be a nice touch. Charm eased the Lady back into sleep before she could even wonder what had happened or what this room was.

Charm folded the letter. She took a sealing ring set with lapis lazuli from the desk drawer. It wasn't hers, personally. She'd found it in the dressing table drawer when she'd been well enough to get up and begin exploring this room, and Orchard House. For a moment she sat, rubbing her thumb back and forth across the midnight blue of the stone. It was not hers, but it would unquestionably be recognized. And it would leave an indelible psychic impression for Mari-Tres if she should have a psychic check it for her; but it felt like sacrilege.

Charm put a piece of sealing wax in her wax spoon, and set it over her lamp to melt, then used her desk shears to prick her thumb. She smeared her blood across the sealing ring. Carefully, Charm poured wax and pressed the seal into it firmly. A little joggle freed the ring, leaving the bloodstained image of a crowned orchid upon the silver wax. The same image that stood above the front doors of Orchard House.

Pain opened the front door of Orchard House and blinked in shock at the figure standing in the early-morning daylight. To Pain, who was used to seeing female Firedrinkers in concealing male uniforms, it was crystallinely clear what she was seeing. "D-Duchess?" The stutter escaped before Pain could prevent it. The person who stood on the steps was certainly the Duchess of Madderley, minus her stunning mass of hair and wearing an army major's uniform.

The Duchess's thin lips twitched in amusement. She did not deny her title. "Miss Charm honored me with an invitation to call this morning."

"I . . . Yes, Your Grace, of course. I'm so sorry. She's expecting you." Pain shook off her shock. She'd been busy with Firedrinkers on the nights Major Nathair had happened to call at Orchard House. "Do come in." Charm had described the major to her, but it hadn't occurred to either Charm or Pain that they could be the same person, that a duchess would serve as an army officer. Pain led the way through the side hall to the conservatory.

"Her Grace, Major Aiglentine Nathair, Duchess of Madderley," she announced, and withdrew with a haste that bordered on flight.

"Mistress Charm, it is ever a pleasure."

Charm stared, but there was no denying what seemed obvious. Pain would not have made a mistake. The slightly-too-long hair gave softening counterpoint to the severity of the features. That sharp face did not belong to just anyone. Nor to more than one person. It was too distinct. The makeup that concealed the deathly pallor was perfect. The masculine impression was absolutely correct, the line of the uniform coat and trousers every inch of elegance. Whoever tailored the major's clothes was a treasure of no small scale. "How does Your Grace prefer to be addressed?" asked Charm. After all, "Major Nathair" and as a man was how they had been introduced, but they had appeared in a gown in the ladies' gallery at the Assembly Hall and been referred to as a woman by Count Seabrough.

Charm's guest hadn't sat down, and now leaned against the conservatory's framework. Long and elegant. As if they were a man and thus utterly unthreatened, completely self-assured. As if they owned the space they took up by right of their mere existence, instead of existing in space borrowed from others. And that, oh genius that it was, that was the surest part of the guise. The major knew their worth to a point of surety that, in a woman, would certainly be overweaning arrogance. As a woman they would not be beautiful. It was their audacity that made them breathtaking.

Major Nathair's thin lips curled up in amusement. "Do you know, no one has ever asked me that?"

"That seems a sad lack of manners in those who have the good fortune to be closely enough acquainted with you. Obviously, I shall refer to you as masculine if I speak of you as Major Nathair to others, and in the feminine if I have any reason to refer to Your Grace by your Imperial title; but as this is a private space, and Orchard House is very good at keeping secrets, is there a manner of address you prefer?" She was treated to what she assumed was a rare sight.

Major Nathair, the Duchess of Madderley, opened their mouth and shut it, twice, thoroughly flummoxed.

"I hope you'll forgive me if the question was rude. It was not intended so. Only, your masculine guise is quite as flawless as your feminine appearance is reputed to be." Charm spoke to give her guest more time to compose themselves. "I certainly didn't make the connection, though I can understand a little better, now, why you wear your masculine hair in such a poetic fashion. Not only is it becoming, but you've only to pin it back under a switch to have a woman's hairstyle."

"I had the hairpiece made out of my own hair that I cut off. I was always told it was my one true beauty, and enough people identified me with it that I thought I could wear it while my hair grew out again." The Duchess lifted their shoulders in a wry shrug. "The day never came."

"I assumed that Major Nathair was Duchess Madderley's son or grandson."

"I never had a son. Only a daughter." But they shook off their bemusement. "This is for a day when we know one another better. And I couldn't imagine that considering me two separate people at once would pose a problem for you." She smiled, an expression practiced—and Charm was possibly the most qualified judge in Borenguard—to perfection.

So. They knew about Charm's boneghosts. What they were. Or had guessed correctly. "We keep many secrets at Orchard

House, but we do not pry," Charm said, returning the smile as if her rounder face could in any way mirror that of this extraordinary switch-blade of a person.

It seemed to work, because the major's chilly smile broke into a grin like a flash of lightning. "So you do, and you certainly do not, Mistress. You have my apology for doubting it."

"And you have mine for Pain's startling you. We are usually more gracious, here. Tea?" Charm invited.

"Yes, thank you. Lemon, please." The major looked around the airy conservatory, taking in the low, slightly wide chairs scaled to Charm's small plump self, the ferns and lilies, the citrus and roses in their pots. Their pale eyes judged it all as they sat down opposite Charm in a chair that, though sufficient, had proportions meant for bustled skirts instead of sleek-lined uniforms. And yet Major Nathair occupied it as elegantly as if it were a throne. "This was an excellent addition to the house, I must say. A lovely way to have a private space in an essentially public ground floor, and to have some decent greenery in this beastly climate."

"Were you familiar with Orchard House in its previous life?" asked Charm, as if this was a perfectly polite morning call and the major had not just implied they were older than Charm's entire residence in Borenguard. She poured, added a slice of lemon, and passed the cup across.

"I'm very familiar with Orchard House. Once upon a time, it was called 'Orchid House,' and it was mine," said Major Nathair with the faintest tension riding their thin lips. They looked out at the bone trees, standing sentinel. "It's easy to understand how the name has metamorphized."

That could not possibly be true. And yet . . . Orchid House. And the seal of the crowned orchid that had been in the drawer, and that same symbol carved over the door. "A member of the royal family with a house below the Uptown wall?"

"There weren't internal walls, in those days. They only put those up at the beginning of the war. Someone told me the geology required they jog the Uptown wall in such a way that my former residence was outside Uptown proper, but I've always hoped that wasn't true. It would have been such an elegant slight on the part of the empress who was overseeing the construction committee that I rather admired it." They smiled as if they were actually admiring it.

Charm asked, "Is that why you were at the gate that night, and subsequently came to the cardroom? To see what had become of your old home?"

"Not entirely," they said. "Mostly, I came to find out how it would feel to see it again. I wanted to know if it would hurt."

The admission was so wry, so open. Was this some deliberate strategy toward putting Charm at ease? Certainly, they could not harm Charm without Imperial repercussions. Probably. At the same time the line itched until, grudgingly, Charm asked, "Did it?"

"A little," admitted Nathair.

"It had been shut up for some time, I believe, before the Emperor gave it to me."

"Only since the beginning of the war. Did the Emperor not tell you about it?"

Something about their face still teased at Charm. She knew them. She was quite sure she knew them from somewhere, but that was ridiculous. Major Nathair had never come to Orchard House until recently. "He said it had belonged to a young cousin of his. There was only one room of furniture left in it."

"Yes," they said with a small tip of their lips. "That was my daughter's room. And no," they went on immediately, "I am not in the least upset. She'd have been very happy, I think, to have it be a haven for such a clever woman."

Charm regathered her wits. "Now you are teasing me. I am, obviously, very curious." She dimpled.

"Yes, I was teasing; which makes me a poor guest as I've no intention of telling all my secrets today. Let us dispense with this to-and-fro before you get me into trouble. May I ask how it is that I can be of service to you? A daylight invitation to Orchard House is certain to be something momentous?"

"You asked me to warn Lord Fergus, which I have done, and now you have sent me quite interesting visitors, I believe."

"Is this where they are?" Major Nathair smiled in apparent delight. "How wonderfully unlikely of the lady. The last person in Borenguard I would have expected to be practical would be anyone married to Lord Fergus. And she came to the last place in the city anyone would look. You know they're watching the harbor and the gates?"

"I didn't, but I did suspect as much. That is where you come in."

The major's mouth made a silent "ah." "And I am an Imperial courier. Any package, cargo, or person I escort cannot even be questioned. And people will certainly think the worst of the situation if it were to be people. Why would I commit such a treason?"

"If not because you have involved me in your concealed treason, then to absolve yourself of the sins that earned you so many decorations in the war," said Charm with a sweet soft smile. "Assuming you are interested in such a thing."

Nathair's pale eyes sparkled, but if it was a warning or if it was amusement, Charm could not tell. Perhaps it was both. "I have always thought that saving you was a significant mark in my favor."

Charm blinked. "You saved me? How did you do that?"

"You'd have died a blithering madwoman without that mindlock. I had to have you carried onto the ship for Borenguard. You were mostly just staring and twitching—which was at least more restful than the babbling and screaming and trying to claw your own face off. I'm impressed you could recover. You must be one of the most tenacious women in the world."

No one could say that Nathair minced words; and there was something hollow-edged, bitter, and rotting in the back of Charm's memory that she couldn't quite examine. She covered her pause with a half-hysterical laugh. It hadn't been her. It had been Shame. "What can anyone do to an empath that's worse than what your empathic Prince Aerleas has done to a whole country?"

"Prince Aerleas doing hideous things doesn't mean that Inshil was a faultless paradise. A fine attempt to divert blame, mind you, but you'd have had to try it on someone who hasn't seen the labs where they produce Rejuv."

Charm herself had no memory of Inshil, and the Lady's memories held nothing but good opinions. Inshil had been as close to paradise as there was for psychics. As good and kind as they could be with dangerous people who without exception died young. "You speak very glibly for someone who's clearly been taking it."

Major Nathair snorted. "You are misinformed. I wouldn't touch Rejuv with an infantry pike. Firstly because it would be cleaner to die of old age, secondly because I do not require it."

Charm stared. It was both entirely possible, and infinitely improbable. Psychic talents were wildly variable, and they certainly ran in the Imperial family. But . . . there was no mindlock in the major's delicate temple. "You have no mindlock, and yet you seem entirely sane."

Nathair's laugh burst out, a weird, almost metallic sound. Skittering scratchily, like a mouse trapped in a pail. "Mostly, anyway."

Charm fingered the spiral of hair at her neck. One could not class unaging as a minor talent, but if it didn't require them to exert their mind perhaps it didn't require the support of a mindlock. "Why do you object to Rejuv, for those who are not so fortunate as you?"

The major studied Charm for long moments with their mouth half open, stilled in a sharp retort. They closed it. Their eyes bored into Charm, pale as a patch of sky reflected on oiled steel. "You may have been sheltered from it before Aerleas, but I know he took you and made you look at what your precious Inshil was doing. He told me so, and I checked it with some of the other officers."

Aerleas had made Pride look at the impalings. What else had Pride seen that she hadn't talked about? But Charm shook it off as the mindlock whirred. It was no part of her. "My memory has . . . gaps."

Major Nathair's thin lips pinched down so that their mouth was little more than a slash in the harsh face. Finally, into the silence, they spoke. Their voice was perfectly level, so calm that the sound of it was terrible. "Rejuv is made from the spinal fluid of empaths. They're kept strapped into special braces and sedated, with a needle in their spine and the fluid dripping slowly out. Not enough to kill them, just a steady drip that their bodies can replace. They are force-fed through tubes. Bucketed clean. When we got there, there was already a long ward full of people gone entirely mad and kept alive far past where they would've managed to kill themselves. Aerleas is a horror, but at least he sedates them."

Charm clutched the arms of her chair as if the grip was all that kept her in it.

Nathair went on. Remorseless. Colorless. Emotionless. "The Emperor decreed the practice should continue, and justified that they were mad or going mad anyway, and after all . . .

they're not Boreners. He wanted to live forever, obviously, and he was willing to let others pay the price of it. Aerleas was insane enough by then to agree; but it was Inshil who invented the process. That was part of why they suppressed mindlocks. If psychics could walk free, empaths couldn't give up their spinal fluid for the good of the state. Those in power could not live forever. The Emperor was a horror. General Aerleas is a demon. And then there is Inshil." Major Nathair's lip curled. Disdain dripped from their teeth like venom. "Inshil spawned them both as surely as swamps breed disease."

"Empathy fluid," Charm managed to wheeze, breath knocked out of her by pieces suddenly falling into place. "The Emperor supplied us with barrels and barrels of it."

"Yes," agreed Major Nathair pleasantly. "I hope you don't waste it. One barrel is, more or less, one empath's spinal fluid production for a year. I imagine that you knew how to make your duplicates because of something your beloved parents were training you to do for the good of the state. There was a laboratory at the palace that, in retrospect, was almost certainly yours. I didn't see that, but the general ordered the entire wing burned, and then he had the ashes scraped up and buried in a massive pit in holy ground. It wasn't one of his more sane units that was assigned to dispose of that lab, but I imagine that was probably for the best."

"I need you to do something," Charm managed.

"Other than save your life and your sanity? How do you plan to motivate me?"

"The Emperor was not a good man. We both agree, I believe?"

Nathair leaned forward, tipping their head. It made them look like some kind of golden carrion bird. "Where is this going?"

"Wait a few more questions and you'll find out. Do you

love Prince Aerleas?" Calling someone a demon didn't negate that Nathair had worked for that demon during the height of the war. It didn't negate Aerleas's power. His hideous empathy. His making others feel as he did.

The golden head slowly tipped the other way, a faint smile lifting the edges of the thin lips. Not in a smile. A baring of teeth. "I have been accused of that."

Charm's question had hit . . . not an old scar, but a wound that had abscessed. Unfortunately, Charm could not be sure of exactly what had kept that infection alive for so long. There was more than one possible source and she could not afford to be wrong. "I would like to take your bare hand and know that Aerleas did not send you to kill his father."

They laughed again, this time merrily. It was in no way an improvement over their previous mirth. The rusty scrape of the sound sent goose bumps down Charm's arms. Major Nathair really should not laugh at all. They should simply be regal. That, at least, suited them.

"I do not think the person who would save Lord Fergus and his family is a person who would poison the Emperor, but I have to be certain of it."

"If I did kill him, you're taking your life in your hands. I am a soldier, after all. I've killed a lot of people." Perfectly level, perfectly deadly.

It was Charm's turn to smile while her pulse tried to beat its way out of her throat. "Yes, but I have boneghosts who are not here." Pain should be doing errands by now. "I have made sure that if anything happens to me, Strephon and Luther will find out. The Firedrinkers will find out, and, I think, be unamused." She'd made no such precautionary arrangements, but wished she had. Pain would, however, almost certainly tell the Firedrinkers. "I won't read further back than I need to."

Nathair shrugged. "On your head be it."

Charm took their hands. They were as cold as marble. There was no warmth at all in them. Charm had handled plenty of the Lady's failed experiments, and she would've wagered heavily that not one pair of dead hands had been colder than these. And so soft, so white, so strong. Justice had hands like theirs.

Psychic gifts weren't a part of Charm. They existed behind the division between Charm and the Lady, so that Charm had to reach into that other mind as an interloper. The Lady reared up, struggling to wake. The mindlock murmured warning, sending little spikes like electric needles in her head, holding her separate from the Lady. Charm wanted to scream and swear, but fought down the impulse. Emotion wouldn't help her. She had only one weapon in this fight. She refocused her efforts. This was the Emperor's order. She must find out. The Emperor's order. The mindlock in her temple gave in a sudden, soft crack. The world disjointed, and instead of the room immediately present around her, she saw the past of the cold hands.

There. The Emperor's hands in those of the Duchess. The Duchess had given the Emperor's hands a gentle squeeze as if in assurance, and put one of her cool hands on his brow, then replaced it with a cold damp cloth. They had visited the Emperor several times, held the Empress's hand. Hugged her shoulders. Combed her hair, and put her to bed and petted her forehead as if the Empress had been a child. There was no sign at all that the Duchess had fed the Emperor anything. No sip of wine or water. No powder or vial of liquid. Lace bobbins flew through nimble dead fingers, clicking out intricate patterns. Leather gloves. Not dainty kid. Heavier, particular. Reinforced and padded specially. Reinforced why? Ah. Fencing gloves. Every day, the major fenced. No slipping of coins to anyone. No packet to a servant. No telltale letter to or from Aerleas.

Something in Charm's mindlock sprang and whirred, the world wobbled around her, and the rain of electric pain crashed into waterfall-agony. Charm released the major's hands and closed her eyes, tears running down her face. The punishment stopped but the headache stayed.

"Do you need a basin? Are you going to be sick?" asked Nathair.

"Maybe," Charm was forced to admit, gagging just at the idea. She breathed carefully.

Nathair took the nearest fern out of its catch pot and put the pot in Charm's lap, then slid one cold hand gently under Charm's hair to lay it on the nape of her neck. They laid their other hand on her forehead.

"That's nice," sighed Charm.

"These are pretty much the only places anyone ever wants my hands if I haven't just been in a hot bath," Nathair said wryly.

Charm managed the sliver of a chuckle. "I'll note that down in case you decide to call upstairs."

"Sorry, Mistress, but I'm not much interested in ghosts. I have enough of my own."

The major's hands warmed up slightly, and when Charm opened her eyes, Major Nathair took their hands away.

"Better?" they asked.

"Yes, thank you." Charm offered a reassuring smile. She put the catch pot aside, and gave in to curiosity. "Why did you let me read you?"

"As I'm sure you realized when I let you do it, I had nothing to hide." Nathair's grin was sudden, breaking across the sharp face like lightning and gone again just as quickly. "And it was the only way you could truly take me into any kind of confidence. I admit it, I am as curious about you as you have said you are about me. You've worked hard to make yourself fascinating, so surely that's no surprise."

Charm smiled. A small, actual expression. Entertainment was what Charm was for, but this was not a ruse or a blind. The major knew too much of that game, clearly. "Not many people realize it's on purpose."

Nathair's scoff was inelegant, but spoke scornful volumes. For all the masculinity on display, it was certainly a noble-woman's sound. "I can neither alter nor explain the lack of mental acuity in the general population. Shall we discuss your plan, now?"

"I need two things," said Charm. "Firstly, I need you to escort the Fergus family to Saranisima. I have someone who can hire a ship, but you are the best guarantee that they will arrive in safety. And Lady Fergus trusts you."

The major's look spoke volumes about their opinion of Lady Fergus. "Even I won't be able to help if Prince Luther is aboard the ship that stops us."

"Prince Luther isn't going anywhere. Strephon doesn't trust him enough to let him take ship and have his liberty for no good reason. He's keeping him close. For now, anyway."

"Mm. And you are in a position to know that for certain. Or did you say something to ensure it?" Nathair tipped their head, examining her.

"I didn't have to do anything. Strephon's paranoia is some-times convenient. And I don't want to make an uproar. Things in Boren must remain at peace as much as possible. With what Aerleas could do to Inshil, I don't want to know what Strephon could make the Firedrinkers do to people."

Nathair shuddered. "No, you don't. Assuming I can ac-complish the first task and not be arrested by Saranisima or taken for treason, what is the second task?"

"You're the Imperial courier, and I need a spy in Prince Aerleas's camp. Someone who can warn me when he takes actions that might disrupt things here." She didn't say "until I can come up with a plan to dispose of him," because there was no point in getting that ahead of oneself. "Would you be able to do that?"

Major Nathair's shock faded into surprise and transformed into thought across the length of Charm speaking.

Charm let herself smile. "Well, it's either this or you get to go back to making lace all day."

"I enjoy making lace. It's very soothing." The major straightened. Hardened. Drew the elegant scabbard of practiced ease off the vicious steel of some internal resolve. "I will get Lady Fergus and her children to safety if I can, and with Prince Aerleas . . . I'll try. His power is heavy. Less so for me than for others, but still. All I can promise is to try."

Charm put on her best dimples and her most girlish enthusiasm, and she burbled. "I only want to know more about him. I don't remember him at all, you know, and he did let you bring me out of that awful place! He's so intriguing, and we know so little of him here in Borenguard! He has worked so hard for the Empire for so long." It was possible that Nathair could use that, if they needed something to say. Tell a true thing that Charm had said and not disclose it all.

Nathair stared, smiled, breathed, "My God, you are superb." It both was and was not a compliment.

"I ask this next only so that I don't misstep and reveal your ruse by accident—do the princes know about this double life of yours?"

They shook their head. "Aerleas, obviously, but he hasn't cared for decades. If any of my fellow staff members know, they pick up on Aerleas's attitude and promptly share it.

Phelan might guess, but I've made sure I didn't meet him as Major Nathair. Luther and Strephon caught glimpses of me in uniform, but haven't guessed. Too self-involved and too unobservant, respectively."

Nathair evidently didn't like their royal relatives. "Excellent. Then I have a little present for you, Major. Can you come out to the lab for a moment?"

There was a long moment of hesitation, but Major Nathair rose. "I can."

Charm covered the small eternity of orchard back out to the greenhouse. She refused to grace the covered tank containing Shame with even a glance. She didn't need to lose control of her body right now. Charm took down the cage that held the first of the Lady's new birds. Sleek and black, the little swallow perched on her finger, regarding her with calm eyes.

Charm turned to Major Nathair. "Just tuck this little fellow into your pocket, and if you have anything that you need me to know before you can arrive yourself, just tell it and let it go. It will come straight back here."

"It talks?" asked Nathair doubtfully.

"Of course not. I'll touch-read what you said. It will be easier if the message is not too long or too complicated. As you just saw, my mindlock has very particular issues."

"Very well." They accepted the bird and smoothed its satin feathers, then slipped it into their coat pocket.

"I'll send you a note to tell you what ship and when, unless you'd rather make your own plans for transporting the Ferguses?"

"Not at all. I'm sure your arrangements will be perfectly sufficient. You're still pale, Mistress, if you'll forgive the observation."

Charm smiled for Nathair's kindness to ask. "I'll be fine,

Major. You'd best go now. If you stay too long, the Emperor may get the wrong impression about your visit." She put out her hand. "Thank you for coming."

Doubt played openly across Nathair's face, but they took her fingertips, bowed with breathtaking perfection, and went.

CHAPTER ELEVEN

Pain made her way slowly down from Orchard House to the Lowtown gate. The distance seemed longer today than it had yesterday morning. Her back burned under her clothes.

"Miss Pain?" One of the Firedrinkers on guard came to cradle her uninjured elbow and guided her gently to a bench beside the gatehouse. "You're not well."

"I will be." It was an effort to force words out past the hurting. She opened her reticule and drew out a thick stack of carefully folded and sealed papers. "Employment assurances for Mrs. Agnes Westmore, Mrs. Maude Hawkins," she croaked, "and for our maids and the rest of our household staff and employees." Letters for brothers, husbands, sons . . . anyone and everyone Charm or Pain knew about and for whom they could dream up theoretical employment. After all, Orchard House could need its windows washed, the lawn mowed, the gutters cleared, and a multitude of other upkeeps.

The Firedrinker accepted the papers and examined them, then took them away without a word. One of the others stepped seamlessly into the space with a cup of water. Pain accepted it, sipped politely. It helped even if it didn't take away the hurt, though whether it was the water or the simple gesture of comfort she didn't know. The only Firedrinker whose visor was pointed in her direction was the one who had brought her the cup, but she couldn't help feeling that they were all watching her.

"I'll be all right," she said again.

"Yes, miss." Not even the distortion of the helmet could cover the lack of belief in the reply.

"Miss Pain!" Round and red-faced, Mrs. Westmore bustled toward Pain from the gate. "Miss Pain, what are you doing here?"

"It was she who brought your papers, ma'am," the Firedrinker supplied. "I will escort you both to Orchard House."

Pain decided that shaking her head would be worse than speaking. "No."

The Firedrinker reached to steady the cup in Pain's hand.

"Don't you touch her," shrilled Mrs. Westmore indignantly. She batted away the Firedrinker and took Pain's hand, cup and all, into hers. Her eyes filled up with furious tears. Mrs. Westmore glared through them at the Firedrinker. "You. You protect those horrible soldiers, let them just take people."

Pain shook her head and regretted it. She could have left more of the day-after-a-beating effect to Charm, but this was her job. To bear it. "They protected us . . . from the army . . ." Pain wheezed. "They can't help it."

Mrs. Westmore huffed disbelief.

Pain waved her free hand in a negative gesture.

The Firedrinker's helmet tipped to one side, as if he were listening. "If you do not wish an escort, miss, we will leave it to your discretion."

"I'll help her," said Mrs. Westmore firmly. "I'm going to take you home and put you to bed myself."

Pain took a gentle grip on Mrs. Westmore and got to her

feet. Slowly, they made their way back up toward Orchard House.

⁓

By Saturday, Orchard House was running short of champagne, several varieties of cigar, the best port, and every kind of amusing drug—all the things that were usually imported via Inshil. Prince Aerleas's difficulties there were beginning to interfere with the accustomed pleasures of the nobility, and they resented it in no uncertain terms.

It had taken until today for Hyacinth to deliver the first white mourning gown. Somehow, somewhere she had managed to procure undyed white crepe. A material so tied to mourning gowns that it could not be mistaken. Not even by drunks in the semi-dark. Severe and plain, the long-sleeved day dress covered Charm from chin to wrists to toes. Nothing sparkled. Nothing shone. Everyone gaped.

Charm was the convenient ear for whining, complaints, and a bit of downright hostility. She made herself smile, flirt, and be sympathetic to men she wished would go the hell away. Of them all, only Count Seabrough and Mr. Anders offered her sympathetic words. When Justice came with Pride's request for aid, Charm was only too eager to escape. Prince Luther stood beside the reception desk.

"Did you want to see me, Pride? Justice said that you did."

"Prince Luther would like me to attend him, Mistress," the boneghost answered calmly.

Charm made herself smile. Pride going willingly to a prince of Boren? To Luther? It was unbelievable. On the other hand, if it wasn't Pride it would have to be Desire, and Charm certainly didn't want to take that risk twice. Pride was doing the right thing.

Charm held on to her pleasant expression. "I'll get Justice to tend the desk."

Pride rose, and put her hand out imperiously. Luther put his hand beneath hers.

"Good evening, Mistress," Luther told Charm blandly, and led Pride away up the stairs.

⤳❦

The next morning dawned cold and wretched. Charm closed her eyes and breathed a prayer to a God she was no longer sure believed in her. She looked at Pain and nodded. Pain whipped the cloth cover off the growth tank that held Shame. Charm sank slowly down to sit on the edge of the tank. Mold was creeping beneath the skin on Shame's face, veining the porcelain fairness with deadly midnight blue. The edges of her wound had bloomed open under the pressure of the growing mass. Whips of the cheese mold floated free like grotesque tentacles in the empathy fluid. The contamination had spread across the bridge of Shame's nose, the color beneath her skin mimicking bruises. It had crept down into the major blood vessels in her neck, and from there it had transformed her breast into a grossly swollen, lumpy tumor.

Ever fragile, Shame had not retained enough connection to her body to fight the infection. She would not be coming out again until a whole new body grew. Something in Charm's mind shimmered for a moment like a heat haze. The mind-lock caught, and the gears ground suddenly, like a pepper mill chewing in her brain until spots danced in front of her eyes. Charm struggled against it, and failed to hold her own. Her frustrated scream cut off abruptly as she was no longer in control of her body.

The Lady woke on the end of a scream, looking at Shame's mangled body. She leaped away from the tank, pressing her hands over her mouth with a shriek. She shook her head desperately.

"I didn't do that," the Lady managed, beginning to cry. Pain gathered her lady into her arms. The Lady buried her face against Pain's breast. "There was nothing I could do. It wasn't me."

Too delicate. The ugly parts of life weren't the Lady's. Charm clawed her way out of the dark like dragging herself up the blade of a bone saw. She eased the Lady back. A headache rose across the back of her skull in mounting waves. Charm began to disentangle herself from Pain.

At the motion, Pain stiffened, pushing Charm away. "You left her to wake up to horror!" she shouted at Charm. "Do you have even a single feeling of compassion left?"

"It wasn't on purpose," Charm snarled wearily. "You know I never let her look until everything's cleaned up and fit for her to see. If I'd planned to let her cope with it, I'd have let her take the cover off the tank."

"The Lady got out on her own?" scoffed Pain. "And how would she do that?"

The Emperor had released almost all of Charm's mindlock. And he was gone. The situation she was made to deal with had been almost all removed. Everything but the last commands. Charm's pulse hammered against the confines of her skull. The Lady had been able to unseat her, and it frightened Charm to the marrow of her shared bones. "I came back the moment I could. You needn't like me, Pain, but even you must realize that I wouldn't do that to the Lady. We're all here to protect her." She rubbed her temples, swallowing against a sudden nausea.

Pain shook her head. "I wish I knew when to believe you."

"I wish you did too." Charm was horrified at the wave of guilt that rolled through her at the idea that Pain didn't trust her. She shouldn't be guilty. That was Shame's job. God, her head felt as if there were white-hot daggers digging into her brain. "Please, Pain, I have a terrible headache," she admitted.

"It's your headache. You keep it." Pain turned and marched away.

Charm was tired to the core of her being, but that didn't change what needed to be done. Resigned, she cranked the body in its cage up out of the contaminated empathy fluid and lowered it onto the table. The finer mold strands broke off and stayed in the tank. The larger dangled and dripped like pond weeds from a drowning victim. It was not, Charm reminded herself dully, the first time she'd cleaned up after one of the Lady's experiments. There had been so many mistakes in those first years. So many bodies that hadn't made it. She'd done all of this before. Telling herself that didn't make it easier. Shame had been alive. Real in a way that all the embodied boneghosts were real. Charm fetched a cloth and laid it gently over the repulsive face that had been the same as her own. As if it would help her distance herself from the body enough to do what must be done.

Charm laid the scalpel against the skin of the bare thigh before her and shuddered so much that for a moment she didn't dare make the cut for fear of damaging the precious bone hidden deep in that flesh. She needed to know if the bones would still be usable. Charm steeled herself savagely. Shrinking from responsibility was the Lady's province. Charm, not being a lady of any description, did not have that privilege. She pressed the blade into the birthmarked skin of Shame's thigh, seeking the big vein there to tell the tale. It was clogged with blue mold along the whole length of her incision, bursting damply and spilling contaminated blood and mold-sludge onto the steel table. If the mold had gotten that far down in the leg, there was no saving the bones. The Lady should've known that the body wasn't recoverable. She'd wasted a whole tank of empathy fluid instead of waiting for new bones to make Shame a new body. Maybe one without the marks, this time. There was enough empathy fluid for one more human tank. Only the one. It was far too rare to count on getting any more now that Charm's emperor was gone. They could afford no more of these mistakes. And Shame would have to remain, sleeping in the back of Charm and the Lady's mind, until the Lady had enough bones to make her a new body. Resigned, head pounding, Charm tossed the scalpel into a long bowl of disinfectant and went to get a sheet to use as Shame's shroud.

⌒∽

Cold rain spat a ragged staccato against the windows of Charm's tower room as the boneghosts filed in silently behind Pain. Their whispering silks seemed only to accentuate their silence. Pain put the breakfast tray across Charm's lap, but no one sat down. They all stood, hovering and uncertain with their eyes downcast. Charm ignored them, pouring her first cup of tea and stirring sugar into it. Her hand shook and the spoon clattered against the china. She put it down. There was no sound in the room except for the drumming of the rain.

"Mistress?" said Justice at last. "What did the Lady say about Shame?"

"She didn't say anything. The body was ruined by cheese mold on the knife. She hadn't washed the wound well enough. Maybe there was no 'well enough,' but Shame will stay with me; at least for a while." When Charm made herself look up, they were all staring at her. Justice huddled against Pain's side like a rejected child, and Desire's green eyes held veiled jealousy. Pride showed only cold and careful neutrality. Charm cleared her throat. "Pain, pick up that pillow, won't you?"

Pain picked up Shame's favorite seat and laid it tenderly on Charm's cedar chest. Slowly the boneghosts settled into their accustomed places, but they perched like feathers; as if the next breath could send them tumbling into the air in disarray. None of them looked at the empty place on the hearth.

"Will the Lady make another body for Shame?" asked Justice into the silence.

Why must she press the point? It would take nine months to grow another human ghost. For Charm's own purposes, it was far simpler to wait until the political ends had been achieved. Less expensive too. In spite of the recent flush, money was not coming in to Orchard House as it once had, and it was going out quickly. Charm said the truth aloud. "We should save our last vat of empathy fluid in case someone who wants a physical body needs healing. Shame can stay with me, for now." Calm words, but the teacup chattered against the saucer when she set it down. "So, Pride, how did you find Prince Luther?" Charm asked, trying to move the morning toward normalcy.

A faint smile began to play around the corners of Pride's mouth. "Desire was correct."

"And that's all?"

Though she could not see, Pride turned a slow, rosy pink under Charm's scrutiny. "He isn't psychic," Pride told them.

"You're sure?" teased Desire, a little sparkle starting to creep into her eyes.

"I'm sure." Pride developed a sudden intense interest in combing out her hair as she added, "But he certainly is perceptive."

The coyness of the ghost stabbed like a letter opener, tearing instead of making a clean cut. Charm clenched her jaw hard against something that felt ridiculously like betrayal. She looked down into the depths of her tea. The boneghosts worked hard, all of them. They bore many of the Lady's heaviest burdens. Her anger was stupid. If Luther was more considerate in bed than his brothers, so what? Her poor ghosts deserved to have a bit of fun if they could find it. That was what she told herself. Twice. She couldn't make herself believe it.

"I've never thought I'd see you go to a prince of Boren willingly, Pride. I thought I'd have to all but twist your arm," Charm said. "Why is Luther special?"

"He treated Desire with consideration. I wanted to know what that is like, if he was the way she claimed." Pride groped for Desire's hand, laced her fingers through Desire's as if they were a sisterhood of two and somehow separated from the others by their experience.

Charm couldn't conceal the bitterness that twisted her upper lip. "And did you like it?"

Pride answered without hesitation. "Mostly. What I didn't like was that he didn't behave as he did out of consideration for me. He did it to be different from them. He wanted to be better than they are, and in the end that is still him thinking of himself, and not of his partner's pleasure." She turned her face toward Desire as Desire winced. "I'm sorry. I wish I was wrong, but I don't think it's ever going to be what you hope for."

CHAPTER TWELVE

When Hyacinth came to deliver a new costume on Wednesday afternoon, Charm had not yet risen. "I cannibalized three coming-out gowns and an unpaid-for wedding dress to put these together," Hyacinth told Desire, laying the bagged dresses across the ghost's arms. "I'm going to have to start charging extra for these last-minute orders."

"You won't get in trouble, will you?"

Hyacinth waved it off. "Never worry about me covering my own back."

Charm did not get up until four. At six o'clock she clung to the bedpost.

Charm's new injuries buzzed against Pain's mind like flies against a window, but she held the sensations out. "You should've let me have the wounds," she told Charm angrily.

"And you are clearly intent on making me suffer for it. No, no shift tonight. I'll wear my corset against my skin."

Pain stared. "You want the wounds, you want to get up and make them worse, and not even wear proper padding between them and your corset, you should have to feel them. Not me."

"I need them."

"The Lady doesn't need them. What will she do when she wakes up with her back in bloody welts?"

"If you fill your purpose, she won't even know they're there.

You might be obstinate with me, but you know as well as I do that you won't abandon her as easily."

"The least you could do is rest and let them heal properly. You have only to say that you are ill." Pain jerked on the laces.

Charm's breath hissed. "I will go down," she muttered through clenched teeth. "I must be stronger than Strephon in the eyes of the nobles. He must not bow me before them, nor keep me away. If they don't see me, they'll be able to forget me."

Pain tied off the corset. "Yes," muttered the boneghost, "Pride was sure you would say that."

"You complain as if I'm doing you some disservice."

Pain sat down on the foot of the bed and leaned her white head against the bedpost. "You make it so that I'll hurt more later on. Should I thank you for it?"

Charm raised her chin. "No. And you shouldn't have to hurt for me at all," she decided. "I should thank you for not sheltering me. The hurting reminds me to hate him every moment, instead of only when I think of him."

Strephon had expanded his original command from no more black to no more mourning, but as that had been predictable, she had been able to order a gown at least a little in advance; so tonight Charm's white gown was an elegant affair. He hadn't said "no white." Strephon liked to try to break her. He had told her so, hissing it into her ear as if it would be a triumph that someday she'd cry. He had been careful, though. He hadn't marred any part of her skin that might show outside her clothes. There was one carelessness, though he hadn't really recognized it. One particularly savage open weal was above the top edge of her corset. Charm rubbed her arms in spite of the warmth of the bedroom. If he could keep thinking he was breaking her, perhaps he would not feel it necessary to break Ylsbeth.

After all, she told herself, *I am a professional whore. His degrading me doesn't matter.* Charm smoothed her hands down the front of the smoothly fitted white bodice and went downstairs to the card parlor.

"Having to write personal letters for every day servant in the house, I tell you it's a demmed nuisance," commented Anders, in his accustomed place at Seabrough's card table. Lord Fergus had not put in an appearance.

"Yes, it is a bit hard. Our servants live in, but most of our people have family in Lowtown," said Seabrough mildly.

"Well, loss of two towns in Inshil does seem to say that Aerleas needs the men," Anders was saying as Charm made her way carefully to their table. He was a tea merchant as well as an assemblyman, and always full of news brought in by his ships' captains. For a foolish man, he did astonishingly well. "It's starting to look rather ugly in the provinces, I understand. There are rumors from Saranisima, all unsubstantiated of course, that they found mass graves in those two towns." He looked up from his cards. "Oh, ah, good evening, Mistress. Do forgive me, didn't see you come up. Hope I didn't upset you," he apologized. His tone was light and breezy. He didn't seem to remember she was from Inshil, and Charm wondered suddenly if there was anyone left who did.

"You didn't upset me, Mr. Anders. I am quite acquainted with Prince Aerleas and his methods." She felt as if it would peel off a layer of her skin to admit more. Charm waved a hand before her face to make the sudden moisture in her eyes seem like a reaction to the smoke that veiled the room. The words tasted coppery, but they served her. "I was born in Inshil, after all." Even as she said it, she realized that it wasn't a lie; but she couldn't remember why. The separation between herself and the Lady wavered dangerously, and the mindlock whirred.

"By gad, that's true, ain't it," recalled Anders in surprise, stubbing out the last butt of his cigar. A thoughtful look worked its way through the general glaze of brandy. "Think there's any truth in this about these two towns?"

Charm touched the mindlock in her temple, fingering the smooth facets. "I . . . could not say."

"By gad . . . I say, by gad," sputtered Anders.

"Oh come now, Anders," Count Seabrough said from beside Charm, "Emperor Strephon gave his personal word that those claims were untrue. Besides, this is hardly a fit topic for a lady's ears."

Charm didn't think it politic to remind them that she was not a lady. Not tonight, anyway. The Count was so obviously trying to both make Strephon out a liar and change the subject at the same time. He had always been a sharp one. As the Emperor's mistress, Charm might repeat criticism, real or implied, of either Aerleas or Strephon. Charm obliged the Count. "Yes, Mr. Anders, shame on you," she teased, wagging a finger and laughing. "You're launching into weighty matters before you've given me a single compliment. Why, you haven't even said you like my new dress."

Lyle, partnering Anders, laughed and clapped Charm on the back in rough good humor. "You may start a whole new fashion."

She gasped a little, fought to keep her smile. Warm wetness soaked along her back. The well-meant gesture had opened her wounds. "While this isn't what I'd pick for myself, I believe I've earned my wardrobe," she managed.

Seabrough looked up at her from his seat. Though he smiled as if he were a bit drunk, his eyes were sad and sober. "I've no doubt of that, Mistress."

Lyle shouted with laughter. The other three didn't join his merriment. Lord Hanover shot Lyle a look of dry distaste over sipping his drink.

"Where is Lord Fergus tonight?" asked Charm. "I have a bottle of wine I was saving especially for him."

"He's decided to stay home this evening and work on some papers. Said he wouldn't be good company," said Anders.

"Two of his little ones fell sick, and Lady Fergus took the family off to the south where it's warmer," supplied Seabrough.

Anders nodded. "Poor fellow is worried half to death about 'em."

Charm made appropriate noises of sympathy and leaned prettily against Count Seabrough's chair, skirts against his arm. "Poor man." Idiot. He should have run.

"Poor fool, you mean," opined Lyle, taking the politically safe track. "He just won't see that Emperor Strephon's only taking these economic measures because of the mess in Inshil. We're all going to have to tighten our belts before this is over."

"Are you going to deal those cards or fondle them, Lyle?" asked Seabrough blandly.

"If I can ask, how is the poor Empress?" inquired Charm as Lyle dealt.

"She is as well as can be expected, with all this upset." Lord Hanover's brows puckered a little. "Why do you ask?"

Which gave Charm a chance to shrug, even though it rubbed her wounds. "She called me to the palace to attend the Emperor's deathbed, and she was so very pale that I wondered if she had been ill even before his passing. Did any of you gentlemen notice it, before the event? Or was it only the strain of that awful day?"

"I wasn't at court that week," said Lyle. "He was annoyed at me, and I'd thought I'd better lie low a day or two, so Anders and I rode out to the country for some shooting."

"Annoying emperors? How brave you are, Sir Lyle," said Charm.

"It would've blown over," Anders assured her. "'Twasn't that kind of annoyed."

Which put both of them out of the running as direct murderers, and bribing the palace staff—regularly scanned by Firedrinkers—was a one-way ticket to the gallows.

"I hope any pallor the Empress exhibited was only the strain of the Emperor's illness," Lord Hanover said. "The Empress is a resilient young woman, but his death upset her terribly." He shot a glance at Seabrough. "Did your wife mention if she'd been ill, prior?" He seemed so honestly worried that Charm nearly smiled at him.

"If you think my wife tells me the Empress's private business, or anything else much, you've not spoken to her recently." Seabrough offered a shrug. "People have apparently seen too much of me here."

"Oh, but Count Seabrough," burbled Charm with a laugh, dipping forward between Seabrough and Hanover so that Lyle and Anders, across the table, could admire her cleavage while she leaned around to look at Seabrough and put a teasing hand on his chest. She purred with a theatrical pout, "I haven't seen nearly enough of you." And gave a bawdy wink around the table as they all laughed to assure them that it was only a joke. It wouldn't do to get Seabrough in trouble with Strephon for something he hadn't done.

Sitting where he had to look at her back to watch her teasing his companion, Lord Hanover's laugh strangled abruptly. The welt above her corset, unrestrained by a shift, must have begun to stain through layers of her bodice.

"Hanover?" asked Anders. "You all right?"

Charm picked up Hanover's empty whiskey glass and held it to her breast like a jewel. "I'll just get Pain to refill this for you."

She turned away from the table, and someone there hissed in shock. Back ramrod straight, chin up, Charm glided between the tables. Silence trailed in her wake. She gave the glass to Pain at the bar.

"Refill this for Lord Hanover, would you? On the house." And Charm went to change her ruined white bodice, smiling. It had been expensive, but worth it.

~☙~

The ladies' viewing gallery of the Assembly Hall was filled with hats, bustles, flapping fans, and dueling perfumes. Pain eased into a seat at the back. Her eyes went wide.

The screen had been removed from the Imperial seat behind the chief assemblyman's podium. Strephon slouched in his father's chair, one foot up on the railing and looking as if he'd like to kick it through the railing.

"The new tariffs have directly impacted Boren's ability to do business with our neighbors," said Lord Fergus, keeping his eyes on his peers rather than glancing at the Imperial seat. "Devarik takes advantage of us by lowering their tariffs to those we offend, pays even less than that on the goods they then pass on to us, and thereby positions themselves to make us dependent on them," Fergus went on, his face full of grim determination. "The international wharves in Borenguard Harbor are empty except for shipping from Devarik, and their prices on goods have increased by forty percent now that they play middleman between Boren and the rest of the world. This situation of favoring Devarik over all others is untenable. We must restructure the tariff acts or risk bankrupting the country."

The Assembly stirred nervously. Finally, a walking stick rose.

"Count Seabrough."

Seabrough stood for a moment, head down, resting his clasped hands on his walking stick as he seemed to compose himself. When he lifted his head, he spoke firmly. "The facts which Lord Fergus reports I do not dispute. His close examination of the financial situations are no doubt superior to my own, but gentlemen, this is not a matter for the Assembly. Matters of external policy are the sole responsibility of the Emperor."

Pain glanced at Strephon. His lips were curled up in a satisfied smile.

"Even with conflict of interest?" asked Fergus.

Strephon's smile snuffed out.

"Does the Emperor Strephon not have personal holdings in Devarik?" Fergus forged ahead. "His marriage brought many such into his hands. No man with conflict of interest may enter the negotiation of a treaty. It is one of the oldest laws of Boren, older even than Imperial law, which legally and explicitly cannot supersede it."

Seabrough leaned on his walking stick as he canted his hands forward a bit. "It's still an external interest, and therefore falls under Imperial law."

"Which precedence of law I have previously mentioned," countered Fergus. "And the treaty affects internal issues of national production and export as well. It is not only an external matter. I maintain that this is a highly questionable issue."

Lord Hanover cleared his throat. "Lord Fergus, what are you proposing?" he asked.

"His Imperial Majesty, I'm sure in all innocence, has overstepped a subtle but ancient and necessary legal principle. We of the Assembly have, as our duty to the people and to His Imperial Majesty, an obligation to see that such matters are handled correctly. Particularly given Devarik is the birthplace of our most esteemed Empress."

A murmur ran around the Assembly.

Fergus went on relentlessly. "I suggest that we consider a request that His Imperial Majesty allow a full review of his finances, which are a part of the national budget. It is a right which we have not exercised recently, but which this Assembly does legally retain," he added loudly over the renewed murmuring, "in order to fully understand the depth of whatever financial conflicts may be present."

Lord Hanover raised his gavel and rapped to still the murmurs. "Given the gravity of this decision, I believe it might be best for all of us to take time to seriously reflect on our vote on this subject. Gentlemen, we are dismissed until tomorrow."

Women in the ladies' gallery stood up immediately, impatient to escape the stuffiness and eager to spread the word among fine parlors and over tea trays.

By the time Pain could see the Imperial seat again, Emperor Strephon was gone.

CHAPTER THIRTEEN

Pain's favorite Firedrinker sat on the edge of the bed with his elbows on his knees, looking into his wine. There were circles under his eyes, and threads of silver showed bright in his hair. Before Strephon's coronation, his hair had been a glossy, uniform sepia. Now and then he reached up to rub the crystal in his temple. It hurt Pain unexpectedly, from the inside; a sensation that was all her own instead of inherited from one of the others.

Pain sat down beside him, laying her cheek on his bare shoulder.

"Can you tell me what troubles you?" she asked softly.

He surprised her by answering. "Lord Fergus spoke against the Emperor's new taxes today."

"I heard." She rubbed her cheek on his skin.

The Firedrinker shuddered for a moment, and his breath hissed through his teeth. A drop of crimson slipped out of his nose.

Pain wiped away the blood with her fingertips. "Don't. Don't do this to yourself. I'm sorry."

He pressed his lips against her palm in a gentle kiss. Pain closed her eyes to block out the sight of his face, concentrating on the shape instead, the way his jaw fitted into her hand.

"Captain . . ." She opened her eyes, looking into his golden ones.

"I may not be able to say it myself, but I think that by now you could use my name."

Pain licked her lips. His name was strange in her mouth, more intimate than touching him. "Oram."

"I . . . want you to know that it was never you. I try not to intrude, but sometimes I'm so tired that my brain feels raw, and you've been touching me, and your thoughts are like silk, strong and at the same time soothing. You're never afraid of me, not even now when you know who I am . . . and I need you to know it's never been that I didn't want you."

Pain's chest burned, and she wasn't sure she could breathe properly.

Oram touched her face with his fingertips, tracing the shape.

Pain found herself unable to speak, so instead she turned her lips into his hand, as he had done with her, to press a kiss against his palm. He stroked her cheek with his thumb. The mindlock in Oram's temple whirred. Oram shivered and dropped his hand.

He reached across to his coat, fished in the pocket for a moment. When he drew out his hand, a large golden watch spun and flashed from his fingers. It was a beautiful thing, with the case all engraved. "Would you keep this for me?"

Pain nodded. "Of course," she managed.

Oram nodded, but didn't pass it to her right away. Instead, he opened it. There was no watch in the case. It held a miniature of a woman. A sepia-haired lady in jewels looked lovingly out at the world with rich amber eyes.

"She's beautiful," murmured Pain. "Who is she?"

"My mother. This is the only picture of her that he didn't destroy, because I'd been playing with it when he came home and she pushed me under the bed. I'd never seen him before that I remembered. He'd always been away at war." Oram was silent for a moment. "He beat her to death because she wouldn't tell him where I was. When she was dead, he started on the portraits, and when he finished with the portraits, he peeled off her face." He tried to speak, gagged, tried again. This time the gag bowed his back and Pain snatched the basin from the washstand, but he held up a hand, swallowed hard, and chose a different tack. "A woman who was close to him came before he found me. She talked him into fleeing Borenguard. If he was in Inshil, she said, the Emperor couldn't implant a mindlock and get control of his mind. So he left. She saved my life."

Pain bit her lip. "How old were you?"

"Seven. I went to live aboard my uncle's ship. He was my father more than my own ever was, even though it only lasted until I manifested as a psychic." Reverently, he closed the watchcase. He pressed it into Pain's hands, holding her fingers around it so hard that the hinge bit into her palm. "I can't stay much longer," he told her. His golden eyes hardened until they gleamed. "If Fergus had been wise, he would have disappeared with his family. Give Mistress Charm my regards and tell her that I said so."

Pain nodded. She forced words out of her throat. "I'll tell her."

Oram lifted her imprisoned hands to his lips. His warm kiss lingered for a moment. Abruptly he released her. He caught up his wine and drained it in two deep swallows. "Take this down to the kitchen for me, Miss Pain? As soon as I've bathed and dressed, I'll have to be on my way."

"Shall I come back up to help you bathe?"

He looked up at her and a tattered smile touched his eyes. "Good-bye."

Pain slipped the watch with the miniature between her breasts, pushing it down securely below the upper edge of her corset. She closed the door behind herself, and all but flew down the back stairs to the kitchen door. The rain-wet grass soaked the hem of her skirts as she ran to the lab building. Desire was just wiping the mud from a shovel before putting it away, and Charm was bent over the empty growth tank wearing her rubberized apron and gloves, wielding a scrub brush. The marble dissection table was still wet.

"What's wrong?" asked Charm, sitting back on her heels. She peeled off the Lady's rubber gloves distastefully and fluffed her indigo bangs. It was a color she'd never been able to wear with black. "Did your Firedrinker want to speak to me?"

"That Firedrinker is Captain Oram," Pain reported. "He's dawdling, but I think he may be going from here to kill Lord Fergus."

"Go. Quick. Get Fergus to Hyacinth's warehouse on the docks, hide him and inform Hyacinth. Desire, finish up here, please?"

Charm hurried to put away her apron and gloves, and smoothed her blue coiffure. Then she took up a post with Pride at the front desk, ostensibly going over the appointment book. Eventually a Firedrinker came down the stairs, sashed in black and as anonymous as every other; but there was only one Firedrinker in Orchard House. Charm's teeth dried, she smiled so determinedly.

"Did you find the services up to your expectation, sir?" she asked.

"Yes, thank you, Mistress." The voice seemed distracted.

"Can I make you any appointments for next week?" offered Charm. "Pain's book fills up so quickly." Anything to keep him for another pair of heartbeats.

"No, thank you, Mistress. My schedule is very uncertain right now."

The front door opened, and Prince Luther stepped in. The Firedrinker stiffened. Luther paused, and stood regarding him. Something touched Luther's emotionless face a moment before he could reassemble his neutral mask.

"Good evening, Your Highness," said the Firedrinker, saluting.

Luther nodded. The Firedrinker, Captain Oram, strode quickly out past him. Luther shrugged off his overcoat and hung it over his arm as he came to the desk.

"What can we do for you this evening, Prince Luther?" asked Charm brightly while she silently cursed him for driving Oram away.

"Under the suspicion that Miss Desire will once again be busy in the kitchen, I believe I would like to see Miss Pain," he told her.

He had an uncanny gift for timing, damn him. "I'm so terribly sorry, but she's not available. As I just said to the Firedrinker who left, she does book out so far in advance. Is there anything else I could tempt you with?" Charm offered. *Say no*, she urged wordlessly.

"In that case, I suppose Justice might be available? Since Phelan isn't here."

Charm laced her fingers into Pride's and held on hard beneath the cover of the desk. She bared her teeth in another smile.

"Justice . . . has only just finished with a customer, Highness." Only Phelan saw Justice intimately, but Charm said a brief mental prayer for Luther's fastidiousness.

"I don't mind."

Damn him to hell. "Then if you'd like the same room as before, I can send her to you immediately."

"Have her bring a pot of tea." He smiled dryly. "Hot, if that is possible."

⁓

Justice guided the tea cart into Prince Luther's room with a shy smile. He was sitting in the armchair by the fire with his long legs stretched out. She limped grossly without her cane, but perhaps Luther liked it. She put the cart by the low table at his elbow. Best to get it over with. With his legs stretched out she couldn't very well sit on his knee, so she clasped her hands behind her back and swayed from side to side. Her short skirts swished around her shins. It was a pose of childish innocence that never failed to rouse Prince Phelan, and the faster she got through this, the sooner it would be over. Luther, however, only looked at her with black amusement.

Justice smoothed her frown before it could do more than twitch her eyebrows. She'd seen him, in Inshil, when he'd arrived with the Lady's father. She'd just finished reading newly emerging psychics, sorting their talents. Consigning them to their individual servitudes. Luther put out his bare hand to her without hesitating. As if he didn't know what she could do and see. She remembered the first clasp, a borrowed memory seen over a wall, back before she'd had a body of her own. Joining hands. He'd just come from his ship. How he loved the sea, and the sounds and feeling of a ship racing before the wind. The hawsers' creak, the smell of the open ocean, and when the sails went up how they sounded to him like the sheets of a lover's bed.

This fresh touch had no vision attached to it. The Lady had kept most of Justice's powers when she'd put Justice out into this hell. Now, Justice could touch-read only in small, unreliable bursts, like a candle guttering before it burned out. It had been decades since she'd tried to do it on purpose. Until now, until the Emperor's assassination, she had wanted to never have to see anything that way ever again; but if they could find the Emperor's murderer maybe . . . maybe she could be free. But the more she strained to feel something, the less was there. This was just a man taking her fingers politely and then letting them go.

"You look at me as if you knew me," said Luther quietly.

"I thought I did, for a moment," Justice said.

"Ah." He didn't look surprised, or insulted. "Did we ever meet?"

"I had not met you until you came in with Prince Phelan, Highness." It wasn't quite a lie. He didn't know who she was. She didn't want him to know. She didn't want anyone to know what she'd done.

Luther poured himself a cup of tea.

"What would you like me to do, Prince Luther?" Justice asked. "Would you like a massage?" she suggested. "I can walk on your back, if you'd like."

He nodded to the bookcase on the other wall. "Pick a book to read to me."

Justice concealed her wariness. What did he have in mind? "What would you like to hear?" she asked.

"That isn't what I asked. Pick a book that you'd like to read. Whatever appeals to you."

Read to him? Read a book that she wanted? "I-I'm sure it would bore Your Highness," said Justice, confusion eroding her professional detachment.

Prince Luther poured himself a cup of tea. "I am willing to be bored."

"As you wish."

Justice went to examine the books. They'd come from In-shil, gifts from the old emperor; but Charm used them as décor, thrusting them away as reminders of the Lady's life that was no part of her. Justice remembered some of the books quite well, others not at all. She pulled down a thick volume of poetry. It had been one of Desire's favorites. She took it back to Prince Luther.

"May I read from this one?" she asked.

"Of course. Come and sit by me." He gestured to the stool on his right, where the light was best. It wasn't quite sitting at his feet.

Justice sat down obediently and opened the book. She expected that he would interrupt her, but after a while she almost forgot him. She enjoyed the poem "Lost Time."

> ". . . A touch, a kiss, and one kiss more,
> yet all that I could wish
> Is a day, an hour, a moment's more
> time lost within a kiss."

Justice glanced up at Prince Luther. He sat with his head tipped back and his eyes closed as if he were asleep, but his long hands were clenched into fists on the arms of the chair.

"Was that all right, Your Highness?" she asked.

Luther let his hands relax. He opened his reddened eyes and smiled bitterly at the ceiling. "You read exceptionally well. Go on, choose another one."

Justice bent her head back over the book. After a moment, she felt Luther's soft touch on her hair, and then it withdrew. She said nothing, just went on reading.

⤮

"I've committed no crime!" shouted Lord Fergus as the Firedrinkers dragged him out of his coach.

Pain pressed herself back into the shadows of the compartment, trusting to her dark cloak to hide her. They'd made it as far as the docks, but not to a ship. Outside, the gaslights in the front of Bern Ostander's shop lit the misty rain like silver threads against dark. They turned the scarlet coats of the Firedrinkers a deeper, bloody shade.

"Captain, you know I'm telling the truth," Fergus reasoned. "All I did was question whether his policies were best for the country!"

The people who gathered to watch the little tableau stood silent. Waterfronters one and all at this time of night, sailors on their way back to their ships or not ready for the night to be over, common whores and others who did their trade at night, they kept a wary perimeter. None of them wanted the attention of the Firedrinkers, but none of them wanted to miss the show.

"Speaking my honest opinion in the Assembly is not against the law," Fergus went on desperately.

"I have orders." Even through the helmet, Oram's voice grated in agony. His gloved hands shook as he drew his pistol. Pain's chest ached savagely for him.

"I swore fealty! I have agreed to the marriage even though I questioned it at first! The taxes he proposes will cripple the population! I have done nothing wrong!" Fergus cried.

Pain dug her fingers into the seat cushion and watched in horrified fascination as a thin trickle of blood slid out from under Oram's visor, shining against the gorget of his body armor. The white armor stained slowly crimson. The pistol wavered, trembling as he extended it.

"Sweet God," muttered a man in the crowd.

The Firedrinkers forced the nobleman to his knees in the road. Captain Oram stood like a statue.

"Please, Captain," Fergus whispered. "You are a man of justice. You do not want to do this."

A second rivulet of blood joined the first. Slowly, shaking, the muzzle of the gun leveled with Lord Fergus's eyes. The clicks of the cylinder rotating punctuated the sharper sound of the hammer locking back.

"Sorry . . . Trying . . ." said Oram hoarsely.

The gun's report was horrible, carrying in the damp and rebounding off the buildings. The echo lost itself in the cries of the waterfronters. Fergus's blood, spotted with lumps of brain and bone, dripped down the carriage door, and the Firedrinkers continued to hold the arms of the body so that it stayed on its knees. For a moment no one moved. Smoke from the gun muzzle curled in the silence.

A ghastly croak tore up out of Oram's chest as he staggered. He went to his knees and clawed at his helmet, dragging it off. The crowd gaped at the suddenly human features of the dread Captain Oram. Dark blood ran from his nose and his left ear, contrasting with his pallid face. He pressed his hands to his temples as if he were holding his skull together. "Orders . . . Do it privately . . . Law . . . be . . . damned . . . Kill . . . Fergus . . ." Oram croaked. His mouth drew out in a silent howl. He began to twitch, shoulders jerking, his back straining in an arch. Oram fell, convulsing, in front of Lord Fergus's kneeling corpse.

CHAPTER FOURTEEN

Pain scrambled out of the carriage, pushing past the Firedrinkers standing silently flanking the dead body of Lord Fergus. Tears burned down her cheeks as she dragged Oram's head into her lap and held him so that his head wouldn't strike the cobbles as he thrashed.

The Firedrinkers looked at each other. The one on the left spoke. "We have no orders for this."

His companion's mirrored visor remained trained on the convulsing Captain Oram for a long moment. "No orders," the companion agreed slowly. "We should go back for further instruction."

They stepped back, letting Fergus's body fall beside the jerking form of their captain. As one the Firedrinkers turned, and the crowd parted to let them pass.

Oram bucked a final time against Pain's hands and went limp. She pressed her fingers to his neck, pushing down inside the bloody gorget to find a pulse. There, a thready flutter. Bern Ostander stepped out of the dwindling crowd. He felt for Oram's pulse as she had.

"Looks like he's gone," Bern told her with never a flicker to betray the lie.

"I won't leave him in the street like a dead dog," said Pain fiercely, and hoped her gratitude didn't show.

Bern looked around, and got a carriage blanket out of the

Fergus family coach. They wrapped Oram up in it. She helped Bern get Captain Oram up onto his shoulders in a fireman's carry. The crowd parted in silence. Pain, and Bern with his burden, headed up to Orchard House through back streets. Pain unlocked the garden gate. She shoved Bern and his burden in the direction of the lab. Then she snatched up her skirts and bolted to the house. Mistress Charm was pacing in her solarium.

"Captain Oram. He tried not to shoot Lord Fergus, but he had to. He's in the lab," Pain panted. "It's bad. . . ."

"Damn it all! Can none of you follow simple directions?" barked Charm. "Fine. Fine, I'll handle it myself. Take a deep breath and wash your face. Go out to the bar and keep an eye on things."

⁓

"Mr. Ostander, what . . ." Charm trailed off.

Bern Ostander crouched beside one of the stoves, feeding up the fire. A pallid, unconscious man lay on the table, covered in a blanket. The mindlock in his left temple screamed that the man was a Firedrinker. Drying blood crusted around it and left rusty streaks from the man's eyes, nose, and ear. The only sign of life in him was the faint rise and fall of his chest. A Firedrinker's uniform, a white sash, and sections of white body armor lay piled on the floor under the coroner's slab.

"Is that . . . ?" she asked in momentary confusion, trying to refuse the evidence of her own eyes. "Where is Lord Fergus?"

"M'lady, Captain Oram," Bern introduced the unconscious man. "I'd have thought the old emperor freed the poor bastard from following Imperial commands."

He could have, thought Charm, clenching her fists in her skirts in frustration. *But he had only one order left in him. He loved me as much as he could, and even that was too much.*

Bern closed the stove door and stood, rubbing his hands on his damp trousers. His lips pinched tight for a moment. "Captain Oram shot Fergus in the middle of the street, in front of a crowd. He was fighting it like nothing I've ever seen. I think he might've partly overridden 'n order. He said something about havin' to shoot Fergus in private."

"Overridden . . . ?" Charm went to Oram. The crystal face of his mindlock was blackened on the inside. "That's not possible," she muttered.

"'Mpossible or no, that's one tough son of a bitch," said Bern with deep respect. "Can you save him?"

Charm stared at the smith in disbelief. "I'm not a doctor, Mr. Ostander, and I wasn't even before I had a mindlock to shackle me."

"I'm further from a doctor than you are. I had surgeons doing the actual procedures. You probably know more about human anatomy than any doctor in Bor'nguard. If anyone can help him, you can."

Charm put out a hand as if to push Bern's words away. She went to fidget with the bottles and instruments on her worktable, straightening them. He didn't realize that she was more than one person.

Bern watched her expectantly. He didn't say anything.

Charm's heart pricked at her. "The lock would have to be removed, and I don't know the first thing about how it went in," she said finally. No lie there. The Lady might have some conception of what to do, or the consequences of such an operation, but Charm had no idea. Restless, she went back to the table.

Oram stirred, opening his amber eyes. They came to rest on Charm, though she wasn't sure he was really seeing her. "I'm sorry. I never got the chance to kill Father." Oram's eyes slid closed. Charm shook him. His shoulder was clammy.

"Captain? Captain Oram, who is your father?"

But he only mumbled, ". . . kill Father," and sank into deeper unconsciousness.

Charm looked across at Bern.

"'Ve no idea. I c'n tell you about mindlocks, though. No one better," he offered.

Charm wound a lock of hair around her finger. She couldn't just let him die, but since she'd gotten her orders the Lady had seemed . . . stronger. Without his mindlock to shackle him, Captain Oram might still be a powerful telepath. He could find out who had killed her emperor much more easily than she could, and she wouldn't have to keep dipping into the Lady's powers, the Lady's memories.

Her mindlock vibrated with the thought, growling by bone conduction in her ear as if something inside wasn't meshing quite smoothly.

Oram could be another ally, if they could save him. "How much of these things are inside?"

Bern either didn't see her pause, or pretended not to. He hurried to her drawing table and picked up her pen. Charm went to look over his shoulder. She hadn't the foggiest notion what to look for. Without the Lady's knowledge, Oram would die. He was her best ally to kill Strephon . . . The mindlock seized.

The Lady blinked. She was looking over a man's shoulder, watching him draw. When she glanced around the laboratory, she saw an injured man on the bare marble table with a thin blanket thrown over him. Only the faint rise and fall of his chest betrayed any life. What was going on?

"One moment, please," said the Lady. She reached past him and touched the bell push on the table, and a few moments later Desire appeared.

"Good evening, Mr. Ostander," Desire greeted Bern politely. "You wanted something, Lady?"

"Yes, thank you, Desire." So, this was Bern Ostander, the man who made the growth tanks. "Would you bring a pillow and some warmer blankets, please? I'd like to make our patient a little more comfortable if we can." She looked back at the drawing, hoping for clarification. "What were you saying, Mr. Ostander?"

"There's not so much to the mindlocks as you'd think." Ostander sketched quickly. "Four prongs to anchor it in the skull, and two tails. The tails're the thing, a'course. They're very fine, very flexible. The old emperor'd use telekinesis to thread in the tails, then connect the lock and set it. This tail is double. It draws 'n' returns power. This single goes t' the pain centers."

"So when the subject fights the lock, they're literally fighting themselves," observed the Lady softly. She hadn't known that before.

"And the more powerful the mind, the harder the fight," he agreed.

"That answers the control aspect, but I don't understand how it acts as a filter."

"A what?"

"It may not be a correct word," the Lady said, blushing a little. "Like . . . colored lenses to protect your eyes from the sun when it is too bright. Mindlocks, what little I understand about them, filter the perception so the psychic can interact with the world like a regular person. One has to concentrate to use one's powers. How does it do that, and why is this pair of wires, this tail, double while the other is single?"

"This end of it draws power," Bern said, pointing, "and feeds that into the works. When a psychic uses their powers, any overflow of energy stores in the springs, just like winding a watch. That stores up in the spring, though the spring doesn't have to be fully loaded before the shutoff trips, and a more appropriate measure of power goes back in down this other fork. The psychic talent is uncorrupted, it's just got less zip. The stored energy gradually releases by use, or, if the subject defies an order or if a certain brain signal trips a switch, it activates the other tail and the energy releases into the pain centers of the brain." He shook his head. "Never regretted anything as much as learning to put in the sec'nd, single tail to the pain centers. It's s'pposed to be a warning system for the psychic to slow down, ease off. The Emperor demanded more than that."

The Lady frowned. "But it can only send to the pain centers what's built up in the mechanism."

"Correct."

"So, if someone were disobeying commands repeatedly, or often enough, they'd have a constant headache; and if they used their power all the time so they were also spending as much energy as possible, there wouldn't be much energy built up in the spring."

"Aye, that's right. The more talented, the more activity, the more energy is feeding into the lock. For a man like Captain Oram . . . no. His disobedience drained his lock until he could speak. Barely. And then it caused, well. Stroke, m'be. Something. We won't know until we go in. He's probably not going to live; but we're certain to learn a great deal more about how his brain may have responded physically to carrying a mindlock all these years. And what happened when it burned out. It'd give me 'mportant information."

Captain Oram was the victim. Now they were getting somewhere. And they certainly weren't going to start cutting into anybody's brain until she knew a great deal more about the situation. The Lady fingered her hair. "So, he's got the lock triggered, and at least for perceptual gifts, you may believe me when I say that pain distracts from input. More pain, less power building up even as he's burning it off," reasoned the Lady, excitement beginning to tingle. "Would that strain the mindlock? Being . . . tripped all the time?"

Bern shrugged. "Gears and springs have a stress limit."

"Is the lock doing him any active damage?" she asked.

"Depends on how it's broken. There's no way to know."

"Could we simply clip off the tails?"

"Nyep. Power'd arc between the tails, and then you'd have a right royal mess. Kill him for sure."

The Lady tapped the desk with her fingers thoughtfully. "The danger as you've drawn this is that the tails curve, and they're embedded in soft tissue. If I pull, the wire will straighten, and slice his brain like cheese."

"But it isn't a raw wire. It's sheathed in gelatin."

The Lady frowned. "Gelatin? Like aspic?"

"A little like," Bern said. "Melts at a hundred 'n' three degrees. That's why it's so dangerous for a Firedrinker to get sick, or for you either. The insulatin' gelatin goes liquid again, and the whole length of the wire touches the brain. 'Swhy most pyros die even after they're safely 'locked. I thought the Emperor would've told you."

"If he did, I've forgotten," said the Lady absently.

Captain Oram's name was familiar. He was an important man. The boneghosts talked about him. The Lady didn't know how Oram had gotten here, or why, but she was certainly not going to let the man die on her table. Besides, she never lost time while she was working. The longer she worked, the longer she would have to figure things out.

To buy herself a little time, she turned to Captain Oram. Hesitantly, she took his pulse at the wrist. His heartbeat was steady and getting stronger. His pupils were even, his breathing deep and rhythmic. The crystal set in his temple was too blackened to see its works, but the skin that had grown up over the edges of the implanted device showed no sign of swelling or bruising.

"I'm hesitant to do surgery until we've given him a little more time, particularly when it will be as dangerous as you describe. He's at least stable now. Could you send me some of the coated wires to experiment with? If we can find a way to safely remove them, and if he doesn't recover on his own, at least I'll be a little better informed on how we might proceed." Something about Bern Ostander's eagerness was off-putting, but she let him think he'd be involved. It wasn't polite to argue with people.

"Tha's sense, I suppose. And if you c'n save him . . . you should." Bern's disappointment showed openly.

"Mr. Ostander, I'm going to give you a very special bird to take home with you. If you need to speak with me for any reason, just let it out and it will come home to roost. You can even tell it a very short message, or even just open the cage." She went to get the swallow from its cage, but beneath its cover, the birdcage was empty. The Lady uncovered one of the little tanks and fished out a new bird.

"So, that's what the little tanks were for, to make talking birds?" Bern asked.

The Lady shook her head. "It's not nearly so dramatic." She fished the bird out of its empathy fluid, holding it carefully over the tank by its feet to let the lungs drain. As the bird had matured, the fluid had thickened into mucilaginous goop. It ran in a syrupy trickle from the limp body. "I'm psychometric. I can sympathetically read objects the way a telepath reads a mind. If you talk to the bird, I'll be able to hear what you said. Nothing too long, please," she reminded him. "Visuals are easy, but it takes a lot of concentration to make sense of actual language."

Desire returned with the blankets and pillow.

"Make a pad on the rack in the human growth tank, would you, Desire?" requested the Lady. "He can be undisturbed, and the empathy fluid blocks psychic impressions. It will keep the lock from building up any more power."

She took the bird to her worktable and put a rubber tube into its beak. With the end of the tube in her mouth, she massaged its ribs with her finger as she puffed, very gently, into the tube. The little swallow kicked, and she held it gently between her hands.

"Just like resuscitating a person," murmured Bern.

"Exactly like that," agreed the Lady. "Most animals want to live. They struggle toward life regardless of their surroundings." She deposited the bird in a cage, a sad smile pulling at the corners of her mouth. "Human beings are more difficult. At some point of trauma, most people just give up and die."

Bern's face changed, something like guilt shadowing his eyes. "Only if they're let to, M'stress."

❦

"Prince Luther!" A Firedrinker voice came through the door.

Justice looked up at Prince Luther, who opened his eyes. "Yes?" Luther asked.

"Prince Luther, Your Highness, it's Captain Oram . . . he's disappeared."

Luther all but leaped to his feet and crossed the room in two quick strides to jerk open the door. The Firedrinker suffered themselves to be dragged in by the arm.

"Tell me," commanded Luther.

"Captain Oram disobeyed a direct command regarding Lord

Fergus, Highness." The Firedrinker's visor shifted slightly, taking in Justice sitting by the empty chair. "He collapsed, and was last seen with Miss Pain and Mr. Bern Ostander. We felt you would want to be informed."

Luther stiffened. "Thank you, Officer. Is the Emperor aware of this?"

"He will be soon, Highness."

Luther opened the door. "Inform His Imperial Majesty that you came across me at Orchard House, and that I've taken the liberty of beginning the investigation."

The Firedrinker saluted and left. Luther turned back toward Justice.

"Well?" he asked with frozen calm. "What do you know?"

Justice closed the book, clutching it to her chest. "They didn't tell me anything about it. . . ."

But Luther was already striding down the hall without bothering to tie his cravat. Justice put the book away and picked up his forgotten coat from the back of the chair. Justice limped after Luther.

⁓

"Mistress!" cried Pain's voice from the direction of the house. "Mistress Charm!" Her voice was crossing the orchard.

Charm pushed the Lady back down hurriedly. The Lady fought slightly, trying to stay focused on her patient, but Charm rolled over her, relentless as the gears of the mindlock.

"Go out the back gate," Charm told Bern. Hundreds of psychics depended on him to make the mindlocks that kept them sane and alive. "Quick! You mustn't be found here."

Bern didn't seem to notice the change, he just obeyed her.

Pain flung open the laboratory door. "A Firedrinker came to speak to Prince Luther about Captain Oram."

"Put those blankets into the growth tank to pad the frame,

and put Captain Oram in it. Drape it so that no one can see into it," Charm ordered.

Charm was only halfway through the orchard when the bright yellow light of the kitchen doorway darkened with Prince Luther's silhouette. He hadn't put on his coat, and his cravat hung untied around his neck. He strode out through the rain to stand towering over her. The rain sleeked his hair, and the shadows of the bone trees cast bizarre planes of light and dark across his face.

"What have you done with Oram?" he demanded.

Oh God, he knows Oram was brought here. Where could she have put him besides the greenhouse? What story would stick? . . . Her eye fell on the newly turned earth in the center of the orchard. Shame's grave, but without a marker and with this rain to tamp down the loose earth, who would know the difference? "I buried him, Your Highness," said Charm calmly, gesturing.

The color drained from Luther's face, leaving him monochrome in the shadows.

Charm tipped her head to one side. There was more to that look than a search for the captain of the Firedrinkers.

"He deserved better." The words ground out of Luther's chest.

"Yes, he did; but he was a Firedrinker, Highness, with no family to claim his body or mourn for him." Luther's big hands clenched into fists. Charm wished he'd understand. "If Captain Oram were buried by the crown, he would be consigned to a nameless and unmarked grave. A pauper's grave. We knew him. My ghosts and I will remember who is buried here among the bone trees," she said softly. "And you are always welcome to visit him if you wish it."

Luther breathed as if the air burned him. He could not seem to speak. Justice squelched unevenly toward them with his coat in her hands. Prince Luther ignored her. He sank to his knees beside the grave. Luther's fine linen shirt had soaked through, and it stuck to his skin. "Will you grow a tree out of him? Make another Oram to go back into service?"

She shouldn't be angry that he didn't understand. Luther was an Imperial prince. Even when he'd been in his father's ill graces, he could count on his freedom being returned to him. "If you are going to insult me, Your Highness, I'm sure you can see the gate from where you are. I would very much appreciate your putting it to use."

Justice put a light hand on Luther's shoulder. Every muscle in Luther was clenched hard, as if some inner world consumed him. She draped his coat uselessly over his sodden shoulders. "What happened?" asked Justice, looking at Charm with big, anxious eyes.

"Captain Oram has died," Charm informed her. "Of attempted disobedience."

It wasn't what Justice had meant, but she saw through the lie instantly. She clenched her teeth together and glared at Charm. Her eyes filled with tears, her slender body jerking with silent sobs. The child ghost whirled, staggering with the intensity of her own motion, and hobbled back toward the house.

Luther didn't move. He didn't seem aware of anything but the muddy mound before him. Well, he might not mind soaking, but Charm possessed no such stoicism. She went to get her umbrella out of the stand inside the laboratory door. Pain sat beside the human tank, her white arm ghostly where she'd slipped a hand beneath the black canvas cover.

Charm snatched up her umbrella, opened it, and went back to Prince Luther. She stood so that the umbrella's far side sheltered him a little.

"You buried him quickly, Mistress," said Luther, his whispered voice as harsh a gull's scream.

Charm's heart pounded. "I had the grave dug for Shame. She wouldn't have minded sharing it with Captain Oram." That part was even true.

Luther stood, the legs of his trousers covered with mud. He kept his back to her. His voice was hoarse. "Do you even remember what color your hair is?" And then he walked away through the rain.

CHAPTER FIFTEEN

Please, Pain, you have to go."

"Do I?" Pain glared up at Justice. She knew that Desire and Pride had bullied their littlest sister into being the one to roust her from the lab. Pain had spent the hours after closing sitting beside the growth tank where Captain Oram lay unconscious. His breathing had grown easier, and his pulse was stronger. She couldn't stand to think of him waking up alone in this place of bones and glass and silver. She stroked Oram's hair.

"You can't just sit there all the time until he wakes up. Besides," said Justice, seizing upon sudden inspiration, "it was Strephon that did this to him, and we need Mistress Charm to deal with Strephon."

"I hate her," hissed Pain, not bothering to fight the frustrated anger in her chest.

"I don't think any of us likes Charm all the time. . . ."

"Both of them, I hate them both. They just, they left him like this. . . ."

Justice wrapped an arm around Pain's shoulders and leaned her cheek on Pain's white hair. "He wasn't strong enough for the operation. If anything, they didn't let Bern Ostander butcher him."

"Stop being so fair," scoffed Pain in a hoarse croak that came too close to tears.

"We have enough reasons not to like Charm without making up new ones," Justice pointed out softly, her own voice hitching.

Pain drew Justice down to cradle the child ghost in her lap. Pain wrapped her arms around Justice, rocked her gently. "What happened?"

Justice put her face against Pain's shoulder and began to cry. "Prince Luther . . . he . . . when Ch-Ch-Charm told him that Captain Oram was dead . . . oh God . . . it was like she t-t-tore out his heart . . ." Justice clutched Pain's sleeve with one hand, hit Pain's shoulder with one impotent little fist.

"Prince Luther?" Pain lifted Justice's head off her shoulder, made Justice look at her. "Did he care what happened to Oram?" His uncle's ship.

Justice's eyes were swollen, glassy with tears. Justice bit her lips, tried to sort memories from the harsh tangle of emotions that she'd read in Luther. "I saw Oram, as a child. Huddled up in a ship's bunk, and he was so miserable . . . then a little older, sitting on the rail, laughing. Not his son, but Prince Luther felt as if he should have been. He loved Oram so much."

Pain stroked Justice's hair, glanced at Oram's pale face. So that was what had happened to Oram after his mother was killed. Luther, who'd had a child thrust upon him, had done the decidedly unexpected thing. He had loved that little boy.

"Please, Pain, I'll sit with him. Let me do something. I have to do something, even if it's just sit with him for you," said Justice. "Charm and the Lady need their body to eat. She's the only one who can help Captain Oram. I'd go get the bread, truly I would, but . . . I don't know how to get to the bakery."

Pain almost laughed at that. So mundane and so simple a reason. None of the others had ever been off the grounds. "All right," she told Justice.

Justice hugged her tightly for a moment, and then let Pain go.

Pain wiped her eyes and smoothed her hair; then went down through the bone orchard to the back gate and slipped out into the street. If she hurried, she would get back to the lab that much sooner. Pain was going down the stairs between two shops that led to the square at the Lowtown gate when a black glove took hold of her elbow. She looked at the Firedrinker, startled. The Firedrinker stepped back into the shadow of a building, drawing Pain along.

"You're late, Miss Pain," the Firedrinker told her softly. "You shouldn't go down to the gate now."

"I'm sorry?"

The Firedrinker took a slightly smashed paper bag out of one coat pocket and put it in Pain's hands. "Mistress Charm's croissants."

"What's happening?" Past the dark shadow of the damp stone buildings, the now-usual crowd was gathering on the upper side of the Lowtown gate, waiting for the army monitors to begin letting them through. There was something awful about that great, guardian stone wall with not a single scarlet coat at the base. The lack of the bright color made her dread what was on the other side of that divider.

"The army is impressing men in Lowtown again. There are not enough of us today."

"Not enough of you for what?"

Slowly, the Firedrinker's gloved hands raised the concealing helmet visor. He was young, not yet twenty; his face square-jawed and familiar. He liked wine so sweet it bordered on liquefied jam.

The nameless man looked down, as if he were suddenly shy, then shuddered in pain so hard the visor slipped and fell, rendering him anonymous again. "Miss Pain, we can't risk you. Captain Oram would never forgive us if anything happened to you."

A chill slithered up Pain's neck. Pain started forward, unsure where she was going, but thinking she should do something. She stepped out onto the little landing that overlooked the square. The Firedrinker caught Pain's elbow, spinning her back against the wall, holding her pinned against the bricks with his body. Past his shoulder, Pain saw the crowd stirring restlessly before the gate.

A wagon stood in the shadow of the gate, covered with a tarp. Two of the army soldiers hovered near it. There were more soldiers, standing in the shadows where the Imperial Way exited the square. Pain's course, along alleys and through the narrowest shortcuts, had avoided the Way. In the square, the waiting people milled slightly, seeming unaware of the ominous change in the army's disposition.

A call of warning rang dully on the Lowtown side of the wall. A man cried out. Shouts came from the far side of the gate. The crowd on the Middletown side started forward, surging toward the soldier-sentries. The soldiers were shouting, now. The crowd fell back, but they did not disperse. The sluggish breeze that carried the salt tang up from the harbor tainted with the smell of ozone and charred meat. The crowd stirred like storm clouds, the low murmuring turning ugly.

The Firedrinker holding Pain pinned above the square leaned the front of his helmet against the wall over her shoulder, his body shivering and jerking inside his coat and armor. The sound of disturbance from Lowtown continued, a horrible and muffled harmony to the shouting that swelled on the Middletown side.

The Middletown crowd started forward again, pressing in toward the soldiers. The officer in charge shouted. The soldiers brought up their rifles. Pain wanted to close her eyes, wanted to look away, but did not have Pride's talent for igno-rance. The crowd hesitated. Several men moved closer to the soldiers. Shots. The men closest to the rifles collapsed. Spat-ters of red danced before Pain's eyes. The mob faltered.

Sudden screaming rent the air on the far side of the gate, and shots sounded there as if in delayed echo of those on the Middletown side.

The mob surged toward the gate, armed with rakes and staves and the implements of their work or whatever else they could lay their hands to, desperate to reach the men dying be-yond the bulwark of the wall. The commanding officer called an order, and his soldiers whipped the tarp off their wagon, jumping to man the tripod gun there. On the Imperial Way, the other wagon rolled across the exit from the square. The gatehouse gun rumbled, and the front ranks of the crowd be-gan to fall. Screaming, the crowd began to turn, to run. New shots as the soldiers in the Imperial Way cranked two more repeaters into action. Smoke roiled up in the confines of the gatehouse. The crowd began to condense in the center of the square, but the guns kept up their thunderous, deadly work. People tumbled down through the growing pall of smoke.

"No!" Pain struggled against the Firedrinker's arms; but sheer horror robbed her effort of strength, and she found herself hanging on to his shoulders instead. "No, no, no . . ." Tears of helpless horror coursed down her cheeks as the peo-ple in the square fell like wheat before a reaper.

The gun at the western side of the square clanked, jammed. The gunners before the gate ripped the smoking feeder out of their gun, fumbling to reload it. A deep and terrible roar rose from the square as the mob split itself and turned on the sol-diers. The first few citizens went down, gutted on bayonets, but those in the back pressed forward, pushing their fellows on. They closed over the soldiers with a howl of bestial rage. The soldiers' screams were short-lived.

Some men sprang to the gate winches. Slowly the massive barrier swung open. Many of the crowd poured through it, but others stood, covered in blood and smoke, too stunned to stir now that the immediate targets of their wrath were gone. Red coats began to come through the gate around the edges of the crowd. Smooth, efficient, calming, they moved among the crowd, helped the injured to their feet, or began swift and certain search among the riddled carcasses for the merely injured.

"What have you done?" Pain whispered to her captor, horror all but choking her.

The voice from the helmet was a weird echo of the muffled words Pain could hear from inside that barrier.

"We've done nothing, Miss Pain." The Firedrinker's automated voice shook. Inside his helmet, he was weeping. She could feel his body jerking against her breasts, heaving with the muffled sobs that his helmet did not transmit. "We've done nothing."

Pain let her head lean against the impersonal smoothness of the Firedrinker's helmet and wrapped her arms around him. Helpless to do anything else, she held him as he wept.

❧

"Mistress? Mistress?"

Charm moaned at the twinge of stiffness in her neck. She opened her eyes looking at her own hands, familiar down to the dimples.

"Mistress," repeated Desire firmly.

Charm raised her head and made her bleary eyes focus on the boneghost. Pain should have been the one to wake her up, but today it was Desire. Where was Pain? Reality swept away the last cobwebby vestiges of a dream, leaving only uneasy hollowness. Today was Tuesday. "What time is it?" Charm mumbled, rubbing futilely at her neck.

"Ten o'clock in the morning."

Charm looked around and realized that she had lain down on the bed to rest until Pain came to help her undress, and that she had fallen asleep still in her clothes. Her corset was digging in under her arms, and her whole body was stiff and sore. This was not the way morning was supposed to go. Some hazy concern tugged at her like the vestiges of a nightmare.

"What's the matter, Mistress?" asked Desire.

Charm pushed the notion away. Today was Tuesday, and it was already ten o'clock. She didn't have time to waste. "As long as I'm up, I want a bath."

Desire went to start the bathwater running. She was just coming out of the bathroom when Pain slipped in.

"Where have you been?" snapped Charm.

Desire took one look at the two of them and retreated downstairs.

"There was a riot at the Lowtown gate," said Pain softly.

"You were in the streets all night? You were supposed to be at the bar!" shouted Charm.

"Oh . . . no, I . . . I sat by the captain after the house closed for the night. The riot was this morning, when I went to get your breakfast."

Riot. Yes. Fine. Today was Tuesday. The Emperor would be coming. "You didn't come to help me undress!"

Pain stared at her. "Mistress, I thought it better to keep watch on Captain Oram. You could have asked someone else; but there was a riot at the gate this morning. The soldiers massacred . . ."

Charm's head pounded with jumbled thoughts, and the mindlock snarled. "I can't do anything about a riot once it's over. The Emperor . . . Strephon, I mean Strephon . . . he will be here before I've had breakfast if you don't hurry up," said Charm impatiently, before Pain could come up with any new way to try to disrupt the morning. If they could get the morning routine back on track, she could get her thoughts in order, she was sure. "I'm not hopeful we can get the crush marks out of this, but do what you can. Did anything else happen after I came to bed?" Charm asked.

"No, Mistress," said Pain, coming to jerk at Charm's laces, "and last night continued to be light after you left. Major Nathair, the Duchess, came by briefly. They had a dispatch for Prince Aerleas saying that Captain Oram died in the act of committing treason. The Emperor ordered Prince Aerleas to stand fast, not to retreat anymore. Several gentlemen sent cards canceling appointments for this week. Count Seabrough sent you a huge bunch of his hothouse carnations with a note expressing his regret that business is keeping him away and his hope that you are feeling improved from the last time he saw you." Pain unbuckled Charm's bustle.

Charm ignored the news of the dispatch completely, peeled off her dress, dropped it and her bustle onto the floor, and stepped out of the heap. "Carnations won't pay our bills. I'll look at the books later, but you may as well give me the full report."

"Orchard House isn't in too bad a position, considering the hit we're taking on private bookings. The customers we've lost are the ones we didn't like anyway. Several of our gentlemen yesterday commented that this is the last place in town to get a decent supper out."

"Thank God for Mrs. Westmore."

"Prince Aerleas has been withdrawing toward Croissonè, though he might stop when he gets his orders. No one's sure yet what the casualty totals are, but they're high. The Duchess took ship to take him the dispatch immediately after stopping here."

Charm went and soaked in her bathtub, washing the blue out of her hair. She examined her collection of colored rinses. Orange? What about bright green? She weighed the bottle of chartreuse rinse in her hand. Luther's comment itched at her like gnat bites. Why should he care about her hair? And what color was it, anyway? Charm dragged the sopping mess forward over her shoulder and looked at it. What color was it? She stared, but the hair wouldn't have a color. Not blond, not brown, not any color at all. It wasn't even light or dark. Her brain refused to register it as any color.

"Such lovely hair." A man's voice, a memory as vivid as if it had been her own.

Charm leaped up, slipped, and sat back down with a splash. Pain burst in, catching her lady's flailing arm.

"Who said that?" cried Charm, staggering out of the tub along with a goodly portion of the water.

"No one, Mistress," Pain soothed. "No one's here but us." She wrapped Charm up in the robe and threw down towels to sop up the mess.

"Who liked her hair?" Charm demanded.

"Whose hair, Mistress?" asked Pain levelly. She didn't look in the least confused.

Charm pressed the heels of her hands against her eyes. *It wasn't me, it wasn't me.* "It wasn't me. He liked her hair, not mine."

"As you say."

"Who was it?" Charm's shriek echoed on the elegant yellow wallpaper. She held her hair in front of Pain's face. Her fingernails bit into her palms. "Whose hair is this?"

"The Lady's," said Pain patiently. "You're distraught," she soothed, guiding Charm to a chair. "It's no wonder with Shame crowding you."

"They're not here," Charm admitted with tears in her eyes. "They left me."

Pain crouched in front of Charm, holding her lady's knees. "What do you mean?" Pain pushed Charm's offending hair back as if the terrified woman were a child.

"I can feel things." Charm caught Pain's hand, lacing her fingers through the boneghost's and squeezing until her knuckles blanched.

Pain had no reaction. "I'll do your hair color for you today." Pain fished the colorant out of the bathtub.

"Who liked the Lady's hair?"

"Many people admired it," said Pain.

"What color is her hair?" Charm hissed, clutching the arms of the chair.

Pain froze. She stood with the bottle of green powder against her chest. "Blond," whispered Pain. "The Lady Charmaine's hair is ash blond."

"What color is my hair?" said Charm, her lips drawn back from her teeth in a snarl.

Pain glanced at the bottle in her hands. "Chartreuse, apparently." She displayed the label for Charm's inspection.

Slowly the world resumed its normal complacency. Charm's heart stopped swooshing around her chest. She settled back into her chair. "Yes," she said aloud, hoping the fact was more real that way. "Yes, that's right. My hair is chartreuse today." She shoved it all down and away. Her hair was whatever color she wished. Today, chartreuse. Her robe was sticking to her back and her breasts, and she plucked at it distastefully. "Good heavens, Pain, I'm all sweaty. I need a bath."

❦

Charm looked for a long time at her last two Rejuv capsules before she took them. Strephon hadn't given her any more. Thank God the years she'd been taking the stuff wouldn't reassert themselves all at once, but the idea of slowly advancing toward sagging breasts and bagging belly, toward wrinkles and stiff joints, was distasteful to say the least.

"So, Justice, I suppose you'll give me a full report on the thoughtful and impressive Prince Luther?" asked Charm. She knew she sounded spiteful, and she didn't care. She couldn't make her hands stop trembling, and it was interfering with her ability to pick up her tea without slopping it all over herself. Her croissants had been crushed into inedibility today, so she only had leftover rolls and butter. Everything was wrong.

Justice pulled Shame's pillow off of the linen chest, hugging it against her body. "He asked me to read to him. He was very nice," she said briefly.

Charm almost laughed in relief. "That's all?"

"You're horrible!" Justice cried, flinging the pillow back onto the chest and leaping to her feet. Her little hands clutched her skirt, knuckles white, as if it was all she could do not to strike out physically. "You don't even care what you did to him last night! You don't care what you're doing to anyone! You don't even care what you're doing to us!"

The cup skittered out of Charm's fingers. It shattered on the floor, splashing her toes with warm, milky tea. For a moment all she could do was cower back in her chair. None of the boneghosts had ever yelled at her before. "Wha . . . what did you say?" she whispered, hoping desperately for continued quiet.

"Prince Luther hasn't done anything to you! If Desire isn't angry with him then you don't have any right to be. You should have told him the truth!"

Charm could only gape at her. No. No, this could not happen. "Don't you dare to breathe a word, you sanctimonious little idiot!" she snapped. "Poor Luther, poor Luther, with his soul as black as pitch and a dried pea for a heart? I did him a favor! He can stand in front of Strephon and tell what he believes to be the truth and the Firedrinkers will confirm to the Emperor that Oram is dead! That is the only way to save Oram! Hell, it's the only way to save Luther, if you really must have that!" Charm's hiss rose to an enraged scream—"I will not jeopardize our freedom and Boren for the sake of Luther's vacillating heart!"

"It isn't part of your command, it's just you! Your vengeance because . . . why? Do you think you've suffered more than the rest of us?" Justice screamed back, but she could not sustain her outburst. "I'm tired of being only a ghost," she said with something like desperation. Sobs jerked their way up out of the little ghost's throat, and tears welled in her blue eyes.

Pain gathered up the pieces of Charm's broken cup. Desire huddled against Pride in open fear, though Pride didn't seem to have noticed the outburst.

"What's wrong with you?" Charm snapped at Justice.

"I will not stay out here!" cried Justice. "You can come and go, and pull the Lady out whenever you want, like a fan to hide behind; but not us! Not us, we have to be here always, always, always and we shouldn't have to be!" Sobs began to jerk their way out of her narrow chest. "I hate Prince Phelan! She makes us into these . . . things instead of just letting us be! I'm not surprised Shame wouldn't come back. I'd rather be dead!"

"She wouldn't have made you like this on purpose. . . . She doesn't know about Phelan." Charm could feel Justice trying to press into her space and she held her competitor out. She'd controlled their body for a long time. Shame might slip in on the sly, but with the two other minds crowding her Charm had quite enough to manage without letting Justice add to the bargain.

"The Lady tricked me out and it isn't fair. She made me the body of a little child so I wouldn't be important, so you wouldn't have to listen to me even if I told on her. So she wouldn't have to know things that go against what she wants to be true." As abruptly as she'd jumped up, Justice's energy faded and she collapsed against Pride, who caught her, cradling the little boneghost tenderly in her arms.

"I want to be real again," said Justice, hanging on to Pride's sleeve.

"You're already real," snapped Charm, but her voice caught on the last word with a squeak.

"Help me, Pride, please?" begged Justice. "Please, Pride, please. I can't do this anymore. I just can't. Please?"

Pride stroked Justice's cheek with her finger, bent and kissed the smooth, childish brow. She slid her left hand under Justice's head, and took Justice's chin with her right.

"Thank you," murmured Justice, looking up at Pride with adoring blue eyes. "I knew that, of all of us, you'd understand."

"Don't," Charm whispered, stretching out imploring hands.

Pride wrenched Justice's head around. There was a sharp crunch. Justice's breath slid out.

Charm threw out her hands as if to shield herself, but the world rocked and roiled and then . . . nothing happened.

CHAPTER SIXTEEN

Charm watched Pride rock Justice's corpse, back and forth, back and forth. Charm whirled around and around in her mind, trying to find Justice, but couldn't.

The sound of the front bell broke over the room. Charm balled her hands into fists, made her arms loosen. She was Mistress Charm. She was the Emperor's mistress, and today was Tuesday. She put her feet down on the floor.

"Pride," she said calmly, "get the door. Inform the Emperor that I will be down in fifteen minutes. Wrap Justice up in a quilt. We'll attend to her body later. An hour won't matter. It isn't as if he takes longer than that. Pain, help me dress."

None of them moved at first. Then Pride took Shame's pillow off the linen chest and arranged it under the head of the little corpse. She rose without a word, and went to do as she'd been told.

When Charm descended to the entry hall, she found that the Emperor was not there. Prince Phelan had been the one to ring the bell. Charm glanced at the tall clock behind Pride's desk. Five minutes to noon. Emperor Strephon should be here any time.

"Prince Phelan, how delightful to see you back in Borenguard. If I may be so bold—what is that, and why is it in my front hall?" asked Charm with a faintly bewildered smile.

The "that" was a man who stood between a pair of Firedrinkers. His hands, bony and age-spotted, were handcuffed, and he'd been hooded. Deep creases ran in fossilized lines across his clothes. He stank from wearing them too long.

"His name is Killarin. James Killarin, to be precise," explained Phelan, his usual charm buried and his eyes suspicious. "We caught him in Croissonè, trying to take ship to Borenguard. He's a damn spy, and he intended to assassinate Emperor Strephon."

Charm's heart thudded. Phelan had brought a spy to see her? What was he about? "And you have brought him to see me because . . . My imagination fails me," Charm said lightly. She tipped her head so that a long chartreuse ringlet bobbed.

"He was carrying this." Phelan passed her a heavy vellum envelope. A red wax seal clung to the open flap.

Charm glanced at the impression on the seal. A thumbprint. The symbol, the wax, tingled beneath her fingers as if it were reaching into her. Clinging to an outward calm, she unfolded the letter.

> *Dearest Charmaine,*
>> *Never doubt that you are loved and remembered.*
>>>> *M-T*

"What a nice note. Should I know this Charmaine person?" asked Charm, bright and stupid as a bubble.

"You did once, I believe," Phelan prompted.

She held up ignorance like a shield. Knowing Charmaine and knowing of her were different things. Charm never actually met the Lady. Spied on her, yes, but never met her. Certainly they hadn't been properly introduced. They didn't even have one another's calling cards. No. "I'm afraid you're mistaken."

"Before you came to Borenguard. In Inshil."

"I came from Inshil," agreed Charm, though she felt she was balancing in a wobbling boat that was too small. The barrier that defined her stretched soap-bubble thin. The Lady stirred under it, stretching and shifting.

"You truly claim not to know the name Charmaine?" Phelan asked.

Charm touched her mindlock, fingering the facets, and dissembled. "My mind is not entirely my own, Your Highness, as all Borenguard knows. It is possible that my emperor could order me to forget something, and I would recall neither the information nor the order." It was possible, after all. She put her hand down in resolution. "I am sorry, Highness, I do not recall being introduced to any woman named Charmaine, and I must ask that you explain to me why you have brought this . . ." She gestured at the unfortunate spy as if it would help her conjure up an appropriate noun. ". . . person into Orchard House."

"Seeing you was his last request. I was intrigued," said Phelan with a dry, unamused smile, "and I had to bring him to Borenguard for Captain Oram's mind reading anyway." He shrugged.

Charm carefully did not glance at the Firedrinkers. It was odd that they hadn't told Phelan anything about Oram. Except that it wasn't. "I thought you would have heard. Captain Oram died last night," said Charm.

Phelan went abruptly still, paling slightly. "What?"

Charm stroked one of her trailing curls with contented fingers. "He defied the Emperor's will," she explained. Oh, it was lovely, watching the play of shock across Phelan's features.

The Prince stood for a long moment. He looked at the Firedrinkers.

"Well, unveil your prize, Your Highness, and let's see what he looks like," Charm interrupted his thoughts brightly.

Phelan jerked his head at the Firedrinkers, who unhooded their hostage. The man blinked for a moment as his eyes adjusted to the light. Charm studied him. He was very elderly, his hair a snowy ring around his head, and his beard had been well trimmed not too long ago. He looked at her, took in the pearl-strewn gown, the display of cleavage, and the mindlock in her temple, then groped for the edge of the reception desk, turning half away. For a moment Charm was afraid he might vomit on her entry carpet. Something hot and sharp prickled up her neck and face. Shame.

"I'm sorry, sir, I don't recall ever having seen you before," Charm managed.

The prisoner sank to his knees at her feet. He wrapped his arms around her skirt and knees, his shoulders heaving in silent rhythm. "Oh God, Lady Charmaine . . . what have they done to you . . ."

Charm's vision seemed to tilt and spin precariously when she looked down at him, so she glared at Phelan instead. This ragged prisoner of his was crushing her clean skirt, and the Emperor was coming. Prince Phelan watched her with narrowed eyes. Memories battered at Charm's defenses. Justice knew this person. Concerns of skirts and carpets, her determined empty-headedness, faltered; but she dared not pull back.

"Might I kiss my lady's hand?" croaked the prisoner into the bone-white satin of her skirt.

Slowly, keeping watch on Phelan out of the corner of her eye, Charm put her fingers in the prisoner's hand. He pressed his lips to her knuckles fervently. Too late, she realized the man's ruse. A sender. Killarin was a sending telepath. Not strong, not strong enough to kill him or bother others much more than if he'd been particularly expressive. With skin contact, he had a solid enough link to force his will past the maze of gears in the mindlock. A jolt of energy burned in Charm's mind on its way through to the Lady. Charm tried to grasp it, to stop it, but it was intended for the Lady, not Charm.

James Killarin had kissed her hand before. He had been a child, a little boy with freckles, kissing her hand in thanks for her judgment that he was not insane, but blessed. For her sending him into a life in the church instead of sending him to "the hospital." The man's tears were wet on her hand. He'd taken Rejuv for a long time. This old age had only come upon him when he'd fled to Saranisima. To Mari-Tres. He had never held a gun. He had only been trying to get to the Lady, to see her and help her. To tell her that Lady Fergus had arrived at an outpost and she and the children were safe with Mari-Tres. He'd come all the way from Saranisima for her . . . for the other her. . . . The Lady jolted abruptly into wakefulness.

The Lady twisted, surging against Charm, fighting toward the surface of their body like a drowning woman, dragging Charm down trying to save herself. Father Killarin's hands were innocent of weapons.

Charm pressed their lips closed more tightly. To say anything about this man would only make Phelan more suspicious. James Killarin was nothing to her. She couldn't save him. But the Lady wanted desperately to save him. Charm simply couldn't afford to, and even if she spoke the truth he'd be killed as a spy. Pressure slammed up suddenly behind her eyes and she had to steady herself with a hand on Killarin's shoulder. Her mouth tried to move. Needed to move. *No!* She tried to shake the man off, but he clung like a limpet.

The Lady struggled wildly to speak, to close the distance between her body and her self, following the line of the sending to grip on her hand. James Killarin must not be allowed to die. It was murder to hang the innocent. It was sacrilege for her to be silent.

Charm began to slip, scrabbled for mental purchase and found none. She slid away from herself. Again. Again, the Lady was winning. Mari-Tres had sent Killarin to help the Lady, not Charm. Just as they'd helped the Lady in Inshil. And worse, Charm could not remember why she knew that or why it wasn't true. Charm clawed and scrambled, but just as in a past she couldn't remember, the Lady bloomed into her brain—polite, kind, appropriate.

It wasn't right that Killarin die for something he didn't do. "This man is innocent." The voice that issued from her lips was soft, serene, sure.

"And how do you know that?" Phelan sounded far away.

"I feel it in his hands. He has never fired a gun."

The words were far away from Charm. She made a desperate lunge toward consciousness, trying to force the Lady back down. Stars burst in brilliant flares behind her eyes. The world reeled as cold encompassed Charm.

Their skirts sounded like collapsing embers as their legs gave out. Charm had no sensation of weight, or gravity, or direction. There was a struggle around the corner of the desk, and James Killarin fell into her line of sight. She must be lying on her side on the floor, Charm realized dully.

Prince Phelan crouched over Charm. "Mistress? Mistress Charm, can you hear me?"

She wanted to say yes, but her lips wouldn't move. She tumbled loose in her own skull. Darkness closed over her.

CHAPTER SEVENTEEN

Bright cold crept slowly into the deep recesses of Charm's shared mind, casting it all in clear, unflinching light as the Lady strove to remember, to make the edges of her memories match up. Charm could feel Shame now, worn gauzy and faint. In a matter of hours she would be gone. Weaker than Charm, with less sense of purpose, Shame had begun to crumble and flake, losing the corners and definition of her personality. The pieces spun into Charm and melted like snowflakes into warm earth.

Charm huddled in the last remnant of dark. *The Lady is not me. She is not me.* Charm's barriers had grown ragged in the last weeks, thinned by her repeated forays into the Lady's territory, and now she pressed herself against the mindlock, clinging to it as to an anchor. She stayed still, still as a mouse, still as death. The definitions of her self grew increasingly fragile. The tiniest jostle might shatter those walls like glass, and then who would she be? Old voices tormented her. She was too brash. Too loud. Too wild. Too troublesome. Too talented. Then what felt like knives in her mind. And Pain. And then nothing for a long time.

The soldiers were coming. Charm could hear them, could hear the screaming and the sounds of battle, coming closer across the city. Their jeers and their slaughtering beat on her mind when they touched her. She couldn't escape, but she could hide. She could curl up deeper and deeper to where they couldn't hurt her, couldn't mock her. Then everything clarified into brutal reality. Every touch of their bloody hands, every mockery they made of her body, was a bruise on Charm's soul. Shame's birthmarks.

⁓

The Lady woke with tears on her cheeks. She had never become conscious voluntarily before. Since the blackouts had begun, since she'd learned the shedding of the other people in her mind, she had never woken up by her own effort. She wasn't even sure when she'd stopped being able to wake herself. Guilt and chills warred with one another. Father Killarin had been going to hang, and she hadn't been able even to speak in his defense. For the first time, her blackouts terrified her. Remorse threatened to swallow her up. What happened when she was not awake? What did that other woman do when the Lady was not in control? Morning light was creeping in the windows of the pretty bedroom that wasn't hers.

Pain came around the screen, saw that the Lady was awake, and smiled. Pain, the first of the Lady's grown bodies. The Lady didn't remember feeling any physical hurt at all. That was still Pain's province.

"What happened to Father Killarin?" the Lady asked.

Pain stroked her brow with one hand. "I'm sorry, Lady, but Killarin died. A stroke brought on by using some manner of psychic ability. His power was so small, and he was over eighty. They didn't even know he was psychic until he'd done . . . whatever he did."

Bits of memory touched the Lady's mind. "Where is Captain Oram?" she asked.

Pain smoothed the covers. "In the greenhouse, in the tank. Desire is with him."

"What does she do?" the Lady asked.

"Who, Lady? Desire?"

She does that too easily, thought the Lady. "What . . ." She stopped, breathed for a moment, and went on. "Mistress Charm? What does she do?"

"You should rest."

"What is Mistress Charm's place?" asked the Lady, firmly.

Pain sat down on the edge of the bed. "She bears the mind-lock." Pain paused for a moment, then said firmly, "She is the Emperor's mistress."

The Lady looked up at the gabled roof over her. Hot darkness lurked around the corners of her memory, but its incandescence was fading, and with that cooling there was a dreadful certainty. *I should recognize this room.* But she hadn't the courage to ask why. She dragged in a shaky breath. "How is Captain Oram?" Apparently Pain only answered the questions she was asked.

Pain answered, but would not meet the Lady's eyes. "He . . . hasn't woken."

"I'm sorry, Pain." It seemed like the right thing to say. The prospect of a patient, of someone who needed her, distracted the Lady from her internal confusion. She was less likely to black out again if she was working. "Help me get dressed. We'll go down together and have a look at him. If he's still alive, he's at least stable. We should try to get some water into him, or some broth . . ."

"Pain?" Pride opened the door and stood in the doorway as if she were a framed portrait. "Emperor Strephon is here. He's demanding to see Mistress Charm. He said we had five minutes to make her presentable."

It isn't Tuesday. There was confusion in the back of the

Lady's mind that wasn't her own. *Yesterday was Tuesday. The Emperor only calls on Tuesday.*

The Lady had no idea who Strephon was, but if he was an emperor it would be very rude to refuse him. "Show him up, Pride," the Lady instructed.

Pride twitched slightly. "My lady?" she asked, uncertain.

"Yes. Go and bring up this emperor, please." One did not refuse emperors. It simply was not done.

Pain brought the Lady a white satin bed jacket. There was a resolute knock on the door, and it flung open. The Emperor was not tall. He had sandy hair and impatient eyes. He had no . . . bearing. He wore his expensive suit with belligerent bravado; like a little boy dressing up in someone else's clothes and afraid of being caught at it. Helmeted guards in scarlet coats stayed on the landing outside the open door.

"I'm glad to see you are awake. When Phelan reported, I was concerned." Strephon sat down and took her hands. The impressions of his hands washed through her in a flash flood. The anger, the beatings, his frustration and his fear, they slammed through her. The feeling of her own skin under his hands made her gag.

It isn't me! That isn't me! The Lady threw herself back inside her mind, twisting away from him, from the recognition in his voice; but she could find no place to hide, no comforting shadows. She pressed herself against the barrier between herself and safety, beat herself against it. She should not have had to plead. *Help me*, she pleaded. *Help me.*

Charm watched Strephon rise to stand over the Lady, fury burning her. They needed a boundary, some thing that the two of them absolutely did not share. If Charm left her shelter without a shield, she might melt into the Lady. She had an assassin to catch. She had to kill Strephon before she let that happen. The Lady was too sweet. She wouldn't be able to kill a man.

"Can you hear me?" asked Strephon.

"She's been in and out, Majesty," Pain told him. She hovered behind the little emperor with her mouth a hard white line.

Strephon reached out toward the Lady, and touched something that seemed to be stuck to the side of her head. "Answer me, Mistress," he repeated harshly. "I am the Emperor! When I give you an order you will do it!"

*As if I *I* would *will* take orders *kill* from *him*.*

Something in the Lady's head clicked and whirred softly, the sound vibrating through the bone of her skull. Her eyes flew open wide. She heard a cry of triumph, dimly, and she felt herself slipping around a distinction as clear as crystal and as fine as a pair of wires. The darkness was soft. Safe.

Charm turned in smooth synchronization with the Lady, coming around to face Strephon like the opposite rim of the same wheel. She wanted to laugh. How simple it was. The mindlock held her. She still had her orders to find the Emperor's killer. Her orders. She did not share any part of those with the Lady. She did not share the mindlock with her. It was her purpose, after all. "I . . . hear you." It was no effort to act weak. Charm didn't fight the inertia of her body. She relaxed into the pillows, watched him smile and wanted to laugh at him. He so loved to be powerful. "Have to tell you," she whispered.

"Yes, my dear. Tell me what's happened?"

Charm shaped the sweet word on her tongue like taffy. "Guns."

Strephon went rigid. "What?"

She whispered as if she could hardly speak, making him

bend close to catch the words. She murmured the words into his ear lovingly. "Paid for . . . with Imperial notes."

Strephon's fingers dug into her arms. "How do you know?"

"Justice is dead," she mumbled, not answering his question.

"Who did it?"

Charm closed her eyes, savoring her triumph. It was as bad as the plot of a cheap play, and he gulped it down whole, like a goldfish with a crumb.

"Charm!" He shook her, a quick, vicious shake.

"Majesty," objected Pain from somewhere in the background, "Majesty, please, if you press her, she may forget in self-defense. Your father's orders . . ."

Charm leaned back against the mindlock, comforted by the new solidity between herself and the Lady. Pain had probably only wanted to protect the Lady, but she had also given Charm the ultimate out. She let her head wobble from side to side. The motion hurt, and her eyes obliged her by filling with tears. "I don't know. I don't know."

"It's all right," soothed Strephon, stroking a streak of dampness from her cheek. He tsked. "Don't cry, my dear. It'll be all right. You have my word."

Charm leveled her finest adoring look at him.

Strephon's chest swelled unexpectedly. "I shall find the ones who did this to a woman of mine, and they will die screaming," he swore heroically. Charm concealed the urge to smirk. "Take the best care of her, Miss Pain."

"I always have." Revulsion burned behind Pain's bloodred eyes.

Pride held the door and Strephon strode purposefully from the room. She followed him on down the stairs. Charm felt quite smug at discovering the trick to retaining her individuality. Pain watched her with silent disapproval. Charm wanted to be congratulated and Pain was clearly not in a congratulatory mood.

"What?" Charm asked, her smug triumph sliding into petulance.

Pain sat down in the chair by the desk. She looked tired. "I just wonder, suddenly, how much of the old emperor is alive in you."

"He made me as surely as he sired his sons," said Charm coldly.

Pain raised one white eyebrow. "And look how well they've turned out."

Charm wavered. Something stirred, pushing. Charm clenched her teeth. A chill trickled down her spine. Was that all she was? In that moment of fear Charm lost her balance. She fell back against the mindlock and tumbled into the dark.

The Lady surfaced gasping, like a diver from deep water.

"Did you hear?" asked Pain.

"Yes." She tried to define the sensation. "Like standing at the bottom of a well and hearing people talk above you. Everything . . . echoed. What was she talking about, with the guns?"

"Are you sure that you want to know?" asked Pain. "It would be easier if you let us deal with all of this. We've always kept Mistress Charm safe. We will keep you safe, Lady."

"Safe? Is that what you call this? With a man collapsed and possibly dying in the greenhouse, an emperor with some kind of mental imbalance, and people smuggling guns? No, I am certainly not safe. You have not kept anyone safe!" cried the Lady in frustration. Something down behind her mind slithered like a waking serpent. The Lady gulped, clenching her fists in the satin coverlet. Snapping at Pain would not get her anywhere. Hysterics would only help that other woman take control of her again. "What has that woman been doing in my body?" asked the Lady.

Pain crept closer, knelt beside the bed. "Mistress Charm has been commanded to kill the old emperor's sons, any of them who try to take the throne. Her mindlock compels her, but I think she would do it anyway. He said it was one of them who poisoned him."

"She loved the old emperor?"

Pain hesitated. "I don't know. She wept when he died."

The Lady swallowed hard. "What is wrong with that Strephon boy? He's frightening. The things on his hands are terrible ..." She paused, breathed. This shouldn't be her. This kind of thing was Justice's job, except she'd expelled Justice. ...

"I'm not sure there's a single name for what's wrong with Strephon," said Pain, shaking her head. "Jealousy, possessive to the point of obsession, sadism—though nothing to touch Aerleas. I can't imagine why Mistress Charm would please him. She seemed to only displease him. You'd know more of him than I would, though. You read him."

The Lady almost didn't answer, but she mustn't run. Firstly, because ladies were not supposed to run. It was important to fulfill one's station in life. There was a right order to things and she had a duty to uphold her station. Mistress Charm did not uphold the Lady's station.

The Lady tried to explain. "I know that his behavior didn't satisfy him because of his actions after the behaviors." Clinging to clinical terms made it easier. It built a degree of distance that felt like a step back instead of flight. "After he'd ... do something, his hands were a little calmer, but still fidgety," the Lady said aloud. Why was he so nervous? He was an emperor. Was he not obeyed? What others would dare disobey him with the Firedrinkers at his beck and call? The Lady shook her head. The illusion of control. Charm was his father's mistress. If he controlled Charm, he felt better. Charm was a sort of symbol for him, probably of the Empire. The mindlock whirred. The Lady changed tack. "Who are the other princes?"

"You would know the eldest as Aerleas. In Inshil they called him the Butcher."

Prickling chills crawled up the Lady's back like an army of frozen centipedes. "I recall snatches of him. Someone else . . . you've told me about him before, I think," she whispered. "He is still in command of the armies?"

Pain nodded. "Strephon doesn't know enough about armies to try to tell him what to do. Except now Strephon's started to send Aerleas actual orders."

"How do you know?"

"Mistress Charm has a spy who sends information to her. She sends it on to Saranisima. Aerleas is losing ground every day."

"And no wonder. Go on," said the Lady grimly.

Pain obeyed. "Prince Luther is puzzling. He is icy to Mistress Charm, but he has been kind to Justice, Pride, and Desire. The only other living son is Phelan, the one who brought James Killarin."

"I remember seeing Phelan with Killarin, but nothing specific," admitted the Lady.

"He has been Justice's province," Pain said quietly.

The Lady nibbled at her thumbnail. "Strephon, he will have people looking for these guns?"

"Without doubt."

"But who will he blame for it?"

"I don't think Mistress Charm cares, as long as it's one of his brothers; but she was aiming Strephon at Phelan."

"Justice is dead?"

Pain crossed her arms, defensive. "She asked Pride to help her, and Pride did."

"Poor thing, she seemed so strong . . . what was the last

straw?" asked the Lady. She could fix it, next time, so that Justice stayed alive and out of the Lady's head.

"Oram was special to Luther, almost like his son. Charm told Luther that Oram was dead. She would not recant it, even though it drove Luther almost mad. Luther had been so good to Justice, and that finally broke something in her."

"And now that she's with Charm, what will she do?" asked the Lady. "What will you do? Will you tell him the truth?"

Pain sat down in the shadowed side of the window seat, looking out over the bone orchard. Her white hair seemed almost to glow in the dimness. "I'm sorry it's hurting Luther to think Oram has died, but if the Emperor finds out that Oram lives, it will be the end of us."

The Lady raised her hand and touched her right temple, where Strephon had touched. She found a cool, smooth surface like a watch face with facets around the edges. The Lady clenched her teeth and did not jerk her hand away. The thing whirred faintly under her fingertips, tiny vibrations betraying complex workings under the crystal. She would have to examine Captain Oram's lock more carefully. Perhaps she could get the scorched face off of it and get a look at the inner mechanisms. Either that or she should speak with Mr. Ostander again. "Is there a hand mirror somewhere?"

Pain fetched the mirror. The Lady stared into it in shock.

"Good God, what happened to my hair?" She ran her fingers through the violently green strands.

"The Emperor, the old emperor, particularly liked your hair. Little rebellions amused him, so she kept coloring it and eventually it became her trademark."

Realization dawned. "No . . . no, I'm sure it didn't amuse him. He knew that if he tried to control every little impulse, she would be able to bleed off the energy in the mindlock," the

Lady whispered, "so he tolerated the little things in order to make sure she would have to follow through on the more major points. Clever, clever of him and clever of her. The question is why does she obey this Emperor Strephon?"

Pain shrugged. "To keep his guard down, so that she can eventually kill him. And he's the Emperor. Saying no would get her, probably all of us, killed."

Yes, well, one didn't say no, but the Emperor was married. She was sure she'd heard that somewhere.

"As long as he doesn't know she's out of his absolute grasp, he won't kill you," Pain told her, turning her pink-red eyes back to the Lady for a moment. She looked down, and went back to contemplating the orchard.

They were silent for a long time. The Lady fingered her hair.

"Chartreuse?" she asked plaintively.

Pain smiled at that. "The color washes out easily enough. She does it a different color every few days."

"For heaven's sake throw this color away, will you? It's hideous." She felt Charm stir indignantly, but the Lady refused to budge and offended fashion sense didn't give Charm enough leverage to uproot her. "I am not going to just let you run over decent people like Father Killarin to commit murder; and as long as we're sharing this hair, you're going to have to live with some compromises," she told her other self aloud. "I'll get you out of there just as fast as I can, believe me."

It was hard to examine her own temple, but the Lady angled the mirror carefully and looked out of the corner of her eyes. The crystal was clear, and beneath it she could make out tiny gears, wheels, brilliant jewels, and something that might have been a spring. Its beauty made it all the more dreadful.

"It never touched any of us because of Mistress Charm,"

said Pain softly. "All that it is and does is hers to bear. We don't always agree with her . . . lately we almost never agree, but Charm is strong. She survives."

The Lady touched the mindlock, fingers shaking. "She was the old emperor's mistress?"

Pain looked down. "The old emperor treated her well enough, but Strephon takes great pleasure in controlling her, and in beating her when she rebels even by the thinnest margin. At first she defied him deliberately, by following precisely what he said without paying any heed to what he meant; but I think in the last weeks we've come to understand that he will always find something which he believes to be defiance."

The Lady put the mirror in her lap and sat still for a long time. It wasn't right to kill people, of course, and being a whore was not moral, either; but obeying Emperor Strephon kept the Lady's body alive, and the Lady certainly did not want to die. The problem went around and around in her thoughts without her finding any way out.

There was a knock, and Pride brought in a tray with tea and scones. The blind ghost set the tray across her lady's knees with uncanny accuracy, then felt her way to the window seat beside Pain. The two boneghosts sat expectantly.

The Lady put a sugar cube into her tea, and tried to think of what they could be waiting for. She finally asked—"What happened? What did Strephon do after he left me?"

"He ordered Prince Phelan's arrest before he was even out of the entry," Pride reported.

"The Firedrinkers told me that after Luther left here, he was given command of some of them and is charged with finding the guns. I expect they'll find them today sometime. The crates weren't very well hidden," said Pain.

Pride picked up the narrative again. "Mr. Ostander has been questioned. A Firedrinker who spoke to me said that

Mr. Ostander had been trying to save the captain's life by bringing him to you. They also knew about the grave from Prince Luther. They didn't know anything about him still being alive. Their telepath must not be very good."

"Or they deliberately didn't ask clear enough questions, or they answered with only surface accuracy," Pain suggested. "Their sloppiness served Lady Fergus very well."

"Prince Phelan is asking to be sent to the front. Theoretically as a support for Aerleas, but Phelan has wanted to take the army from Aerleas for years; and now there are more atrocities." Pride shrugged.

"So Phelan looks like a good alternative to Aerleas, but only if he is cleared of the gun-smuggling charge," reasoned the Lady thoughtfully. She poured herself a little more tea.

Pain spoke up. "The people of Boren are growing uneasy about Aerleas just as he is taking heavy losses in the war. His troops send press-gangs into the lower city. There was . . . there was a massacre. Other than that incident, Firedrinkers have kept things under control."

"Other than that, there's only the preparations for the Festival of the Masque being held for Her Majesty's birthday," Pride went on with a disdainful sniff. "Strephon is sparing no expense. . . . Oh, and a boy brought a note from Countess Seabrough." Pride stared unblinking into the bright day. "She wondered if she might call upon you to pick up the birds she ordered."

"The little canaries in the lab? Yes, they're perfectly ready for animation, but . . . Countess Seabrough? Do noble ladies come here often?" the Lady asked. It seemed strange for a lady of high station to call at a gentleman's club.

"Countess Seabrough's never been here before, but her husband hasn't called recently so I suppose she feels it's all right now," said Pride calmly. "What's strange is that she didn't order the birds." She put gentle emphasis on her next words. "Lord Fergus ordered them as a gift for his wife."

The Lady shook her head. She obviously ought to remember Lord Fergus, but there was nothing. Mistress Charm stirred in irritation. She could take far better care of this situation.

"Lady? Lady, you look pale," said Pain.

"I'm all right. I'm just . . . I'm afraid I don't remember about Lord Fergus." She took a hurried sip of tea and put the cup down with resolve, wiping her sweating palms with the napkin. "We'd best try to get me ready to receive Countess Seabrough."

CHAPTER EIGHTEEN

The canaries sang sweetly in a white wire cage, their liquid melodies wrapping around the light percussion of the bones in the orchard. The Lady sat at a graceful little table in the solarium surrounded by ferns and orchids. Pain had done her hair the color of lilacs, and the white mourning gown she had on was the least showy thing in Mistress Charm's wardrobe.

"Countess Seabrough," announced Pain from the door.

The Lady rose.

Countess Seabrough bore herself with noble grace. Her beauty was sharpening with age, and her eyes kept their own haughty counsel.

"Welcome to Orchard House, Countess Seabrough," the Lady said simply. She didn't curtsy to her guest, and Countess Seabrough was not inclined to shake hands. "Pain, I am home for no one but the Emperor while Countess Seabrough is here."

"Yes, Lady," murmured Pain, curtsying and backing out. The doors clicked behind her.

It had been easier to be brave and righteously outraged in the privacy of a bedroom, even one that was not hers. The Lady's courage wavered under Countess Seabrough's scornful eye. "I was a little confused by your note," said the Lady, gesturing to the white wicker chair across from her own. When in doubt, courtesy was always the right answer.

"I imagine that you were." Countess Seabrough did not smile and she did not sit. "Mistress, I came here to warn you. The Empress does not like you."

"That is hardly surprising." But Mistress Charm seemed surprised. The Lady lifted her chin. "I trust that Her Majesty is not offended in any way but the usual?" Mistresses were usually considered offensive by wives, after all.

"Not that I am aware of, but the last person to displease the Empress was Lord Fergus," explained Countess Seabrough a little sharply.

"I see." The Lady did not understand at all. Neither did Charm. "Why tell me this?" she asked, covering her cowardice by pouring two glasses of lemonade.

Countess Seabrough flung her words at the Lady like stones. "I will be as frank as I can be, Mistress. I know perfectly well that my husband comes here for more than cards, and I know that he goes nowhere else. I know that one of your . . . creatures"—her lips drew back from the word as if in revulsion—"attempted to help Lord Fergus leave the country. I do not know how he managed the escape of his family, but I suspect that you had something to do with it. I have come to urge you to follow Lyra's very sensible example."

The Lady set down the lemonade pitcher. Leave Borenguard. To simply go. They could escape somewhere, anywhere, that people would not know her as Mistress Charm. The mindlock whirred, and deep within her Mistress Charm cried out. The echo of pain slashed down the Lady's spine, taking their shared body to its knees. Their fingers spasmed on the stone floor.

"It seems I cannot leave," the Lady managed.

Countess Seabrough lifted the cage with the birds in it from its stand. No trace of pity touched her eyes. "Then I am sorry for you." She swept past the Lady. The knife-pleated silk of her skirt brushed across the Lady's hands.

Pain came and helped the Lady to her feet, half supporting the Lady back to her chair. "Are you all right?" Pain asked.

The Lady shook her head. Her eyes spilled over, tears sliding down both sides of her nose. "I can't do this. I don't know what made me think I could."

Pain crouched at her knees. The familiarity of it was airy and fragile as a blown egg. "The world isn't all towers of white marble, and it isn't all gardens of perfectly trimmed grass," said Pain softly. "Whether we want to look or not, we cannot escape from the world. We can retreat for a while, but always it is there."

"Mari-Tres wanted to go to Saranisima so that she could see what lay outside Inshil." The Lady wiped her cheeks with her fingers. "She said she wanted to go somewhere that she could be part of the world instead of only a voyeur, but she wasn't psychic. She could leave. Psychics have to be careful."

"I have been outside the walls of Orchard House, Lady. The things that are bad within this house, and even the things that are wrong in the city, are not bad and wrong everywhere; any more than Inshil's perfection existed outside the walls of its palace," Pain told her. "When you see a larger world, there is room for good things as well as bad." Her red eyes almost glowed in the filtered light of the solarium. "There are no perfect men, but Lord Fergus was a good and honest man who stood up for his principles. And Captain Oram and Count Seabrough are at least not cruel."

"Seabrough? The Countess's husband?"

"I think he's a man who pursues his purposes with the most practical course. He doesn't get into political fights he can't win. Some think he supports the Emperor because he says nothing."

Saying nothing is not solving the problem, and all Seabrough's practicality has brought is trouble. If Boren had fewer practical men and more Ferguses, we would not be where we are now, thought the Lady.

More thoughts came to the Lady unbidden, slipping around the mindlock like spiteful whispers in a crowd. *At least he's doing something besides getting himself killed.*

The Lady pushed the thoughts away. She didn't know Seabrough, and this Mistress Charm person was obviously no great judge of character. "What would his wife know about the Empress?"

"Everything. She's the Empress's lady of the wardrobe, her closest servant."

The Lady's head ached. She didn't want to think about it, didn't want to know anymore or fight anymore. She was so tired already. How did people live like this, with all the ugliness? The Lady was not supposed to have to live like this. "You came to see me for something?"

"Prince Luther is here. He says that he has questions to ask you, but I'll tell him you aren't well."

"Well enough to see Countess Seabrough, but not well enough to see a prince of the blood royal?" The Lady smiled wanly. She used the arms of the chair to lever herself up.

The Lady's ivory taffeta petticoats rustled around her feet as she went down the long flights of stairs. Taffeta petticoats were not tasteful, but Mistress Charm hadn't had any quiet clothes. By the time she reached the ground floor, the Lady had herself somewhat in hand.

Prince Luther stood in the entry hall with one thumb tucked into his broad belt, drumming his fingers on the leather. Four men in scarlet with closed helms flanked him. Her heart pounded. She knew him. Luther. Luther, whose father was her country's enemy. His father had sent him to try to talk her family into giving him the designs for the heretical mindlocks, but Luther had been better than that. He had been kind to her. She reminded herself to breathe, and not to lock her knees. She wanted to fling herself from the stairs into her old friend's arms, to beg him to keep her safe; but she stayed standing two stairs up. Ladies did not indulge in unseemly displays. It was up to the gentleman to approach.

"Good morning, Highness. Pain tells me that you wish to question me?" the Lady asked, her voice low.

Prince Luther's dark eyes narrowed for an instant. "That was my intention, but I wonder now if it would do any good."

He knew. He knew she was not Charm. He'd guessed it instantly. His gaze bored into her. She remembered that sharp, falcon look. He glanced at one of the Firedrinkers, but they said nothing.

She could not feel any touch directly on her mind, but there were other ways Firedrinkers could test for the truth.

"A large cache of guns has been found hidden in Uptown. The Emperor seemed to think that you knew of it."

Ladies did not lie. It was beneath them. The Lady was not, however, such a dimwit as to think that the truth would not get her body killed. One must have a body. She said calmly, "I told him what I knew." She had, after all, told him everything she'd known at the time; which was nothing.

"Prince Phelan's hair was found on one of the guns. It had been test-fired."

The Lady closed her eyes for a moment in disgust at so stupid a mistake. "That is sad news."

"Is it?" Luther snapped, suddenly angry.

"Forgive me, Prince Luther, but I still don't understand why you're here." True enough even to say before telepaths.

The Lady came all the way down the stairs. Luther was very tall, and she had to cock her head to one side to look up at him. She saw the gesture strike home in his face.

"Phelan professes his innocence." Luther's voice rasped.

"Is he innocent?" The words were bitter on the Lady's tongue, drawn through the hot white lines of the mindlock wires. She pinched her mouth shut, hard. As if it would make that other woman in her head shut up.

Luther didn't flinch. "The Firedrinkers who listened to his statement say that he is telling the truth as he knows it."

"How many children must he rape before he's guilty of a crime?" Charm burst out bitterly.

The Lady whipped back into control of herself. Ladies did not lose control. This lack was intolerable, but tolerate it she must.

Luther ignored her. "Phelan has been known to frequent Orchard House. It would not be difficult for his hair to have been collected here and planted on the rifle."

The Lady shook her head and let her disappointment at his opinion of her sound in her tone. "Prince Luther, do you believe for one instant that I am so stupid, having managed to buy and import the illegal firearms you describe, that I would plant a hair in a rifle lock? Particularly knowing, as I of all people should, that any skilled telepath would be instantly able to confirm Prince Phelan's innocence or guilt merely from his statement? And that the hair itself would give me away if there was even one other psychometer in Boren? I hope that you do not think so slenderly of me."

"I believe I have passed the stage of underestimating you, madam." Luther's smile was cool enough to freeze a serpent's heart.

The scarlet-coated guard nearest his left elbow leaned

forward, tipping his helmet close to the Prince's ear. Luther partly turned his head, keeping his eyes on the Lady.

"Very well," said Luther. "I was instructed, Mistress, that, should the Firedrinkers fail to find you at fault in this matter, I was to deliver the Empress's compliments and this invitation." He took a thick vellum envelope from his jacket and extended it.

Mistress Charm wriggled and strained. *If you touch his hand, you can find out if he murdered his father. We can tell the Firedrinkers honestly what you see. We can be safe. And free.*

The Lady did not consider Charm running around loose to be something that would improve public safety. She took the letter from the opposite end. There was little else she could do without arousing suspicion, anyway. Particularly after the Killarin incident.

Luther turned and went out. The Firedrinkers saluted and followed, letting the door close behind them.

Frustrated, the Lady sat down on the bottom step and opened the envelope. In gilt and scarlet ink, the enclosure commanded the recipient's presence at the Empress's birthday masquerade. Gentlemen, it assured the reluctant, need not appear in costume if they did not wish to. Down at the bottom of the card someone with a lovely hand had written in plain black—"Please come, Y."

The impression of cool, slender fingers turning the card over and over, nervous, and then suddenly, quickly, putting it in the envelope.

Charm stirred. *Empress Ylsbeth. She is alone and afraid.*

The Lady frowned. *Why would any woman invite her husband's whore to her own birthday party?* It made no sense at all.

"What's that?" asked Pain, coming down the stairs.

"The Empress has invited Mistress Charm to her birthday ball."

Charm stayed quiet in the back of the Lady's skull.

"Is she going, or are you?"

The Lady shivered. Orchard House was bad enough. To go to the palace, to have everyone stare at them and know the Lady's disgrace, was far worse. Disgraced women lived quietly. Out of sight. But it was expressly asked, and one did not disobey one's superiors. "What . . . what do you think I should do?"

Charm sniffed, settling into sulky obstinacy. *You wanted to be in charge. Go ahead. Tell her no and cower in your laboratory. Let's see how long they'll leave us alive.*

"If you're going to the Empress's masquerade, you'll need a gown. Shall I speak to Hyacinth Barker?" Pain asked the Lady. "She made all of Mistress Charm's gowns, and half the noble ladies in Borenguard call her in on the sly. Even the Empress has sent for her."

"In that case I suppose you should call her. Do you think Mistress Charm will come back next Tuesday?" asked the Lady aloud, though the question was more for the interior listener. There was no answer, but perhaps that was a problem for later. The immediate crisis had passed. "Do you think she would go to this party?"

Pain's lips twitched as if she wanted to laugh. Or scoff. "Since the old emperor brought her through the gates of Orchard House, Mistress Charm has only been off the grounds once—at the Empress's command. Well, the Empress has asked, so I suppose she would go. About Tuesday, Mistress Charm will do as she chooses, the same as always."

"I can't face that man, Emperor Strephon. I can't," the Lady whispered, pleading with her other self. Nothing. "I'm sorry," she whispered. "I'm sorry."

I'm sorry, I'm sorry, mocked Charm's voice in the back of her head. *Why don't you just go back to sleep and let me handle things? Go back to tinkering around your lab and be happy with your ignorance.*

"Because Killarin woke me up," hissed the Lady, impotent anger building to a low burn under her sternum. "How can I go peacefully on with my part of our life knowing what you do? Prostituting yourself and settling for whatever vengeance you can get instead of doing what's right. The Emperor of Boren was our enemy. You shouldn't run his errands for him. And you're letting innocent people like Killarin die for things they haven't done . . . you've pleased your emperor at the cost of everything else."

The mindlock . . .

"Is an excuse!" shrieked the Lady, hitting at the air as if she could get at Charm that way. "To whore and flaunt yourself and your immorality! You could shoot Strephon and say it was his father's command and the Firedrinkers would swear it was the truth before whatever judge because no one can check on their story! Your stupid command would be done; but that doesn't satisfy you. Oh no! You want vengeance!"

I want to live, snarled Charm. *What would happen if the princes thought there could be hidden assassination orders waiting behind my mindlock? I'd be a threat. I'd hang and what good would it do? Just Strephon dead? Should I die so cheaply as disposing of that one piece of trash? Should I make every Firedrinker suspect along with me? Never.* Charm's laugh stung savagely around the inside of the Lady's brain like a storm of hornets. *I waited decades for this chance to come along. Being a martyr is lovely in chivalric tales of woe. All of Inshil's martyrs didn't help anyone as much as my being alive here and now. The Princes of Boren are a stain on the face of creation. Aerleas will die, and Phelan, and Strephon, and I don't care how they die or why as long as they die, but I'm going to find that assassin, and then before*

God I will see those three pay for their crimes in hell; and if Luther gets in the way I'll see him dead as well.

The Lady screamed in frustration. Tears ran, scalding, down her cheeks. "Shut up! Shut up." She sank down onto the floor, sobs tearing out from beneath her ribs. The world spun and rocked crazily.

Pain watched her, helpless to cut off the exchange she could hear only one side of.

"I should have just died. . . . I should have . . ." She looked up at the boneghost, standing still and white like a statue of an avenging angel. "Won't you help me?"

Pain's face was as rigidly uncomprehending as stone. Her bloodred eyes never flickered. "Of course, Lady. I'll go fetch Miss Barker at once," said Pain, and left the Lady collapsed in the crumpled pool of her skirts on the floor in the entry.

And no one came to help her get up.

CHAPTER NINETEEN

It took the Lady several minutes to drag herself to the bottom stair. The entry was tall and dark and foreign around her. What should she do? What could she do? The hair in the gun had been stupid. The princes knew, now, that someone was conspiring against them, trying to set them on each other. Charm of all people should have known that the Firedrinkers would find out Phelan hadn't handled the gun. Any telepath should be able to read innocence or guilt in a statement. Prince Luther knew that too. Did he think she was hiding Charm? And what would he have done if he'd been faced with Mistress Charm?

It seemed irrationally safer to speak aloud than to keep the words in the privacy of her crowded skull. "Even if what she knows can't be read, surely they could still touch-read the gun."

I didn't touch the guns, nor did I directly touch the hair, said Charm patiently. *The order was placed anonymously, and the men who placed the guns don't know where the hair came from. Besides, the Firedrinkers can't read me. The mindlock protects me. Now we'll have to hope it protects you, too.*

The thick vellum card on the floor drew the Lady's attention. "Do you want to go to that?"

Charm scrabbled for purchase and found none.

"I asked if you wanted to go, not if you wanted to put me back to sleep."

The quiet in her mind turned thunderous.

"I may be weak, but at least I'm not petulant," the Lady muttered.

The Lady retrieved the card and hauled herself to her feet. She wandered out to the orchard to stand among the trees. Her trees. A cat skeleton that she'd found in the bushes by the greenhouse was a pretty little tree now. The swallow's wing bone had grown into a sentinel corner tree. A weird little bush grew soft fruit that hardened into frog bones.

She smiled and laid her hand on the trunk of the tree in the center of the orchard. The tree of human bones. She remembered planting a small round disk of bone she'd found when she woke in the greenhouse for the first time. She hadn't thought about where it had come from. The Lady lifted her hand to finger the crystal face of the mindlock. She knew, now, where that disk had come from. The other trees were not so personal. The Lady wrapped her arms around herself and inhaled as far as Charm's corset allowed. The air was still. It smelled of damp wood and grass. The bones hung silent.

Desire came out the door of the greenhouse. "How are you?"

"Uncertain. Prince Luther was here. He clearly recognized me, and he knows that I am separate from Charm, but he's angry too. You, Pride, Pain, Charm, and I. Only five left. Charm was the Emperor's mistress. Pain and Pride have other experiences. What is it that you do?"

"I remember loving Prince Luther . . . and what came of it."

"Oh." The Lady sat down on the bench by the greenhouse.

Desire's voice was soft, wistful. "I have been with him once here, but he has not asked for me again."

"If you were in this body, would you love him?"

"That's what I do, Lady. Where I am isn't important."

"And do you think he would love you?"

Desire shrugged. "I don't know. Mistress Charm found the whole thing idiotic," she admitted. "She used to point out that he didn't come back."

"Mistress Charm has so many sharp points she ought to be a pincushion. Could he have come back?"

"Why would he? How could he? He was in Fortress Isle, and wasn't released until the conquest was over. His father took Mistress Charm, and no one knew about me. I didn't even have a body until you grew this one a few years ago."

The Lady glanced up at the boneghost. "Do you like the body I grew for you? I'm sorry she makes you sell yourself."

Desire was silent a moment, then sighed. "I'd hoped that Luther would come sooner. Maintaining this house and the laboratory is expensive. . . . Charm asked me to accept a room on the second floor. And I agreed to do it."

"She's disgusting. She and her emperor both."

"The old emperor was horrible in many ways, but he did love Mistress Charm," said Desire, leaning her head against the doorframe and watching as the wind stirred through the orchard. The horse bone tree groaned under the strain of its heavy fruit.

"Loving the power he had over her, lusting after her, and loving her are all different things, Desire."

Desire smiled gently. "Why do you think men come here?"

"What do you mean?"

"Barring those whose minds are deeply injured, the men who come here do not want to have to be clever, or to provide initiative, or to do anything except relax and possibly show off to people who will not fail to admire them. Sex they could legally demand from their wives if they truly wanted only that. Mistress Charm is good at all the other things. And, because of the mindlock, the Emperor could trust Mistress Charm absolutely. It must be hard for emperors to find someone to trust so perfectly. That's why he asked her to find his killer."

"Is that what Prince Luther wants? Someone he can trust and everything simple?"

Desire walked to one of the bone trees, a delicate, arching little tree, and stirred her finger thoughtfully through a cluster of half-grown cat's bones. They sounded lightly, almost chiming. "I don't know what Luther wants," she admitted sadly, "but I don't believe anything could be simple between us. It's all . . . complicated."

"You said that loving Luther was what you did, but what is it that you want, Desire?" asked the Lady, curious.

Desire's eyes went glassy with tears. "Forgiveness, Lady."

"For what?"

Desire would not look at her. The tears spilled over, tracing paths down Desire's face.

Chills chased around a blank place inside the Lady's skull, dazzling and flashing. She swallowed and looked down at the pleated hem of her skirt.

Desire wiped her eyes on her sleeve.

"I'd still like to know how you can say that the old emperor loved Mistress Charm," the Lady insisted.

Desire came back to the doorway of the laboratory, looked inside briefly. "It was not an unselfish affection, but with Mistress Charm he could be truly at ease. And being magnanimous to her assuaged his guilt. That's what he wanted most of all, so she gave him that. In return, she had safety, and this house, and a kind of companionship even if it was with her jailer and her customers. She made the best of what she had."

Surprise and a small warm feeling grew in the back of the Lady's mind as Charm heard Desire's defense of her.

The Lady could have ground her teeth together, and now

it was she who turned away. "It is wrong to kill people, like the ones who smuggled in her stupid guns, in order to accomplish the orders of one deranged old tyrant!"

"I beg your pardon?" asked Pride from the kitchen door.

The Lady leaped up and spun to face her, turning so abruptly that the momentum of her skirts made her stagger when she stopped and they did not. "People are dying in Inshil. It isn't right!"

"Of course it isn't," Pride agreed patiently, "but Mistress Charm didn't make the war. If anything, Mistress Charm has saved Saranisima tens of thousands of lives by informing Saranisima of Aerleas's orders. She has possibly saved that city from capture, and saved your sister Mari-Tres by doing so."

The Lady shook her head, trying to clear it. Would she have sent men to die, to save Mari-Tres? Soldiers died to defend the innocent. If the attackers died instead, it was surely not wrong. It was hard to think. "She is committing treason."

Pride's laugh came out as surprised scorn. "Against whom? Certainly not against Inshil. If we are captives here, then destroying our captors is not treason, and if we are citizens of Boren then she is still right carrying out the will of the old emperor." Pride smiled a little. "Label Mistress Charm how you will, there is no treason in her."

"But we don't know who it was," the Lady shot back, pouncing on the one kernel of fact she could find. "There is no proof whatsoever about who is responsible, she only assumes it's one of the princes, and even if it's not them, she'd want to kill them anyway."

"Everyone who could have done it will be at the Empress's birthday masque, and dancing requires touching. If you truly want to know who is responsible, and as long as you can get around their gloves, you will have an ideal opportunity to find the guilty person," suggested Desire.

"I can't." The Lady's ferocity melted. They were ganging up on her. She turned back to the orchard. The trees shivered as a breeze stirred through them. Overripe bones dropped in a pattering shower. The Lady wrapped her arms around herself, not wanting to have to face either of them. "All those people looking at me, staring, thinking that I am a whore . . ."

"It would not bother Mistress Charm," said Pride with uncomprehending calm. "Why should you be so ashamed of her for finding a way through the Gordian knot?"

The Lady's eyes burned as if they could burst into flames within their sockets. "Why should she have been happy as an imprisoned whore in Orchard House when I was taken the best care of and miserable?"

"Oh, my lady." Pity made Desire's eyes shine. "You were more a prisoner than Mistress Charm has ever been."

"Blasphemy!" the Lady hissed, rounding on Desire again. "That is blasphemy!"

Pride snorted and went back into the house, shutting the door with a diminutive and dismissive click.

"Did the mindlock bind her any more tightly than expectation and tradition bound you? Charm's emperor never, ever laid a violent hand upon her." Desire reached out, touched the Lady's hand with her own maimed fingers. "Can any of us say the same about Inshil? My hands are Boren's work, and the mindlock that of Charm's emperor. Strephon beat Mistress Charm, but your back was scarred first in Inshil. If we were so holy, what right did they have to do such a thing?"

"That wasn't me! It wasn't me! I would never do anything so wrong."

"Only your father, the Chancellor, could have beaten you to such a degree. Do you really not remember?" Desire frowned.

"It wasn't me. The lot of you, creeping around when I can't see you, doing horrible things. You're no different. It was you that betrayed our position," accused the Lady. "It was you who let him seduce you!"

Desire closed her eyes, half turned away as if the words were a blow. "If you say so, my lady."

"Stop it."

"Lady, I am guilty, if you call it that, of loving him and of having an affair with him. I know that I'm guilty of failing myself and the only other person in the world who loved me; but though I am the one who spent our time together, I am not the one who first befriended him." Desire's voice died to a pleading whisper. She did not look at the Lady. "You cast me off, to be sure, but I was you until you were discovered. You only minded it when you were caught."

There was nothing there, nothing to take the Lady's treason away. She had gone to Luther, betrayed all her training, all her duty, everything that was rightfully expected of her. She might not have the memories of the encounters, but she had cast off Desire. The Lady didn't want it. It wasn't her, it couldn't be her. The mindlock caught in a metallic whine.

The Lady denied it. No! It wasn't her, she wouldn't let it be her! She hadn't gone to Luther. But she could not make herself believe that, because there stood Desire. The mindlock, cold and mechanical, held her together. She couldn't find anyone who was responsible except herself. The Lady clawed at the crystal in her head, but could not get her fingernails under it. She'd get it out. She'd throw out Charm and everything she'd done so wrong with it.

The mindlock whirred, tiny mechanisms spinning. Charm writhed and fought for control of their body. *You will never get rid of me, you insufferable little moralist! Pull it out and I'll still be here, and so will the past.*

Desire pushed her broken hands beneath the Lady's fingers to her temples, keeping the Lady's scrabbling hands away from the lock. "Don't, Lady, please don't. I'm sorry. Let me take it from you. I will carry it. I can. Let it go. . . ."

A horse's skull dropped from its overburdened tree. The released branch rushed back up in a sudden whoosh, leaving a fluttering fall of coppering leaves and the smell of damp leaves.

"It's all right, Lady," Desire soothed. "I am not Shame. I am not such flimsy stuff. I can carry it."

But Charm caught up the memory of that treasonous meeting. She remembered being sixteen and how it had thrilled her, dressing in her room to escape to Luther. She didn't care anymore about the rules and expectations that bound her. He was going to set her free. Twice a week she sat in court, and every day she tended the gardens. She'd be dead soon in spite of all she could do, her own power gradually chipping away her sanity and her health. She wanted an adventure, to get out, to have a life of her own for just this little while. But Luther hadn't been there to meet her that last day, only a note in their message place behind a brick. His father had heard of their affair. Luther answered his father's demand and went home without her.

"Be silent! It wasn't me, I'm not a whore! I would never betray my country! It was Charm, all Charm even then! God, if I had known you'd all babble so, I would have made you mute!" the Lady cried, tears streaking down her face. She stormed back through the orchard and into the house, slamming the heavy oak door closed behind her. The glass panes shattered with the force, and skittered around her feet in a wash of glittering edges.

CHAPTER TWENTY

No one but Firedrinkers stirred on the streets Thursday morning as Pain went through Middletown toward the Lowtown gate. No servants carrying messages, no street peddlers with their wares, no ladies walking out. The Firedrinkers moved up the Imperial Way in ordered pairs, pausing at some doors, passing by others. One pair nodded to Pain, polite but not pausing. The girl at the desk of Hyacinth's shop told Pain that her employer was at the warehouse in Harborward.

Reluctantly, Pain continued down through the city. Near the Lowtown gate a scent crawled along her arms and prickled over her scalp. There was no wind, but the stench seeped slowly up the streets in defiance of the dead air. Blood, feces, and the acrid smell of gun smoke roiled together in a battlefield reek. Sounds of crying carried more honestly in the damp air. Pain clenched her fists in the folds of her skirts and forced her feet to move. One step toward the last corner. Another.

The Firedrinkers were helping clusters of weeping people find their loved ones among neat rows of corpses. On the south side of the square lay a dozen mangled bodies in army uniforms. On the north side, rows of townspeople. Men and women walked along the rows of dead or sat beside the bodies of their loved ones, weeping. One of the Firedrinkers approached Pain.

"Miss, can we help you?"

"They're . . . still here."

The Firedrinker nodded. "We had to attend to the wounded and to the city, first. By today the rigors had all gone, and we could get them sorted and laid out decently to be claimed."

"How many?" she asked.

"Of the army, fifteen. Of the townsfolk, one hundred and six killed, and more injured."

"Why . . . ?" The broken word leaped out of her mouth, leaving silence behind it.

"Because the army had repeating guns, and the townsfolk only what they could improvise."

Pain shook her head. "Why weren't you there? Why did none of you even try to keep the peace?" she hissed, tears of rage and helplessness burning in her eyes. "I know some of you are pyrokinetic! You could have kept the guns from firing!"

The Firedrinker spoke softly. "There were no good choices, miss. If we had been on this side of the wall when it began, the people would have assumed we were on the side of the press-gang. We would have been forced to defend ourselves and onto a side of the conflict that we do not want to join. As it was, we were able to hold the rioters in Lowtown to a confined area."

"How did you know?" asked Pain, unable to look away from the carnage in the square.

"One of us read the plan in Colonel Fletcher's mind. It was his intention to stir up enough trouble in the lower city that Prince Aerleas would have an excuse to come home and declare martial law. Lowtowners have been walking a thin line. It was only a matter of time. We did what we could on that side of the gate, suppressing the violence in the soldiers. People were going to die, but at least this way some of them were Prince Aerleas's men."

"And by being the ones to come in and bring things under

control, by taking Colonel Fletcher away, you are, at the least, still seen as the ones defending the people."

"It is all that we can do, miss. It was that or suppress the people endlessly. That is not our goal. That is not even the spirit of our orders."

The central square had been cleared but for the grotesque pattern of streaks that radiated out across the gory cobbles, left by the heels of the dragged bodies. Bile rose in the back of Pain's mouth. She swallowed hard.

Most of the soldiers had been torn almost apart. Their faces were grossly bruised and broken. Their limbs twisted in places they should not have. They were hardly recognizable as men. Four soldiers lay with their eyes wide and staring, without marks of violence on their bodies. One smoking body still had a few bright uniform buttons showing among the charred husk. "Those men, the . . . just . . . dead ones, the burned one, they weren't killed by the crowd."

The Firedrinker's answer was calm. "They were in the act of assaulting citizens of Boren, Miss Pain. They did not desist when given fair warning. They died by psychic means."

"And Colonel Fletcher?"

"He and the remainder of his unit are under guard in Fortress Isle."

"Aerleas will not stay away from Boren now," said Pain, unable to keep the bitterness from her voice.

"He will come because no matter what is said of this, he will make it an excuse. What we have accomplished is to keep the goodwill of the people and we will be here to defend the city against him as best we can. That is what will be important in the end, and it is what the captain wants."

Pain stared at the mirrored visor, trying to glimpse the face behind it, but all she could see was the ghostly pallor of her own skewed reflection. This Firedrinker was the same height as Pain. Pain let her gaze slide down the figure in the scarlet coat. The hips were a little wide in proportion to the shoulders. Small, narrow hands inside the gloves, fine-boned wrists. This was probably one of the women, then.

The expressionless helmet betrayed no waver. "We are not people, miss. It is only you who ever thought of us as more. Now, after Captain Oram had shown his face, the lower orders of the city were reminded that the Emperor's hounds were human once."

"But you must still follow the Emperor's orders," she pointed out softly. "It was disobedience felled Oram."

"We have always followed the captain's orders, miss."

Pain went still. "What of the Emperor's orders?"

"Captain Oram has his orders, miss. We have ours."

Pain's pulse roared in her ears. Oram had told her himself, weeks ago. "My Firedrinkers have not had the same orders." Oram was the one who commanded them. The Assembly had chosen Strephon to be emperor in part for fear of having no one to control the Firedrinkers. Strephon's control now that Oram had been laid low was only illusion, the same as his control over Charm.

There was a faint gentleness in the voice behind the visor. "He will need you, miss."

Pain blinked. "I'm sorry?"

"You have errands to run, miss, and I know that you value your privacy, but you should have a guard go with you. I would be honored if you would allow me that privilege." The Firedrinker who was probably a woman inclined their helmet.

Pain shook her head in disbelief. "Why must you all ask that so formally? I'm sure I've been with most if not all of you."

"No matter who has come to you, you are still the captain's. We know that others do not value you as we do."

"Someday," promised Pain, forcing a smile through the sudden ache in her throat. "Someday, I promise, I will accept an escort."

"But not today."

Pain reached out, touched the side of the helmet that hid the Firedrinker's mindlock. "I promise."

The Firedrinker inclined their head in an almost-bow, and returned to their post near the corpses of the soldiers.

Pain started across the square, holding her skirts carefully around her ankles so that they would not drag in the grotesque mess that the riot had left upon the cobbles. Halfway across the killing ground she stopped. Standing abandoned in the shadow of the Lowtown wall was a familiar pushcart. Baskets of laundry still stood in it. A man coughed, a racking sound that snapped Pain's head around. He was crouched over a woman's body. Maude. Slowly, Pain's feet dragged her toward him.

The man with Maude did not look up as Pain approached, but put his face in his hand in misery. There was a bloody patch on Maude's skirt that showed where a bullet had struck. Once she had fallen, the panicked crowd had apparently done the rest. The dead woman's clothes showed the bloody marks of merciless boots and shoes.

Pain felt strangely empty, looking down at the laundress's corpse. It was only a body. It was the semblance of Maude that made the corpse terrible, the tangible reminder of the woman who was not there anymore, and the physical reminder of her suffering. Maude's body was not unlike Shame's body, or Justice's.

The idea shook Pain. Not so unlike. Flesh and blood and bones, without mind or soul or whatever it was that animated such a collection of tissue. Human babies were born. They had their own minds, their own thoughts. They made their own memories. Boneghosts were grown in a womb of glass, their memories those moments of the past that were too much for the Lady's peace of mind.

Pain carried no memories, no history. She had been only a hollow place. Pain's memories were those of her own making, her thoughts springing from the experiences of her own body. Did human babies have that? Were they but potential and hollow, or was there some ephemeral moreness to them? Was there anything more to Pain than experience filling a void?

The man looked up then, eyes swollen, chest heaving as he tried not to weep aloud. "Ye're Miss Pain," he managed. "My Maudie allus . . ." His voice broke in a sob that turned into a coughing fit.

Pain rubbed her hand along his heaving shoulders, a habitual soothing action. "Your name is Jim, isn't it? Do you need help with her?"

Jim shook his head. "I've no money for the funeral, e'en if I could afford the plot. No, Maudie'll have to go with the rest to the paupers' pits." He scrubbed his sleeve across his eyes.

"I wish I could do something." The words felt empty.

"There's nothin', miss."

Something. There must be something she could say, something she could do. "Come to Orchard House later. I'll give you the money for a decent grave." She'd steal an Imperial note from Charm if she had to, though Orchard House could ill afford even the cost of a grave at the moment. "And if you ever need a new place, or if your family does, come to Orchard House."

Jim nodded. "Thank ye, miss. Could ye please go now, miss?" He touched Maude's head. "They'll bring the carts soon, and I want . . . I want just another bit with her. . . ."

"She isn't really there, Jim," murmured Pain, her eyes prickling hot in their sockets.

"I know, miss, but this is all I've left of her to say good-bye to.... Please, miss ... please go." He was weeping again, silently and through his bared teeth.

"I'm sorry. Of course." Polite noises she wasn't sure he heard as she turned away.

CHAPTER TWENTY-ONE

Pain passed the bakery by. She could get croissants on the way back. On the Lowtown side of the gate, Pain found the cobbles no less begrimed. The bodies of those who had been taken up by the press-gang lay in neat rows, still in leg-irons. They'd been shot.

Middletown had been silent, but Lowtown was awash in whispers. Clusters of people huddled in doorways and on the narrow steps of their tenements, shoulders hunched, heads together. They watched Pain pass, conversation dying as she approached, rising as she moved away. The Firedrinkers on the road to Harborward nodded to her and let her pass without speaking.

There were more Firedrinkers on patrol along the docks. On Monday, the prison transport had been heavy in the water, nearly ready to depart. This morning, Prince Luther stood on her deck, speaking with her captain, and the ship rode high and light. Pain managed a smile. Someone in authority, prob-ably Prince Luther or the Firedrinkers, must have ordered the release of the conscripts. At least there was a little good news for Lowtown today. Bern Ostander's shop was dark and closed as she went past. The warehouse that held the shipping portion of Hyacinth's business was only a block beyond it.

Hyacinth's warehouse smelled of cedar chests and lavender. The silence of the streets and the docks seemed to have crept into the warehouse as well, like smoke under a door. The first man who caught sight of Pain shouted, his voice sudden in the stillness. "Miss Barker, it's Miss Pain!" As if that one voice had broken the spell of the silence, a babble of questions poured in from all sides. Thick, sweating bodies closed around her.

Hyacinth hurtled out of her office, swatting her workmen aside to smother Pain in a voluminous hug, holding the boneghost to her ample bosom. "Thank God you're all right."

Abruptly enveloped, Pain stood for a moment with her hands flapping uselessly in the air before patting at Hyacinth's broad back. Hyacinth's cheek pressed against Pain's.

Hyacinth pushed Pain abruptly back, holding on to Pain's forearms and giving her a little shake. "The baker's girl said you hadn't come in to get Miss Charm's croissants for two days in a row. . . . I sent people to the square to look for your body!" she accused, towing Pain out of the press of workmen and into the paper-filled warehouse office.

High, battered filing cabinets stood half bursting with ledgers. Shipping bills lay impaled on a long spike on the desk. Hyacinth's filing system was theoretical at best. These, after all, were only the legal records.

Hyacinth was not done scolding. "You scared me out of half my life!"

"I'm sorry I frightened you," said Pain dutifully. "We've been a little disrupted. Mistress Charm has been invited to the Empress's birthday masque. She'd like you to make her costume."

"I can come later this afternoon. I need to be here for now, for my men."

"That will be fine, thank you." Pain stepped close, lowered her voice to a murmur. "Have the Firedrinkers found the last two caches of guns?"

Hyacinth shook her head. "They seem to have stopped

looking when they found the first one." She studied Pain's face for a long moment. "Why?" she asked finally.

"Because the army is trying to promote disorder in the city so that Aerleas the Butcher will have an excuse to come here. It will work, sooner or later. The Firedrinkers may have body armor, but there's a limit to what they can prevent. Psychic talents won't stop bullets. If the mob gets those guns, they won't be careful who they shoot. When the city starts shooting itself, we're done. Aerleas will have the excuse he wants. The guns will keep right where they are, for some day when we need to arm people."

Hyacinth sucked her teeth thoughtfully. "What does Mistress Charm say?" she wanted to know.

"I only found out on the walk down, and Mistress Charm is angry at me just now," admitted Pain.

Hyacinth smiled slightly. "I can well imagine it. Sharp as a well-stropped razor, that woman, and testy. Tell you what, I'll mention it to her when I come up to Orchard House and we'll see what she has to say." Hyacinth fished in a fold of her elaborate skirt and came up with a sealed envelope, which she passed to Pain. "This came for you, by the way, with my latest shipment."

Pain had never gotten a letter before. Puzzled, she looked at the name on the envelope as if somehow Hyacinth might have misread it. "Lady Pain of Orchard House, care of Miss Hyacinth Barker, Borenguard, Boren." Hyacinth was watching her. "I've been ennobled," Pain joked faintly, sliding gloved fingers across the inscription.

Hyacinth smiled her broad smile in answer, the expression kind. "It's from Miss Fergus. She tracked down one of my shipping friends in a certain port city. Said you'd been good to her, and she hadn't even thanked you. She seems to be a most resourceful and polite young lady. Impressed my ship's captain. If you'd like to answer her, I know a ship going out in a few days that could take it."

"Thank you," managed Pain.

"Go on, get back home and read your letter. Tell Mistress Charm I'll be up late this afternoon."

Pain made her way back up the Imperial Way to Orchard House, and found the Lady up, dressed, and sitting in the solarium cradling a cup of tea in her hands. There was a tea tray on the little glass-topped table beside her.

"Pride helped me make it," the Lady said into the silence. "I did all right to put water in the kettle, but I didn't know where to find the tea."

They looked at one another warily for a moment. There were scabbed scratches around the Lady's mindlock.

"Miss Barker will come late this afternoon," Pain told her. And hoped Charm could hear her.

"Thank you."

Pain began to turn away.

"I'm sorry for my outburst, Pain," the Lady said. "I don't know what came over me."

Slowly, Pain turned back. "Lady . . ."

The Lady cut her off. "Thank you for not taking me at my word. I wanted all of this to . . . to just stop."

"Shame died half a dozen or ten times trying to make it stop, but you kept bringing her back."

The Lady looked out at the sunny orchard of bone trees.

"You dying wouldn't stop Phelan from preying on children, or stop soldiers dying on the front, or stop Strephon from ruining the people he rules. To stop those things, we need to live. You want what's right. You want things orderly, but we need to live for that to happen. Mistress Charm was correct. To change any of this, we have to live," said Pain.

"As if any of us will live through this, or want to if we do."

"Mistress Charm has done at least one thing right. When Prince Aerleas comes here there will be people willing to fight him, and there will be guns to fight him with."

"You're angry at me."

"I just . . . I hoped that if you were ever free you would somehow right all wrongs at a stroke. It was unfair of me," Pain admitted. She tried to smile, wasn't sure it had gotten to her lips, but couldn't summon a better effort.

"It's so strange . . . to know all of you. The lab was never like this. I didn't have to know you, didn't have to consider how I affected you." The Lady looked at her with thoughtful eyes. "I'm afraid," she admitted. "I'm afraid of being without you. Possibly more than any of the others, I depended on you."

Pain's eyes prickled at the corners, and she closed her eyes. What did she have in common with the Lady now, except a building, and a situation? The sweet, troubled face of her maker watched her. Pain knew what the Lady wanted to hear. The Lady had given what she thought was a compliment, and she would want an acknowledgment of it. Pain dragged air in through her nostrils as a fuel for her courage. She gripped the stair rail so tightly that her hand was numb, aware of her treason. The words came out thickly and tasting of bile—"I don't want to hurt for you anymore. I just . . . don't know how to stop."

The silence lasted so long that Pain opened her eyes.

The Lady caught the look, forced a trembling smile. "I was thinking that you would not have said that before you had a body. I was wishing I had not let you out."

Abrupt anger flashed through Pain.

"It is selfish of me, is it not?" continued the Lady.

"Yes," Pain told her, "it is."

"How did you do it?" the Lady asked wistfully.

"Do what, Lady?"

"How did you escape?"

It took Pain a moment to decide. She wasn't sure she liked the answer she found. "Well, first of all you threw me away. And now I am becoming too much my own self to belong to someone else. I've become possessed of my own self." She paused. "I am afraid, too. We are the same in that, at least. I don't want to go back to sleep. I don't want to be only an empty place. I do not think I can do it."

"Ah." The Lady fell silent, and seemed to turn her thoughts away from Pain.

Pain forced her hand to release the railing. She climbed slowly to the little attic room she had shared with Justice. It felt hollow, empty without her smallest sister in it.

Pain settled onto the window seat in the gable. When she looked down, she could see the glass roof of the solarium, the bright white of the Lady's gown, and the brilliant blue of Mistress Charm's hair.

Pain looked at her letter. A letter addressed to her. Not to Charm, but to Pain herself as if she were a real person. She took off her gloves and lifted the thick envelope from her lap. It promised a kind of comfort in being not-quite-alone, though remote from the writer. Inside the envelope a letter was wrapped around a second sealed note. There was no address on the second missive. Pain laid the inner message aside and read the outer letter.

Dear Miss Pain,

Forgive my writing to you without an invitation, but your kindness has emboldened me to look upon you as a friend. I hope it will not trouble you that I felt I should write to tell you we are all arrived in safety. Our voyage was long and not altogether comfortable, but our welcome in Saranisima has been wonderful. Lady Charmaine's sister, Mari-Tres, is a great lady here. She is very grand and dignified, and I should not have been surprised to find her a very ancient lady. Of course she has not had any Rejuv to keep her as young as Mistress Charm is. She has been very good to us, and has insisted on our staying with her. She asked many questions about the Lady Charmaine. I do not think we understood the circumstances from which your Lady comes until now.

Mari-Tres seemed very curious to know all about the boneghosts of Orchard House. I do not think any in Boren have realized how unique you are. Mari-Tres seemed to think that human boneghosts could be little more than idiotic—less even than animals—and was at first very distressed to hear of your existence. I told her that you were every bit as intelligent as anyone I knew, and quite a lot brighter than most. I told her as well that I hoped you were my friend. She was surprised by this, but on further questioning seems to believe my reports.

News of the war is everywhere, here. The testimonials of Prince Aerleas's behavior confirm all of my father's worst fears. They say in the papers that Aerleas's influence drives the men around him insane. The captives from the Boren Army are considered lunatics. One might discount such rumors if they did not, within a few weeks, suddenly become filled with horror and remorse at their own past actions. Many have killed themselves, or have taken up holy orders and lives of service in an attempt to somehow make up for what they have been a part of. I spoke to one such fellow myself, and his tears and regrets moved me very much.

Saranisima's psychics live a much different life than Boren's. They are given into holy orders, where they live out what is considered their naturally short lives. It seems very cruel to me, though I wonder if it is not more cruel to be delivered into Imperial slavery; for what are the Firedrinkers if not slaves of the Empire and the Emperor? They are very interested, here, in the mindlocks. There is nothing we can tell them that is not common knowledge in Boren, and nothing that my father had not told them during his tenure here as the Emperor's ambassador. I'm not sure whose course is better to help psychics live with their abilities, but perhaps that is a conversation for later.

In this letter you will find another that I shall shortly write to John. If you can get it to him, I will be even more deeply in your debt. There is no one else who can know what we go through if it is not you.

Your Grateful Friend,
Anna Fergus

Pain traced her fingers across the last lines of the letter. She could imagine the stroke of the fountain pen's smooth gold nib on the paper, the way it broadened on the downstrokes. She wanted to think that Anna Fergus would have written her the letter even without the enclosure for John Seabrough.

CHAPTER TWENTY-TWO

Hyacinth Barker examined the Lady with a suspicious eye. Furbelowed in brilliant yellow and lime green, the dressmaker seemed to fill up the red parlor. Her energy pressed into the Lady even from a polite distance.

"You're taller," Hyacinth announced at last.

"That's a nice fantasy," said the Lady with a cheerful smile.

Hyacinth would not be put off the track. "You're all the same height according to my tape measure. Well, except for Justice. You're standing more upright, is all; less curve in the spine, less sway in the hips when you walk. You look about as seductive as a Firedrinker."

Charm smirked briefly from behind the mindlock.

The Lady retaliated by standing a bit straighter yet. "I'm nervous." That, at least, was true.

"I'll keep it in mind when I do the design. I don't imagine you'll be any more relaxed at the palace. What do you want to go as?"

"A Most Holy of Inshil." The words slipped out of her mouth without her conscious thought.

Hyacinth laughed a great, broad laugh. At the Lady's puzzled look, she went on. "Your showing up dressed as Inshili . . . that's guts." Admiration rang in her voice.

Uncertainty whirled in the Lady. It was very daring. Too daring . . .

"You really want to go as a Most Holy of Inshil?" asked Hyacinth.

Indecision warred at the Lady. Her first impulse was to say no. It was so hard to think. It was hard to decide.

Yes.

"Yes," said the Lady. Once the word was out, it was much easier to think. "In something like the old styles. Do you know them?" asked the Lady.

Hyacinth huffed, her yellow-and-green-brocaded bosom heaving up indignantly. "I can build the dress, if you can provide the proper jewels."

"I have my jewels, yes."

"Oh." Hyacinth fidgeted with the edge of her bodice. "I see. It's all true, then."

"Stop it," said Charm, rising to defend her friend from Hyacinth's apparent notion of what station Charm held. "They're worth money, of course, but they might as well be paste for all the good they've done me."

"Did Strephon hit you in the head or something?" Hyacinth asked, eyebrow rising.

The Lady laughed in spite of herself as Charm faded back. "You could say that."

"Hmph. Well, whatever happened, I'll have that dress for you. Don't lose an ounce or loosen your corset."

"I'd hoped to go without a corset," admitted the Lady quickly.

Hyacinth snorted. "If you want your dress to fit, you'll wear a corset. Besides, it'll make your costume fashionable enough to make the nobs drool. You want to impress, to brand yourself onto their brains as the most elegant thing they've ever seen. This isn't re-creation, this is theater."

"True." The Lady bit her lip in nervousness.

"Did you hear Prince Phelan was arrested?" Hyacinth

didn't disguise her glee. "They tossed him in the clink on Fortress Isle!"

"The Firedrinkers have said he was innocent of the gun situation."

"From what I hear, that isn't holding much book with Emperor Strephon," proclaimed Hyacinth happily. "He doesn't think so much of the Firedrinkers since that Captain Oram go-round."

"He should hold Phelan for raping children, not smuggling guns," Charm snapped through their mouth.

The Lady clenched her teeth together. She went to the sideboard and poured two glasses of wine.

"That would assume that the law is equal for paupers and for princes," said Hyacinth with a snort of scorn. "As long as it happens in private, people can ignore just about anything. You ought to know that better than anyone. Your bleeding-through-your-bodice stunt set them on their heels."

The Lady passed one of the wineglasses to Hyacinth. "Strephon beat Shame for years before he became an emperor."

"They didn't have to see it. It was always quietly taken care of, which is what the Emperor and the princes preferred, but now that the nobs have seen the results with their own eyes . . ."

"They haven't come back to Orchard House," observed the Lady.

"Doesn't stop them from talking in their own smoking rooms. They all know I do your clothes, and I've had more calls from nobs' wives for the Empress's ball than I have ever contemplated. I've had to hire six new seamstresses. No one is supposed to know, but I'm even making the Empress's costume. She must've liked the day dress I did. I'm going up tomorrow to show her some sketches, and to take her order and her measurements."

"The Empress sent for you?" The Lady was appalled.

"You've turned green. What's wrong?" asked Hyacinth, puzzled.

The Lady paced the room, skirts sighing around her ankles like waves on sand. "I don't know, quite. Doesn't it seem wrong to you that I should be invited to this celebration at all?"

"She can't like Strephon. Maybe she wants to embarrass him," Hyacinth suggested.

The Lady didn't add that it was peculiar for an empress to send for a dressmaker-to-whores. There was no point in insulting Hyacinth. Charm's profession wasn't Hyacinth's fault. "Most wives would consider it embarrassing to themselves to be seen alongside a mistress. He's the Emperor. He could have her killed if he wanted to."

Hyacinth looked more closely at the Lady, tipping her head. "She's fairly safe. Their marriage guaranteed peace with Devarik, remember? With Inshil in open rebellion and Saranisima beating up Aerleas, he can't afford to divorce or abuse her. He needs Devarik peaceful."

"I had completely forgotten," the Lady said with a shake of her head. "I don't know what I was thinking," she covered for herself. That was why the Empress could be so bold, but the whole thing still bothered her. Why parade her husband's strumpet in public?

"You're not losing your nerve now, are you?" Apprehension touched the dressmaker's features.

"Certainly not!" snapped Charm, bobbing up on a bubble of outrage.

The Lady forced a smile and snatched her mouth back. "Even if I was, I certainly wouldn't let any of the guilt for this scheme fall upon you. You've been a good friend when no one else would be and I don't treat my friends that way," the Lady told her. "Do you regret . . . ever . . . what you've done for . . ."

The last word dragged out of the Lady's mouth tasting of bile. ". . . me?" She fingered a lock of lavender hair. It had been for that other woman, really, but Hyacinth wouldn't understand that.

"I did it for me, not for you," Hyacinth shot back instantly. "And as to regretting it—hell no!"

"You did not begin this. Ultimately, it is not your responsibility."

"I came into it with both feet."

Yes, but you were only hired. You did not have any viciousness in your belly to begin this conspiracy, thought the Lady.

She didn't have the tools to get the job done, Charm sniped from the background of the Lady's mind.

The Lady forced a smile. "Well, one way or another we're in it now. I still don't like it that the Empress invited me to her birthday masque."

"I'll keep my eyes and ears open for you when I go to the palace," offered Hyacinth.

This was to do with the Emperor's order, and Charm surged forward. She spoke plainly. "They know that the hair in the gun lock was planted, Hyacinth. They know someone is plotting against them. Emperor Strephon will be searching for the conspirators, and we must seem innocent."

Hyacinth laughed a great, expansive laugh. "Honey, they're looking for men," she said, shaking her head. "Men always do. How do you think I've been in a man's business so long? Not even the Firedrinkers think to look for women in relation to serious business, and a lot of 'em are women themselves. Trust me, no one has the slightest idea that it's two poor, weak women who threw the wrench into their works."

"Prince Luther brought Firedrinkers to make sure that I hadn't supplied the hair for that gun," Charm told her. Somehow she must make Hyacinth understand.

"They must've believed you were innocent, or you wouldn't be here," reasoned Hyacinth. "Wish I'd seen that, it must've been a pretty dancing job."

"Don't ask a single leading question, Hyacinth. I won't risk you," Charm said.

The Lady was mildly appalled that Charm had put her trust in this garish creature, even if she were the greatest dressmaker in history.

"Nobody is more protective of me than me," Hyacinth assured her. "What I want to know is what our next move is. What do you want done with the rest of the guns, for instance?"

"I'm not sure yet," said the Lady, buying time. Charm had no comment.

"It's a secret that won't keep, Charm. The men who hid those crates for me are loyal, but they're human. Now that word's out that the first cache was guns, sooner or later one of 'em is going to talk."

"How is Lowtown?" the Lady asked.

"Fragile. Plenty of Lowtowners are just ordinary people that work honest jobs, have nice kids, and go to church on Sundays. It isn't only the press-gangs that are the problem. It's their taxes, and the price of food, and a half a thousand more things that add up to they're worse off now than they were just a month ago. Things almost came apart this morning. The Firedrinkers managed to hold the situation in check, but a lot of folks died. Lowtown's hissing like an overheated boiler. It needs an outlet. Soon."

The Lady nodded, pacing restlessly. "Pain tried to tell her . . . me . . . she tried to talk about it earlier. Is it really that bad?"

Hyacinth shook her head, skirts enveloping a little gilded chair as she sat down. "Once the mob's blood is up there won't be anything that anyone can do, not without Captain Oram. They'll have to shoot people that on any other day would be just going about their lives, and that's just what Aerleas will do if he gets here. He spreads violence like a disease."

"Aerleas coming here would be a disaster." The little the Lady remembered of the briefings in Inshil told her as much. "Will your people know if he heads toward Boren?"

"Moving an army is hard to do stealthily. We'll hear, or you will," Hyacinth added.

"The last person who tried to bring me a message is dead," said the Lady. "It can't go on," she decided abruptly. "I'll have a chance to try to read the people who attend the Empress's masque. I may be able to find out a great deal there."

"Just as long as you don't have a fit in the ballroom," Hyacinth advised. "Pain nearly had one, some weeks back. Didn't she tell you I put her in a cab? I thought she would've, but either way: it won't do for you to break down, now."

And the Lady couldn't help the tiniest wince at the truth of that.

⌘

Evening gathered thickly over Borenguard, though the eerie stillness of the midday was beginning to break. A few servants hurried on errands, and an occasional carriage rumbled along the cobbles. Pairs of Firedrinkers kept up their obvious patrols, so it didn't take Pain long to find some.

"I need you to deliver a message for me," she told them.

The helmets turned toward one another, then reoriented on her. "We can do that, miss," one assented.

"Tell John Seabrough that I have a letter for him, from Anna."

"We can deliver the letter, miss, if you have it with you."

Pain took the letter from her pocket, keeping hold on it for a moment longer. "It's a very private letter," she told them.

"No one will handle it with bare flesh until he does," the Firedrinker promised.

Reluctantly, Pain passed the letter to them.

"Can he send a return by you?" asked the Firedrinker.

"If he would like to reply I'll do what I can to see that it arrives." Pain paused. "If you cannot say your names, how do you know which of you is John Seabrough?"

Pain could almost feel the Firedrinkers' smiles, hidden behind their visors, though the one that spoke did so with precise care. "Even if we were not a barracks full of psychics, we would have recognized him. Nobles don't marry into families with psychics in them, miss. Only two of us ever came from Uptown."

"And those include . . . ?"

"John Seabrough, and the captain."

CHAPTER TWENTY-THREE

Pain slipped into the laboratory. Pride was there, sitting beside Oram in his coffin of glass and silver.

"I expected you earlier," said Pride, turning her blank eyes toward the door.

"I had to take a letter out. How is he?" Pain knelt beside the growth tank, lacing her fingers together in her lap.

"He stirred a little while ago, as if he dreams. Are you staying? There is little point in both of us sitting here," Pride pointed out.

"I'll stay. Thank you for sitting with him." Pain looked into the tank, at Oram's long, still face. His eyes moved slightly beneath their lids. Did he know she was here? She took off her gloves and slipped a hand in beside him, threaded her fingers through his. Skin contact. Squeezing the trigger. Trying not to. Agony jerking his muscles. The pistol bucking. Pain's breath hitched. "It's all right," she whispered to him, or to herself, stroking his wrist with her fingertips. "Next time your hand will remember me holding it."

Pride rose, giving her skirts a brief flick to straighten them. She touched the back of the chair, walked the two paces to the table along the wall, let her fingers trail along the edge until it stopped, and transferred her hand to the railing on the open side of the steps. She paused there for a moment, turning back toward Pain. "What will you do, if he dies?"

Pain tipped her head, looking up at Pride, trying to read behind the smooth, controlled features. "Be destroyed for a while, probably, but after that I'd try to help the Firedrinkers."

"Help them in their own lives, or help them with their work?" inquired Pride.

Her tone held only distant interest, but Pain found it odd that Pride would take any interest at all in Pain's life or plans. Pride seldom spoke. One question might have passed by Pain unnoticed, but two in succession was strange to say the least.

"Either," Pain answered, "or both, depending on what I find I can accomplish."

"Why would you do either, or both?"

"Because they need me."

Pride seemed to consider this. Silence stretched out. "Does the Lady not need you?"

"I don't need her."

"That isn't what I asked."

"She thinks she needs me. I wish she didn't. I wish she'd make someone else to suffer for her, if she can't stand it herself." Pain couldn't help the smallest bit of bitterness.

Pride angled her face down at Pain, so that if she hadn't been blind she would have been looking down her nose. "For a woman who has made herself out of nothing, you are almost irretrievably stupid."

Pain stared. Where had all this come from? "What are you saying, Pride? That I should go back into her? You'll pardon my impatience, but if you have something to say I wish you'd just say it."

"You have developed a certain knack for independent action and self-concern," said Pride. "You will, if you feel it necessary, disobey both the Lady and Mistress Charm, whom you used to acknowledge as your betters." Pride already stood tall, and so could not draw herself up higher, but her chin lifted a fraction, and her mouth twisted into a curl of defiance and challenge. "We were made pale, crippled, blind, and lame so that we would be clumsy and ridiculous, but the Lady has underestimated us." The last words rang in the dank of the laboratory as if in marbled halls. "I love you, Pain, as a sister; but I will not suffer you to take my place. Do I make myself clear?"

It took Pain a moment to remember to close her mouth. Never in her wildest imaginings could she have conjured up the notion that Pride was . . . jealous. "Take your place?"

"You've grown in leaps and bounds until you think you can challenge everything. You challenge Mistress Charm's decisions, encourage the Lady to step outside of her right boundaries. I will not have it, Pain. We are falling back together. Do not try to stop it."

"What about Mistress Charm?" asked Pain. "She is still there, you know, even if she is letting the Lady cope with everything other than Strephon."

Pride's mouth smoothed again into a cool, flat smile. "Mistress Charm and I are closer than we might appear."

"And the Emperor?"

"Is her business, and she will do as she must."

"Kill him, you mean?"

Pride's cold smile turned almost dreaming. "Strephon wanted so badly to take responsibility for his country, who am I to deny him the reaping of what he has planted?"

"It doesn't matter to you whether he killed his father or not, then?"

"Responsibility for a country's actions must ultimately rest with their government," said Pride calmly. "In Boren to date, the Emperor is the government."

"And Aerleas? It was him did the actual slaughtering."

Pride's eyebrow rose. "I was there. Boren has not troubled themselves to deal with him, so we must."

Oram stirred in the tank. An incoherent sound escaped his lips.

"Stay with him, Pain," said Pride, suddenly gracious. "He needs you." And on those words, Pride swept up the stairs and out into the orchard.

Pain shivered in Pride's wake, holding on to Oram's warm hand. His grip tightened slightly in response. Pain wished she could trust that response, wished it meant he was waking; but boneghost bodies did such things, stirred and held on to an object in their palms, even before there was a conscious self in the body. She lifted Oram's hand up to the rim of the tank, laid her cheek down on it.

A wild flutter of feelings whipped around inside Pain like leaves in a windy corner. They were all her own, frightening and exhilarating emotions that had nothing to do with anyone else. Her thoughts tumbled out of her mouth born of her own confusion, her own fears.

"I'm afraid, Oram," she murmured aloud, speaking to him as if he could hear her. "I was never afraid before. Pride . . . I was never afraid of her, or for her, until now. She's been so quiet for so long, quiet and polite. She seems threatened by me now.

"Shame is dissolved, Mistress Charm plots her own plots, and Desire can't think of anything but Prince Luther. They're all falling away from me. I don't want to be the Lady. I'm just learning how to be me. I don't want to go back to the Lady, to being an empty nothing. I'm afraid."

Mindlock. The word drifted across her mind, so faint that it felt like imagining.

Pain raised her head to look at him, catching up his hand to keep contact with him.

"Captain? Oram?"

But Captain Oram did not stir.

. . . *lock*. No mistaking it this time. A strained thought not her own.

"Wait for me," Pain told him. "Wait." She laid his hand down and ran for the house and the Lady.

⌗

Pain held Oram's hand. She watched the Lady lay fingers on his neck. After a moment, the Lady bent carefully to put her ear against his chest. The lock in Oram's temple made a faint, grinding noise. The muscles around his eyes spasmed.

"Whether or not his mind is aware I cannot say," the Lady pronounced, drawing the blanket back up around Oram's shoulders, "but his pulse is strong, and he is breathing well. I believe he may live."

Pain exhaled. "When will you be able to remove the lock?"

"Pain, I haven't ever operated on a real human being."

Pain's eyes blazed at that. "You operate on us."

"It isn't the same," said the Lady sadly.

"Why not?" cried Pain, hands going up in open frustration. "Why isn't it the same? Our anatomy is human."

The Lady shook her head, rising from her stool at the edge of the tank. "I'm sorry, Pain, but your body is artificial. I grew it in this same vat."

"Don't human babies grow?" Pain demanded.

"That is not the point. Anesthesia is dangerous. Inducing a fever is dangerous. Even if all that goes well, the shock of taking the wires out of his brain may kill him or drive him mad or render him an idiot."

"And if we leave him like this, he will still die," said Pain through clenched teeth. "He lies there, trapped in his own body, wasting away. Can his chances get better?"

"N-no," admitted the Lady, "but if we filled the tank the

rest of the way with empathy fluid and changed it regularly . . . it would sustain him indefinitely."

You ruined a whole vat of fluid with Shame. We can't get any more. The words in the Lady's mind came unbidden.

Go away, said the Lady. *No one wants you.*

Cold crept over Pain, leaching her clean of illusion. For the Lady, stalemate was better than risk. Pain wrapped both hands around Oram's, keeping it fast against her belly as if it would help to keep him safe. "Bad enough to be an empty place in a living body. To keep a whole person unconscious and trapped in a lump of flesh and bone forever . . ." Pain's voice choked down to a thready whisper. "I'd kill him myself to keep him from that."

The Lady hesitated for a moment. "You'd kill him when you wouldn't kill me?"

Pain stared down at Oram's hand, at his fingers tangled with hers. She didn't dare alienate the Lady. "You're the only one who can save him."

"We can operate in the morning," the Lady said softly, "but I want you to understand that his chances are very poor."

Pain nodded. A strand of Oram's hair lay against his cheek, displaced by the Lady's examination and caught on the stubble of his growing beard. She thought of Maude, whose body had been more outwardly damaged, but she hadn't been less still than Oram was now. A sudden, unbidden jerk of Pain's diaphragm threatened to become a sound. It battled against the back of her teeth. Pain bit down and the sound did not escape. It was hers. Only hers. She lifted the wayward lock of hair, stroking it back into place along Oram's temple.

"Will you come and help me dress, Pain?" asked the Lady suddenly.

Pain looked up at the hesitant tone.

"I wouldn't ask, but Hyacinth sent up a new gown today and I don't want to hurt her feelings by not wearing it. I'm sure word will get back to her if I don't. Pride can't see the buttons and Desire can't possibly manage them. Would you help me?" The Lady winced a little at her own choice of words, a blush rising in her cheeks. "With my buttons?"

Pain forced a smile. "With your buttons, I can help."

CHAPTER TWENTY-FOUR

The Lady examined her white evening gown in the mirror. It was too heavily ornamented for the Lady's taste, but she did have to admit that Hyacinth Barker had an artistic turn. A massive, crystal-encrusted brooch gathered the overskirt at the Lady's left hip to create a fluid curve of motion. The graceful drape of the cloth gave it all direction, turned what might have been an overwhelming splash of decoration into a swirl like a storm of ice. The thing displayed every inch of cleavage legally possible, of course, but it was art in its outrageous way. She wouldn't ever have been able to wear such a thing in Inshil.

"Are you sure you want to go to the parlor tonight?" asked Pain from behind her.

"If Charm hadn't had any desire to remind people about Inshil, she would never have worn black," the Lady opined. "The gesture was well made, but white is far more striking for evening, don't you think?"

My hair stands out better against black, groused Charm, but she didn't sound entirely displeased.

Pain interrupted, "You could choose to be diplomatically ill."

Absolutely not. I have too much to do.

"This is what's expected," said the Lady.

"It's what's expected of her," pointed out Pain.

The Lady shook her head. Crystal pins flashed in her softly pink hair, like dew on roses. People would've suspected something wrong if her hair had not been colored. This was the least outrageous color Charm had owned. "I don't see how she plans to find a murderer when she hasn't any experience of anything but tasteless displays."

"You think Mistress Charm is only foolish frippery? That she doesn't plan in advance? Do you think that's how she's made Orchard House what it is?" asked Pain.

The Lady shook her head at the tone of disbelief in Pain's voice. "Charm is clever after a fashion, and even I won't deny it, but without her emperor there's nothing here for her. I shall have to make my own life. It's unfair I have to rehabilitate hers at the same time. Are you coming down with me, or are you going back to the lab?"

"I'll go back to the lab, if you don't mind; but I'm expecting a Firedrinker this evening."

The Lady shuddered slightly. "I don't see how you stand it, if you really love him."

Pain looked at her as if she'd sprouted antlers. "You wouldn't understand, Lady," she said finally.

"I'd really rather not." The Lady went down the back stairs, shaking her head at Pain's perverse mood. Mrs. Westmore was still presiding in the kitchen. The heat was stifling. Charm glanced in the direction of the parlor.

"There were two for supper this evening, Lady. They're still at table," Mrs. Westmore told her. "I only just now sent in coffee."

"What did they have?"

"I gave them potted shrimps for appetizer, and since the only chicken available was an old bird, I casseroled it slow with bacon, beans, and mushrooms to make it tender, and served it with crispy potatoes, crisped chicken skin, and wilted chard salad. I cut a few herbs in my garden and brought 'em up with me to make the chard more interesting than just bacon and chard. 'Tisn't what they're used to, but I gave them soufflé for dessert, and they sent their compliments."

The Lady didn't frown at the woman. One did not feed important people old poultry that might be tough, but it was not the cook's fault.

We only have chicken because our grocer supplies Uptown.

I said go away! There's no emperor here. How did one order groceries? Was that something the Lady would need to do?

Two girls came up out of the cellar. One lugged a pail of coal, the other carried a bottle of wine. They stared at the Lady, mouths open in twin expressions of surprise.

Mrs. Westmore rescued the wine, giving its bearer a light swat on the back of the head. "Don't goggle at the lady, you look like fish. Put that bucket by the stove and the both of you get to them pots."

Chastened, the girls scuttled to the sink, casting glances at the Lady as they set to their scrubbing.

"Sorry, Mistress. With Sally and the others working cleaning, now that Miss Shame and Miss Justice are . . . resting, I needed more help."

How much are we paying them?

"Are . . . are we paying them?" the Lady asked, hesitating over the subject. Well-bred ladies did not speak of money.

"Just their suppers, and soup to take home. The gents always leave a good bit on their plates, and with the carcass it will make fine soup. Lowtown's hungry, Mistress. This is a good thing for them," Mrs. Westmore assured her. "I'd like to lay in a few extra hams, and bacon and some potted beef. It'll last, and meat isn't getting more common in the city."

A slight chill admitted itself into the Lady's blood. She tried to tell herself she was relieved. The cook would order groceries. "Yes, of course. Whatever you think is best."

The Lady caught sight of herself in a window, a creature all glittering and unnatural, corset putting the soft curves of her breasts on display and making her waist look smaller than it was. It seemed suddenly as if passing the door into the front of the house would make everything real. She had felt daring, letting Pain recolor her hair pink, donning Mistress Charm's dazzling clothes. It had been easy to be daring in private.

The door between the private back half of Orchard House and the public front seemed suddenly terrible. If she passed through that green-clad portal into the front of the house, there would be men there. They would see her dressed like this. They'd think of her as a low woman. Fallen. They would stare, as the girls were still doing surreptitiously. Heat flooded up the Lady's exposed bosom, and she fled out of the heat of the kitchen into the orchard. She ran until the iron gate in the orchard wall stopped her. The Lady leaned her hands on the bars. The night was cold on her arms; but her face, her exposed throat and bosom, those were still hot with humiliation.

What royal pretentions, Charm taunted her. *Run and hide, by all means. Be a whimpering prisoner and be grateful for the scraps they throw you.*

"This isn't what I am!"

Isn't it? Admiring yourself in the mirror, weren't you? Didn't you think you were pretty? That was you making that curl on our neck lie just so. Oh, and those are my hairpins you were admiring the effect of a few minutes ago.

"It's . . . yes, it's pretty, but it's so . . . on display."

Charm's laugh rippled like the refreshing breezes that Borenguard didn't have. *Where should "it" be? Women have few enough advantages, and we have even fewer. Our advantages* include *nice hips, a trim waist, and a frankly magnificent bust. I'd be stupid not to use it to advantage.*

"It's tacky. Nice women don't want this. I don't want this," bit out the Lady.

It doesn't matter what you want. At this moment it doesn't matter what I want. Those men will be done with their coffee soon, so if you're going in you need to go. We need those two guests in the dining room to stay and have a good time. We need the money they're going to spend. It is not a question of what you want. We have got to have that money if we're going to be able to pay our grocery bill. If you can't stomach my life, you'd do much better to turn control back over to me.

But the Lady wasn't ready to give up control. As embarrassing as the dress was, it was trivial beside Charm's assassination plots. "How did you run out of money so quickly?" sighed the Lady, pushing away from the gate. "And a lady shouldn't think about money all the time."

Have you seen the dress you're wearing? Fifteen women worked on it for a week, probably ten or fifteen hours a day because Hyacinth tries to give them good lighting. When Strephon gives his orders about how I dress, he doesn't think for a moment how hard those women had to work, and how much it cost to buy even this one gown.

"You should have sent him the bill."

A mental chuckle warmed the back of the Lady's mind. *As if he'd pay it. You better be careful, though, you're starting to sound practical.* Charm's thoughts were teasing.

It felt like Mari-Tres's teasing when they were girls. Familiar and oddly comforting. "Having morals doesn't make me stupid." The Lady was still feeling stung.

Lady, stupid is the one thing I will never call you.

The Lady had the uncomfortable feeling that there were quite a lot of things Charm would call her. As if a public strumpet's opinion should bother her. She walked slowly back toward Orchard House.

The orchard was silent around her, its bone fruit fallen in a sudden rush of time and wind. A few dogged leaves still clung to their skeletal branches. Bones lay scattered in the orchard grass, a pallid litter of little deaths. She should have picked them up, laid them up carefully sorted in their proper baskets. These bones were ruined now, autumn's molds creeping into the pores of the cortex, all their potential lost. A human skull lay in the grass beneath the orchard's center tree, the empty eye sockets staring up. Most of a human skeleton was carefully stored in the laboratory. It was short only a few vertebrae. Were those bones here somewhere, tangled and wasted in the autumn grass?

The Lady paused, looking down into the dark holes. "I could grow you a separate body," she offered.

The mindlock is in this body, and the lock is mine. I wonder if you could grow another body for yourself?

It was a tempting thought. Shed this body and its frightening sensuality . . . In so many ways this was more Charm's body than hers. It was Charm who had crafted this bright bauble of a woman. Charm's body was like a disguise that the Lady was wearing. Yes. Yes, this body was a disguise. It was all a charade. A cold wind gusted through the orchard, and the bone trees stirred with it. There was no pretty music now, only the black fingers of the branches creaking and murmuring. The bones had all fallen away. The Lady straightened her shoulders, lifting her chin. She turned away from the ruined skull and went back to the house.

⁓

When the knock came on the door, Pain closed her book of poetry, put it in her pocket. She rose to greet her guest. The

Firedrinker gave Pain a nod of greeting and turned to close the door. He stayed facing the door for a moment. His hand lingered on the cut-glass knob.

"What is the dilemma?" asked Pain softly.

"I don't know," he admitted. He lifted his hands, took off the concealing helm. He was the Firedrinker who'd held her against the wall during the massacre at the Lowtown gate. "It's difficult to be here, when I know that she knows you," he admitted. John Seabrough turned to face Pain with a blush of discomfiture riding his cheekbones and across his mother's aristocratic nose, now that Pain knew who he was to identify its origin. "She wrote that she's met you. She says you're her friend."

Pain nodded, partly to herself. "Strange how much difference that makes, isn't it? Come and sit down." She poured him a glass of wine, and one for herself. "Do you have a return letter for Anna?"

"No." He came into the room, hovered near a chair. "It isn't that I don't want to, believe me, but it's not fair to her. If I write, she'll only keep hoping."

"But you care enough about her that you are embarrassed to be here," said Pain.

John Seabrough sank into the chair, raking his hands through his short, sandy hair. "She ought to marry someone else, move on." His misery at the idea rode every line of his body. He shrugged. "She wouldn't listen to me."

"Situational deafness runs in her family. She inherited it from her father."

John didn't laugh. "It killed her father. I wanted her to be wiser."

"Can you teach someone like that to be less brave without breaking them altogether? The more the odds were against Lord Fergus, the harder he fought."

"Did he come up with anything useful?" asked John, his smile twisting with bitterness.

"He was trying to avoid violence."

"That isn't going to be possible."

"I know that," said Pain, trying to keep the snap from her voice. "There will be a fight, there will be deaths, and there will be someone who wins the day. It's fairly clear to me that the Firedrinkers do not support Emperor Strephon. What I want to know is who you do support."

The young man was silent for a long time, and Pain was sure he wasn't focusing on her.

"We follow the last orders the captain gave us," he said at last. "We would do so even without our mindlocks."

"John." The name felt strange in her mouth, and he flinched at it as if she had struck him. How long had it been since anyone said his name out loud? Pain tried again, softly. "John, I want to help, but I don't know how. Tell me how," she whispered.

"We follow our orders, Miss Pain. I'm sorry." He hesitated for a long time, mouth half open. "Stay with the captain, miss. Save him, if you can. That is what you can do."

Pain closed her eyes for a moment. "Very well."

"What will you tell Anna?"

"That's up to you; but if you're determined to break her heart, I wish you'd do it yourself," admitted Pain.

"I . . ." The young man broke off. His voice cracked. "I'll write to her," he whispered.

"I can't imagine it will be an easy letter no matter what you write, so I'll leave you in private. There's paper and pen in the desk. Leave your letter there, and I will do what I can to see that it reaches Anna." Pain left him to make his choices alone.

CHAPTER TWENTY-FIVE

The Lady smiled at the man who was coming out of the dining room.

"Mistress, it's good to see you looking so well." He took her hand and kissed it. "You are well again, are you not?"

His concern is genuine, the Lady realized. His hand told her that he was Philip Anders, that he was accustomed to eating in Orchard House, and that he usually played cards. He was deeply fond of Mistress Charm, as if she were a favorite eccentric aunt. "I am well, Mr. Anders, but a little worried." She tucked her hand into the crook of his arm, conducting him, or letting him conduct her, toward the cardroom.

The little woman, clinging to his arm, Charm observed in amused tones. *Isn't that the manipulativeness you despise in me? Do nice women resort to such things?*

Anders looked down at the Lady with puzzled surprise. "What worries you, Mistress?"

"I recalled your saying that many of your servants lived in Lowtown. Are they all right?"

He said it where I could hear, not you, said Charm. *Stop using what I know.* But something seemed to occur to Charm, and she fell silent in the Lady's skull as if thinking.

She took wicked delight in Charm's frustration. *You used my memories, I'm using yours. Sauce for the goose, you know.*

Yes, said Charm thoughtfully. *So it is.*

The Lady didn't have time to worry properly about Charm's thinking so hard, because Anders's merry foolishness turned grave.

"Several of my people were injured, Mistress, and my cook and her daughter were killed." It seemed to honestly distress him. "I'd be demmed surprised if this was the end of it."

"I am very sorry to hear that." The Lady shook her head. "I think there will be few households in Middletown that are not touched by this one way or another." Charm's stony silence told her she'd misstepped, but she couldn't think what she'd said that might have been wrong.

The front door opened as they passed through the foyer, and Count Seabrough came in, shaking accumulated damp off his cloak.

"Evening, Anders," he greeted his confederate, passing his cloak to Pride. "Quite an evening. There appears to be a storm blowing in." He stepped forward, took the Lady's hand, and kissed it. "How is our luck? Can we can dig up a fourth this evening?" he asked her.

Lord Fergus was his partner.

"I'm afraid I don't know, Count, I only just came down. Did you see any likely partners in the dining room, Mr. Anders?" asked the Lady.

"I'm afraid there were only Sir Lyle and myself. Bachelors, you know, we felt a need for some company tonight. Lyle should be . . . ah, there you are, Lyle. Cards?" Anders directed his question to the man coming from the dining room.

Sir Lyle was of moderate height, in his early twenties with a round, serious face. He was replacing a cigar case in his inner breast pocket, fingering the unlit cigar in anticipation of entering the cardroom. "Sounds very pleasant. Have you a partner, Seabrough?"

"I daresay Lady Charm might be pressed into taking a hand

of cards with us," Seabrough suggested. "I would be honored, Lady, if you would help me thrash these young pups." He offered her his arm as a replacement for Anders's.

No one had ever asked Charm to play cards before. Certainly no one had ever called her "Lady." Noblewomen played at court card parties, or at genteel gambling parties. Whores in brothels watched men play as luck charms. They were never given equal status across a table. Seabrough's arm was like a handhold up. Or it meant he'd nothing to lose by the gesture. Charm wondered which, but she wouldn't refuse the gesture, particularly not from Count Seabrough.

Do you know how to play cards? the Lady asked her inner companion, tipping her head and offering the Count of Seabrough a smile that echoed some of Charm's bewilderment.

Scorn. *I should hope so. I've been watching them for years. With Seabrough as a partner, we can't lose.*

Do they play for money? the Lady asked, suddenly hesitant. She'd never gambled before.

They'd better. We need some.

Maybe you . . . began the Lady.

Dark amusement, and Charm's low laugh vibrated in the Lady's mind. *Not if you beg on your knees. Seabrough's calling us a lady for the first time, and you're a lady. Just do what I tell you.*

Why are you so helpful suddenly?

Would you rather I wasn't?

"Pride, have I any specific concerns to see to this evening?" the Lady asked Pride, who had hung Seabrough's cloak on the huge and ornately ugly coat tree that lurked in the corner of the entry.

"A Firedrinker has called upon Pain, Lady, and I have an appointment for a massage. There are no other bookings this evening."

"Poor fellows, they've had a rotten few weeks, I daresay,"

said Anders. "Send him up a bottle of the '65 we had at dinner, will you, Miss Pride, with my compliments?"

Interesting, observed Charm.

That's interesting? The Lady scoffed. *He's common as an old penny and not as bright.*

Charm's snort was inelegant and not a little smug.

The Lady smiled to keep from gritting her teeth in frustration.

Pride inclined her head to Anders with no flicker of emotion.

"Count Seabrough, I should be delighted to partner you." Charm lent the Lady a graceful curtsy, and the Lady lifted their fingers from Anders's arm and transferred them lightly to Seabrough's cuff.

Anders laughed. "We're in for it tonight, Lyle."

Seabrough led the Lady into the cardroom and held her chair. "You made quite an impression on my wife the other day, Lady Charm," he told her.

Charm considered from behind the Lady. He'd picked up on Pride's address of them. She was to be neither Mistress nor Madam. He was willing to grant her a noble title because he had heard Pride use it. Playing along with what he must see as Charm's bid, like any good card partner.

"Shall I leap to the assumption that her impression was a good one, or that it was bad and you are deliberately provoking her by being here?" asked the Lady. She could feel Charm sharing her eyes without pushing or trying to take control.

"It was an impression, anyway. She suggested that since she was not at home this week, she hoped I would find some way to amuse myself in the evenings."

That was not a good sign. Not at all. "How very thoughtful of her."

Seabrough smiled faintly. "I thought so."

Anders and Lyle caught up.

"Shall we fleece these innocent lambs, Lady Charm?" asked Seabrough.

The Lady fingered the spiral lock of hair that hung against her neck. He made her feel daring. Charm grinned from behind the Lady's eyes, and lent the Lady her throaty laugh. The Lady smiled brilliantly at Charm's aid. Charm wouldn't let her fall. Charm would help her. If she had help, it would be all right. It would be like playing dress-up, pretending to be Charm with Charm herself to help. And she didn't have to do any of the things she didn't want to. The Lady looked at Anders and Lyle as Charm gave them a raised eyebrow and a smile. "I think a light shearing might be in order."

At Charm's prompting, she excused herself to bring a brandy decanter to the table, and a little glass of sherry for herself. Seabrough held her chair for her to sit down.

The Lady sat erect when Charm would have leaned back. *A lady's back and the back of a chair should never be on speaking terms*, she corrected Charm, and was disconcerted that the aphorism seemed to get Charm thinking again.

"Lady Charm, a while ago you reminded us that you are from Inshil. Given the recent difficulties there, I've an interest in how Inshil treated their psychic citizens. Given your clear abilities, I wonder if it would be too painful or if you wouldn't mind telling us about your upbringing there?" asked Lyle as they contemplated their first hand of cards.

Charm studied the cards through the Lady's eyes while the Lady talked.

"You must understand, Sir Lyle, that in Inshil any psychic was considered a gift of God. The moment a psychic talent was displayed, the child was taken to the capital to see what application might suit their abilities, and how powerful they were, and so on."

"And you possessed the ability to grow these bone trees and produce artificial creatures?" asked Seabrough, and added, "Two spades."

"No, I never grew a bone tree in Inshil. I am what was called a 'sympathetic psychometer,' which is a widely useful talent without being at all powerful. I cannot light fires nor make ice nor read a man's mind. In Inshil our activities and schedules were very carefully monitored so that we would not injure ourselves. We had special living arrangements, beautiful gardens, music rooms and books. It was a very gentle life," said the Lady wistfully.

"So Inshil had a lot of people like your very charmin' ladies?" asked Anders.

"No, and not many animals. Empathy fluid was too costly, for the most part. We had it, of course, in my father's house."

If you wave a "daughter of the Chancellor" flag, I promise you I will scream.

I wasn't going to. One should not have to brag in that way. "But human boneghosts were not something of which Inshil could boast. I'm quite proud of them, you know. They're my greatest accomplishment."

"And our great good fortune." Seabrough offered her a little seated bow from across the table.

"Is it true you weren't allowed to go outside?" asked Lyle as the bids moved around the table.

"How silly. Of course we could go outside. I could walk in my father's gardens at any time. I did not go past his walls, of course. An uncontrolled environment is too dangerous for both the psychic and the people around them. I, of course, was not in the official government cloisters."

"Don't sound much like more than a gently outfitted prison, if you'll pardon my noting it, Lady," Anders said.

"Three clubs," bid Lyle.

The Lady blinked and hesitated. "I suppose it might be looked at that way, but there are few hospitals, I think, as perfectly lovely as ours, and fewer inmates in them as contented as we were."

Liar, discovered Charm, and relished being able to call out such a failing with certainty. *"We" weren't content. If we had been so perfect, we wouldn't have needed Desire.*

You wouldn't know anything about it, the Lady told her with a sniff. *You weren't there.*

Charm faltered and acquiesced. But it nagged at her. She was certain of what she knew, but she wasn't sure how, and not knowing frightened her.

"Er . . . no bid," Anders said, scowling a bit at his cards.

"What was the life expectancy of psychics in Inshil?" asked Seabrough quietly.

"More extreme talents could expect to live to be twenty or possibly twenty-five before they destroyed themselves or went mad. For more controlled and minor powers, some could live as long as thirty," said the Lady, puzzled by the question.

"And when they died? How was that?" asked Seabrough quietly.

"It depended on their abilities. There were special wards for pyrokinetics and telekinetics. Places they could not hurt themselves or others when they . . . at their end. For those with mental gifts, well, when they went mad, they were removed to a different special ward to be cared for. Eventually gifts like mine would lead to stroke."

It was a lie. Or not quite a lie, but it was not true. It was what Inshil had always told the world, but it was wrong. Duchess Nathair had told the truth, and Charm wasn't sure how she knew, only that she was so certain that rage burned in her at the thought of this . . . this false belief of the Lady's; and yet she did not dare rail. The conversation, this card game, they were too important for a confrontation now.

"We are very fortunate, in Boren, to have mindlocks for our psychics. The life expectancy of the psychics here is a natural span," Seabrough said, without looking up from sorting his cards. "A full and healthy life. With Rejuv, their life expectancy is virtually unlimited. They seem to me at least as humane as the methods of other countries."

"You seem to know a lot about the devices," commented Lyle. "I never took you for a scientific man."

"I admit I have an interest in that particular subject," said Seabrough. "I think I could manage to go six hearts, Lyle."

Lyle shook his head, smiling in confidence now. "You may have that contract, Seabrough. Let's see if you can fulfill it."

CHAPTER TWENTY-SIX

Pain sat down beside Oram, threaded her fingers through his, and took the book of poetry from her pocket. Several poems later she became aware that she had read the last three lines twice. A groggy haze clung around the corners of her vision. Her chest hurt, and her head throbbed with every stuttering beat of a laboring heart. She drew in a deep breath, felt her ribs expand against her corset and lift her breasts. She knew that she was breathing, but couldn't seem to convince herself that she was drawing in enough air. The haze intensified, and the pain in her chest. It was crushing her, grinding her slowly between the gears of the mindlock.

Mindlock? *Not my heart*, she realized. *Not my lungs*. Oram.

She tried to get up. She must reach the bell pull and hope that Pride could bring help. Pain forced her legs to push her upright, but couldn't catch her balance. She fell forward, half into the tank, her face coming to rest against Oram's neck and shoulder. She felt him, felt his joy at her touch. His mindlock jolted him with a sudden burst of agony. Pain let the searing sensation wash into her. His pulse under her cheek steadied slightly. Oram's mind twisted, trying to block the punishing screaming of his nerves, trying to protect her. With her last conscious thought, Pain defied him. She wrapped herself around his hurt, curling up tight so that none of it would get out, and let his agony take her into immobile silence.

⤳

"My lady, there is a caller for you in the solarium." Pride's murmur in the Lady's ear was threaded with tension.

"Gentlemen, may I beg your indulgence for a few moments?" The Lady picked up a wry thought from Charm and voiced it with a smile. "It will give you a chance to have the cigars you have been so thoughtfully not smoking."

Seabrough smiled. "Don't stay away too long, Lady Luck. I haven't had such a run of cards in recent memory."

The Lady dimpled happily at his praise, rose, and glided after Pride.

Hyacinth Barker paced the dark solarium, rubbing her big hands together. Her wildly black-and-white-striped skirts did nothing to lend her an air of calm. "Charm, thank God. Thank you, Pride," she added to the boneghost.

The Lady took Hyacinth's hands and stood on her toes to touch her cheeks to Hyacinth's. The dressmaker's hands were like ice and her cheeks not much warmer. Hyacinth's turmoil rolled through the Lady with the contact. Hyacinth had kept her hands calm and still through measuring tapes and pencils. Writing numbers in a book. "Pride, bring Hyacinth some brandy. You're so cold," she said to Hyacinth. "What is the matter?"

"She wants to come to her masquerade as you!"

"As . . . as me?" The Lady didn't understand.

"The Empress wants me to make her one of your black dresses to wear to her birthday ball. That's why she asked for me. I'm your dressmaker, and she wants to come to the ball as you. Charm, I tried to explain to her . . . she's going to look like hell in black. It'll make her look sallow. Your clothes are all wrong for her, she's built like a boy. She wouldn't listen to me, and it's going to be my fault if she looks bad." Hyacinth was almost hyperventilating.

The Lady tried to think through the panic that battered at her through Hyacinth's grip on her hand. She stood fast against the buffeting, but it wore at her, tried to catch at her lungs and make her heart race in sympathy with Hyacinth. She needed some way to block it out. She could not reassure Hyacinth if she herself were panicking. She needed some way, some way to block it out.

Let me take this one. I'll give you the body back, I promise, said Charm in the Lady's head.

Hyacinth's emotions battering at her, she let Charm have their body.

Charm whipped a brisk, not too hard, slap across Hyacinth's cheek. The Lady gasped from her place in the background of Charm's mind.

Hyacinth rubbed her cheek, swallowed hard.

"Breathe," Charm told her, "and sit down."

Pride appeared with the brandy, put it into Hyacinth's hands, and retired back to her post in the front hall.

Hyacinth sat down in one of the little wicker chairs. It creaked threateningly but did not give way. She downed a swallow of brandy. Her laugh was still a little shaky. "Oh God, Charm, she's going to look dreadful. What am I going to do?"

"Think," said Charm.

"She's doing it to mock you," said Hyacinth fiercely. "You should have seen her, Charm. She's so angry and . . . and bitter."

I knew she couldn't be as benign as you thought. The Lady was smug.

Adding prophecy to your skills, now, are you? Charm shot

back. Charm took Hyacinth's hands. "You're the one always saying 'don't lace down, pad up.' Can you pad her up?"

Hyacinth shot her a look of disgust. "Well of course, but the black won't do her a single favor, believe me. Her kind of blond looks awful in it, especially by candlelight."

"Surely she knows that herself." Charm tried to follow her own advice and think. "Did she say why she wanted to attend as me?"

Hyacinth shook her head. "Only that it's a vast secret and that even Countess Seabrough mustn't know about it."

"Take her two sketches, one of the ones you've done for me that you could alter just slightly to be more flattering, and one that would be designed especially for her. Explain to her that you fear that her more regal figure will not be most flattered by something designed for me. Let her choose." And if for some reason the Empress did want to look bad, if the Lady was right, God help them all.

"If she looks terrible, I'll never make another gown in Uptown!" protested Hyacinth.

Hyacinth shouldn't suffer for this, the Lady fretted. She gave Hyacinth's hands a squeeze, focused on consoling Hyacinth.

Oh bosh, snapped Charm. *She's done better than fine for years without Uptown. Dressmaking is her hobby, not her true profession. She only needed the cloth shipping to smuggle things inside the bolts. She's just flattered and seeing piles of money vanish before her eyes. Even if she does lose the Uptown market, Hyacinth will be fine.*

"How much of your income would you lose?" blurted the Lady.

Hyacinth drooped inside her corset. "Not any I had before, I suppose, but it's a chance, Charm. A chance to be respectable."

Why she would want that after all these years, I cannot imagine. You'd think she understood society better. Charm sighed. "We can't control what the Empress does, Hyacinth. If what you say is true, she could have you killed just for warning me."

"I know." Hyacinth's jaw firmed suddenly. "I couldn't let you go in there without telling you. She's doing it to mock you, I know it."

"If that's all she has in mind, well, I've borne worse than a little laughter. We can only hope it's me they laugh at. You do what you can to protect yourself. We'll let her lead. It's the only safe thing to do."

"You still want to go as a Most Holy of Inshil?" asked Hyacinth, hesitant. Anxiety came off her hands to the Lady so strongly that Charm could feel the whispered edges of the emotion.

"Did she ask what I was going to come as?" asked Charm. Hyacinth nodded.

"Did you tell her?"

Slowly, the nod again. "Countess Seabrough, this was before the Empress sent her out, said it was dressing . . . well . . . she said it was an insult to Boren."

It was kind of Hyacinth not to repeat the exact wording. "What did the Empress say?"

"She said—'I do think there are better choices for Mistress Charm.' And then she sent the Countess away."

Charm pressed her hands against her belly. *The Emperor said I underestimated her. He was right. God, do not let me be wrong to trust that.* "Then I want to change my costume. You are making her one of my gowns, make me one of hers."

"What?" Hyacinth didn't quite shriek.

"Utterly correct, stiff brocade in some pale tone. If she wears my clothes, I wear hers. If she changes her mind, you remake the costume for her into clothes for me, and the reverse. You'll be out no money."

Hyacinth stared. "That is not the point!"

"I must go back to the card table. If it comes to the worst, even common jailers will not treat me worse than Strephon does."

"You're sure?"

"I've been dealt into the game," Charm said with a faint, dry smile. "I can't afford to fold."

Hyacinth rose as Charm did, her eyes bright. "You've got guts and brains, Charm. You should have been a man."

"So should you, except that if either of us had less bust, men might think we had brains and we would have been caught by now," said Charm with a teasing wink.

Charm walked Hyacinth out through the kitchen and kissed her cheeks. She fixed the goggling pot girls with a stern glance that set them to scrubbing with renewed vigor.

The Lady watched Hyacinth go out, and only Charm's grip on their body kept her in the kitchen. The Lady wanted to run and lock herself in the laboratory and never come out.

Pull yourself together, snapped Charm in irritation. *We're going to go play cards and make conversation that will lead to talking about the Empress's birthday masque. You must get someone to ask what we're going as. I don't care if he asks you, or you ask his advice, or how it happens, but it absolutely must happen. Hyacinth's life depends on people knowing the costume was my choice and not hers.*

That is a nasty reminder, accused the Lady bitterly.

If I thought that self-preservation would stiffen your spine, I'd remind you that our life depends on it, Charm said briskly, gliding toward the front of Orchard House. She paused in the entry, where it would be as embarrassing as possible if the Lady tried to bolt. *You're on.* And she gave up control of the body.

The Lady drew in a shaky breath.

I am still here. I will help you, murmured Charm from the back of her mind. *You can do this.*

The Lady stepped forward. One step at a time, going back to her chair at the card table.

"I hope it was nothing serious, Lady Charm?" Anders rose and held her chair for her as she sat down.

"My dressmaker wanted to speak to me," said the Lady. "Is it my deal?"

"No, it's mine," Lyle told her with a generous smile, picking up the deck.

"Don't let her sandbag you, Lyle," said Anders, giving her a grin. "She remembers perfectly well whose deal it is."

"Praises my memory and card playing while criticizing my guile. Hmmm." The Lady took Charm's prompt and tapped a finger on her chin. "I will take it as a compliment," she decided.

"What on earth is Miss Barker doing out at this time of night?" asked Seabrough.

The Lady was slightly surprised that Seabrough knew of Hyacinth, but recalled his wife's run-in with Pain before she embarrassed herself. "Miss Barker is working on something for the Empress, I understand, so naturally she does not put me first in her dealings this season; but she came to consult on my costume."

"Your costume . . . for the Empress's birthday masque?" One of Seabrough's eyebrows rose.

"Why yes, Count."

Anders stared at her in open shock, but Lyle had the tact to take a sip of brandy instead.

Who'd have thought honesty was so useful. Nicely done. That's put a cat among the pigeons, commented Charm in a pleased tone.

"You will . . . be attending?" asked Lyle.

"The Empress was good enough to invite me personally, so yes."

Lyle glanced at Seabrough. Count Seabrough was studying his cards without expression.

"Did you know of it, Seabrough?"

The Count looked up from his cards, favored the Lady with a faint smile before looking directly at Lyle. "I had no idea, but is there some reason why she should not invite the Lady Charm?" he asked.

He's very good at that, the Lady observed. *They daren't criticize the Empress, and it would be rude to their hostess, and it would cast aspersions on Seabrough too.*

He's not still alive for nothing.

"I hope that the famous Miss Barker will be rising to her usual exquisite standards for you, Lady?" Seabrough asked her, relieving Lyle of any need to frame a response.

"I do assume so."

And you tell me you don't enjoy being coy? Charm gave a short laugh.

It was Anders who fell to the bait. "What will you be going as?" he asked.

"It's a surprise. I can only say that Hyacinth didn't approve."

"Well damn me. Did she have the temerity to disagree with you?" asked Anders.

"She disagreed with my choice in the strongest possible terms, but I wouldn't take no as an answer. And even when she disagrees with me, Miss Barker has never let me down," said the Lady.

Seabrough glanced at his cards, and changed the subject. "Two hearts."

The Lady tried to be careful not to watch him in particular, but if Charm was looking for someone who could commit an assassination, then Seabrough, who didn't seem to mind that Boren had slaughtered Inshil to get mindlocks, was certainly at the top of the list.

CHAPTER TWENTY-SEVEN

Desire clasped and unclasped her hands, rubbing fretfully at her twisted knuckles as she paced up and down the second-floor hallway. Luther had sat on his horse in the rain in the drive for almost half an hour before he'd come into the house. When he had come in, he'd asked for Pride. Again. The door opened, and Pride slipped out.

"I didn't think he'd come back, after Captain Oram."

"Well, he did and all he wanted was a massage," reported Pride crisply. "He was extremely tense."

Nothing unusual in that, and Pride was a sought-after masseuse. "Is he dressed?" asked Desire.

"He said he was going to get in the bath to wash off the oil. Are you going to scrub his back? I'm sure he'd like it," offered Pride.

Desire flushed at the unexpected sympathy from stiff Pride. "Mistress Charm will be angry at me. She doesn't want me to talk to him."

Pride raised one cool eyebrow. "Scrubbing does not require talking."

"It's all changing, isn't it?"

"I don't know what you mean."

"Justice is gone, and Shame."

"I have been unable to avoid that realization." Pride seemed to take the deaths in stride.

"Don't you want to be whole again, Pride, not even a little bit?"

"I have no idea what you mean," said Pride loftily.

"Do you think that Luther would have come back if I looked like the Lady?"

"Have you looked in a mirror recently?" countered Pride. "And the fact remains he didn't take you with him when he left Inshil." Her lip curled until it showed a flash of teeth. "He didn't come back to you, he didn't come to save you. He only chose to come see you when it was safe."

Desire chewed on her lip. "Pain tried very hard to save Lord Fergus. As much as she tried, he died. That wasn't her fault."

"I have no doubt that she did all she could," Pride said with a tone of strained patience.

"I tried, too. I truly tried." She still had nightmares about Evlaina sometimes, about her baby's tiny, tortured body. Aerleas had thrown her baby away like rubbish.

Pride groped for Desire's hands, held Desire's twisted fingers gently. She held them up before Desire's own eyes. "No one has ever doubted it."

But Pride could not see those hands, couldn't see how ugly, how useless they were. She never had to see anything. She was the sentry at the gate, blind to save the Lady from seeing things she could not bear.

"Pain couldn't save Fergus, but she tried to, and we still love her. Do you think that Luther could still love me? Even though I didn't save the baby?"

Pride's thin lips lifted into a faint smile. "He doesn't deserve anything from you. Not. One. Tear. Cry for yourself. Not for him."

Desire looked at the door. "He knows something. We're supposed to help the Lady, and if we can find out who killed the old emperor . . . we'd be free."

"What a good excuse," said Pride, cold. "Go in, then. If you really must face him."

Very slowly, she reached for Pride, and slipped her broken fingers into Pride's long, smooth, beautiful hand. "I wish you could make me stronger."

Pride kissed her head and offered a small smile. "As do I."

CHAPTER TWENTY-EIGHT

Desire squared her shoulders and went into Luther's room. A screen concealed the hearth and fireplace. From behind it, Luther's voice was mildly annoyed.

"Who is it?"

"Desire. I can go if I am intruding. . . ."

Silence for a long moment. Then, "Come here."

Desire went to the screen, hesitated, and didn't go behind it. What would he say? It was hard to know what to do without the others. Desire pressed her hands against her bodice. Feeling the boning against her palms. Extra bones, to hold her up. Straight, springy, resilient. She would be like those bones. "You asked for Pride, and Justice, and you asked for Pain even though she wouldn't book you. . . . You've asked for Pride twice. I'm sorry." The words came out small and shaking, so she tried again. "I'm sorry."

Desire looked up as Luther came around the end of the screen in a dressing gown. Lean and fit, she knew every plane of him; remembered the warm taste of his skin.

"What's happened to make me worth talking to?" he asked.

"You did not speak to me, either," Desire said, wounded.

"Sauce for the goose." The way he said the words made her think they meant something special to him, but they meant nothing to Desire.

"I wanted to talk to you," said Desire with quiet desperation, "but Mistress Charm was afraid of what you might do. She said that she'd see me in the tank if I didn't keep silent, and I wanted to be with you. It was the only way, so I promised not to say anything because I wanted to be with you."

"I don't suppose you came in here to explain that, so ask your question," he told her.

Desire shrank back from his anger. Oh, how she wished she were Pride, who didn't know how people looked at her. She wished she were Pain, who was so strong, or even Mistress Charm. "I don't understand you," she whispered.

Luther's laugh was bitter as walnut hulls. "Nor I you."

"I'll go. I wanted . . . I'll go." She'd wanted him to be honest. To speak of their past. To tell her it hadn't all been just a pretense. He didn't ask for her. Only the others. How stupid she'd been. She began to turn back toward the door.

Luther took two steps, closing the distance between them. He picked up Desire's hands. He pressed a kiss into each palm, held them so tight it ached. Luther's hands were worn and callused by the sea, strong hands. Desire clung to them as well as she could, knowing it was futile, letting herself pretend, if only for a moment, that she could keep hold of him.

Luther rubbed his thumbs gently across the distorted lumps of her knuckles. "I don't quite understand. Why aren't Mistress Charm's hands maimed? You were in that body at that time, weren't you?" he asked.

"You knew, then." And still he'd said nothing.

"I figured it out quickly enough. I'd be surprised if anyone who sees you didn't figure it out, though your hands confused me. They still do."

Her pulse thundered in her throat and her belly. The world spun in swirls around her. The floor rose up under Desire and stopped abruptly beneath her seat.

Luther sat down in the nearest chair, frowning a little as if in concern. "Are you all right?"

She looked up into his ink-dark eyes. A chair. He wouldn't even touch her. "I loved you."

Luther's thin lips twisted in a bitter smile. "If you were all together, would you feel the same? I seem to recall that some of your parts are not too fond of me. Mistress Charm is one of you, isn't she? The one who makes you be prostitutes."

No, Charm had never been like them. Desire's heart twisted. She didn't really answer him: "Mistress Charm has always carried the mindlock. She asked for our help. We agreed. We had to survive." Desire searched his face for any reaction.

He bent down, leaning his elbows on his knees. "I admit to a certain amount of selfishness. It is much more convenient for me to be in love with you when you are alive," teased Luther in his cool voice, a trickle of amused sarcasm relieving the tone of any sting.

It was like her best memories, as he used to be under the blooming pear trees in the cloister orchards. Desire fancied she could hear the low buzz of the bees. She reached to touch his face with her fingertips, and he flinched a little. It was too sweet to be real. Any moment now he would slip away from her.

"Do you think I would have kept coming back if I did not care?" he whispered. "I have hesitated in the drive for so many hours I believe my horse thinks he's a lawn ornament. I sit and repeat to myself all of the reasons that I should not come in, should not torment myself by only having a sliver of my lover at a time."

The words were exactly right. They matched the fanciful pear orchard of the past.

"I'll ask Mistress Charm to give you back the hands you ought to have. I'll make her, if I have to."

Pride hadn't been wrong. Luther hadn't come back. He was being kind, but only because she was part of a whole. He hadn't asked for her again because he didn't want her twisted hands. It sank into her. Settled into her broken bones with an ache that wasn't mourning. Desire went still.

"That is not the reaction I was looking for," Luther observed.

"The Lady is far too pretty, too cultured to have such ugly, useless hands. I wanted these bones, so we helped each other trade them. These hands are ugly, but they're mine." Desire's throat tightened, aching around the words, and she hugged her hands against her breasts as if someone could take them away.

"Why would you want them? Why not have a fresh start?"

How could she make him understand. "Justice said that you wept when Mistress Charm told you Oram was dead. Why did you cry for him?"

"He was my cabin boy, from seven until his telepathy came on."

He wasn't telling her everything, she could see it in his stillness. "You raised him?"

"As if he were my son." Luther kept his emotions contained.

Desire bit her lip.

"What do you know of Oram?" asked Luther, suddenly sharp.

"Captain Oram's secrets are, or were, his to tell you if he had wanted to."

"Ever faithful with secrets, are you?" Frustration tinted his voice.

"With your secrets too," Desire whispered. The bitterness in his eyes seemed to soak, stinging, into her skin. "If I didn't keep his secrets, you could not trust me with yours."

"You I could trust. Justice I could trust. Pride I can at least predict. Mistress Charm is another matter."

"Would you trust the Lady?"

"Mistress Charm is up to her big blue eyes in some scheme, I'd stake my life on it. Even if I could still trust the Lady, they're living in the same skull. That seems like close quarters for secret-keeping."

"I'm sorry, Luther, I am not the most intelligent of us. I don't know how to overcome that." She let her head tip sideways, and offered, "If there is any quality of the rest of us that Mistress Charm shares, it is loyalty."

"She is loyal," agreed Luther with a sharp, hard laugh. "She is shackled to my father by that damned lock even when he's dead."

Desire couldn't think anymore, didn't want to. He did not want to hear or believe what she said, and so she said nothing.

"I give you my leave to discuss with the Lady how to trust Charm, if you think she might have some light to shed on the conundrum."

"It would hurt the Lady, to think that you don't trust her. I am not here to hurt her. You say she doesn't know you, but you're wrong. You were her friend. She only didn't tell you because she was trying to protect you."

"Do I need her protection?" he murmured, stroking her hair with a gentle, roughened hand. "It's hard to trust someone who thinks there's a threat to you, but who won't tell you what that threat is."

Desire shivered. "It's hard to know what to do. The Lady is forced to change, and Pain is acting as if she's a whole different person. It's all drifted . . . gotten confused, somehow."

Luther's rueful laugh rumbled in his chest. "That it has."

Desire held up her twisted hands, examining them. Did he know? Desire assumed he did, but now she wasn't sure. But still. He wanted trust. Secrets did not breed trust. "I had a baby."

Luther froze for long moments while Desire's heart thudded in her chest. Finally, "What happened to it?"

The last word struck her like a blow. She could hardly breathe, gasping.

And then, "Was it mine?"

She wasn't as smart as Charm, wasn't as strong as Pride, but she understood now. Desire closed her eyes, drew in breath, glad for the whalebone stays that supported her.

And he said, into the silence, "I must go. Strephon and Phelan think that I'm merely playing where I was not allowed before. I don't want to draw their attention too much."

"Close your eyes," whispered Desire, standing up as he did.

Luther closed his eyes.

"Think of my true face, of my true body."

Luther nodded shortly, throat working as he swallowed.

Desire kissed him, savoring the taste of his mouth, feasting on his low groan. She slipped out of his arms and opened the door, stepped into the hall. "Good-bye." Firmly, she closed the door.

Desire went slowly down the back stairs. Once she was outside of the kitchen door, breath burst up out of her in a sudden, deep jerk that turned into a sob. Fog had risen, veiling the bone orchard in a frosty cloud. Like a madwoman she flung out her hands and walked through the thick white mist, the dampness on her face like tears. "Pain?" she called as she went into the lab. "Please, I . . . I need to talk to you."

"Here." Pain managed a croak. She lay with her upper body on top of Oram as if to shield him from something, half in the empathy fluid.

"He asked me if Evlaina was his."

Pain's eyes glittered with tears.

Desire tucked her hands up warmly under her chin. "I told my parents I'd kill myself if they didn't let me keep my baby." Everything was so jumbled. "I loved Luther. I truly, truly did. And then I couldn't save Evlaina. I wanted to."

Pain's mouth worked, but nothing came out.

Desire went on slowly, emptily, "She was crying, and Prince Aerleas broke my hands because I kept holding on to her, and then because I kept reaching for her," Desire managed. "I've tried, Pain. I tried so hard, but Justice was right and it's too much for just me."

Pain spasmed abruptly, back arching and mouth opening in a soundless gagging. Her pink eyes focused into nothing, and she gasped and fought for breath. Their hands tightened in unison on one another, knuckles going marble white.

Desire leaped up, tumbling her chair off its feet. Had she done this? She touched Pain's shoulder gently. Whatever was wrong, she didn't want to make it worse by jostling the two of them. "Pain, what is it? Pain, can you talk?"

Pain twitched. Her mouth worked again for a moment. Then her teeth bared in a grimace of concentration. The voice that came from between her pale lips was a man's; hoarse, but definitely male.

"Help. Tell her. Take. Out. Lock."

CHAPTER TWENTY-NINE

Lady! Lady, wake up!"

Was someone calling to her, or to someone else? Waking was strange, blurry and confused. The card game had gone on into the early hours of the morning. Seabrough had been a brilliant and entertaining partner. The night had gone on and on and she hadn't wanted it to stop; but even when it had, the glow of being clever and admired lingered around her like the scent of smoke on her gown. It had been pleasant, basking in the afterglow of a pleasant evening and the unlooked-for accomplishment of not a little fresh money tucked into the safe behind Pride's desk. The person calling gave her a sudden shake.

"Lady! It's Captain Oram!" said Desire desperately. "Pain is with him. You must come!"

The world firmed up around the edges as the Lady threw off the gauzy haze of dreaming. She slid out of bed as Desire threw a robe around her shoulders.

"Quickly, Lady, quickly."

Desire hustled the Lady down the back stairs. The bone orchard was buried in fog so thick that the Lady could not see from one tree to another. It limned the trees in silvery damp. The Lady's thin slippers soaked through, and the hem of her robe stuck to her legs. The warm, close familiarity of the lab banished the last uncertainty.

Pain lay half in the growth vat, sprawled across Captain

Oram. She panted slightly, lips taut. She managed to roll her head to look at the Lady and Desire as they came in, her eyes bright with agony so intense that the redness of them seemed to throb with her pulse.

The Lady laid her hand on Oram's forehead. She could feel his body straining against the mindlock, each heartbeat fighting past the grinding teeth of its cogs.

"How is he?" asked Luther's voice from the greenhouse door. "So this is Oram's secret. He's still alive." He glared at Desire, who was carefully not looking at him. "You bitch."

"Actually, he's dying if we don't get the mindlock out," the Lady corrected. "You and Desire can spat later." She snatched her rubberized apron from its peg and began pulling it on. "Get Pain on top of him, so we can winch them up and get them onto the table."

Luther worked the crank and the Lady and Desire balanced the awkward load as Captain Oram and Pain rose out of the growth tank. Carefully, they swung the metal basket over the dissection table. Luther let the rack down one notch at a time until the basket settled on the table.

"Mr. Ostander said that a mindlock is a crystal-cased gearwork with two curved wires coming out of the back." The Lady pulled out the corner pins of the rack so the basket's shallow sides fell flat against the table. "And the wires are coated with gelatin." The Lady fingered her hair. "So, if the coating melted, it might slide the wire along like a lubricant instead of producing tension to make it slice. We'd have to raise his body temperature, and then if we clip off only the pain wire there's no power getting into the nerve centers. We clip the pain tail, and draw the feeder out still attached to the lock's body. We draw the pain tail last," she finished. "Yes, yes, I think that's the only way. Desire, I need a surgical tray, a syringe, and that blue glass bottle."

Luther stayed standing on the step. He did not stop looking at Oram on the dissection table with Pain sprawled across
his chest. His face was utterly neutral, as if the expression had
been carved into his flesh.

"Prince Luther, would you please take the razor over there
and shave around the mindlock. Then I'll need you to track
his temperature while we work," the Lady said briskly as she
went to the shelves that held the bones from the orchard.

"You'll kill him," managed Luther, his voice rough.

The Lady braced both hands on the shelf in front of her for
a moment. He could easily walk to the door, go to his brother
the Emperor, and turn them all in for treason. Certainly he'd
seen enough here to make Strephon act.

Pull yourself together, snapped Charm from the back of her
skull. *There's a loaded pistol on the second shelf from the top. If he
turns to leave, shoot him.*

Don't bother to bully me, he isn't leaving. The Lady straightened, then turned to face Luther fully. "He's dead already if we
don't operate. Captain Oram chose to probably die in agony
instead of go on one more moment as Strephon's pet killer. All
I can do is try to save him, and possibly Pain. If I fail, at least I
will have tried." The Lady turned back to the shelves, dragging
out the bottommost basket.

He's going to leave, hissed Charm.

*If you try to take over now, Captain Oram will die. You
need the captain, so you'll just have to trust my judgment. Luther
wouldn't leave when there's a job that needs doing, and he certainly
won't leave Oram to die.*

Most of a human skeleton was piled in the basket, bones
she'd gathered and dried over the course of two years. It was
short only a few vertebrae. It had been intended to be her
last creation, to free her from the periods she now knew to
be Charm's. The Lady couldn't feel Shame as a separate en-

tity anymore. There was only herself and Charm. Who would have ended up trapped within the bones? Could she have escaped, if she had found those three small bones? She rummaged through the basket until she came up with the skull.

Luther was still standing on the step, as if unable to make up his mind what to do.

Keep him here, urged Charm.

"Shave Oram or kindly leave," said the Lady, reminding him of his choices. She took a fine bone saw from the pegs along the side of the shelves.

Luther peeled off his coat and hung it on a hook by the door. "Should I move Pain?"

"No, let her be. We don't know what the connection between them is, precisely. We shouldn't jostle it," the Lady told him.

Desire, assembling the surgical tray and watching, let out her breath and visibly relaxed.

The Lady used the fine saw to cut out a piece of bone roughly the same size as Oram's mindlock. There was an irony to her work. Cutting out a piece of her skull was exactly what the old emperor had done. That little bone disk had grown into the tree in the center of the orchard, from which this skull had fruited. She was cutting a disk from her skull to put into Oram's skull. If not for Charm's mindlock, the Lady could not have saved him.

She put the bone into a bowl of sickly-green empathy fluid, said a brief mental prayer, then pricked Oram's finger and let a single drop of his blood fall into the bowl. The chartreuse fluid flushed blue. A positive reaction. The Lady breathed a little easier. In a growth vat she would have used a bellows or stirred, but with just this little bowl and this single bit of bone she didn't want to introduce too much air. The Lady blew gently across the surface, just rippling the fluid, watching as the tint blushed lavender, then began to pinken. The Lady put the bowl gently down on the instrument tray when the fluid color was just on the edge of being a pure pink.

Desire arranged padded blocks around the captain's head, and adjusted the lamps carefully. She pulled a tall stool over for the Lady to sit on. A rubber guard kept Oram's teeth apart enough for the thermometer to be taped into his mouth. When all was in readiness, Luther took up a post as the instrument nurse. Desire stood by the head of the table, looking down at Oram and Pain, both so white. The Lady filled a syringe and injected Oram.

"His temperature should start to rise in just a few minutes, Prince Luther. Keep an eye on that thermometer," the Lady instructed.

The Lady scrubbed carefully, then scrubbed the patch Prince Luther had shaved. She took her seat on the stool.

"Scalpel," requested the Lady.

Carefully she slit the skin around the burned-out crystal, clipping flaps of scalp in forceps and laying them back. She packed the edges of the wound carefully so she could examine the setting prongs.

"His temperature is starting to rise," reported Luther. "Ninety-nine and two-tenths."

"How long will the fever last?" Desire asked.

"Ten minutes or so, but if this is going to work it will only take a few minutes." The Lady's attention never wavered from her work. "The prongs are gold."

"Is that bad?" Desire asked.

"It's good, the metal is soft. The next forceps there, please, Prince Luther." She cut through the prongs, holding the crystal steady with her free hand. "How are we doing with his temperature?"

"A hundred and one degrees," Luther said briefly.

The Lady worked the four setting prongs out of the bone with forceps. His scalp was bleeding fairly heavily, but head wounds always did bleed that way. They always seemed to be bleeding too much. Always, the Lady reminded herself firmly. She replaced the packings. The blood crept around her fingers, and impressions of Oram ran along her nerves. Pain's connection to him hovered somewhere through a mist, drawing a veil across the sensations of his body. The Lady could feel the wires of the mindlock like the cold edges of a sword in his brain. She bent her head in close, concentrating on the tiny machine under her fingertips. Listening to how it existed, to how that changed. The tension of the leads began to ease.

"Temperature?" she asked.

"One hundred and two."

The bell that Pride used to signal Charm when there was a particularly important customer chimed sweetly through the greenhouse. Someone was in the lobby of Orchard House. Someone that Pride thought she needed to warn them about. Charm fretted in the back of the Lady's head.

"If I stop, he will die," said the Lady, half to Luther and Desire, but half to Charm as well, "and I need another set of hands to help me."

Desire darted toward the house.

⤥⤦

Desire slipped up through the green baize door to the entry. Prince Phelan loomed over Pride, who would not have shrunk away even if she could have seen his face.

"I do not know anything about Major Nathair, Your Highness," said Pride, her tone faintly patient. "He has not been here in some time."

"Whom does he see when he stops here?"

"He saw Justice last, Highness," Desire told him from the hallway door.

"Justice?" Phelan's eyes raked her. "He sees my girl?" repeated Phelan, as if he could not believe it. He took two swift steps toward Desire. He snared her by the jaw, pinning her head back against the doorframe. His thumb dug in painfully.

Pride slipped, unnoticed by Phelan, toward the kitchen.

"What did Nathair want with her?" hissed Prince Phelan.

His grip on her face made it hard to speak. Desire told the truth, but a partial truth only. "He had a private room. Only Justice could tell you exactly what went on."

"Where is Justice?"

"Dead, Your Highness." Desire took a deep breath. "She killed herself." Since they were each a part of the Lady, it was even true after a fashion.

A bright, wild light in Phelan's eyes gave them a frantic energy. His fingers trembled against Desire's jaw. "Dead?" For a moment Phelan seemed not to believe her. Then rage curled his lip and flared his nostrils. "How?" he hissed through his teeth. His fingers squeezed her jaw.

Her words were deformed by his brutal grip. "She asked to die, Highness."

"What did he do to her?" Phelan jerked her forward and slammed her back into the doorframe. "How did he drive her to it?"

Stars flared and danced behind Desire's eyes. Darkness misted around the edges of her vision. "Wasn't . . . him."

"Who was it!" he roared. This time Desire managed to take the blow of the doorframe against her back and shoulder. "Who drove her to it?"

Desire looked into Phelan's eyes. "You."

Sweat rolled along the side of the Lady's nose as she craned her head over to see more clearly. She slid the wire cutters beneath the crystal, held her breath, and clipped. Oram's heart stuttered, stumbling forward as it gained erratic speed and strength. Pain shuddered. The Lady lifted the crystal fractionally, and used forceps to take hold of the wire that was still attached to it. She gave a low cry of triumph as it began to draw out of Captain Oram's brain. The gelatin, slick as oil, guided the wire through the delicate tissue.

She could feel a faintest easing in Oram's brain as the first wire came free. The mindlock clashed onto the metal tray with the twinned wires flopping. Instruments seemed suddenly too crude, too impersonal. The Lady caught the second tail with her bare fingers. Blood-slick as it was, she had to pinch hard with her nails to get a solid grip on it. Once she had it caught, the pain tail slid smoothly free.

The Lady scooped the bone disk out of its empathy fluid and pressed it against the hole in Captain Oram's skull. It didn't fit, but she didn't want it free-floating in the hole anyway. "The chisel with the curved blade." The Lady pressed the chisel blade hard against Oram's skull, carving around the edge of the hole to make a lip. His heart beat in struggling double time, counted seconds in the background of her mind. She tried the fit again. Not quite. "File!"

Luther snapped the file crisply into her hand.

The Lady worked with quick, easy strokes, reducing the size of the disk. Three passes of the file, four. The Lady dropped the file on the floor and fitted the piece of her bone into Oram's skull. She laid the skin flaps back around the edges of the disk. The skin had just enough give to cover the implanted disk. "Suture."

Oram's pulse began to find a rhythm. One stitch at a time his heartbeat smoothed. Ten stitches were all she needed to close the wound. It seemed such a very small repair. The Lady sat back. If his mind had held through the procedure, he would live.

Pain lay limp and unconscious on Oram's chest, her face sheened with sweat and her skirt tangled about his legs.

Something scrabbled at the upper corner of the door. Luther opened the door, and startled as a bird darted past his face. The swallow dropped into the Lady's lap, wings sprawling. Its heart hammered in staccato time against her palm as she picked it up.

Vision flashed across her mind. It was warm and dark, but the swallow could hear and smell things. It smelled a kerosene lamp, and someone's supper that the Lady could identify as roasted pork. "Your Highness, it is my duty to tell you that Captain Oram is dead." Long silence. A great noise and the smell of gun smoke. Falling.

The bird tumbled out of the dark warmth of cloth. A youth's narrow features with his pale eyes going glassy and his golden hair, too long, half fallen across his face. Blood in a great pool. Darting up into the framework of the tent, clinging to the canvas. Prince Aerleas loomed over the body, pistol clenched in his bony hand; his narrow face was twisted in rage and his too-bright eyes burned with madness. More gunshots, a roar like a cannon, and shouting outside. A man in a command uniform threw open the tent flap. "Highness, we are under attack!" Past that officer, the swallow saw open sky, albeit dark. It flashed out into the night, driving up and away, north toward the bone orchard that had birthed it.

The Lady shook off the vision with a shudder. "Did Mistress Charm have a quite young man working for her?" she asked. "A soldier in a brown uniform with fair hair?"

"Major Nathair," Pain managed in a thready whisper. "He's a courier between Prince Aerleas and Emperor Strephon."

"Then Mistress Charm has used him ill. Major Nathair is dead," said the Lady. "Prince Aerleas killed him." The poor young man hadn't done Charm a jot of good, and she'd gotten him killed.

Luther closed his eyes for a moment as if he were hurting. "How did Nathair provoke him?" asked Luther.

"He was sent to break the news to General Aerleas that Captain Oram was dead." Charm's lie. How many people would be hurt by it?

"Then Aerleas is coming here. How long ago was this?" Luther's question was sharp, jerking her out of the thought.

"About . . . several days? I don't know exactly. There was a battle beginning," she added without real hope that the detail would be useful.

Luther nodded. "I may still be able to cut him off. Oram will be all right? You said he'd live, but that isn't the same thing."

"It depends on how his mind adjusts to the removal of the lock," said the Lady. "On how much damage the fever may have done and what we injured drawing the machinery out . . ." The Lady trailed off with a weary shrug.

Touch his wrist.

What?

Touch. him. You can, right now. Be nice. Be comforting. You can find out if he killed his father!

The Lady had forgotten all about that. Well. Yes. Even though she still thought it might have been Seabrough, at least this would be a little proof for Charm that the Lady was correct. She laid her hand on his wrist, just inside his cuff.

The cascade of images was rapid, clean. He hadn't even made landfall before the Emperor fell ill. It wasn't the right time frame. He'd seen his father before the man died, but he could not have been the assassin. His isolation on his ship had been complete.

I told you so, the Lady said, smug. She smiled gently at Luther. "I can't make predictions for a surgery I've never done and which I only partly understood. It's more chance than he had before. I'm sorry. I can't guarantee more."

Luther nodded. He turned toward the door.

"Use the small gate in the back of the orchard," said the Lady to his back. "That's the one that Pain always uses going toward the docks. It's shorter than going through the front."

Luther vanished into the fog outside the door without a word.

Well done, said Charm in the back of her mind.

"Well done in what way? The surgery? Luther? The bird?" the Lady asked aloud.

All of it. Charm was apparently not inclined to say more on the subject. *Are you just going to leave them on the table?* Meaning Oram and Pain.

The Lady sighed. "No, they might fall off. I have to wait for Desire's help to get them into the tank."

Pride stepped out of the mist at the top of the steps. Her voice, usually so cool and calm, was underwritten with urgency. "Lady, Prince Phelan is in the entry. He's demanding to know about Justice. Desire is speaking to him, but I'm afraid he'll kill her."

Before the Lady could even think of it, Charm was bolting to their feet. Not pushing the Lady aside, not bothering with argument or struggle, just moving. The Lady caught up their skirts so that they didn't stumble on the stairs up out of the greenhouse. The orchard trees loomed out of the mist, trunks and low-hanging branches appearing in her path. Charm and the Lady in their single body dodged around them, through them, racing toward Orchard House.

CHAPTER THIRTY

Phelan flung Desire away from him with a bellow of denial. Desire felt herself falling, but it seemed very slow. She could step with her left foot, redirect her momentum up, put out her hands and catch herself on the edge of the desk. Desire smiled. It would be all right now. She turned her temple in the direction of the desk edge, and let herself fall.

The Lady burst through the green baize door to see Desire falling. She leaped forward to catch the boneghost, but too late. Desire's temple impacted the corner of the reception desk with a muffled crunch. Her head snapped awry as her body continued its plunge. Desire hit the floor limply, and didn't move. Blood poured from her split temple.

Desire's mind broke over the Lady and Charm like a wave, the force of her own want smashing her into drops. Desire ran into Charm, leaching into gaps in the shielding facets of the mindlock. Desire understood loving. She understood loyalty. Staying loyal was part of what Desire did. Desire did not fight the mindlock. She yielded, soaked in around its edges and eased its gears and mechanisms. Charm reeled, stunned. Desire added to herself gave Charm a new weight, new solidity.

The Lady threw herself back, away from Charm's presence in their mind, as if Charm had been somehow contaminated.

Their body stumbled. Charm's hands slapped into the pooling blood. It soaked into her robe at knees and cuffs, wicking into the soft wool. Charm looked up at Prince Phelan with bright spots wheeling madly around in her vision. The Lady cringed back in their mind as if she could somehow escape their skull.

Phelan stood staring at Desire's body, breathing hard. He oriented on Charm. His eyes were hectically bright.

"Where is Justice?" he demanded.

"She's dead, Highness," snapped Charm. She sat back on her heels.

Phelan half snarled. "Why?"

Charm met his eyes, kept her voice firm and level. Like a tutor explaining something incredibly simple. "Because she could not stand to live anymore."

"She was mine!" His big hands balled into fists.

Charm staggered to her feet. She leaned against the doorframe, but her hand was slippery with Desire's blood. Strands of hair were stuck on the doorframe. Charm remembered Justice's pleading, her need to leave behind the things that had been done to her. Desire had helped the Lady peel the scalded skin from Justice's thighs and groin, taking off the dead tissue to prevent infection when she was in the tank. Pain holding Justice's head so the child ghost didn't have to feel the surgery. Shame, mold from the cheese knife making her hideous, deformed. A body become a corpse. Charm clutched the front of her robe around herself, drawing up.

"I think you should leave, Prince Phelan," said Charm, her voice shaking with anger. She wanted to scream. Instead, she held her voice to a conversational tone. "I will have Pain and Pride take the body out to the orchard and bury it. The Firedrinkers needn't know."

"Needn't know what?" Phelan frowned in confusion.

"That you have murdered Desire." Charm spoke patiently.

"Shame might be explained as a fit gone wrong, and Justice was not your doing in the mechanical sense, but Desire you have killed outright. That is murder." *Whether or not Strephon will see it that way.*

"You can bring her back . . . you can bring Justice back. Bring Justice back," he ordered, the urgency in his voice rising with repetition.

"Justice is not coming back," repeated Charm, enunciating the last three words with vicious satisfaction. "You can't have her anymore."

"Bring her back!" Phelan lunged at Charm.

Charm jerked away. His fingers caught air where she had been. She hurtled through the green baize door and tried to brace against the far side. Phelan hit the door with his greater strength and weight. Charm staggered into the kitchen. She collided with Pride coming in from the orchard.

Phelan snared Charm by the hair. She screamed, clung to his wrist as he dragged her back.

"Give her back, you manipulative bitch!" he howled, shaking Charm.

Pride caught at his arm and face. She tried to pull him back from Charm, her fingernails digging bloody trails across his cheek. Phelan threw Pride off with a roar of rage. She collided with the stove, still hot from the coals banked in it. She screamed, with no Pain awake to take the burns, falling off the side of it and down behind Phelan in a crash of metal.

"You killed Justice!" Charm shrieked at him, struggling against his grip, clawing at his wrist. She scrambled in the mass of her skirts as she tried to get her feet under herself. "She was me, mine, not yours, and you will never have her again! She's safe in my head now, and you can't take her from me!"

Phelan hauled her up, the pins in her hair pulling. He

looked past Charm to the cutting board and the knife block that stood beside it. His eyes gleamed insanely bright.

"I'll get her back," he said. A horrible smile pulled his lips back from his teeth. He snatched a knife from the block. "I'll cut her out of your head."

Pride flung herself at him from the side, flailing with burned hands, got her arm through the crook of his knife arm and pulled, staying the strike midmotion.

A biscuit jar rose above Phelan and smashed across his skull, scattering pieces and biscuits. He went down heavily, colliding with Charm and driving her to her knees as he toppled to one side.

Pain stood behind him, no longer eclipsed by his bulk.

His arm jerked out of Pride's hand. Her burned palm went with Phelan's sleeve and Pride screamed, keeping her hurt, driving herself with it as if it were a lash. She pawed the air with the raw, bleeding hand to try to locate him as she got hold of the stove poker with the other.

"Pride, stop! Stop!" Charm staggered to catch her upraised wrist.

"Never again!" hissed Pride. "If I have to beat him to death, he will never touch any part of me again!"

Charm caught the poker.

"Where is he?" demanded Pride, pawing the air past Charm, spattering blood on the floor and Prince Phelan.

"Pride. Give me the poker." Charm pried the makeshift weapon from Pride's bloody hand. It clanged on the floor.

Charm took Pride by the elbows and steered her into a chair at the kitchen table. "Stay there," she commanded. Charm crouched by Phelan. She laid two fingers against his neck. A pulse. She was no judge of the quality, but she was willing to settle for a pulse of any kind. She stepped out of the back door into the dampness of the fog, sucked in a breath so deep that her corsetless ribs expanded and ached, and then screamed at the top of her lungs.

Pain leaned on the kitchen table, wobbling.

"What are you doing?" asked Pride, voice strained, rocking slightly.

"Calling the Firedrinkers. We can't hide this, so we might as well face it, and it's better that it look messy." Charm stepped back over Phelan to Pride. She took the boneghost's wrists, turning her palms up. The left was raw flesh oozing blood, the right a mass of blisters.

Pain turned, if it was possible, whiter.

"Pain, please try not to faint, I have too many patients already. We need ice and water," requested Charm.

Pain staggered toward the front hall. She came back with the ice basin from the bar, the chipped remains of last night's block of ice and water, and put it in Pride's lap. She sat down at the table, wrapped her arms around herself. Focused on something within, or far away.

Charm gave Pride's shoulders a one-armed hug of support. "It will hurt, but it will numb quickly."

Pride's sightless eyes filled with tears and her breath shuddered out when she put her hands into the bowl. She did not raise her hands to wipe her tears, but sat straight in her chair as the tears ran down her cheeks.

"You felt Desire's death?" asked Charm, taking a towel to wipe her tears and her running nose.

"The Lady doesn't want her, or any of us, but I will not give up any part of me," hissed Pride fiercely. "I will never give us up."

"Oh, we're not going to start giving up now," Charm assured her. "Desire's safe with me." She applied the towel hurriedly to her own eyes and nose, then gave Pride's wrists a gentle squeeze.

A pair of Firedrinkers burst out of the mist and through

the kitchen door. The door in the front of the house banged open. The Firedrinkers in the kitchen stopped. One stood in the doorway, blocking it. The other crouched by Phelan, stripped off gloves, and pressed two slender, white fingers against his neck. "Alive. Take him back to the Isle."

Four more scarlet-clad bodies came in through the green door from the front of the house. They picked Phelan up, the ones at his arms cradling his head carefully. They took him out through the front door.

"He attacked you," said the Firedrinker with bare hands. Not a question. The hands looked feminine at first glance, soft and white; but they'd been in gloves for who knew how long.

"He killed Desire, then he attacked me. Pain and Pride saved my life," Charm told them.

The Firedrinker's partner nodded, short and sharp. "That is true."

"Does it matter?" Pride's lips twisted with bitter smile.

The mirrored visor turned toward Pride. "Yes, miss," the Firedrinker told her in the calm, mechanical voice of their helmet. "To us, it matters."

Pride looked away, shaking her head slightly. Her lips pressed into a flat, silent line.

The Firedrinker's helmet reoriented on Charm. "We will see to Prince Phelan and Miss Desire. Take Miss Pride and Miss Pain away and let us work."

Pain stood up, and fainted.

⁓

Pain tumbled in the jangling world of thoughts and emotions crashing into Oram's mind. Herself, the Firedrinkers in the house, Prince Phelan, Prince Luther. The city full of people. No regulation, no buffer, just the wild cacophony of other minds pounding into Oram's from every side. The throbbing agony of his brain poured into Pain. She wouldn't let go, wouldn't let herself be shaken or fall away.

There was no sense of time, no passing of moments, just a continuously deafening babble of minds. It hurt, but he was hunting desperately for something, for someone, reaching out with his freed mind even though the city was tearing him to pieces. A touch on Oram's shoulder, or her own, Pain wasn't sure, brought an approaching hollow in the storm into clarity.

"Pain, wake up." Charm. Her mind was hidden in the shadow of the mindlock, but her touch connected them enough for Oram to feel who she was.

Pain/Oram watched Charm, her shielded strength behind the Lady. Charm gave them an anchor in the gale of minds. The Lady was a single note, thin and flat as a badly tuned violin string. Charm shone brighter, her strength a brilliant growing chord. There was a trace of Shame there, the guilt for things she'd done, and more for things she hadn't. Desire and Justice too, like complementary notes. They moved in tight synchronicity, Charm and her other personalities, so close that their edges blurred into one another and made them more than the sum of their fragmented selves. They were Charm.

"Pride, sit down. I have to get Captain Oram into the growth vat. Empathy fluid should insulate him from other minds until he's healed enough to have some defenses."

Pain felt half of herself fall up, away from her. There was a jolt at the top of the fall. Some tint of connection remained, a line that Pain clung to doggedly. She took the hurt from him. She could not take away the thundering roar of the city around him, but she could help in this one, small way.

"All right, on three. One, two, three."

Oram's hurt swung left, lowered. Pain forced her eyes open. The Lady used a wooden block to raise Oram's head slightly and winched him down into the vat. The precious, thick fluid rose around Oram's flanks and ribs.

Pain shuddered. It was cold. The fluid began slowly to block out the noise, inch by inch insulating him from the mad whirl of others' thoughts. The fluid picked up the signature of Oram's own mind, protecting him from the thoughts battering him, reinforcing him.

Something hovered in Pain's mind. It was an indistinct memory, haloed in fire. That image, the blackness and the running blood, choked Oram's mind with a need to defend at all costs. A drive to kill or be killed so strong that even with the lock broken, it had driven him almost to heart failure.

Pain blinked, jerking up with a gasp of relief as Oram dropped into true unconsciousness. She found herself lying on the floor beside the glass coffin that protected Oram.

The Lady turned off the tap on the empathy fluid when the level of the mucilaginous goo reached Oram's temples. She fetched the blocks from the dissection table to prop the sides of his head so he couldn't turn it and drown.

Pain dragged herself up against the smooth glass of the side. "Air?" she croaked.

The Lady shook her head. "He's breathing for himself. If there's too much air, things could go wrong. I don't know why it is, but it's a mistake I made with Pride. I won't repeat it," she said, glancing at Pride.

Pride blinked, turning her head toward the Lady. "A mistake?"

"Yes." The Lady sat down on the stool by her writing desk. "Your body was the only one that was perfect. I was so close, with you, but growing a human being is harder than growing an animal. With Pain I didn't uncover the tank, and with Shame I let the light in too soon. Justice's bones were not fully grown when I assembled her because I just couldn't wait to pick. She made me feel so . . . guilty; and I couldn't wait for a perfect thighbone, so she limped. It took a few years to figure out what I'd done that blinded you, but it was too much air in the mix. It injured your eyes in some way."

Pride opened and closed her mouth, turned her head away.

"It doesn't mean much to you, I'm sure, but I am sorry."

Pride managed a brittle smile. "While it is utterly unacceptable that you would put any of us out into bodies that you wouldn't want for yourself, I neither need nor want your apology. I do not find my lack of sight such a great disadvantage."

The Lady rubbed her hands together, looking at them for a long time. "I thought that if they weren't crooked anymore, I wouldn't have anything left of her. I thought it wouldn't hurt me anymore. It didn't stop, because the ugly bones were always there . . . so I took the crooked bones out, and put in ones that were straight."

"You cannot make them not part of that body," said Pride calmly. "Desire held them, but they were your bones. Your memories."

"They weren't mine. I was a good girl. They shouldn't be part of me. I didn't want them," whispered the Lady, tracing the fingers of one hand along the faint white lines that ran so precisely up the palm of the other, matching finger to finger. Tears filled her blue eyes. "They hurt. They weren't mine. They're not. They never were."

"That's hurt I can't help you with," Pain said, making her way gingerly to stand beside the Lady.

The Lady turned away from the memories with a shudder, bringing Charm to the surface.

Charm's breath caught under her ribs like a hot coal. She gasped for a breath, but it jerked out of her control, and she wept. She buried her face in her scarred hands. "Oh God . . . my baby . . ." Like a child herself, Charm turned her face in to

Pain's dress, hanging on and beginning to sob. "They killed my Evlaina. They killed her."

Pain stroked Charm's head gently. Her body ached with the aftermath of Oram's ordeal. Her heart ached with the wrenching sobs that had belonged to Desire and now were Charm's.

The Lady twisted suddenly, fighting out of Pain's arms and to her feet. She screamed to the air, to herself, "No, I won't go back to sleep! I didn't do any of that! It wasn't me, and I won't be her!"

Pain took hold of the Lady's shoulders. "Lady, it is her right to weep," said Pain firmly, not to Charm but to the Lady behind Charm's face. "If she wishes to weep for her child, it is simple decency to allow her to do so."

Slowly, Charm's body relaxed. Her eyes still shone, but she lifted her hands to wipe away the tears instead of to cover them. "I've wept before, and probably even enough, but it . . . I feel raw. I'm not sure if I'm more her or more me."

Pain's knees began to give way from sheer exhaustion, and she sank down into the chair that Charm had vacated. "You are you," she assured Charm.

"But I'm not," said Charm, her voice veering back toward hysteria. "I'm not one me. I'm two? Four? Six? How many? Who am I? I'm not who I was and I don't know who I am or who is me."

Pride snatched at Charm's arm. She spun Charm around and gave her a swift shake, her bloodily bandaged hands clutching Charm's arms. "You are the mother of Evlaina. You're Charm, enthraller of princes and emperors, feared by bestial men who abuse you in order to expiate their own weakness." Pride's teeth bared in a fierce hiss—"You were clever enough to grow into someone who could take her shocks in pieces that could be dealt with instead of dying of them. You were strong enough not to die when anyone else would have. You are *Charm*." She shook Charm again, viciously, heedless of her own injuries. "Stand up and act like it!" She let go and slapped Charm. Her bandages left a bloody smear on Charm's face, and on the sleeves of the white robe. Red on white skin, like Shame's birthmarks.

Charm stood as if struck into stone. For a moment she didn't seem to breathe or blink.

Pain looked at Pride, took in her tight lips, the muscles hard in Pride's jaw. The burns didn't matter to Pride as much as standing upright. Pride accepted hurt as a price for her action. She passed none of it on to Pain.

Charm managed a breath, touched the blood on her cheek. "You're right," she managed. Her disorientation and the sight of Pride's bloody hands slid her into the back of her mind.

"We need to treat your hands," said the Lady, coming out of her trance. She took Pride by the wrists and drew her to a stool. The Lady ignored Pride's loathing look and began to collect linen, tweezers, a jar, and bandages as if nothing at all were wrong. She began to gently peel the tattered remnants of loose skin from Pride's bloody, blistered hands. "Tell me if I'm hurting you."

Pain put a hand over her mouth to hide a smile as Pride's lip curled in utter scorn. "I'll take it, Pride," she said softly.

Pride turned toward Pain, her chin coming up in spite of the tear that slid down one cheek. "No. I earned it. It's mine."

The Lady smoothed gel reduced from empathy fluid onto Pride's burned hands. She wrapped them in gauze and turned a pair of gloves inside out but for the fingertips. She rolled the gloves gently right side out over the bandages. "There. Give them a day or so and we'll change the gauze."

"Lady . . . let's not hide from each other. Pain and I have assaulted a prince of Boren. I won't need the bandages changed," said Pride.

Pain stared at her sister ghost, but couldn't contradict it.

"I clawed furrows into his face, and Pain struck him down," Pride said with surreal good humor. "He killed Desire, and he was trying to kill Lady Charm. From his collapse, I assume Pain struck him in the head." Her mouth turned up faintly in cold satisfaction. "The Firedrinkers did not arrest us, but I will be surprised if Emperor Strephon is as understanding."

The Lady did not acknowledge Pride's comment. Instead she shook her head as if trying to clear it. "I think I must be tired. Yes, I'm tired. I think I'll go get a little sleep before morning. Pain and Pride, are you coming?" she asked. "I can get undressed by myself, but you need sleep too."

Pride stood as if too disgusted to argue anymore. "I believe the Firedrinkers will have finished in the house by now."

Pain touched Oram's cheekbone in a brief caress of promise. She didn't know what he had seen, what was so deadly, but she knew that the Firedrinkers were both their best defense and themselves at risk. "I have some things to attend to, but I'll be back as soon as I can."

CHAPTER THIRTY-ONE

Pain went up the back stairs from the kitchen and found John Seabrough's letter waiting on the desk in her second-floor room. He had used his thumbprint in place of a sealing ring.

Pride sat at her desk in the front hall, at her post. She could not see the dark stain on the marble floor, there at the end of her reception desk. There was no sign of Desire. Pain wondered what the Firedrinkers had done with the body.

"What are you up to, Pain?" Pride's head didn't turn.

"I'm taking a letter."

"For someone made to resist torture, you're a poor liar," Pride told her bluntly. "You're part of us. You should want what we want. I understand that you are made to be obstinate, but this is too far to take it. Why persist in things that do not interest the rest of us?"

Pain found her hands balling into fists against her skirt. "You may not care, but I do." The memory of Maude's bruised, trampled body burned behind her eyes as if it had been branded on Pain's brain. Maude's body, Jim's tears.

Pride hesitated. "Do what you think is best, then. When it comes to the city you know better than any of the rest of us."

And Pain knew suddenly and with perfect clarity that the idea of the city falling had concerned Pride enough to make her let go of some control. Pain came down the last three steps. She had always thought that Pride was taller than she was, but of course Pain's eyes were level with Pride's. "I didn't think you'd admit that there was anything that anyone else might be better at."

"There's a funny thing about sitting here at this desk so much. It gives one a great deal of time to think, and to come to fairly precise terms with one's strengths and weaknesses." Pride's voice held dry humor instead of the bitterness that Pain expected.

Embarrassment was a strange emotion, to Pain, coming with a flush of uncomfortable heat.

Pride's lips quirked slightly. "A little blindness now and then would have been far more comfortable."

A laugh rose up from Pain's diaphragm to her lips. "It would be at that." She patted Pride's shoulder.

Pride lifted her gloved hand, covered Pain's with it. Their fingers laced together and for a moment they hung on to each other. "It's falling apart," said Pride quietly. "The Lady is growing more fragile. Charm's display today was disturbing. She's not usually so weak either."

"She has a lot of things to face, with so many memories back suddenly. She wasn't coping very well just then, but she's strong enough for it. We all learned to live with our memories, and the skill is there whether she knows it yet or not."

"A day for surprises. I never thought I'd hear you praise Mistress Charm." Pride's voice held tired, black amusement.

"Charm is far stronger than she used to be. Whether I agree with her or not."

"Ah." Pride sighed, nodded as if that answer eased her mind in some way. "Go on, then . . . and would you please tell your Firedrinkers that I would appreciate it if they were the ones to arrest me instead of making Strephon send the army?"

"Thank you," said Pain softly. By asking for them, Pride

might delay Strephon finding out how little control he had over the Firedrinkers.

Pride flicked Pain's hand off of her shoulder with an impatience born of defense. Imperious Pride again. "You reassure the Lady just by being here that she is still protected. We can't afford for her to break down, so we can't do without you. Not yet."

Pain's lips trembled and she didn't know if she smiled with hurt, or relief, or anxiety. Whatever it was, she pushed it down. She glanced at the front door, hesitated, then hurried through the kitchen, out the back door, and into the fog. The air was so thick with moisture that halfway across the orchard she could see neither the gate ahead nor the house behind her. She made her way through the shrouded trees until the gate loomed up suddenly before her.

A figure in a telltale scarlet coat stood silently in the fog beside the gatepost, keeping watch. "Miss Pain, you'll be tired. You should get some sleep," advised the Firedrinker.

"I have to take a letter."

"I'm sorry, Miss Pain, but you may not leave the grounds." The blank visor was trained on her, waiting.

"I'll only be a few minutes."

"I'm sorry, miss," the Firedrinker repeated.

"I must take this letter. Please," said Pain with soft urgency. "I promise I'll come back. I won't be even an hour."

"Miss Pain, if you will accept an escort, I'll summon someone to take you to wherever you go and bring you back here. If you will not, then we must ask you, respectfully, to remain here," insisted the Firedrinker.

"No. This is personal business. You have more important things to do."

"Miss, at this time there is nothing more important to us than keeping you safe and guarding Orchard House."

"I must take this letter," Pain insisted.

"If we cannot go with you, then it will have to wait," said the Firedrinker firmly.

"It's a letter from John Seabrough to his friend."

A pause. "We're sorry, miss. He does not want you to risk yourself. The army is not something we can control. We can deny them access to Orchard House so long as they do not have an order of arrest from the Emperor, and if they bring such an order we can at least ensure that they behave appropriately; but if they take you on the street without our presence they may do anything. They grow more restless, more violent. Prince Aerleas is getting closer."

"How . . . Are you sure?"

"Miss," said the Firedrinker in a tone of faint disappointment. "We saw the captain's vision. He sent it after the lock came out and before he went silent." The Firedrinker spoke so softly that even standing close Pain could hardly hear the mechanically cloaked voice. "Is he all right, miss? We felt him again, for a little while, and now . . . now there's nothing." Quiet urgency that even the helmet could not disguise.

Pain put her hand on the Firedrinker's arm, on the fine red wool sleeve. "He is alive, and I hope he's recovering. You only can't hear him because the Lady felt it best to insulate him while his brain heals."

The Firedrinker seemed to inhale as if to speak, then made a choked sound, shoulders bunching forward.

"No, no, don't," Pain said hastily. "Don't," she said again.

"I'm sorry, miss. We can't give you a better reason to trust us than what you have already. We want you to be safe. Trust us."

Pain gave the arm under her hand a gentle squeeze. "In the rest of this whole city there is no one who knows you better than I do. If I had never seen any of your faces but one, if I had never known any of you but one, that one would be enough to make me trust you."

"It's . . . it's hard with him gone, Miss Pain. Since he was brought in he's always been with us. Now he isn't. We aren't . . . whole." Even through the helmet, the Firedrinker sounded miserable.

Charm was in despair over being many, while the Firedrinkers were injured by the loss of one. "It will not be forever," Pain told the Firedrinker softly, and hoped it was true.

"We can wait, miss." There was a soft, choked sound from inside the helmet.

"Stop it," said Pain. "Don't hurt yourself. If I've been taught nothing else by knowing all of you, it's to sometimes trust what isn't said." Pain paused. "Pride would like the Firedrinkers to please arrest her, if the Emperor gives the order. She doesn't want the army to do it." She tipped the Firedrinker a wry smile. "She must have come to the same assessment of you all that I have."

"Miss Pride predicts him very well." The Firedrinker paused. "I don't think he will send the army. We are still following his orders."

But not because you have to, thought Pain grimly.

The Firedrinker was a little taller than Pain, but only a little. Pain looked at her own pale reflection in the polished visor. "May I ask you a personal question?"

"Of course, miss."

"Have you visited me?" Pain lifted her hand and reached up beneath the helmet to touch the edge of the Firedrinker's jaw. The skin was satin smooth. No stubble. She was a woman.

"Yes, miss."

"Can you tell me which one you are? Don't hurt yourself, but I would like to know if you're able to tell me."

"I am . . . the woman with the blond hair, miss."

Pain knew her by description instantly. Short, bright gold hair that curled at the tips and around the nape of her neck. She had gray-green eyes and she liked a hard massage using oil scented with roses. She could light all the candles in a room at once, and her bathwater never went cold. "Thank you."

Slowly the Firedrinker nodded.

A quartet of Firedrinkers appeared out of the fog from the direction of the Uptown gate. Their shoulders were pulled up slightly inside their scarlet coats, their strides stiff.

Pain smiled sadly. "I'll take you in to Pride," she told them. "We've been expecting you." She led them through the gate and the veil of fog in the yard.

Pride looked up from the appointment book and inclined her head to the Firedrinkers in grave welcome. "I believe the book is in order. Charm shouldn't have any trouble with it." She closed the book and stepped around the desk, fingers lightly on the surface for reference. "I've been told that the ride to Fortress Isle is very cold. Perhaps you would wait in the solarium while I fetch a shawl?" Pride gestured graciously in that direction. "Lady Charm is there, I'm sure she would appreciate your speaking to her. I'll be down promptly."

The Firedrinkers bowed slightly and stepped through the sitting room to the solarium. Pride put out a hand, touched Pain's shoulder, stepped forward and laid her smooth cheek against Pain's. Something whispered in Pain's mind, but she could not quite catch it, could not decipher it.

Pride smiled briefly, turned, and glided up the stairs.

"Would you like me to help you find a shawl?" asked Pain.

Pride paused, spoke over her shoulder. "Your other shawl is still in the trunk in your room?"

She meant Pain's attic room. None of them thought of the second-floor, working rooms as theirs. None of them would have left any personal thing on the second floor. Cold curled through Pain's blood. Something uncertain that she didn't like. "I'll get it for you."

"I can fetch it," said Pride firmly. "This is something I need to do for myself, Pain." She turned away, ascending the stairs with her back straight and her head high.

Pain stood frozen for a moment, then trailed after the Firedrinkers half in a daze. They stood, speaking quietly to each other near the sideboard. Charm wasn't here. In the greenhouse probably, and it wasn't wise to send the Firedrinkers there.

"Is Miss Pride all right, Miss Pain?" asked a Firedrinker. "She seems a little detached."

"Yes," said Pain, going to look out into the orchard. The mist was starting to recede, as if it were flowing out the gate and down the alley toward Lowtown. The beginning of a fine rain made tiny needles of water on the glass.

One of the Firedrinkers came to stand at her shoulder. "Is there anything that we can do to help, miss?"

Pain risked a look at them, but saw only her white reflection in the visor. She looked back out at the bone trees, bare in the fading light of afternoon. "Could you take us away somewhere? Not to Fortress Isle?"

"The Emperor will know if you don't arrive, and that would endanger both of you and Mistress Charm. I'm sorry. There are some very pleasant rooms at the Isle, if that helps."

Pain leaned her forehead lightly against the cool glass. "Pride has never been outside the gates of Orchard House." A pointless thing to say, but important.

Light changing caught her eye, made her look up past the honeycomb of hexagonal glass panes that formed the geodesic solarium roof. Pride stood silhouetted in the open dormer window of Pain's attic bedroom. The hem of her dress lifted as she stepped up on the little iron railing on the outer sill, balanced for a moment with her hand on the point of the dormer.

Pride let go of the dormer. She fell forward, plunged past high windows of the third and second floors, and smashed against and through the geodesic glass dome.

Pain felt Pride's impact, the daze of her head striking the glass, agony as a support rod slammed through between collarbone and shoulder. Her ribs splintered with the rod's exit and her weight tore the bolts free and brought the rod down still in her body. Her bones shattered as Pride smashed into the flagstone floor. Pain's world went gray. The floor seemed to tilt and wobble under her. The Firedrinkers stood frozen for a moment. Then one spoke, indistinctly. Three moved toward Pride, one turning to Pain, blurs of red coalescing into their proper shape as she focused past Pride's injuries. She ignored the hands held out to her and staggered to Pride. Pain went to her knees beside Pride's broken body, catching her flailing gloved hand and holding on.

Pride blinked at nothing, on her side on the glass-strewn flagstone. She coughed and bloody froth ran down her cheek. "Charm was . . . supposed to . . . be here . . ." Pride managed. She struggled to inhale around the iron transfixing her, but instead her breath ran out in a long bloody trickle.

Pain snatched her hand away, threw herself back into the legs of a Firedrinker, but Pride's personality slipped into her mind like a serpent of ice and fire. A double image swam before her as both of them tried to see through their now-shared eyes. Too much light, too much color, too much too much too much . . . and then darkness.

CHAPTER THIRTY-TWO

Miss Pain? Miss?" The Firedrinker's concerned voice was followed by a touch on her sleeve.

You're not Charm! What are you doing here? demanded Pride from inside Pain's head.

This is my body, give it back to me, Pain said. She tried to push Pride aside.

If I could get out I would, Pride snapped, pushing back. *You weren't supposed to be in the solarium! And where is Charm?*

Give me back my eyes and maybe I can tell you.

And why am I blind still? The Lady said it was because of my body!

Pain struggled, squirmed, and light began to filter in, dark blobs and light streaming around them. *Apparently, she was wrong.* Her skull felt too full, as if it would explode from having too much inside of it.

I told you you were becoming too much your own person, Pride hissed. *You have too much definition of you as . . . not us.*

What were you thinking, jumping like that? Everywhere Pain and Pride touched it was like fingernails on glass, shrill and ragged and irritating.

I thought there wouldn't be anyone but Firedrinkers and Charm in the solarium! Pride jerked their arm away from the Firedrinker who tried to take it, overbalanced because she didn't have control of their legs, and they would have fallen if the Firedrinkers hadn't grabbed both her arms.

"Easy, miss, you'll cut yourself on the glass."

At least let them get us into a chair, Pain said in exasperation.

Icily, Pride let the Firedrinkers guide their body to sit down.

"There, miss. Just breathe deeply, and . . ." The Firedrinker paused. "Miss Pain, are you there? Can you hear me?"

Pain worked her way toward the light, where the mirrored visors of the Firedrinkers were gathered around her. The abrading rasp of Pride squeezed Pain's throat until she couldn't speak. She managed a jerky nod.

"There is nothing wrong with my ears," Pride informed them through Pain's lips.

"No, Miss Pride, I expect not," the Firedrinker said respectfully.

The Lady came running from the kitchen, stopping with a shriek of horror as she caught sight of the crumpled body lying in the middle of the solarium amid the broken glass and iron rods. Blood pooled out from it in a dark slick. She took in Pain/Pride. "What were you thinking, Pride?" she cried.

"'That you would be in the solarium, and that Pain would have gone back to the greenhouse. Do not dare to ask me if I am all right, I certainly am not all right," Pride told her stiffly.

Pain tried to speak but all she could do was make her mouth move silently.

"May I, miss?" asked one of the Firedrinkers, removing his gloves. He crouched by the chair and took her hands. His touch on her skin made a gentle touch on her mind, as light as a brush of feathers.

Will you keep watch on the house? asked Pain. *Just . . . in case Charm needs you.* But she didn't mean Charm and the Firedrinker knew it.

"Yes, miss," said the Firedrinker gently. "Don't be afraid. We won't let any harm come to Orchard House."

"What in the world is going on?" the Lady asked fearfully.

This is intolerable, Pride sighed. Her voice from Pain's mouth was steel-certain, but tempered. "We attacked Prince Phelan in defense of Lady Charm. Under Emperor Strephon, we can hope for no fair trial. We know that no plea of defense will stand to overcome the charge of attacking a prince of Boren. I do not wish anyone else to suffer for it, and Pain feels as I do."

"We understand, miss," the Firedrinker assured her solemnly. There was momentary silence among them.

"Lady Charm," said the Firedrinker holding Pain's hands, "Miss Pride is correct. There were crimes committed both in the assault on you and in the attack of Prince Phelan, even if it was a crime of defense. Emperor Strephon has demanded an arrest be made. Though it is unjust, it will make Miss Pain and Miss Pride safer just now if we comply with our orders. It is possible that by this evening, a fair trial can be more assured or the charges dismissed altogether. Can you walk, misses, if we help you?" he asked.

Awkwardly, clutching the Firedrinker's hands, leaning against and bumping into each other, Pride and Pain managed to get their body out of the chair.

Now look, you step with the left, then I step with the right, Pain suggested. *I'll call it since I can see, and you follow my lead, all right?*

All right, agreed Pride after a moment.

Ready? Me, you, me, you . . .

With a Firedrinker on either side to help her balance, she

took the few steps into the entry. Pain balked as they began to turn her toward the front door. "Please, I should go out the back. It's less fuss that way. . . ."

The mirrored helmets all looked at each other, and then they gently turned her around.

"You're . . . really going to just . . . take her away? Just like that?" asked the Lady, her soft voice shaking with anxiety. "But . . . what . . . what will I do without anyone to help me?"

Charm soothed her. *I'm right here and I'm not going anywhere. Tell the nice Firedrinkers we'll manage. After all, you've been trying to get rid of Pain and Pride for years and now you have.*

The Lady fled down into the dark, weeping.

Charm sighed. *Oh honestly.* She caught their body before she could do more than stagger. Charm imitated the Lady's halting speech. "I-it's all right, gentlemen . . . and ladies, I'll . . . I'll manage." They couldn't leave Pride's body lying around in the house. Charm drew in a deep breath and let it out, then went on in her own tones, as if she'd pulled herself together. "Do you need to take Pride's body?"

"No, miss," one of them told her.

"In that case, would you take it out and lay it outside my laboratory, please? It will keep better out there."

Pain went on counting, trying to feel Pride's action and respond to it smoothly while Pride tried to do the same. She sounded out each of their steps. *Me. You. Me. You.*

One step at a time, the Firedrinkers helped her into the kitchen. Mrs. Westmore was just coming in the back door with Sally.

"What . . . did she do, sir?" asked Sally, taking in the disastrous kitchen and the spattered blood.

"I attacked Prince Phelan when he tried to kill Lady Charmaine," Pride told her, head high.

Sally's pinkly scrubbed face twisted. "Good," she said.

Mrs. Westmore snatched Sally back and shook her arm. "Hush, you! Be sensible."

"No! No, I'm glad!" cried Sally, twisting free and clenching her slender fists. "'E was a beast an' I hope she killed him! He left poor Benna Abrams to bleed to death! You were sorry, you said, you couldn't do nuthin' about him you said," she raged at the Firedrinkers. "Why would you take away Miss Pain over that sick bastard if you were so sorry!"

Charm wrapped an arm around the angry young woman's shoulder. "It will be all right, Sally. You're right, of course, but you misunderstand. The Firedrinkers are taking Pain into custody to protect her. They won't let anything happen to her." She glanced pointedly at the greenhouse, then looked back at them.

"We wouldn't let anything happen to her in any case, miss. The captain wouldn't have liked it," said the Firedrinker on Pain's right.

"There, girl, you see? Now hush," Mrs. Westmore urged.

Pain and Pride had themselves smoothed out a little by the time they'd crossed the orchard. Her walk was a little odd, with a pause at each step. The pair of Firedrinkers took Pain out the garden gate and closed it gently behind her. Pain/Pride slowly disappeared from sight.

"The laundry lady, Maude? Didn't she have a husband?" Charm asked Mrs. Westmore as she led Sally, and the other girls by example, into the kitchen.

Mrs. Westmore nodded as she took off her bonnet and shawl. "Yes, Lady. Jim's 'is name, Lord love 'im. A good man, strugglin' since Maude was killed."

"I need a grave dug, and a new tree planted, and the roof of the solarium repaired. Perhaps he'd know how to fix it. Could you spare Sally to go inquire if he could come tomorrow?"

Sally paused in taking her shawl from her shoulders.

She . . . she'll tell everyone . . . whispered the Lady in terror.

I'm depending on it. We want the Lowtowners to know that Pain . . . well, as far as they know that body attacked Prince Phelan and we want Strephon to think they'll riot if anything happens to her. We need to take every trick now, and risk is part of that.

Sally looked at Mrs. Westmore.

"Yes, Lady, I kin spare her, but . . ." said Mrs. Westmore slowly. A sharp look broke across the plump face and she put her hands on her hips, nodding. "Yes, Lady, I kin spare her." She bent a stern gaze on the maid. "Don't ye dawdle, girl, git!"

Sally jumped, bobbed, and darted out the back door as if she'd been fired from a gun.

"I'm afraid there are no open bookings for you gentlemen this evening," Charm told the two Firedrinkers who came out of the hall carrying Pride's corpse in a rolled-up rug. "If you'd put that by the greenhouse, please. I have private guests coming this evening. I hope you won't deny me company?"

"No, Lady, we've no orders to do that."

"Very well, then I must change. Mrs. Westmore, if you have a cup of tea to spare for these fellows when they've finished so kindly helping me, they've had a hard day." Charm went up the back stairs to change.

The Lady whispered at Charm, *You were wrong about Luther. I tried to tell you that you were. He's a gentleman.*

Not from where I'm standing.

CHAPTER THIRTY-THREE

Slowly Pain began to be able to predict Pride somewhat, and to trust tenuously that Pride would keep walking. The Firedrinkers didn't take her by back alleys. They helped her down the Imperial Way. Partway through Middleton, Sally dashed past them, running with her skirt caught up around her ankles.

What . . . began Pain.

Mistress Charm or the Lady or both. Playing to the crowd, Pride suggested with a warm admiration. She drew up within their body, standing taller. *No shrinking,* she chided Pain. *Stand up straight. The Firedrinkers need to look like they're assisting us, not arresting us.*

We are being arrested, Pain said.

And what will the people do if they think the "white angel" that feeds the little urchins with the extra bread she buys every morning is being arrested? What will they do to your Firedrinkers? Without Captain Oram to act as a focus and keep the mob calm?

A chill ran down Pain's spine like ice water. She knew the Lowtowners far better than Pride ever would.

Exactly, said Pride crisply.

By the time they reached the Lowtown gate, a crowd had begun to gather. Four more Firedrinkers joined Pain/Pride's escort. The Lowtowners stirred restlessly. Pain duplicated Pride, tall with her chin up.

Pride smiled at the people she could only hear. *What are they doing?*

They're just . . . milling. Pain knew this look. Like before they'd rushed Aerleas's guns.

"Ye ain't takin' 'er!"

A man grabbed at one of the Firedrinkers. Pain knew him. A cargo loader from the docks. The Firedrinker intercepted the hand smoothly, turning the man's wrist. The cargo loader went to his knees, and then it was a blur. Struggling bodies pressed against the Firedrinkers, who stood with their backs against Pain, trying to defend her and one another. Without Captain Oram, they could not suppress so much anger. The world began to fall away from Pain, and the assault tore and ripped at her.

"Stop!" cried Pride, voice carrying above the struggle. "You should be ashamed of yourselves! Stop!"

The outward struggle stopped, Firedrinkers and Lowtowners all looking at her in surprise. Pride could feel the weight of their gazes even without Pain to see for her.

Pride supported her voice from the diaphragm, so it carried. "Captain Oram's men are helping me to Fortress Isle while Prince Phelan's incident is investigated. I asked them to take me. It is the law, and I've agreed to go. You are all very good, but you needn't worry for me." Pride smiled gently at the people she couldn't see. She imagined she could feel them, warm and comforting around her. "The Firedrinkers do their duty to protect us as best they can. They do all they can to shelter us from abuse and if they fail in it sometimes, we must remember that it is through no fault of theirs. They follow their orders. It is up to all of us to aid them. I am guilty in self-defense only, and they take me for my own safety."

The crowd didn't know what to make of that, but a familiar voice called from behind her. Bern Ostander's voice shouted, "God keep ye, Miss Pain." The sentiment began to be echoed.

"Let us proceed, gentlemen," said Pride to the Firedrinkers, regal as a queen.

They took her forward again. Ostander's words seemed to spread through the murmuring as if her skirts brushed the words from the cobbles into the air like dust. "God keep ye, miss. God keep ye." As they approached the docks, the men who were wearing caps began to pull them off.

Thank you, Pride, Pain whispered.

Pride caught the words "Cap'ain Oram's gal" from someone in the crowd.

"God keep ye, miss."

It isn't me they're responding to, Pride told her, the warmth of her regard easing Pain a little even as it made their eyes go misty with emotion. *They see you. They see their lady of mercy who brings bread to the sick and feeds the children. They calmed for the sake of the city's "white angel."*

Alongside the dock a little pinnace stood ready for her. The Firedrinkers lifted Pain/Pride lightly across the gap between the dock and the deck.

"Would you like a chair, miss?" asked the Firedrinker on her right arm.

"No, thank you," Pride said at once. "I believe I'd rather stand."

The water carried the last words of a dockworker to them even as the little ship pulled away. "It's a steady, brave soul 'as Cap'ain Oram's gal, God keep 'er."

CHAPTER THIRTY-FOUR

In the privacy of her tower bedroom the Lady found the courage to look at herself. She smoothed the white silk shantung of her bodice, and checked her reflection in the mirror. It had taken her far too long to find a dress that buttoned up the front. Without help, she couldn't do up back laces neatly enough for formal company.

Stop fussing. Your hands are sweating, and you're going to get it dirty.

"Closets full of black ones and we have to wear this. You couldn't choose a color?" The Lady shut the events of the day out of her mind. It had been Charm's day. It hadn't happened to her. It hadn't.

Charm gathered up the dissociated memories, collecting them carefully, keeping to herself and trying to sort them into some kind of order. She didn't jostle the Lady. There were too many little details of behavior that Charm didn't know well enough yet. *A color would clash with my hair,* she said mildly.

The Lady looked in the mirror at the glossy chartreuse hair held up with pearl-tipped pins and bit her lip. *This is the tackiest color you own. I thought I told Pain to throw it out. I don't see why you're so attached to it.*

It amuses me and it amuses others. With me for amusement and you for manners we can't miss. Besides, we do have to actually pay Mrs. Westmore, and Sally, and the other girls. If we play very well, we might be able to hire you a proper lady's maid.

The Lady brightened at that. She went down the long flights of stairs to the front hall. The empty desk made her stop cold just as there was a knock. Charm sighed and opened the door herself. "Count Seabrough, good evening."

"There are four Firedrinkers at your front gate, Lady Charm," he greeted her. "They only let me in because I assured them I was supposed to be playing cards with you this evening. I made sure to ask that they let in the rest of our table and they said that because it was your invitation personally they would."

She gestured him in. "Come in, Count. Please forgive the state of things this evening. It's been an eventful day." The ludicrousness of that understatement made her laugh a little.

Seabrough took in the empty desk and carpet newly arranged in the front hall. He glanced into the card parlor. There was no boneghost at the bar, there were no players at the tables. By this time of night, Orchard House was usually full of talk and merriment. Tonight it stood silent, and Charm was painfully aware of it.

"What's happened here?" Seabrough asked.

The Lady quailed, and Charm spoke for her. "Prince Phelan had a fit of rage on finding his abuse had killed Justice. In his fit, he also killed Desire. I . . . don't know quite what to do, but we're muddling through."

"Mm." Seabrough looked her up and down. "You'll forgive me for saying so, but you are not in a state to entertain this evening, Lady Charm. You look quite pale and tired."

"It has been a difficult day, but it sounds as if the Firedrinkers will be limiting my guests. I hope you'll stay for supper and for cards if anyone else braves the gate?" Charm tipped her head in invitation. "Otherwise I shall have nothing to do but sit and worry."

"We can't allow that," said Seabrough with a smile. "It would be rude of me to leave."

Charm's laugh slipped out, low and warm. "Yes, I know."

He gave her a grin. "I rather assumed you did." Seabrough sobered. "Can you tell me what happened today? Would it be a relief to speak of it, or does it distress you too much?" he asked. "You know I would aid you if I can."

The words warmed Charm. A wobbly smile found its way to her lips and she had to blink hastily. "Thank you, Count, but you're taking enough risk by staying this evening and I think you know it. Your friendship is a great solace."

Another knock. The Lady went to answer it. Anders and his partner for the evening, Lord Hanover, greeted her.

"I finally persuaded Hanover to come have a round of cards," Anders announced to Charm proudly. "I promised him that your excellent cook was still in top form."

"You're too flattering, Mr. Anders, as always," said the Lady with a dimple. "Lord Hanover, welcome back." The Lady greeted him more quietly, with Charm's prompting of title and previous visits.

He and Seabrough have sparred from time to time in the Assembly. He hasn't been back since the night I bled through my gown. I suppose it's safer now that we don't offer upstairs amusements, but if he's here, it's for a political reason, Charm told the Lady.

Then ... he wants to be seen to have come here to meet Seabrough? But I thought ... I don't understand.

Neither do I. Let's figure it out.

Should we really be involving ourselves in gentlemen's affairs?

Charm managed not to laugh. *It's a bit late for that. Remember, we're trying to stay alive?*

"Forgive my lack of staff this evening, won't you? I promise that even if my ghosts are not here, my cook is," she said, answering the brief glance Hanover made toward the empty front desk. "And as you see, Count Seabrough has decided to brave my servantless state, so I expect courage from both of you, too." The Lady gave Anders a bright smile.

"Seabrough is the man of the hour, Lady!" enthused Anders. "Quite the man of the hour! Wouldn't miss seein' him for the wide world! Ah, there he is! Damn me, Seabrough old man, well done, sir!" Anders exclaimed as he caught sight of Seabrough in the card parlor. He left the Lady hanging up his cape as he went to clasp Seabrough's hand and shoulder. "Well done!"

"What has the Count done?" the Lady asked Lord Hanover, collecting her less enthusiastic guest's cloak.

"Didn't he tell you? He's gotten enough leverage to make the Assembly elect him prime minister. All perfectly legal," Hanover told her quietly.

"But . . . Emperor Strephon won't like it." The Lady glanced at the Count and Anders as they went through the red parlor and into the dining room, leaving Hanover and her in momentary privacy. Anxiety made her fidget with one of her dangling curls.

"First he helped put Emperor Strephon on the throne, and little by little he's been nibbling away at the underpinnings of the Emperor's authority by picking up what Emperor Strephon deems not important enough for his attention and returning it to the Assembly and himself." There was admiration in Hanover's voice, along with dry amusement. "A small concession here, a vote there, a bit of decision-making given to him . . . until now I'd say Seabrough has all that he needs." Hanover shrugged, smoothing his steel-gray mustache thoughtfully with his left hand. "At least a prime minister must have his actions voted on. He can't do worse than the Emperor has, certainly. Strephon's pissing away the treasury in spectacular fashion. Unfortunately for Seabrough, the Assembly doesn't meet again until Tuesday."

Hanover wants to be seen as friendly with the rising star. Toasting his rival in good spirit, Charm commented. *Smart man.* A realization grew in Charm's mind like the slow dawn. "But . . . they're voting on Tuesday?" Charm said through the Lady's lips, and admired their gall.

The Lady took the opportunity to quit the field and give their body over to Charm.

"His Imperial Majesty has been requested to come to the Assembly Hall Tuesday morning at ten, and if he's smarter than a hitching post, he'll come. As long as things stay legal, Seabrough's got him dead to rights on this." Hanover gave her his arm as Seabrough looked around for the tardy pair, and strolled Charm toward the dining table.

"Lord Hanover has been telling me of your triumph, Count. I gather I am to congratulate you," said Charm to Seabrough, smiling.

"Well, I'm not sure it's my triumph," Seabrough told her. "Without Lord Hanover's support I very much doubt the rest of the Assembly would have found their courage."

"They're both too dem modest, Lady Charm," said Anders. "They argued like a pair of hyenas from different sides until the whole Assembly met them in the middle. It was brilliant!"

Mr. Anders has remarkable perception, commented the Lady.

No wonder Anders wins when I let you play, Charm said. *Anders has always, always been a good cardplayer. It's why Seabrough likes to play against him. It's a challenge.*

Anders wasn't done with his assessments yet. "Strephon could try to send the Firedrinkers after him like poor Fergus, but the city'd rise up and even the Firedrinkers couldn't protect

Strephon then. By now I assume you've heard that the Low-town mob has gotten their hands on a large shipment of guns?"

"No, I hadn't heard," the Lady admitted, bobbing up in puzzlement while Charm blinked in surprise. "I must not be very bright. I don't understand how you've accomplished all this, Count."

Sally brought in consommé and there was a pause until the little maid went back through the padded green baize door into the kitchen.

"Seabrough's banking is partly in banks in Hemmerholm, so it's secure. With Imperial marks fallen so low in value be-cause of the Devarik trade deals, he's got enormous leverage, now. He bought the controlling interest in the banks that hold the Emperor's rather substantial loans," Lord Hanover explained. "Tomorrow the Emperor will have control of his Imperial allowance left, but little else; and privately he'll be lucky to keep a bent sixpence of that if the Assembly chooses not to defend him when debt collectors demand repayment."

"So Hanover argued for the Assembly to remove Stre-phon's powers of finance on legal grounds of incompetence. Beautiful arguments," added Seabrough. "And when they got done with that they had to decide who could manage things for the Emperor." He shrugged. "If he decides to be sensible tomorrow, he will formally ratify the vote."

Seabrough's looking at us. Smile for the man, he's brilliant, Charm prompted her counterpart.

Charm retreated after dessert, sweetly pleading business with her scant staff so that the gentlemen could smoke. She congratulated Mrs. Westmore, Sally, and the two dish maids on managing an elegant meal out of such simple ingredients. Their smoking concluded, and the Lady carefully paid atten-tion to the drinks and the amusement of the gentlemen so that Charm could concentrate on the cards. Over the course of the evening the two of them managed to make Lord Hanover laugh and smile with apparently real enjoyment and Charm counted it a definite coup.

Seabrough lingered in the front hall after their competition had been sent weaving benignly to their carriages. "Have you thought of anything that I can do, Lady Charm?" he asked seriously. "I make no promises, but after tomorrow I think the Emperor may have to begin appointing assemblymen to administrate various portions of his authority. The Assembly is demanding that he give up the supreme judiciary seat. I might be able to see to it that the new appointees were favorable toward you."

The Lady had gone the whole evening without thinking about the dead boneghosts and the injured Prince. She sucked in a shaking breath as her eyes filled up.

Charm whipped over the top of her and hastily blinked, letting the breath out and settling their body. "I don't know," she said. "The Firedrinkers have taken Pain into custody. That is as safe as she is likely to be."

The Lady spoke up, letting her words carry on from Charm's as if they were the same thoughts. "Thank you for staying this evening, but I think it isn't wise for you to come again. With your new position, it would be best for you to be very morally upstanding. Orchard House isn't known for that."

Seabrough stood for a moment. "Thank you for your concern, but I wouldn't dream of allowing a cad to prevent me from enjoying the company of a lady. I will be back tomorrow night. I believe I can find a pair of fresh sheep to shear," he said with a trace of a smile, "but even if I can't make it sooner, I shall depend on dinner on Thursday. My cook has had Thursdays off for six years and I doubt she'll countenance a change at this late date in her employment."

Charmaine smiled, shaking her head at him so that her

ear bobs swung a little. "I trust you won't do anything foolish, Count."

"I've been a fool once and survived it," he quipped as he put his gloves on.

"In which case I will look forward to dinner on Thursday."

"I have a little present for you, also." He fished in his pocket and produced a small enameled box.

Charmaine accepted it with a chiding smile. "You shouldn't give me gifts. Emperor Strephon won't like it and from the conversation tonight I'd take it you've raised his ire quite enough." Her breath caught as a vision passed behind her eyes. Slim white hands, holding the box, clutching it. The hands relaxed suddenly, and passed the box to Seabrough.

Seabrough smiled. "Well, as I understand it, he isn't giving you this, so if it's just between the two of us that's fine."

Slowly the Lady opened the box. A gleaming heap of capsules lay in it, half filling the box.

"Rejuv . . ." Charm breathed the word in relief past the Lady's lips.

The Lady stirred the capsules curiously. Shattered flashes of impression skittered over her mind. Slim white fingers, one with a gold ring cast in the shape of a loop of violets. Each capsule being opened, emptied, refilled, closed. She jerked her hand back and would've spilled the Rejuv capsules all over the floor if Seabrough hadn't caught her hand with the box and steadied it.

"What's the matter, Lady?" he asked, frowning.

"Who . . . Where did you get this?" the Lady managed.

"From my wife, who found it in the old emperor's belongings. She suggested I give it to you since she was sure our young Emperor Strephon has not thought of your Rejuv."

"How very thoughtful of her." The mindlock spun and whirred. The sound of it whispered in the stillness.

Seabrough smiled, the expression slightly forced. "It still works, I see."

"Yes," admitted the Lady, "but there are only a few commands left that matter."

Someone is trying to kill us!

Don't be ridiculous, it could be left over from killing your emperor. The Lady smiled at Seabrough. "Thank you, Count. This is very, very kind of you. I hope the Countess won't be in trouble if they're noticed missing," she said, closing the box carefully.

"You can count on my wife to cover for herself," Seabrough assured her dryly. "She has never been a fool." He smiled. "Good evening, Lady." Count Seabrough shrugged on his cloak and stepped out into the fog, closing the front door.

The Lady sat down on the top step with the little box in her lap. *What do we do? It was a woman. It could be any woman.*

Charm could feel the mindlock, set hard on this new information. *It might be left over from the Emperor's murder, but if it is then either the Empress or Seabrough's wife killed him. One of them wants us dead as well. No other women could get access to the Emperor's private supply, and no one finds a dead monarch's enameled boxes just lying about. They both have cause. How will we decide between them?*

Countess Seabrough doesn't have cause, so that leaves the Empress, the Lady said.

Charm shook her mental head with a despairing laugh. *For someone who is a woman, you really don't understand them.*

And you do?

Better than you, said Charm in irritation. *Ylsbeth was Empress for four years before Strephon. She had plenty of time to be angry at me about a much better husband. I don't believe for a moment she'd murder me over Strephon's attentions.*

*Maybe she murdered your emperor over your attentions.
What are we going to do about it?* The Lady fingered a dangling
curl.

*You're going to test one of these Rejuv to see what's been added
to them,* said Charm. *Or would you need to know what Rejuv is
made of?*

*It's perfectly simple to test Rejuv. It's the same test I'd use to
test empathy fluid for contamination before I use it,* the Lady said.

It is?

*Well, more or less. Rejuv is a by-product of manufacturing
empathy fluid. It's a purified form of the crystals that grow around
the inside of a vat as the fluid level evaporates.* The Lady started
toward the back door and the laboratory. *It takes hundreds of
gallons to make enough to fill this box.*

Only Inshil ever made empathy fluid. A wave of nausea
rolled through Charm, as she thought of the empaths whose
spinal fluid she now knew it to be. There were that many. . . .

*Well, while I test this, you can think. With Pride and Pain
away we need a lady's maid.*

Charm rolled her mental eyes. She knew this dodge better than anyone. Pretend trivia was important, try not to think
about important or upsetting things. *We'll send a message to the
Ferguses' former lady's maid. Someone must know who she is. For
that matter, we could hire as many of their old staff as we can afford.*

The Lady paused, and they blinked slightly with her surprise. *How completely sensible.*

*I'll have one of the girls take a note. In the meantime, though,
let's go out and you can explain these chemical tests to me.*

The Lady got up. "Let's put on the white mourning first.
It's already ruined. This dress is pretty and I don't want to get
it stained."

The test, to Charm's surprise, wasn't very complicated.

Dissolve the powder from the capsules in a tube of water and add drips of various things to see if the solution turned colors.

Four test tubes of colorless water later, they dripped in two drops from yet another little bottle and the liquid in the tube bloomed bright yellow. "Atropine," the Lady whispered. "Belladonna."

CHAPTER THIRTY-FIVE

ike the plant?

"Yes. This is made from that plant. You . . . I . . . In Insh . . ." The Lady broke off.

In Inshil? provided Charm.

"Yes. The Most Holies used to use it. It comes as a powder like this. A grain or two, when it's diluted and dissolved, just makes the eye relax and look bigger. It's useful for making people think psychics are very mysterious. To make an eyewash you only use a very tiny amount in a lot of water," emphasized the Lady. "This is almost pure atropine. It's extremely poisonous. This much taken by mouth would make all the muscles relax. Relax until you couldn't breathe and your heart would beat less and less strongly until finally you'd die of it."

That's how my emperor died. His heart and lungs failed even though he'd never had heart trouble before.

"This wasn't put into these capsules a long time ago," the Lady said reluctantly. "The impression on just an object would have faded if it had been as long ago as that. We still don't know if it was Strephon behind his father's murder. And this woman wants to kill us. Added into it, this is a poison that we would use. She can make it sound like an Inshili thing."

If you touched the hands of the woman who poisoned these capsules, would you know it was her? Charm's mind voice was low and urgent.

"Yes, why?"

Because we'll have a chance to shake a lot of hands at the Empress's birthday masque. A thought and Charm surged to the surface. "Oh God . . . Seabrough! She might not be after us at all!" Charm snatched up their skirts abruptly and ran up out of the greenhouse.

What?

"Count Seabrough may have kept some of the Rejuv! She may have counted on his doing so, or he could have been given some separately." She bolted through the orchard, through the house, hurtling herself out of the front door and down the steps, down the drive to the gate.

The Firedrinker posted there looked at her in surprise. "Lady . . . did you want . . . to speak to me?"

"I need to get a message to Count Seabrough immediately. The Rejuv he got for me is poisoned. He mustn't take any of it," explained Charm, panting a little.

The expressionless helmet lifted for a moment. "The patrol nearest the Seabrough house is going there immediately. Thank you, Mistress."

Charm didn't relax even slightly. "The Emperor . . . he hasn't given you any orders about Count Seabrough, has he?"

"No, Lady." The emotionless voice was at odds with the curious turn of the helmeted head.

They stood in terrible silence, Charm twisting her fingers together in anxiety.

The Firedrinker stiffened. "Mistress, what kind of poison is it?"

"Atropine . . . belladonna. Is he all right?"

"What should we do until the doctor arrives?"

The Lady stared at the Firedrinker, at the open street spreading out past them. The cobbles seemed to yawn out, a huge expanse of the unknown that threatened to swallow her.

He's going to die. Because of us he's going to die . . . beginning to panic.

"Mistress, please!" said the Firedrinker urgently.

Charm whipped over the top of her. *Tell me. Don't look. Think. Atropine poisoning. What would you do for atropine overdose?*

Inside her own skull, the frightening world shut safely out, the Lady shivered. *If . . . if he just took it, they need to make him vomit. If the doctor has activated charcoal in his lab, he needs to bring it.*

Charm repeated the instructions.

The Firedrinker just stood, statue-still. They nodded absently now and then.

Charm snarled internally for more information until the Lady gave in, repeating the advice. "You may need to breathe for him until the doctor arrives. Can one of you put up your visor?"

The Firedrinker shook their head. "Only in private with Miss Pain."

Fireplace bellows, said the Lady. *It'd be better than nothing if they can keep his lips closed enough around it and pinch off his nose. Make sure they tip his head back so his airway is open. They'll do best if they can use it in synch with his own breathing, to help him. Try not to interfere with his own breathing, and be gentle. Don't burst his lungs.*

Charm told the Firedrinker. "You could take off the tube and just use the broad gasket at the bottom of the bellows," she added, "if that's easier to seal his mouth around."

The Firedrinker nodded slightly. "I've told them."

Charm paced.

"The doctor is there, Mistress," they announced.

"What does he say?" Charm asked. "What's going on?"

"They are trying to get the charcoal down him, Lady. It's

hard for him to drink it without vomiting more." The tension in the Firedrinker's body made them look like a statue in a coat more than a human being.

The Lady looked out through Charm's eyes like a child peeking around her mother's skirts.

It's all right, Charm told her. Then, slightly sourly—*You can come out now.*

If you wouldn't mind . . . I'd rather stay here. I can think here.

Are you going to do this every time we look past the gates?

I'm not up to the outside world. It isn't my responsibility, countered the Lady.

Charm snorted with brief amusement. *How slow could that doctor possibly be?* She paced again, and the too-long grass whisked wetly at her skirts.

If we were in Inshil it would not take so long.

It would take just as long, snapped Charm. *Strephon hushed his father's murder up. He must've. The end symptoms aren't something a competent doctor could miss . . . but why would he do that if it wasn't him?*

Emperor Strephon didn't do it. It was a woman's ring. A woman's hands. As to the lesser symptoms, this emperor of yours could've had a lesser dose.

The Firedrinker's helmet lifted slightly then sank a bit as if they'd inhaled deeply and let it out. "The doctor asks us to tell you that he believes Count Seabrough will be all right thanks to your advice." The stress drained out of their shoulders. "It will still be a bad night for him, but he's expected to recover."

The Lady echoed the Firedrinker's sigh of relief.

"Thank you," said Charm. She reached out, breaching common protocol, and squeezed the Firedrinker's forearm warmly. "Thank you," she repeated, looking up into the mirrored visor as if she could see through it to the face inside.

"Please go back to the house, now, Lady; or to the lab."

The Lady reached to pick up their skirt and turned them back toward the house. *Now we just have to figure out who's trying to kill whom this time, and why. You do realize this could mean Strephon didn't kill his father at all. He could easily have been someone else's pawn.*

The mindlock spun and whirred.

Charm retreated into their skull, since the Lady seemed to be doing the walking. *There's still the command that none of his sons inherit his throne.*

"Who will you put there instead? You seem determined to ignore that point."

Did you have a candidate in mind? asked Charm, half reasonable and half waspish that she was being picked at.

"What about that Seabrough of yours? He certainly has the political acumen." The Lady frowned. "At least you're not sleeping with him."

I'm not sure he'd like being emperor.

"It isn't a question of liking it."

CHAPTER THIRTY-SIX

Fortress Isle loomed at the mouth of Borenguard Harbor like a dull gray threat. Its guns, combined with the batteries at either end of the harbor's crescent, promised death for any country bold enough to try attacking Borenguard by sea. It also housed criminals too dangerous or too important for the stockades. Pain/Pride surveyed the place as their boat pulled up to the pier. Somewhere in this gray place, Colonel Fletcher and his men were imprisoned. Possibly even in the dungeons. Prince Phelan was supposed to be here as well.

Pain/Pride steadied themselves with the Firedrinker's offered hand, careful as Pain put her foot on the damp stone step, accepted their body's weight, and Pride lifted the other foot out of the boat. *That was quite good,* Pride congratulated her companion. "Do you need to take me to my room immediately?" she asked, as they helped her through the inner curtain wall.

"No, miss. Is there something you wish to do or see on the Isle?"

"I'd like to call on Prince Phelan," Pride said.

"If you wish to, miss, but he . . . has become quite unbalanced."

"Thank you, I'll make sure to let you stay between him and me," Pride assured them. "We're unsteady enough without being attacked."

Prince Phelan stood as the Firedrinkers unlocked his door. The inside of his cell was a simple bedroom, but all the walls were padded with thick quilting. His tension faded as he saw Pain. "You're making calls to the prison now?" he asked scornfully. "How much are you charging?"

"I wanted to ask you about Justice," Pride explained through Pain's lips.

Phelan's mouth twisted up in a frustrated snarl. "Your bloody witch took her from me. She thinks she's so clever, but she's not. I want my Justice back and as soon as Strephon tracks down how you're framing me, I'll have her back. I won't let you keep her locked up away from me!" He bellowed the last words at Pain/Pride.

Pride drew herself up, all shocked dignity, drawing outrage from a vast, long-buried store. "Highness, Orchard House has been pleased to offer you our very best for decades. Nothing in that has changed. No one there is framing you for anything. Who told you such a terrible thing?"

Not going to talk about us keeping Justice from him? Pain asked, amused in spite of herself.

Naturally not. That's true.

Phelan's anger faltered, as if he were unused to being taken seriously. "Strephon said it was you bitches, keeping her away from me."

I suppose we're going to talk about it after all. Pride held in an impatient sigh. "Is Strephon's word to be taken so infallibly? Was he infallible before he was emperor?"

Phelan frowned, rubbed his scarred temple, and raked his hand into his hair. "Strephon? He's always been a rat-faced little liar, but . . . someone's been doing . . . something. Strephon suspects me of gunrunning, even though the Firedrinkers

SARA A. MUELLER

know I didn't. I never did that! There's some damned woman at the bottom of this, you mark my words!"

"Miss, in this state he has an ongoing paranoia of women to the point that he won't eat if one of the more obviously endowed among us brings him food," murmured the Firedrinker standing guard. "It is a deeply buried, ongoing symptom. He is fixated on Mistress Charm right now, but it has been other women in the past."

Pride licked her lips, thinking. "Your Highness, tell me about Father Killarin?" she requested.

"The damn bitch, she set me up," said Phelan. "Killarin, he was wise to her tricks. He told me all about it. How the bitch we see was the 'undesirable' element that their mind-fuckers locked down when she was a kid in Inshil." He laughed bitterly. "They made her into their loyal woman. That's funny twice, isn't it? A loyal woman and how they locked her down, but my father let her loose with a lock? Yeah, I know Inshil's precious Lady Charmaine is in there, plotting and planning against us. That's how she dodged the Firedrinkers and Luther. I know it all," he hissed.

Pride tipped her shared head to one side in curiosity. The action made Pain wince. "Have you told this to Strephon?" she asked.

"He's so fucking sure he's got the Firedrinkers dancing on a string. Says he knows they're loyal because of Oram." Phelan laughed again. "Oram. I went first, so when they got to him they'd practiced the surgery. By the time they got to Aerleas's brat and the whore they had practice, but me? Father ruined me!" he bellowed savagely, slapping sharply at the scar on his temple. "It should have been ME on the throne!" Phelan paced the room. He stopped in front of what looked like a firm cushion fixed to the wall over the end of the bed and slammed his fist into it. "I was. ME! That miserable bloody butcher Ostander, telling Father they could help me, but they didn't. They RUINED ME!" He slammed his fists against the cushioned wall.

"What was your talent, Highness?" asked Pride calmly.

Tears in his eyes made Phelan stop shouting and turn away from her. He sat down on his bed facing the padded wall, huddled in his misery. "I was telekinetic." His breath hitching made his broad back heave. "I was going to be like Father, and I practiced to get it under control. Fine, you know, like his? Father could sign his name with his telekinesis. He could set a watch from across the room. I could lift a wagon of bricks, but I couldn't do what he did. I practiced and practiced, but I never could. And they ruined me."

"Did no one warn you that it was dangerous to overuse such a massive power?" she asked. "That it could cause damage to your mind as well as your body?"

Phelan's back shuddered. He was weeping. "I had to be like Father. They just wanted to make me weak. Father said the surgery would make the headaches stop. He said it would make the rages stop," he rasped through his sobs, pummeling the padded wall with an impotent fist. "They ruined me. I was their goddamned experiment." He snarled, slamming his fist over and over into the wall. "They worked it out in time for the fucking Firedrinkers, and for Oram and for her. And now she's taken Justice away from me. They all want Father, the bitches; but the little ones, before they grow up to be bitches, they still like to play with me."

"Thank you," Pride said to the Firedrinkers. "I've heard quite enough."

Prince Phelan was still ranting when the Firedrinkers locked the door.

CHAPTER THIRTY-SEVEN

The day of the Empress's birthday masque, Charm examined their reflection in her mirror critically. Hyacinth and the hairdresser she'd found, and young Sally, matched Charm's review. Charm's hair sported a new color: pale ashen blond.

"You've done a superb job with the color of my hair," Charm praised the finicky little man with his curling tongs. "It is the Empress's hair exact."

The hairdresser beamed at her in the mirror. "My dearest Mistress Charm, I had only to let nature take her place; though she is not so extravagantly courageous in her ways as you," he said, bowing.

It was bizarre to see herself so, but Charm had to admit the hairdresser had done his job with exceeding skill.

It is my hair! My hair that you cover up with your colored powders, snapped the Lady. *Your precious emperor had a certain type of coloring he liked in his pets.*

Charm shook her off and considered herself in the mirror again.

Not less strange than the hair was the tasteful, restrained gown. Oyster satin and gold brocade enriched the pale hair. The beauty of this gown was not in the decoration, but in the draping. The way the satin lay in gentle folds as a counterpoint to the stiffness, the richness of the heavy brocade. A new corset with not a little strapping-power restrained Charm's bust-line somewhat. The ripple of the oyster satin, and a collar of diamonds flowing in an over-lavish cascade, helped hide that no corset was truly up to that job. It had taken some care to achieve the look of an elegantly restrained evening gown ruined by gaudy jewels, as Pain and Hyacinth had both reported of the Empress's wedding gown. No one would mistake who Charm was costumed to be.

"Are you sure?" asked Hyacinth for the seventh time.

Charm smoothed on a touch of colorless lip conditioner, and hooked the wires of her pretty gold mask behind her ears. "Don't be silly, Hyacinth. I've already sent my acceptance, and I've nothing else to wear. How is the Empress's dress?"

"It's better on her than I thought it would be. And she requested some padding that's helped," admitted the dressmaker. "She's refused to let anyone see it. When I delivered it this afternoon, the Empress threw Countess Seabrough out while she tried it on, and had me wrap it back up. She said she wouldn't leave it alone for a moment for fear of someone seeing it. She wants it to be a complete surprise."

"Does she know about my dress?"

Hyacinth bit her lip, and then nodded. "She asked me."

"How did she seem?"

"I don't know." Hyacinth threw up her hands. "She's a cipher in a woman's skin. And Countess Seabrough is seething around making sure no one else can get near her."

This is a terrible idea, insisted the Lady, but she didn't make any attempt to take over their body.

Can you dance? Charm asked her, rising.

Of course!

Then I hope you'll help me with it. I never learned.

There was a quality of surprise to the Lady's moment of silence. *I . . . Yes, of course.*

Charm wished she knew whether her counterpart was flattered by the request, or was simply trying to get them through the evening intact.

At seven, a coach arrived without warning. The same plain carriage with its mismatched horses. The driver gave her a smile as he put out a hand to help her into it. With Pain's much-too-plain greatcloak enveloping her and hiding her hair, Charm took her courage and her gall one in each hand, and got into the carriage.

The carriage delivered her to a back door of the palace, where a trim maid in a starched cap and apron was waiting. She curtsied very politely as the driver helped Charm down. "Good evening, Mistress. Her Imperial Highness asked me to meet you and to see that you had a chance to refresh as you'd like. She asked that you forgive her asking you to come in so stealthily, but she wishes to enter the masque with you." The maid dimpled.

"What is amusing you?" asked Charm, smiling openly back beneath her mask.

The maid looked flustered. "Oh, no, Lady, I wasn't laughing at you. And I don't know why she wants it this way. Honestly. No one knows. Not even Countess Seabrough."

"How did she get dressed in any complex gown without assistance?"

"She hopes you will come and lace her up. The hairdresser just left, and I've got her into all her underpinnings. She's all ready. She only needs her gown on."

"I have money to wager that Countess Seabrough's not very pleased," Charm whispered naughtily.

"I couldn't say, Mistress." But the maid's dimple told the tale. "I'm sorry, Mistress. I'd get in terrible trouble for familiarity."

Being too friendly with you won't do the poor girl's reputation the least bit of good, the Lady pointed out.

"I understand," murmured Charm to both her interior critic and the accompanying maid.

"Thank you, Lady."

The maid took her to the Imperial chambers, and the familiarity of the trip made Charm's throat tight. This time, though, lamps shed more golden light, and the staff were hustling back and forth. Every single one stared at her. She couldn't see their faces around or under the deep cowled hood, but the weight of their eyes pressed and slid off the concealing cloak. The Empress's chambers were off the sitting room Charm had seen when she came to say good-bye to the old emperor. Countess Seabrough, costumed as the sun in glittering gold lamé, came out of the Emperor's room as Charm hurried through the sitting room with its fireplace blazing. If anyone had the impertinence to come to the Empress's birthday dressed as the sun, they might at least do something about having the same boring, ash-blond hair, Charm observed. She kept her head down, relying on the concealing shadow of the greatcloak, hurrying in the maid's wake.

"I don't know who you are, but if she is less than stunning, woman, I will have you and that slatternly dressmaker beaten," hissed the Countess, as if her words were knives thrown at Charm's anonymous back.

It seems strange that Count Seabrough or one of the others didn't try to find out from us, the night Hyacinth interrupted their cards, fretted the Lady.

Of course they didn't tell, Charm murmured, blinking quickly to be sure she didn't tear up and spoil her subtle makeup. *They're my friends.* Though she hadn't realized it before, and wasn't sure if it was absolutely true.

Perhaps they're afraid of the Empress, suggested the Lady.

Charm snorted internally. *Perhaps they don't care for Countess Seabrough.* Count Seabrough had not told his wife about

Hyacinth's call, maybe because she hadn't told him about the Rejuv being poisoned. An old story of marital issues. A hundred men had told it, over the years, in Orchard House's cardroom. What would a man like Seabrough do once his trust was broken?

The maid knocked on the door opposite the Emperor's, opened it at Empress Ylsbeth's quiet bidding, curtsied as Charm passed her, and closed the door with only the smallest click of the latch to denote the fragile privacy between this room and the glittering, sun-robed Countess.

Empress Ylsbeth rose from the stool before her boudoir. Her usual pale hair had been powdered brilliant chartreuse. It was braided up the back, with smooth flat bows of hair between the twists to better display the unlikely color. Whoever had done the Empress's hair knew enough to make sure Charm's trademark spiral of hair trailed down the Imperial neck. There was enough padding in the corset to put every bit of the Empress's bust as high as it could possibly be, near indecency, so that she appeared to have much more endowment than she actually did. Padded hips were simplicity by comparison.

Charm curtsied. She lifted the cloak hood carefully from around her own pale, elegantly swept-back hair and untied the bow that held her cloak closed. "Good evening, Majesty."

"Good evening, Mistress." The Empress surveyed Charm with a wan smile. "Thank you for attending." She put out a slender, white hand.

Charm took the bare Imperial fingers and curtsied. This was not the hand that had poisoned the Rejuv capsules. But if not Ylsbeth, then who?

Ylsbeth raised her up and went to the massive, brocade-draped bed, where a sheet of silk covered the black gown laid out upon it. "I felt sure you would understand. I'm pleased that you did."

"I'm not sure I do understand, Majesty; but I would like to," Charm invited as she went and took up the underskirt to help put it carefully over the Empress's head.

"Oh come, Mistress, which of us is whom? By the time I came to Borenguard you had been the Emperor's wife in all but name for more than fifty years." Arms and head free, she held the waistband so Charm could fasten it around her padded hips.

"We were not what it seemed, Majesty. We were only friends until the last handful of years." She wrapped the overskirt onto the Empress. "The only Empress I have actually offended against is you."

"He was kind," Ylsbeth hastened to add to her first, embittered words, refusing Charm the blame, "but Devarik sent me as a hostage to avoid his wrath, to avoid Aerleas the Butcher."

Charm held the bodice up and hurried behind the Empress to lace it where Ylsbeth couldn't see her. "Inshil refused to pay that price, and much good did it do them," she said stiffly.

"Did you love the Emperor?"

Charm didn't imagine for a moment that Ylsbeth meant Strephon. He had destroyed everything any of her ghosts had ever loved. "I did my best to make him love me, of course, because, honestly, it was in my best interests." And that was, after all, what Charm was for. It felt off in her own mind, now, when a few months ago she'd been sure of it. The Lady winced back, but there wasn't time to examine why. The Empress was waiting with calm, sweet patience. "He was a pleasant jailer, and he was as kind to me as he could possibly be. I didn't mind him. I very much looked forward to his coming to see me; but I certainly did not love him."

The Empress's voice was quiet. "I asked him, once, how he'd learned to be a friend to a woman. He said he learned it from you."

It touched Charm unexpectedly at the same time that she concealed the urge to snort. But at least he'd learned it. She supposed that was something. A sad, limping something. "When our emperor died, why did you not go back?"

"Devarik needed to hold off Aerleas as much as ever, and I am spoiled goods for every other possible marriage."

My family wanted to keep me. They cared, said the Lady. *When this is over, we could go back . . .*

There is nothing to go back to, or you wouldn't have made Pride. Charm tied off the lace at the top of the bodice, carefully on the inside where it wouldn't trail down the back of the gown and ruin the line.

Empress Ylsbeth put on her mask. "Good likenesses of one another, are we not?"

Charm forced her head up, made herself step to the Empress's side. It was a good illusion, for all Ylsbeth was tall and she was short. "Miss Barker has outdone herself," she admitted, "but even in three inches of heel, I'm too short to truly be mistaken for you."

"I counted that into my idea," the Empress assured her. "Your earrings are too understated. Take them off. You'd better put them in your pocket, I wouldn't want Seabrough to make them vanish out of spite. She's horribly frustrated about my keeping this a secret." Ylsbeth went to the great jewel cabinet on one wall and brought out the massive earrings she'd worn at her wedding to Strephon.

"Majesty, I . . ." Charm started to refuse.

The Empress's certainty faltered. She forced a small smile. Restrained. She couldn't seem to break out of that ladylike restraint. "I'm sorry. Of course. It would get you in terrible trouble," Ylsbeth whispered. For a moment, very much her young age.

Charm made herself laugh. She'd done it so often at Orchard House. It was more difficult to make it sound natural, here. "Oh Majesty, no. No, I was only going to say I didn't deserve such a gesture. I'm happy to be 'in trouble.'"

"We have shared everything else. Earrings seem little enough." Ylsbeth came and took off Charm's earrings, slipped them into the pocket in the seam of Charm's brocade skirt, and one at a time hooked the great, glittering monstrosities into Charm's ears, arranging cunning wires over the tops of Charm's ears to help support the weight. "If they get too heavy, you can change them partway through. Keep them, though. My gift for your courage to come tonight."

"They will feed a great many people," Charm told her, and offered a real smile. Offered a long pause for the Empress to object, or take back her gift. But Ylsbeth only nodded. Charm swallowed a sudden lump in her throat. "I'll make sure Lowtown knows where it came from."

You forget who you are, accused the Lady. *You are not Pain.*

Ylsbeth hooked her arm through Charm's, let her hip tilt a little. In the mirror, a very good impersonation for all the Empress was obviously taller. And this was only the second time she'd seen Charm.

Charm did laugh then, and drew the young empress's arm in closer. "Come, then, Majesty. Let's go make your position clear. And if it goes wrong, remember you can blame me."

You're going to regret that generosity on Tuesday, when you don't have Pain to protect you, said the Lady.

That is mine to choose, not yours, snapped Charm. *I didn't always have Pain's protection, and some things are worth the beating.*

But even as she thought it, she wondered when. When had that been true? She couldn't remember. It must be the province of one of the boneghosts.

Arm in arm, the brocade skirt of her disguise light against the Empress's raven black, they went out through the sitting room. The little maid who'd showed Charm in waited there, and stared when she saw them.

"The Countess and Emperor Strephon have gone to the ballroom together, so that you may enter last, Majesty," she reported.

The Emperor had entered his wife's birthday masque with another woman on his arm.

Below her black mask, the Empress's smile was thin. "How kind they are."

Charm had never been in the great public spaces of the palace. Amber wooden panels, polished until they shone, reflected the candle and gaslight. The reflected light enriched Charm's brocade until the gold threads all but glowed and the oyster gray glimmered like tarnished tears. By contrast, the Empress's black satin was rendered into an inky void overlaid with gleams. The harsh glitter of black sequins and the sheer organza teased the viewer with all the fine creamy skin of her shoulders and the column of her throat and then the pink diamonds and the bright elaborateness of her hair.

They might be two new boneghosts: Elegance and Comedy, thought Charm. Deceptive Comedy and treacherous Elegance. The doors of the great ballroom loomed ahead in the golden light, all beveled crystal and gilded lead. Those doors alone would buy Orchard House five times over.

The Lady quailed, panicking. *I can't do this. I can't. They'll all see you and think I'm as immoral as you are.*

Survival is not immoral. Winning our freedom is not immoral. We must know who poisoned my emperor, and who poi-

soned Count Seabrough. *We've found out nothing from listening in Orchard House. We need to be here. This is not only for our freedom. It is our life at stake, now. No one will know who we are if we don't tell them.* It was not true, of course, but if the Lady would believe it that was enough to get them into the ballroom.

"Are you all right?" asked Empress Ylsbeth.

"Nerves," Charm admitted. "I'm not sure I remember how to dance." But she wasn't sure, as she said it, if that was true. If it was herself or the Lady who'd learned. The definitions around her were as misty as the black organza around the wrong shoulders.

Ylsbeth squeezed Charm's arm as the crystal doors opened before them and they stepped out on the Imperial balcony that overlooked the ballroom.

The chamberlain rapped three times with the butt of his staff, his basso carrying over the vast crowd of the court. "Her Imperial Majesty, Empress Ylsbeth, and Mistress Incognita."

There was quiet for a moment. Coming in with their arms linked, there was little to choose between them save for their height. "Charm" tall and "the Empress" small. Emperor Strephon, paused in the act of murmuring into Countess Seabrough's ear, stood with his mouth half agape.

The Empress fluttered her ebony fan, and by pressure of her arm and hand cued Charm so that they sank into identical curtsies.

Lord Hanover clapped, firmly, loudly, and Sir Lyle put down his glass to laugh and join the applause. Slowly the rest of Borenguard followed their lead, until the applause at their feet was thunderous, laughing, and the party swirled back into life. Strephon hurried to meet his wife. He hesitated, looked from one to the other of them.

"Is this what you've been up to, my dear?" he asked, the

endearment clunky and obvious as the nobility began to whisper all around the massive ballroom. "You have hurt Countess Seabrough's feelings by not confiding this to her. . . ."

"I hoped she might enjoy the joke," said Ylsbeth.

"But come now, tell me who this lady is." Strephon gestured in impatience at Charm.

Ylsbeth's soft, rouged mouth dropped open slightly, and Charm's, without any colored cosmetic, did the same. Hyacinth had designed their Colombina masks, and though they showed the lower face, each mask had wings that covered their temples. No one could see Charm's mindlock. Charm hardly dared to breathe in her anonymity. She did not coquettishly flutter her fan. She didn't tip her chin up. Instead she lowered her chin slightly, turned her hand out, let it fall, and curtsied to the floor. Impeccably precise. A lady could not afford to be sloppy.

Silence resounded like a tolling bell.

This precise moment was what Ylsbeth wanted, Charm realized. Not the entrance. This tableau for all of Boren to see. "The Empress," by many inches the smaller figure, curtsying to "the Mistress," who stood beside the Emperor. Each dressed as the other. The courtesan with the Emperor, and the Empress forced to curtsy to it. Charm's breath caught at the audacity of it, at the brilliance. Ylsbeth had forced them all to see. Charm's whispered status was a thing they must now all own.

She has humiliated you!

She's brilliant.

Like a confused youth at his first ball, Emperor Strephon glanced toward Countess Seabrough, drawing every eye to the Empress's lady of the wardrobe. Countess Seabrough, in her splendid gold, far more expensively dressed than either Empress Ylsbeth or Charm, clutched the stem of her champagne glass. Charm wondered briefly if it would shatter.

Slow red crept up Strephon's neck. "Ylsbeth, what have you done?" he hissed at his wife.

"Is Your Majesty not amused?" Ylsbeth's soft voice was dulcet as she put out her hand to Emperor Strephon. A commanding, slender hand. The glorious room and walls, the palace around them, was Empress Ylsbeth's domain, clashing magnificently with her gown and her hair and the contradictions of seeing the Emperor's mistress so. "They are holding the dancing for us?" Empress Ylsbeth prompted her stepson-husband. She waited, all serene patience, hand suspended in open air.

Strephon's fist flashed before anyone could move.

Ylsbeth didn't flinch, though the backhand flung her head to one side.

Multiple faint hisses, and then the ballroom, crammed with Uptown's finest, was utterly silent with the Firedrinkers ramrod-straight in punctuation at the doors.

Slowly, Ylsbeth turned her head back to face her seething husband. The blow had raised a teary shine in her eyes within the mask, but her hand did not move. Waiting in patience.

Strephon struck her again, open-handed on the other side.

Ylsbeth turned her head slowly back, blinking in a quick flutter, hand never wavering.

There, thought Charm, was courage. A picture of herself bizarrely not her.

I could make someone like that, offered the Lady, until Charm could easily imagine someone so elegant and so much more suited to this deadly regal game than a common whore. The Lady whispered temptation into Charm's thoughts. *The mindlock won't let me do it, but you could make a Courage. It would be easy. She'd be better at this than you are. You could just close your eyes until you're safe back at Orchard House. . . .*

How easy it would be to fall back, to let someone else do

this. The mindlock whirred softly. Charm clawed the idea down even as the Lady leaned, pressed until Charm wanted to scream. She locked her eyes on Ylsbeth, standing brave and defiant in Charm's clothes. *Is that how Ylsbeth sees me?*

No one wants you.

The mindlock ticked and whirred softly as the Lady stirred, tried to do . . . something.

You just need to ease the mindlock, tempted the Lady. *Let me do this, and it won't be our problem anymore.*

Charm took care to keep the snarl well away from her face. *No. I'll make no ghosts on purpose.*

The Lady fled into their mind.

"Imperial Majesty," said Lord Hanover softly, though it was uncertain which Imperial Majesty he meant.

Emperor Strephon stood, fuming, furious and red-faced. Around the room, the Firedrinkers didn't move, but the nobles glancing at them gave all those scarlet coats sudden weight. It was Ylsbeth who broke the standoff. She turned her hand gentle, head turning meek and modest. Turning back into herself in a costume of Charm.

"I'm so sorry, Majesty," she managed, soft voice trembling. "I thought you'd enjoy my little joke. Forgive me. Dance with me even though I'm stupid? For my birthday?"

The Firedrinkers remained frozen. Unnaturally still.

There was nothing else Strephon could do without leaving the field entirely in those slender, soft fingers. Emperor Strephon put out his hand in an impatient snap, and Empress Ylsbeth laid her meek fingers, so at odds with costume and hair, on it. The Empress turned her hand, lowered it to Charm in dismissal. Strephon paused to hiss something to a server. The man paled and slipped out. The music struck up as Strephon led the Empress to the floor, and the Imperial couple danced. Strephon in a temper was a terrible dancer, jerky and unsubtle.

Lord Hanover led a striking older lady costumed as a pale green moth, presumably Lady Hanover, to the floor. The assembled nobility of Boren came slowly to life, beginning to move.

Charm rose from her curtsy. She must remember to send Lord and Lady Hanover flowers.

It would be an insult, coming from you, hissed the Lady. *She would never accept them.*

Do you think she would accept them from the Empress? Charm didn't bother to keep the archness from the thought.

The Empress is ruined by your touching her. Emperor Strephon will divorce her, now.

He can't, and she knows it, Charm realized. *The Firedrinkers obey her as well as him. It was she who sent for me to attend my emperor's deathbed.*

Or else they did as she asked simply out of respect for her!

Charm surveyed the Firedrinkers around the ballroom. *And that should frighten Strephon even more.*

CHAPTER THIRTY-EIGHT

Other couples trickled gradually onto the floor after Lord and Lady Hanover's example.

You've served the Empress's foolishness. You should go. The longer you stay, the more your emperor will be sure you had a part in his embarrassment, hissed the Lady.

He is not my emperor. Just the thought made her want to growl in outrage. But at the same time, she could feel the eyes of every woman in the room on her like biting ants. Their very dignity eroded by her presence. No one approached her. A yawning gap of space surrounded her, as if to touch Charm was to be infected by her.

Around the room, the green baize doors that divided the palace from the servants' halls, quiet doors hidden away in corners, opened. More Firedrinkers in their scarlet coats came in, silent and causing no commotion. A loose ring around the ballroom. Pairs moved around to flank each of the public doors two on each side and the base of the Imperial stairs. One, emerging from the door under the Imperial stairs and stationing himself silently at the base of the stairs, wore a white sash under his broad black belt. He stood at quiet parade rest.

Is that Captain Oram? asked the Lady. *Did he come out of his coma?*

Not that I'm aware of.

Emperor Strephon must've replaced him. They need a commanding officer, after all.

Or he wants Boren to think that Captain Oram can be replaced.

Movement toward Charm caught her attention. At the wall of the ballroom, a tall figure in an admiral's uniform took one more step, and hesitated as several people around the room saw him, recognized his motion. The looks caught and spread around the room, several noble ladies openly craning to see if the Prince would approach this stranger dressed as the Empress. Prince Luther's eyes met Charm's. Recognized her. His jaw clenched. Then he turned away. Snubbing her before every eye in Uptown.

The mask didn't help, now. There was no Shame to protect Charm, or perhaps Shame had bled entirely into her. Uncertainty stalked around the edges of Charm's mind behind her concealing mask. Desire was dead. Perhaps Luther thought their past had died with her. Or perhaps the Lady was right. This wasn't Charm's place, but hadn't she first woken to her emperor's face? Wasn't it her place to deal with emperors? The Empress, dressed as Charm, danced with Strephon. Charm had danced with Luther that way, once. The memory came unbidden. Charm stayed quiet and still. When they'd all stopped staring, she'd go.

Philip Anders looked from Charm to the departing Prince Luther, and stepped into the gap to offer her his arm with a beaming smile. Just as if it were Luther giving him the honor. "By gad, Mistress, that was astonishing. She's set the lot of these old sticks properly on their heels, ain't she?" he said merrily.

"It is no wonder you aren't married, Mr. Anders, if the first words you say are to praise a woman other than the one you're with," managed Charm in reflexive teasing. "And should you not be dancing with one of the pretty young ladies who'd like to cure your bachelor state? You won't please their mamas lingering here with me."

"But by gad, Mistress, if I take a glass of champagne with you, they'll all want to dance with me to find out if you're actually the famous Mistress Charm." Anders gestured toward the long table laden with refreshments.

"I'm sure you mean infamous." She forced a grin.

"And it looks wonderful on you, Mistress," he assured her.

Just past the dancers, a little knot of noble ladies gathered around Countess Seabrough at the far end of that same table, whispering and pretending not to look at Charm and Anders.

"None of their men will admit knowin' you even if they recognize you behind that mask, and none of the ladies would recognize you even without it. And everybody suspects who you are. Come and help me tease 'em."

The devilish invitation gave her refuge. A reason to stay. To enjoy, just for this little while, taunting these people. Charm smiled, let her chin duck as if she possessed any sort of modesty. "On one condition."

"What's that?"

"Introduce me to the ladies at the refreshment table?"

"That's right, by gad, you don't know any of 'em! Poorer they are. Let's enrich 'em." Anders angled her toward them.

"You are so stylish tonight that I suspect you are setting me up somehow, Mr. Anders," Charm murmured to him.

His eyes sparkled. "Dem me, if people are seein' through me, I must be more stylish, not less!"

"How cruel of you. You already put them all to shame. What is your reason, beyond getting virtuous women to drape themselves in your arms, to be speaking with me?" teased Charm, lifting her chin in a so-slight burlesque of courage. Let all the onlookers read in what they would.

"I'd've been glad of any chance to escort you, Mistress, but as it is I did promise to keep you entertained until your surprise arrived." Anders seemed, in the midst of an Imperial tantrum and with the Emperor's fitful wrath hanging over them all, to be having a wonderful time dancing in the lion's jaws.

Charm pressed her lips together in a pretty moue, eyes narrowing a bit behind her dainty mask. There was something she wasn't seeing. "And what is this surprise?"

"I think you'll like it, Mistress. Had strictest instructions to send for it if you attended. Lurked in the back stable yard all evenin', hopin' to see you come in."

"How intriguing of you."

The ladies at the refreshment table looked at one another in uncertainty, but they didn't move away as Anders brought Charm over to them. He introduced her as they worked their way along the table as "Mistress Incognita, you know," grinning and merry. As if there were not Firedrinkers hovering around the room. Names flitted past with Charm hardly noting them. It was the hands she wanted. Their hands, ungloved to enjoy their refreshments. They had to shake with her when Anders introduced them, in spite of her suspected identity. Not one was familiar. Not one was the hand that had poisoned the Rejuv Seabrough had brought her.

"It can't possibly be her, there'd be a great lump under her mask," whispered one lady a little too loudly behind Charm and Anders. Obviously she'd never considered that Firedrinkers could put helmets on, which argued against mindlocks being a large bulge.

"Countess Seabrough! Felt you should meet our Mistress Incognita," said Anders jovially.

Charm looked up at the dour countess. "Countess." Charm bent her knees by a precisely respectful amount and rose, then put out her hand.

The Countess took Charm's hand with exactly as much evident pleasure as she might have laid hold of a dead fish. A small, familiar ring adorned her hand. The image of capsules flashed through Charm's mind. Once, with the pretty box that had come to Charm. And once before.

Charm's heart stuttered, but she kept her feet. This was how the Emperor had been poisoned. In his Rejuv. The one thing he would ingest with absolute certainty. The mindlock came to life softly under Charm's muffling mask, the whir no more than bone conduction.

I told you Seabrough couldn't be trusted! I told you! hissed the Lady in her mind.

Charm pushed the idiot notion aside. *I sincerely doubt he'd poison himself.*

He might have had the remedy at hand, and intended already to take it; or he might have taken a less-than-lethal dose.

The Countess dropped her hand. Charm covered her falter by fanning herself. "It is already so hot. Mr. Anders, we're intruding on the Countess, and you promised me champagne," she said sweetly up to him. "Countess." She bent a knee again, and Anders led her to the other end of the table.

"You all right, Lady?" he asked.

"Oh yes, just unaccustomed to grand events." She didn't look toward the Countess. To do away with an emperor of Boren seemed suddenly easy. Strephon would come to Orchard House, one way or another. She only had to be willing to hang for his death. To kill the Countess was more difficult. Their two spheres never touched. It would have to be tonight and she had no weapon, no method.

The waltz ended and Strephon marched Empress Ylsbeth to one side. Couples began cycling past them, eager to appease the Imperial temper.

Charm carefully did not grind her teeth in frustration.

The half box of poisoned Rejuv lay in her desk at Orchard House. Foolish, foolish, foolish. She should have brought it to poison the guilty party's wine. The Countess's wine. And Strephon's. The Countess had tried to kill Charm and possibly her husband. And certainly the Emperor.

The Lady pounced on the thought. *Every woman here believes you're humiliating them with their husbands. Is it any wonder they want you dead?*

The barb only made Charm want to roll her eyes. *They all know perfectly well I have only one intimate client. If they want that one, they are more than welcome to him.*

Anders gave her a glass of champagne. "Last of the stuff in the whole city. Hoarded for the occasion."

"Shame about that. We could've been drinking it over cards and supper," Charm muttered, careful it wouldn't carry and spoil her mysterious identity. She sipped some of the last champagne in Borenguard.

"Have mercy on my income for one night, Mistress! You and Seabrough are too canny for me," murmured Anders, mouth puckish with trying not to smile.

"Bosh. The reason he partners with me is because you're the one man in Boren who can give him decent opposition."

Anders grinned at her praise. "Ain't nobody can hope to beat Seabrough. I'd be proud of givin' him a challenge."

"You are in league with him up to the tip of your devious nose, and cards are not the game," Charm accused, and laughed softly for his cleverness. She let her voice rise a little so that others might hear. Lest she and Anders should be mistaken for being well acquainted and tip the audience to Charm's identity. "You are very silly, Mr. Anders, and possibly the most amusing man in Borenguard."

Anders clasped a hand to his chest. "Wounded, by gad! Wounded! Only possibly?"

"If your surprise is amusing, you shall hold the title without peer."

In the pause between one musical set and the next, the chamberlain rapped his staff—a gesture more than an hour out of place—and with stentorian voice announced, "Count Seabrough."

CHAPTER THIRTY-NINE

Every eye turned toward Countess Seabrough, standing behind the Emperor and Empress. Some curious, some confused, some sharply observing for any sign of weakness. Emperor Strephon choked on his sip of wine.

The Countess turned four shades paler. Pale enough for Charm to see the color of her face powder as slightly darker than Countess Seabrough's current bloodlessness. Her husband had not sent for her to enter with him. He had deliberately arrived without her. It stirred fans to life as if they would hide the sudden murmur of whispers rising to swirl around the ballroom like a restless breeze.

Count Seabrough moved slowly, with an ivory-headed walking stick to help support him though his clothes were perfect and his posture upright. He bowed low, rather stiffly, to the Imperial couple.

The Empress, apparently unable to see her lady's distress, put out her hands to him. "Count Seabrough, how surprised we are! We had heard you were still ill!"

"Your Majesty is very kind, and kinder still to one arrived late. I am past the worst, and would have risen even from my deathbed to do honor to my emperor and empress." With the faintest grimace, he straightened. Still, he did not acknowledge his wife's presence.

"Well, good of you, Count Seabrough. We've had our

moments, but we do very much appreciate this courtesy to our wife," said Emperor Strephon.

"Your Majesty is gracious to recognize that the dissenting voice may be one of even greater loyalty than those of more agreeable assent," Seabrough replied.

"Did you see the other half of my wife's costume?" Strephon said, gesturing to Charm across the room.

Charm sipped her champagne thoughtfully. Strephon was trying to brazen it out a little too late, but perhaps he'd carry it off if he could make people forget he'd struck Ylsbeth. They'd all be happy to forget it, to not speak of the swollen bruises forming. It was an incident between a man and his wife, and none of their business. Among the men, the most that was likely to happen were comments about Strephon's bad taste. Among the women . . . that depended upon their own marriages. The bruises rising on the Empress's face, however, were on Charm's side rather than the Emperor's.

Count Seabrough examined Charm dressed as the Empress from across the room, smiling politely. "A foil. Even more inspired than your initial clever likeness," the Count said, smiling and inclining again to the Empress dressed as Charm. "Extremely well played, Majesty."

A compliment that could be mistaken as courtesy.

"He really is good," murmured Charm to Anders.

"Toss-up, dem me, between him and old Hanover; though Hanover's a bit hidebound," Anders agreed. "How's my surprise?"

"You are the most amusing man in Borenguard, and hold your title in splendid, glowing solitude," she assured him, laughing a little.

Seabrough murmured some polite leave-taking to the Imperial couple, backing the appropriate two steps, and turned away toward the refreshment table. Ylsbeth shifted to one side, so that she wasn't in Countess Seabrough's way, clearly expecting Count Seabrough would put out his arm for his wife to take. The Count, however, did not pause his turning away. He didn't acknowledge his wife at the Empress's elbow. He behaved as if the Countess was utterly invisible. Color rushed back to the Countess's cheeks and reversed her pallor, leaving her crimson with powder on top, as if she'd dipped her face in flour.

Ylsbeth bit her lip, glanced at the Countess's high color, at the Count's back, and cringed inside her sumptuous black evening gown. Afraid of her lady of the wardrobe? Charm didn't believe Ylsbeth was feigning, but with that little motion she'd supplied for the entire ballroom the inescapable conclusion that the Count's gesture was exactly what it appeared. Seabrough had socially cut his own wife, so much more richly dressed than the Empress, and left her standing alone in her brilliant costume. And he'd done it in this most public possible of places. No one could fail to see, nor fail to understand.

Count Seabrough made his slow way, nodding to greetings and greeting his friends, toward the refreshment table. "Good evening, Anders. Lady, I wish that I could request a dance, but alas I am not yet so recovered as that. May I ask you for a quiet turn about the conservatory?"

"It will give Mr. Anders a chance to ask some young lady of eligible character to dance instead of spending his time squiring me." Charm smiled up at Anders, and put a grateful hand on his arm. "Thank you for the surprise, Mr. Anders. It was lovely of you."

Count Seabrough and Charm were not the only people in the winter garden, but it gave more scope for private conversation than the ballroom. Potbellied oil heaters made the place tolerably warm for the tender plants huddled together in the beds. The Count led Charm strolling slowly beneath the palms and potted citrus, the plants all slightly sickly with Borenguard's overcast skies, along circuitous paths that some garden designer had managed to imbue with a bit of grace.

"I hope you don't mind that I tasked young Anders with being my eyes to spy you out," said the Count.

"In no way. He is entertaining company and altogether a triumph as your protégé."

Seabrough chuckled, the lamps rendering his once-red hair less roaned by silver. "I don't think many people would phrase it quite that way," he admitted dryly.

Charm strolled a few more steps, until they were well away from the couples lingering by the doors of the garden. "A few days ago, after Mr. Anders had gone home, you asked me if there was anything you could do to help me."

"I remember." He watched her, but without any wariness that Charm could detect.

"Given your greeting to the Empress tonight, may I make so bold as to ask a favor?" requested Charm. "I'd like your permission to reveal a truth."

"Does the truth require my permission?"

"When it is about John, yes." She didn't bother to dissemble as to her motive. "I assume you had good reasons for your silence about him, but I need a weapon that will drive your wife out of her post and into the open where a charge of murder might be made to stick. It will not stick unless her peers are primed to be outraged and demand a case be brought. I might tell the Firedrinkers she tried to poison me and did poison you, but though they would be able to detect the truth, I cannot hope that Emperor Strephon will be obliging and hang her without some public uproar calling for it."

"May I ask how you came to know this truth?"

"From a young lady who recognized him in spite of his helmet and body armor."

"Anna Fergus?" He smiled, a trifle wistful.

Charm nodded. "Only two Firedrinkers ever came from Uptown, and she identified John. Between that, my emperor's appetites, and the distance in your marriage . . . and having played cards with you I already know you can count to nine." But she watched his face carefully anyway, in case he'd never cared to count before.

Seabrough's face betrayed no surprise, and no pain at it.

"Why were you silent all these years? Why let her continue as your wife?"

"At first I was beginning to rise in the Assembly, and having a wife in the palace was useful. Being a cuckold just as my career was beginning was not something I wanted to advertise, in my youth and my pride. Later, I was silent because I love Johnny more than anything in the world; and no matter that she hardly saw him, Johnny loved his mother. The idea of her, anyway. I didn't want to hurt him, so I kept quiet and prayed he wouldn't be psychic. He fought it so hard. He said he didn't want to be anyone's son but mine." The Count's voice rasped with emotion for a moment, and there was pain at that memory before he went on more normally, "The only other person outside the Firedrinkers who knows is Anders. He and Johnny were best friends until the very last day. He was there with me to hug Johnny goodbye."

Charm stared, and it made Seabrough smile down at her. He didn't have to smile very far. He was of only middling height, though his presence made up for the fact.

"You already know Anders is cleverer than he sounds," Seabrough said.

"No one is that irretrievably stupid. And anyway, you'd never play cards with a stupid man, though it took me an embarrassing amount of time to realize that."

"Well, I did ask to be able to aid you in some way." He

drew a breath, and nodded. "I give you full leave. If you want some help in your aim, bring it up around Anders. He's kept his promise not to tell for years, but he's got explicit permission to tell all if it becomes known. Insurance that someone would take my side and explain things without my needing to be defensive," explained Seabrough.

"I assume you don't mind my saying that the Countess poisoned you."

His expression was dry as dust. "Not in the slightest. It was her, then?"

"Yes. I saw the hands that handled the Rejuv. The woman was wearing a distinctive ring, and the Countess wore it again tonight. It wasn't the first time she'd doctored Rejuv. I can't prove she gave the first poisoned batch to my emperor, but I am sure it's what happened and that a good telepath could testify to it."

"Then I am doubly glad I've set the stage for you. May I ask you an indiscreet question, Mistress?" asked the Count. "I'm not entirely sure you would know. It is more Miss Pain's province than yours. Do you know if . . . Is Johnny all right?"

"He's all right, though I think he still mourns Anna Fergus. You raised a fine man." Since the Count had already known of the connection, there seemed little point in denying.

"Then it was you who got Fergus's family out of Boren?"

"How did you guess?"

He tipped his head at her. "That is the only way Anna Fergus might have come into contact with you. Lady Fergus is not too proud to save her children any way she can, and she had no cause to worry about her husband's calls at Orchard House." His mouth lifted faintly at the corners.

"And your reputation is not stuffy?" she couldn't quite help teasing him.

Seabrough laughed. "Ah, my dear. I promise you would

be my first choice on every occasion, but it has long been my impression that would be quite a fatal effort; and any part of you is more than enough fortune for any man."

Charm's cheeks warmed a little. "And wise as well." Oh, he tempted her to be bold. She hesitated only a breath, did not examine before she leaped. "You make me jealous . . . of myself."

"Jealousy is an occasional hazard of being human. For instance, I was a little surprised that you were not dancing with Prince Luther when I arrived." He said it casually. Carefully casually. "Were I he, I would not have missed this chance."

He'd done his research and put the obvious historical points together. How long had he known? She might have teased him about his insecurity, but couldn't quite bring herself to it. She was going to hurt him, with her revelation. And maybe hurt John. Gibing him now seemed . . . grotesquely small. Instead, she forced a smile and shook her head as their feet crunched gently along the winding path. "Prince Luther has no interest in being seen with me. He made that perfectly clear."

"No?" Seabrough sighed, his mouth wry. "No. Perhaps not. Try not to think too harshly of him. If we succeed in ousting Strephon, the Assembly would have likely tapped him next. If his reputation is good, it might assure him the throne."

"Ah." Of course. They had had no one else. If she revealed John Seabrough as a royal prince, even an illegitimate one, they had someone else to propose, to Seabrough's mind. He didn't know of her emperor's command regarding royal sons, and he loved Johnny more than anything in the world. "It was courageous of Anders and you, then, to associate yourselves with me."

"Fergus managed the association without damage. He received some smirking for his prudery, but still. I think Anders and I will survive. After all, half the city knows I spend my unengaged evenings at Orchard House."

"Particularly on Thursdays, when your cook has the day off," she recalled with a slight grin.

"Mrs. Westmore is a treasure. If anyone ever tries to hire her away from you, I shall be glad to deal with the blackguard's body once you've done with him," Seabrough teased her, and returned the smile. He was not aesthetically lean. Nor young, as Rejuv had kept Luther; but his teasing warmed her. Even better, in the teasing he hadn't said that he would deal with it for her.

He should have. He should do things for you. A lady shouldn't soil herself as you are so eager to do. You are telling him you want to kill his wife! And for all you know he's the one who orchestrated poisoning the Emperor and trying to poison you, and only lightly poisoned himself to cover up and be rid of his wife, accused the Lady.

Seabrough flickered a glance at her hidden temple, at the mindlock. "Did it hurt you, just then?"

He'd noticed some reaction. Was she growing so transparent? Charm covered with a quick renewal of her smile and a shake of her head. "I was contemplating something rather unpleasant. That your wife might have meant to poison you, not me, and that she may be at this moment poisoning the ears of the court against you." Charm watched his face.

"I was the adjunct, I think. I had a moment of vanity, but I hope it's not something she would count on. It was you she wished to remove. Strephon sees you over her objections. I had believed she and I were still at least political partners, but she has thrown in with Strephon far more completely than I'd supposed. She is still a striking woman. Perhaps she has hopes of more Rejuv. I was a fool to bring you anything from her hand. I hope you can forgive me." He strolled her slowly toward the doors to the ballroom.

"There was no harm done to me, so there is nothing to forgive. Even if I were prone to blaming, I'm much too grateful to see you recovering to indulge it. I would have missed our card games dreadfully," she admitted.

In the concealment of some palm fronds, he lifted her knuckles to brush his lips across them. He'd kissed her hand often enough in the open. Charm wrapped the silence of this gesture closer than she would have a thousand lover's caresses.

"Shall we go out? I would more happily stay here," in concealment with pleasant company, "but you have work to do tonight or your former political partner will try to bury you," she said, not hiding the regret in her voice.

"Unhappily, that is sensible. I suspect I will have to dine with various supporters this week; but I shall see you Thursday at least?"

If he survived Emperor Strephon's wrath after Tuesday's vote. "I hope you will bring me someone new to practice my card playing on, or else bring someone you need and I will endeavor to serve them up for you," Charm said lightly.

"Orchard House does have the most elegant china service in Borenguard." Count Seabrough delivered her back to the refreshment table, and as if to prove the particularity of the concealed action, kissed her knuckles firmly and with a laugh as if she'd said something witty.

The Lady read him in a hard flash, hunting savagely for signs of his guilt, but the kiss was brief and he was gone. He let a gentleman politely take him off to discuss a bill of some kind.

Well? Charm asked her.

I know it's there. He was just too quick for me.

Or, as with the Duchess, there was nothing for him to conceal.

You only say that because you want it to be true, the Lady sulked.

And you don't?

Philip Anders, escorting a young lady costumed as a rather insipid rose, drifted up to the refreshments to give his companion, and then Charm, glasses of champagne.

The rose was eager to console Charm. "Poor you! I don't know how you could bear speaking to such a cruel man. The Empress is trying to control the damage, but there's no doubting the Count has ruined his wife."

Idiotic enough to speak aloud, the rose gave Charm a weapon. Not a killing weapon, but a start. "You think him cruel?" Charm kept her voice so carefully sweet, cultured, confused, everything a lady's should be. "How peculiar. Do you not find he's been stupendously tolerant?"

"Tolerant?" The rose blinked stupidly.

The Firedrinkers themselves had told Pain. "Well, you know, only two Firedrinkers ever came from Uptown. One of them was John Seabrough." Though it wasn't, she delivered it in the tone of an aphorism. In all of Uptown, only the Imperial family had ever been psychics. No other noble family carried that "taint" in their blood. Whoever had sired John Seabrough, it wasn't the Count.

Two more stupid blinks. Charm lifted hinting shoulders to help the young lady's confusion along the path to Charm's intended destination. Several eavesdropping nobles got there a step ahead of her, by the looks on their faces.

"You know, Johnny was my best friend when we were nippers," said Anders. "Shared a schoolroom with him, until he started to have fits. He would have kicked off, of course, if the Count hadn't called Captain Oram to come have a look at things. I was there when Captain Oram called round the

Seabrough house." His silly voice went a bit rough with the memory.

Charm smiled sympathy to him, and reached to squeeze his arm gently, prompting the rose to do the same.

Anders drank a long swallow of champagne and offered the pair of them a tight smile and nod. "Seabrough asked me that day to say nothin' unless someone else did first. Not for the Countess's sake, but for Johnny's. Didn't want Johnny to have to face such a thing said of him; and no matter who sired Johnny, the Count loves him as his own."

"Count Seabrough is a great man," said Charm softly. "He must be such a man, to love a child so much he bears his own betrayal in silence."

Bitch! hissed the Lady. *How could you do this to another noblewoman?*

She sneers at Pain and scorns injuries she never had to feel. How can I do this? It was all Charm could do not to show her laugh. *Easily.*

"But . . . I don't understand. Why cut her after all this time?" asked the rose.

Give the rose credit, at least she'd followed the hint through to its conclusion. Innocent, but not entirely dim. Perhaps that was why Anders had danced with her. Charm leaned toward the rose as if they were friends and whispered too loudly as if to speak over the music that had come back up, "I suppose coming into the ball on the arm of yet another emperor after trying to poison him was a step too far even for a man as fair-minded as the Count."

The rose, and every other lady and gentleman within earshot, turned and stared.

To be stared at for this was something Charm minded not at all. This was a show exactly like what she might do in the cardroom of Orchard House. She fluttered her fan as if flustered at being overheard. "I had it through one of the Count's own servants. The doctor made the Count drink charcoal. They only use charcoal for poison." There was little chance that a doctor the Firedrinkers trusted would reveal anything; but if he did, it was likely to be the truth.

The rose, and every other person within earshot, pivoted to transfer their stares to Countess Seabrough. And then to Count Seabrough, where he stood chatting with Lord and Lady Hanover. Lady Hanover laughed at something, making Seabrough look pleased.

"Got to think Lady Hanover isn't fussed by Seabrough cuttin' his wife. Dem me, Lady Hanover can freeze whiskey at a thousand yards if she wants," said Anders, "and since she ain't, she must not want to."

A young man—Charm didn't remember his name but he liked his brandy, barbarically, with a squeeze of lemon—came to ask the rose to dance and took her off. The rose was speaking in low, excited tones to him almost at once.

Strephon strode to one of the Firedrinkers, said something, then stalked back to put out a hand and, as if to prove his timing thoroughly abysmal, led Countess Seabrough onto the floor for a dance. One of the gentlemen begged a dance with Lady Hanover and swept her away.

"Go to the Empress," murmured Charm to Anders. "Don't let her look abandoned. Be as kind to her as you were to me?"

"White-knightin' ladies is my profession, Mistress," said Anders heartily, bowing to her. He drifted her over to Count Seabrough and Lord Hanover, then took up a glass of champagne and went to the Empress, gathering up a gaggle of friends along the way so that the Empress was surrounded by young noblemen to talk to.

The Firedrinker wearing the captain's sash detached himself from his post and approached Count Seabrough. They didn't keep their voice particularly low, and it carried well enough under the music. "Forgive me, Count. The Emperor wishes me to tell you that, as you are so obviously ill, you are dismissed. We're to see you home."

Charm's breath caught in her chest as if her lungs had snagged on a knife. Lord Hanover's hand shot out to Count Seabrough's forearm. The naked defiance on his face didn't appear deliberate, but it spread like wildfire through the nearest nobility.

"No, Lord," said the Firedrinker. "Nothing like that. Our only orders are to take him home. On my honor. We have no orders save to see him safely home. And we will strive to keep him that way."

"Never fear, my dear Lord Hanover. I shall go along quietly into my disfavor. Hanover," he said, taking his leave of his friend with a nod. "I'll hope very much to see you on Tuesday."

One more Firedrinker detached from their post and the two walked Count Seabrough slowly out. Every eye watched them go, and whispers erupted.

In the general murmur and stir, with Strephon smirking on the dance floor, Charm didn't notice Luther until he touched her elbow.

Luther tucked Charm's hand through his arm wordlessly, and drew her back into the relative privacy near the base of the stair.

She blinked up at him, shocked and not a little appalled. What in the world was he trying to do? Get her beaten to death?

"I want to ask about you and my father."

Charm's mouth dropped open in shock before she could do anything else.

"I think I have a right to know."

She narrowly restrained the urge to gape at him. "Why would you believe that?" she asked incredulously.

"Because we were in love with each other. Or is that some other one of you I haven't met yet?" he snapped. "Considering that, I think I could expect the common courtesy of an explanation." His voice softened. "I know you didn't have a choice, and I know you were a prisoner, I'd just like to hear it from you."

Charm shook her head. Feeling sorry for him wasn't love. If he really did know she'd had no choice, he wouldn't have injected a second half onto his sentence. He should not need her to drag all her private pains out and put them on display for him. It was long past time to let go of the fairy-tale romance. God knew it was past time for both of them. "Luther, try not to be an ass if you can possibly help it. What could he have done with me? I was losing my mind, and I was a prisoner of war. Someone that, if free, might escape back to Inshil or Saranisima and become a central figure for rebellion. Instead of letting me die, your father saved my life and my sanity with this mindlock. And yes, it restrains me quite as much as bars and stone walls might, but you will forgive me that I find being alive in a quite comfortable prison preferable to being impaled by your elder brother. Your father was, if nothing else, a considerate captor."

"How can you not hate him?" Luther's exclamation cut through the nearest low conversations.

CHAPTER FORTY

Charm waited while the people who turned to look had turned away again. What fine gossip she and he would be tomorrow. "If you could not shout, Your Highness? Your violent reactions will make people believe that you are my lover. Having been thoroughly abused by your elder brother, kept a prisoner by your father, and forced to weekly degradation by your youngest brother, am I now to be publicly endangered by you? Perhaps you could remember that we are at a ball? A ball where the Emperor, who will certainly be around to see me again, is glaring at us."

Luther opened his mouth, seemed to struggle for a moment, then said quietly, "How can you not hate a man who was holding you prisoner and using you as his whore?"

Charm shook her head at him. "Firstly, your brother is now using me as his whore and is far less pleasant about it. And secondly, think about the situation. Goodness knows I've had time to do that. Your father couldn't let me go. He couldn't afford to have me somewhere that people could form plots about me, where some fool might use me as a figurehead. I was a witness to atrocities that he was responsible for. I was a survivor of them. I was a threat to his reign and to Boren. He could have simply killed me. Or let me die. It would have been as easy as tossing me into a nice aristocratic room and doing nothing. A mindlock couldn't cure me, but it could stabilize me; and if it killed me, well, I was no great loss and he could tell himself he'd tried."

Luther scoffed. "He used you as his second experiment with the mindlocks, right after he was finished butchering Phelan."

"You're bringing up Phelan to try to equate us because you're trying to drum up outrage. From me? For a man who made one of my ghosts commit suicide, and who murdered the other? You're wearing your outrage the wrong side out." She met his eyes squarely, and waited while he opened his mouth and closed it again. "I am not responsible for your father's decisions. I can only speak for myself. I was going mad, or more mad than I was already," Charm told him tightly. "When I was recovering from the surgery, your father came to Orchard House to sit with me every day. Was it partly to track my progress? Probably. Was it out of guilt for Phelan? I didn't care then and I don't care now. While he was with me, he did everything I needed with his own two hands. I recovered, and he kept calling. Every Tuesday. Say whatever else you want, he came every single week. I am not so stupid that I was going to spit in his face for it when the other choices were Fortress Isle or beheading."

"Did he tell you he loved you?" challenged Luther, his dark eyes angry. "Did you love him?"

Charm considered it a triumph that she didn't laugh in his face. "Given you told me that and then abandoned me and your child, I'd be careful about what high ground you're choosing to stand on. It's slippery."

"I did love you."

"You very much want to look back and be a romantic hero, but a man of twenty-eight seducing a sixteen-year-old isn't heroic, and as I've had to live with the consequences of that, the least you can do is live with a little guilt." Charm went on, remorseless. "Charmaine was sixteen, and, to her, you were worth tearing her own mind apart so she could love you and be her daddy's perfect, uncorrupted darling at the same time."

"Which one of you is Charmaine?"

He brushed past the self-mutilation of the Lady's mind as if it was nothing. As if it hadn't been important. The Lady had done violence to herself. Knowing that, still all he was interested in was validation of his ego. Charm fanned herself instead of slapping him. "Which 'me' it was doesn't change my age at the time. It doesn't change your running back to Boren and not taking me with you." And then her fury slipped through, the spite slipped out. He had no right to any of this, and she had given it to him anyway, and he had no remorse for anything. Luther was as ruined as all the rest of them. Charm smiled sweetly into his eyes. "And, as you asked, I enjoyed your father's company. I counted the minutes of every Tuesday morning waiting for him."

"How touching," managed Luther through stiff lips. "How long was it before his attention turned physical?"

"I cannot imagine, Your Highness, why you presume I would discuss my intimate life with you." She remembered how the Emperor had laid his head on her shoulder after, and his arms around her and his weight in the cradle of her hips. The feeling of his tears against her neck as he had wept for John Seabrough—his last son; though she hadn't realized, then, why he wept. All she knew was that she had become his solace, and he was the only security she had.

"Would you have bedded him if you'd been whole?" demanded Luther. "If you'd remembered me?"

Charm breathed. Men did not respect anger in a woman. They labeled it weakness. "You ask a question designed to ferret out or create guilt, because you're convinced your best dramatic stance is to be hurt because I've 'spurned' you. Have

I got that right? You want me to feel as hurt as you do? Well, I don't, and I'm not going to. I won't mourn my surviving. No one has the right to ask me for that. Certainly not you so that you can feel nobly blameless. You seduced a child, and got a child on my body. And you abandoned us both. My child and my body and my ghosts had to pay the price for it. You didn't even have the decency to come see me until after your father was dead."

"I was at sea . . ."

"Someone broke all my fingers once, but even Desire managed to relearn how to hold a pen and write a letter."

"He swore that if I stayed away he'd protect you!" snarled Luther.

Charm rolled her eyes and fanned herself. "Which makes exactly one man in your family who was good to his word."

Luther looked at her for a long time. "That part of you is completely dead, then? That loved me?"

She stared at him. He kept right on going back to his lines so that later he could tell himself he'd been noble. She didn't even bother to keep the scorn out of her voice anymore. "I'm not going to play pretend with you. I'm not going to act as if nothing's happened in between then and now. Could you look at me and not see your father's mistress? When it was a pure girl who loved you"—she camped and fluttered her eyelashes like a damsel on the stage he seemed to want—"and it was only nebulous other men, that was one thing. Could you make love to me and not think of your father? Of Strephon? Or of Aerleas's troops? He didn't rape me, but quite a number of them had a go. I'd already been your whore, after all, so clearly it was fine for them to treat me like one."

Luther couldn't meet her eyes, but she'd known the real answer from the moment he asked about her physical relationship. Even if he hadn't.

"I am not pure, and I stopped pining for you a very long time ago. Even Desire wasn't pining anymore. She loved you, and she mourned you, but she wasn't sobbing into her pillows at night."

"Would you still run Orchard House if I can persuade Strephon to leave you alone?" Luther finally asked.

If Charm had ever been angrier than at that moment she could not remember it. How dared he dangle such a hope, like a carrot for some dumb beast. He would not, had not acted to make it so. At least his father had acted to make good on his promise. She forced another sweet smile below her mask. It was so familiar an expression it didn't even hurt. "Of course I would still run Orchard House. An income allows one so many of the little things. Food, as an offhand example." Enough was enough. "Since your father died, only one member of the royal family has paid their bills. Yours isn't the one that's up to date, if you wondered. There's a little slot in the top of the reception desk. Feel free to pay your account at any time. And now, as Strephon is still glaring daggers this way every other minute, I would appreciate it if you would leave. Otherwise, I shall be forced to walk away from you, which would be far more embarrassing for you than this conversation has already been."

He hesitated.

"Fine. Excuse me, Your Highness." She turned and walked away from him. She put every bit of her body language into simmering outrage. It wasn't difficult.

You're a monster, whispered the Lady in her mind. *He gave you every chance.*

Oh yes, he gave me every chance to feel guilty and small and come crawling back to him. He has no one to blame but himself. In Inshil, he thought if he had had the Chancellor's child, and without protection, mind you, the Chancellor would be out of choices.

Luther would have a sweet, perfect, adoring biddable wife with spectacular breasts and childbearing hips, get mindlocks for a wedding present, and be lauded throughout his fairy-tale land for it.

You must see that his pain is real, at least.

Not nearly real enough.

Ladies were not supposed to wander ballrooms on their own, but Charm made her way to the refreshments and helped herself to one of the dainty choux pastry canapés filled with cream cheese and smoked trout.

It was Lord Hanover who, after a few moments, detached himself from respectable company and came to incline his head and shoulders to her. "Mistress Incognita. My wife has asked to make your acquaintance. May I present you to her?" He did not instantly put out his arm. He did not take her agreement for granted.

"It would be my very great honor, Lord Hanover. I'm sure she must be a very splendid person to be your chosen partner in life."

He offered his arm and she put her hand on it, beaming.

Lady Hanover smiled at her husband's introductions, and murmured the polite "so lovely to meet you." Lord Hanover went to bring them punch. Charm looked at Lady Hanover with smiling wariness, and Lady Hanover returned the look. The nearest nobles all looked at them looking at one another.

The longer they stood tongue-tied, the perversely funnier it got. Charm's smile tucked in at the corners and she struggled not to snicker. Lady Hanover's eyes began to sparkle, crinkled, and that highborn and dignified matron gave a sudden laugh that verged on a giggle. She offered in a rush, "I believe your gown and Her Imperial Majesty's were designed by the same seamstress?"

"Hyacinth Barker," said Charm with relief, blinking against tears of mirth, grateful that Lady Hanover could find a safe topic. "Yes. She isn't generally known in Uptown, but she has a really wonderful eye for proportions."

Chatting about clothes drew other ladies in, and Charm found herself, much to her own surprise, enjoying herself. Lord Hanover fetched back two cups of punch. Charm gave the man great credit. When he did a thing, he did it handsomely. He was declaring to Borenguard that he was backing Seabrough via Charm, and that he was certainly not backing Prince Luther. Lady Hanover was also declaring, tacitly, that Charm was perfectly respectable, and possibly more so than Countess Seabrough.

The massive main doors of the ballroom eased open a crack, and a familiar figure in an army uniform came through. Charm stared. Major Nathair scanned the ballroom, just as alive as they had ever been. They strode to salute Emperor Strephon crisply. "Imperial Majesty, General Aerleas is sailing for Boren on tonight's tide with twenty ships." Nathair did not keep their voice down.

There was a single moment of shock among the silent crowd; then a glass shattered and pandemonium broke over the ballroom. Ladies shrieked, and several collapsed in faints as the bluebloods of Borenguard broke and rushed for the doors that the Firedrinkers had already closed. People fell, and others tripped on them. The lady next to Charm nearly knocked Charm down in the rush to escape. Lord Hanover steadied his wife, and Charm. The Firedrinkers stepped mechanically in front of the crowd, a human cordon so the masquegoers could not even touch the doors.

"Cowards!" roared Strephon at the shoving, panicked nobility. "Cowards, you'd all run where? To huddle at home? Flee to the country? Do you think that will save you from him? Did you truly think he wouldn't come?"

The stampeding nobles hesitated. Stared at him, aghast.

Charm no less than anyone else. Not only did he throw this outrageous masked ball, with piles of food and case after case of champagne while Lowtown and Middletown struggled just to eat. He had done so while he knew that Aerleas was coming.

"I knew this would happen, you fools! This was the plan! I forced him to come! I'm the one that can put him down!" shouted Strephon.

"He's mad." The horrified words escaped Lady Hanover on a soft breath, and she clearly didn't mean General Aerleas.

"Frothing," agreed Charm, and earned a tight smile from Lady Hanover; but Charm wasn't looking at the shouting Strephon. The Firedrinkers didn't calm the crowd. Just as they hadn't calmed the crowd at the Lowtown gate. Charm's fingers gripped Lady Hanover's wrist, and Lady Hanover wrapped a firm hand over them. The Firedrinkers had not calmed crowds since Captain Oram's collapse. Without Captain Oram, could they counter Aerleas's projected insanity? Charm's lungs squeezed inside her costume and corset. Memories seethed under her like a cauldron of flames. They were not Shame's or Desire's, now, nor anyone's save Charm's. She had nowhere to hide, no way not to fear. She shook her head, drew herself up, breathed, did not join the crowd packed against the Firedrinkers' arms at the massive double doors.

Prince Luther, who hadn't bolted, paused to lift a collapsed lady to her feet and then left her to go to Emperor Strephon's side. He murmured in his brother's ear.

"Yes, perfect. On your way, Luther. Let him out," Strephon called to the Firedrinkers. "You stay, Major," he added, calm and beginning to smile. "Play a waltz," Strephon said, flipped as if by a switch into something reasonable again. "Ylsbeth, come dance." He put out a commanding hand to the Empress.

Empress Ylsbeth, swollen bruises showing through her

powder, went meekly to her stepson-husband's summoning hand. And the orchestra struck up the commanded waltz while the nobles of Boren huddled against the barrier of Firedrinkers and watched the monster they had made.

He isn't wrong, mused Charm, drinking down her last swallow of punch and setting aside the cup so she could open her fan and put it to use. *We are all cowards.*

Major Nathair bowed in the Imperial couple's wake, then came toward Charm and the little huddle remaining around Lord Hanover. "Lord Hanover." Nathair's bow was spectacularly perfect. "As the Emperor has commanded dancing, I wondered if you would lend me this lady for a dance. . . ." They tipped a slender hand toward Charm.

"Mistress Incognita," supplied Lady Hanover.

"As the lady wishes, of course," said Lord Hanover.

"Mistress Incognita? It would be my great honor," Major Nathair said, asking her directly instead of letting the deferment stand.

It was rather marvelous how the Duchess had not forgotten what it was like to be a woman when they'd put on trousers, reflected Charm. "I fear I am not experienced at the waltz, Major, but I would be delighted to learn more of the skill." She folded her fan so it could dangle from her wrist, and extended her hand.

Major Nathair danced well. A firm lead to help Charm not go amiss, and the Lady conquered her fears enough to help. If once or twice her slipper got entangled with their boot, Nathair was dexterous enough to avoid disaster.

"I was convinced that Aerleas had killed you. I'm relieved that I was wrong," said Charm under the music.

"I'm relieved you were, as well." Nathair smiled, but the expression turned faintly artificial. "I suspect it won't be long until this dance irritates Strephon, so please forgive my abruptness, but Aerleas is blaming you for Captain Oram's death. It has penetrated his mind to a depth that I've never seen. He is coming to Borenguard, Mistress, but he is coming for you in particular."

Cold raged up Charm's spine like a blizzard, and she shivered before she could stop herself.

"Pay. Attention," hissed Nathair in their perfectly aristocratic voice, snapping Charm's focus back to the present before ghostly memories could swamp her. "Do you have any means to defend yourself?"

"Only what every woman has—my wits and my body— but Aerleas cannot bend me. I have my orders to protect me."

Realization crept into Nathair's pale eyes, and they breathed in admiration, "The clever old rotter." Nathair hesitated. "Does that skirt have a pocket?"

Charm snorted. "Hyacinth Barker would never send a skirt out without pockets. It's the second reason I love her work."

"I won't be able to shoot Aerleas. I'm too conditioned, and it's . . . I simply can't. Even though he needs to be put down. Even though it's best for him. I've tried, in the past, and couldn't. I only hope you can. I'm going to take you back to Lord and Lady Hanover. On the way I'll put my revolver into your pocket. Get as point-blank as you can before you use it. You mustn't miss."

"I really don't want him to get that close to me."

Nathair's narrow, handsome face was grim. Their eyes were as colorless as ice. "At this moment, Mistress, I sincerely doubt you're going to have any choice."

CHAPTER FORTY-ONE

The Lady woke on Tuesday morning, to the sound of thunder. Thunder? No. Cannon fire in the distance. Dread skittered through her, and she turned away, hiding inside, where it was safe.

Charm snatched their robe off the foot of the bed and went to the window to open the shutters. From her tower room she was high enough to see past Fortress Isle, and the day was perversely clear and bright. Far off across the harbor, off the point of Fortress Isle, there were ships' sails. White puffs of smoke plumed from a ship, and the roar of her guns came after it.

Aerleas. She was shudderingly certain.

The Lady made a trembling sound. *Is Luther as good as that? Do you think he can stop Aerleas? If the Butcher has gotten ships this far . . .*

Charm shivered a little. "He's not a significant threat at long range. It's when he's close that trouble will start. Unless we'd like to trust Strephon, we'd better hope Luther keeps his distance and lives up to his reputation; or that Luther's gunners live up to Luther's reputation."

We need to run, urged the Lady in her mind.

We've had this discussion several times. I don't know why you think it's going to come out differently. Charm pulled on her robe and stood at the window, watching as the ships swept back and forth across the bay. Now and again one foundered. Sails bloomed in bright fire. They beat each other to smoking tatters. Gradually one knot of ships fell back, slipped away down the coast. The remains of the Imperial fleet followed behind it. Charm's fist hit the window frame in an impotent thump.

"Luther can catch him," the Lady said hopefully.

We better hope he can.

The ships' sails disappeared around the point.

Charm put on the day dress that buttoned up the front, carefully putting Major Nathair's revolver in her pocket. It was a lovely thing. Half of a dueling set, possibly. Gleaming blued steel chased with gold and the grip of mother-of-pearl. It didn't seem like a thing that would belong to the battle-worn Major Nathair, and somehow it did not match any vision she could summon up of Nathair in their more female aspect; but however it had arrived to Nathair's hand, they had provided it and Charm would carry it. She balanced it with her keys in her other pocket, went resolutely down the back stairs, and found that Mrs. Westmore had raised Sally, the most competent of the kitchen girls, to the lofty post of parlormaid and left her on duty to polish the silver, bring hot water for tea, and lay out lunch and supper whenever Charm wanted them.

"An' not to worry, m'lady, I've errands to do when the Emperor calls," Sally assured Charm. "I won't be underfoot or anathing."

"Thank you, Sally," Charm said. "That's very fine planning."

The girl beamed and went vigorously on with her polishing.

Charm fetched the account books for herself, settling in the red parlor to go over them while she waited. It was, after all, Tuesday. Touch, tally, and check. Working down the columns of figures. Come storm, siege, or strife, the Emperor called at Orchard House on Tuesday. Thunder, or the cannons at sea, rumbled in the distance. Had the Assembly been put off? Or were they voting even now.

Do you think he'll come today? asked the Lady nervously.

I have no idea. I suppose that between the battle and Seabrough, Strephon may be busy with other things today. But in spite of her denial, Charm waited. And waited. And when the accounts were finished she found herself just sitting. Waiting for the emperor.

The clock in the hall chimed sweetly. Four o'clock. *I don't think he's coming,* the Lady said with quiet relief.

It's Tuesday, said Charm.

The Lady rose. "Well, perhaps while we wait we should look at some of the clothes that Justice, Pride, Desire, and Shame left. I'm sure that there are people we can give them to." She went into the kitchen. "We should pack up Pain's things as well. She'll want them at the Isle. Sally!" she called.

"Yes, Lady?" The girl came in and bobbed.

"Would you run find Jim, please? That Mrs. Westmore mentioned? If he's at liberty, I'd like him to come mow the orchard. . . ."

The front door slammed open. "CHARM!" Strephon's roar carried from the entryway.

An emperor. Not hers, but enough of one. She could hear his boots going up the stairs. Charm resurfaced from the depths of her own mind. "Never mind, Sally. Ask Jim to come tomorrow, and take the rest of the day off. I'll pay you for your day, never fear."

"Yes, Lady." Sally fled, leaving the green baize door swinging in her wake.

Charm rose, brushing her skirts straight. Strephon shouted from far up the stairs, from her room. Charm's lips tightened in annoyance. She hurried up, and stepped into her room with a smile.

Strephon clenched his right hand into a fist and back-handed her. The force of the blow whipped her around and to the floor. Charm blinked at the flowers in the carpet for a moment as the initial numb sting burst like stars across her cheekbone and set her eyes swimming.

"You knew, didn't you, you bitch!"

Charm stayed down, taking only the risk of pushing up to her elbow. "Knew what, Majesty?" she asked.

"Seabrough comes here, he plays cards with you!"

"Majesty, he can see the mindlock I wear. He knows my loyalties are inviolate," she said shakily. Charm looked up at Strephon with tear-filled eyes. "What has he done?"

Strephon hesitated.

Charm blinked at the tears. She must hold to her alleged ignorance. Thunder again, but it went on longer this time. Not thunder, she realized. Cannon fire again. From the southeast. Landward. *Aerleas.* Her blood went ice cold. *He's drawn Luther away with a sacrifice of ships. The fleet was a ruse. He's duped Nathair, or had a few ships peel off, landed somewhere else!*

"What are you still down for, whore? Go get me a drink," he snarled.

Seabrough's play must have succeeded, Charm thought, *but too late.* "Majesty, that's at the gates. Prince Aerleas is attacking the city!"

Strephon snorted. "And about fucking time, too. Soon as he's done cutting that bloody Assembly down to size I'll be fine."

"But . . . the Assembly made you Emperor . . ." the Lady quavered.

"Are you getting me a damn drink sometime today?" he snarled.

The Lady was silent, retreating down deep beneath the mindlock, cowering.

Charm sighed and got up. "Would you like whiskey or wine?" she asked. "The whiskey is local, and quite good. The wine is terrible." Which was all she had left save for a few bottles of Blood Fields. And she'd be damned and dead before she would give him that.

"Whiskey."

Charm dipped a curtsy and went to fetch a whiskey decanter and a glass from one of the second-floor rooms. When she returned, Strephon had her little enameled box of poisoned Rejuv in one hand, and two Rejuv capsules in the other. He flipped the box closed and put it in his coat pocket. Charm glanced at her desk, at the top he'd left standing open.

"Still had a stash, I see," he said with a cold smile. "I knew that you'd have extra you were holding out."

"There is none at the palace?" Charm poured him two fingers' worth of whiskey.

The Lady stirred.

"What, Luther hasn't told you?" he sneered. He tossed the capsules into his mouth.

The Lady jerked at the sight. She reared up in Charm's mind and began, "Majesty, you mustn't . . ."

His slap whipped her head around. "Shut up. You talk too fucking much."

The Lady spun around the mindlock and into hiding again with a whimper.

OW, snapped Charm, and snatched control back. She touched the side of her mouth gingerly.

"Stop shaking, you damn whore, I can see perfectly well you don't know anything. You never have, have you?" he muttered around the capsules, then downed them and his whiskey in a gulp. He wiped his mouth on his sleeve.

It looks as if it wasn't Strephon using the Countess trying to poison us, Charm observed blandly to her counterpart. *Even if they did conspire to kill his father.*

"Vote of no confidence my ass. I can still outlive that bastard Seabrough," he muttered. He went on to Charm—"There isn't any Rejuv left in Boren and there isn't going to be any more for the foreseeable future. Aerleas has bungled it, and the labs where they make it blew up and burned down."

He'll die! You have to warn him! You have to get him to vomit them back up!

I have to do nothing of the sort, Charm replied calmly.

"Gimme that." Strephon snatched the decanter from her and poured himself a second glass, full this time.

He mustn't drink any more until he vomits! The alcohol will dissolve the gelatin capsule faster and it will dilate his blood vessels even more.

He keeps drinking like that and vomiting won't be a problem for him, Charm shot back. "Majesty, please, surely you'd like some water?" she suggested.

His backhand returned her to the carpet. Charm blinked at the stars dancing behind her vision.

We have to warn him! the Lady cried, struggling.

When you're willing to be the one being beaten every week, you're welcome to object, Charm snarled. *Strephon is at least partly to blame for his father's death. I haven't forgotten my order even if you have.* The mindlock whirred, holding down her counterpart brutally as the delicate gears caught and held firm as a fortress wall. Outside, the cannon fire went on. She watched Strephon drink and pace. He muttered to himself, wiping his mouth on his sleeve. *If he doesn't vomit and keeps drinking like that the alcohol'll kill him before the atropine does,* she thought with savage amusement.

You're enjoying this! You don't know he killed his father and you're enjoying it anyway!

Yes, I am, said Charm serenely. *I'm enjoying watching an abusive traitor die. I'm enjoying knowing that he'll have done it himself because he's a thief. It isn't nice,* she mocked, *but watching him get what he deserves by his own hand . . . oh yes. I'm savoring every. single. second.*

Murderer! The Lady hissed the accusation.

Strephon threw himself into a chair. The blue velvet one that used to be Pain's chair in the mornings. "Come here. Don't get up. Crawl."

I didn't force the pills down his throat. I'm not tying him to a chair and pouring whiskey down him. Tempting though it sounded. Charm gathered her skirts above her knees so she could crawl toward him. She kept a wary eye on his boots.

"You're not remotely beautiful, you know," said Strephon. "Really. You're fat an' cheap."

Charm didn't answer, since it wasn't a question.

He flailed a foot at Charm, but she scuttled to one side and he missed. He didn't seem to notice. "Got everythin' I wann'ed. Go' the crown, go' the untouchable whore, go' the wife, go' rid of Phelan . . ." He laughed for a moment, a wheeze.

"Phelan?" asked Charm. She started to frown, but stilled the expression with a wince. She touched her swelling mouth with tentative fingers.

Strephon laughed. "Yeah. He was really crazy for that little one you had. So I got him." He smirked with satisfaction. "He wasn' so tough . . . ol' Phelan, it was easy to make him soooo mad. Now, Phelan's crazy for good. But Aerleas can' get me. Not me, thash my talen' . . . none of it works on me." So drunk or so drugged it was hard to understand him. Strephon laughed. "I go' him. Go' ever'shing. None of itsh ever any good." His face puckered into a childish pout, and then he smirked. "But I'm gonn' get Lusher . . . Loser Lusher . . . Aerleas never fergave 'im for taking Oram away." Strephon chuckled wetly. "Steal a man's shon . . . he isn't gonn' forget that."

"Wh-what?" Charm blinked.

Strephon smirked. "Dinn' know that, did you, stupid fat bitch. That's right. Oram was Aerleas's brat. Aerleash los' his mind an' Lusher took 'is brat out to shea 'ntil Oram was ol' enough to mindlock."

Charm listened to Strephon's rapidly deteriorating speech and resisted the urge to prop her chin on her hand.

He's going to hurt Luther! cried the Lady. *I know you loved him! I know you did! You're Desire too, I know it! You can still do the right thing.*

Luther's safe at sea. It's his element. If he can't survive there, I can't help him. Strephon's going to be much too dead to hurt anyone ever again.

"My wife's beau'iful." Stephon glared at Charm. ". . .'Sbackward. My wife's beau'ful and my whore's not." He frowned at the whiskey decanter. "Sheabrough's such a liar. Shaid it'd be okay. 'Snot okay. Like marrying my sishter."

Charm frowned. "Seabrough said . . ."

"'Snot fair. I'm the Emperor!" He put effort into the shout, but it didn't carry. It didn't ring. It soaked quietly into the carpets and heavy drapes and was gone.

"Majesty, what about Seabrough." Charm reached up to touch his wrist.

Strephon tried to raise his hand and strike her, but his arm flopped limply. "Wahs wrong ish me . . ." His frown wouldn't quite form, and a sudden flare of concern made him try to get up. He couldn't.

"Other than the heavy drinking, you mean? The Rejuv you stole from my desk was poisoned by someone who wanted to kill me," Charm told him calmly, standing up and shaking her skirts straight. "I'm afraid you've taken far more than a lethal dose. Out of curiosity . . . did you know your father was going to be poisoned?" she asked.

Strephon's eyes glittered with malice. "Sheabrough sh-shaid . . . it would be . . . ho-kay . . ." His slurred speech trailed off.

Seabrough. All this time, the man you've been playing cards with, and . . . and flaunting yourself with! accused the Lady. *Seabrough used Strephon, and betrayed him. He's the one who ordered the poison. He lied to you! We only saw that poor woman doing what she was told!*

Impossible. If he knew it was tampered with he wouldn't have poisoned himself.

An innocent man is dying!

Innocent? hissed Charm in sudden rage. *Innocent? And you want me to do the "right" thing?* Charm drew herself up, borrowing the Lady's most regal posture as the Lady had borrowed Charm's smile. She looked down at Strephon with his slobbering mouth starting to hang open as he struggled to breathe. "We, of the Most Holy of Inshil, Servant of God Almighty, do hereby pronounce this as our last judgment. We find you guilty of rape, assault, treason, and conspiracy in the murder of His Most Imperial Majesty, the Emperor of Boren."

Strephon made a massive effort and slurred out, "Bitsh." He managed almost to smile. "Aerlash'll . . . huv fun wish you . . ."

Charm went on with clarion chill in her voice, ". . . and do hereby sentence you to die." She folded her hands in front of her and stood, simply watching, making herself watch as Strephon of Boren slowly asphyxiated. She watched his eyes, the panic in them, the desperation. Those emotions eroded as he drew in less and less air, dulled as his head began to loll.

The Lady huddled under the mindlock, weeping. *How can you stand it?!*

This isn't the first man we've condemned to death and to worse than death in Inshil's laboratories. You wanted to please your father and have his praise, but needing to be such a dainty lady at the same time, you had to make Justice to do this for you.

Strephon's breathing grew shallower. Little gasping pants growing weaker.

Even if I had done it myself, I wouldn't stand there and watch!

"Maybe you should've," snapped Charm aloud, angry now. "Maybe you should have had to watch, even once to see what you made someone else be responsible for! Maybe you shouldn't have had to go through all the things you did, but you didn't even go through them! We did! We've gone through it all and you gave us away, shed us like so much dead hair that you didn't want anymore. You'd have shed me too if you could have done it."

I don't want you! I don't want any of you! In a massive effort, the Lady tried to cast out everything that wasn't her—Charm in her entirety and all the others who were associated with this vile house.

Charm stood against the onslaught like rooted stone. Her eyes prickled with tears at the burdens her ghosts had carried. Her soul burned with them. For all these years she'd done her best to keep her selves all alive, and even when they hated her they'd still done their best to protect her. She wouldn't turn her back on herself now. Not any part of herself. Of herself. *Not part of her, they're . . . part of . . . me.* Charm reeled at what she found in the Lady's panic. *I'm me. I'm Charmaine.*

I won't let you be part of me!

"Part of you? I've never been part of you. Never," spat Charm. She sank mental fingers into her rival, forced open the Lady's fear. Raked and clawed for the first thing the Lady remembered. The mindlock clicked and whirred, reinforcing Charm's demand, grinding the Lady's defenses in the built-up power of decades of tiny resistances. Hair color. Black gowns. Card tables and sharing herself out to whomever even when she was reserved only for the Emperor. *What do you remember? What is the first thing you remember?!*

The Lady screamed and fought, twisting, trying to escape with nowhere to go.

Charm's hands curled into fists at the perfection of the betrayal. "They made a Most Holy who was perfectly good, who never wanted anything inappropriate; but I'm the center. Me. I wasn't made to deal with my emperor. I wasn't created to deal with the mindlock. That's what you said, what you believed, but that isn't how a mindlock works. It stabilizes the mind. It resurrected me after Inshil's telepaths buried me. I'm the core! I chose to call myself Charm, because it was a shortening of my own name. You never really existed. They made you up."

Shut up! raged the Lady. *That isn't true, I'm nothing like you. I'm no part of you! I'm a Most Holy of Inshil!*

"You exorcised the others. You threw away shame and pain and pride . . . even justice. Everything that interfered with being their obedient little dolly. You kept me locked in and did whatever they asked, and you never had to pay the price for any of it because you had parts of me to do that for you."

A trickle of fear from the Lady. A flicker of memory, of the telepaths, smiling so kindly at her as she opened her eyes, "cured" of impending madness. The Chancellor, Charm's father, so eager to tell the country. They built her a laboratory, brought her the cavalcade of dead psychics, hoping she could reanimate them as she had her sister's pet squirrel. Corpses who'd turned into rotting meat in vats of spinal fluid. They'd wanted her to make vat-grown empaths. It hadn't worked the way they'd wanted. But still she'd been praised and petted and seated next to Prince Luther of Boren at his welcome supper now that she could be trusted not to say or do anything inappropriate.

"They made you! They made you to control me! A childish woman who lives to be good. To be proper. To be appropriate! To do what she's told! And every time I came to the surface you split that 'me' off! It isn't the mindlock that kept you from throwing me out, it's that I'm Charmaine and you were never any part of me. And I won't feel guilty anymore for what was done to us! I won't feel guilty about surviving! I won't be ashamed of what was done to me! I won't be ashamed of remaking myself. And I won't turn my back on myself," Charm hissed. "There is no Inshil anymore. There are no church telepaths trying to read discontent that I need to hide from. Aerleas and his army slaughtered my family for what they did and I wouldn't see it, wouldn't weep. He killed Evlaina. They beat me and raped me, but they couldn't break me. I tore myself apart so they wouldn't destroy me, but I can stand it now." Tears traced down her cheeks. She bared her teeth and wouldn't stop. She wouldn't spare herself. Better wild grief than this meekness with no passion. "Pain . . . she was how I stood it then, but I can remember it all, now. I can stand it all by myself because I won't let you win. I won't let what someone else made me into be what I am. I love this me I've made myself into. I'm proud of me. And I damn well won't give me up to you."

The Lady reared up against the mindlock with a scream.

A long, last bubbling breath sighed out of Strephon as he died.

The mindlock released and the gears spun, ripping out of control.

~◦~

Pain/Pride's cell was more like a comfortable bedroom with a sitting area. The door was thick and of course locked, and the window was barred, but they had a beautiful view down on the harbor. They practiced walking, growing gradually smoother until they flattered themselves that they looked quite normal. It didn't even take thought between them as long as they shared their intentions.

The Firedrinkers who brought her breakfast told her that the thunder at dawn had been a naval engagement. "Prince Luther's in pursuit of Prince Aerleas's fleet."

The renewed boom of the cannons drew her to the window. Puffs of smoke rose from outside the thick gray-white ring of Borenguard's massive outer wall. Answering fire came from the emplaced guns on that old siege defense. With the antiquity of Borenguard's emplacement guns it was only a matter of time before Aerleas was close enough to force some innocent to open the gates.

"How clever of Aerleas," commented Pride aloud as they watched the smoke puffs and the roofs of some buildings exploding under the impact of the shells.

Do you have any feelings? Pain snapped.

"Of course I do. Even if we loathe him, it is clever. He's drawn Luther off, and without Oram there's nothing between him and taking Borenguard except the Firedrinkers," Pride reasoned, but Pain could feel the quaver in her now. "The population may even do his work for him and slaughter one another. That's part of how he did it before. His people got in somehow, or he controlled someone and threw all the gates open. He made everyone all over the city start to kill one another. That's what he unleashed at Inshil. That was his influence on the people. And once he had the city, he did so much worse than anyone else."

Are you all right? Pain asked.

"Of course I am!"

All right, all right, don't shout.

People, small specks surging together like sand running in

a glass, crowded the Imperial Way in the city. They flowed up-hill like an improbable tide toward the Lowtown wall, fleeing to higher, safer ground in Middleton.

The heavy lock in the door opened with a thunk. Pain/Pride turned. A Firedrinker bowed. "Miss Pain, if you'd come with me, please. We need you to wake Captain Oram."

Pain/Pride hurried with them, down through the fort to the wharf. Aerleas's mental seeking slammed into Pain as she passed out of the thick stone of the fortress. *Where is my son?! Where is my son?!* Pain/Pride staggered. The Firedrinkers lifted her by the elbows, up and onto a small skiff. The sound of the cannons swelled. As they neared the docks a massive roar rose above the ongoing booming.

"The armory," said the Firedrinker across from her, jumping to the dock to tie up the skiff. The helmeted Firedrinker helped her out, almost tossing her up to their comrade. "He's shelling the emplacements and the munitions storage. Hurry, miss," they urged.

Aerleas's mental assault grew stronger. *He's very close . . .* Pain whispered.

Pride caught up her skirts and ran. Pain curled up around the white-hot barbs of Aerleas's seeking. She concentrated on keeping her eyes open and let Pride run for them. The Firedrinkers urged her up through the streets of the harbor district. A barricade stood across the Imperial Way, manned by men with rifles. Bern Ostander was with them, shouting directions. He gave her a grim smile and a salute as the Firedrinkers hustled her through the last opening in the barricade and the Lowtowners rolled a wagon across the gap.

The Firedrinkers helped her run, arms under hers when the hill began to take its toll on her speed, dragging her on until a milling crowd of people trying to get through the Low-town gate forced them to let her catch her breath.

The crowd shouted, cried, howled. "Where is my son?" "Angie, have you seen Angie?" "Where's Charles?"

The Firedrinker who was directing the crowd faltered, helmet swinging left and right searchingly. "The captain . . . Where's the . . . ?" He shook his head suddenly, staggered, and leaned on the wall. "Keep moving!" he called to the crowd. "Everyone will be reunited in Cathedral Square. Quickly, now, keep moving!"

Aerleas, whispered Pride in their shared mind space. *Seeking his son. Projecting onto the crowd. It will get worse with no one to counter him.*

How is he affecting the Firedrinkers? Shouldn't their mindlocks protect them? For that matter, if we're partly shielded by Mistress Charm how is he hurting you?

Pride's mental snort might've been amusing at any other moment.

They need Oram, realized Pain. *They don't have orders as Mistress Charm does. They need Oram to be their buffer. And I'm too different now, too differentiated for Charm's shield to help me.* She curled up tighter as Aerleas's seeking raked over her like metal claws.

Just hold out Aerleas, Pride said. *And keep your eyes open for me. I'll take care of the rest.*

Pain had little choice but to trust her.

"Keep moving along, orderly if you please," a Firedrinker at the gate was shouting. "Keep moving up if you please once you're through the gate, on up the road!"

"The . . . the guns?" Pride managed as they panted for air in the crush of frightened people.

"Bern Ostander had them!" The Firedrinker on her left

had to shout for her to hear them. "Prince Luther had the others!"

Someone looked at her. "Miss Pain! Miss Pain's back!" People started turning, pausing.

"Let Miss Pain pass!" bellowed the Firedrinkers at the gate. "Keep moving, keep moving! Move on and let her through!"

The crowd kept flowing through the gate, dragging Pain/Pride and the Firedrinkers with it now, pressing forward, jostling and struggling. The Firedrinker on her right and then her left were swept away in the sea of people.

Pain felt some panic rearing up in her. *Oram. We have to get to Oram. I have to get through the gate. If we can just get through the gate . . .*

Pride kept them on their feet doggedly. She shook the shoulder in front of her. "Please! Please, we must get through!" she called.

"'Ere, miss, we got you!" Two burly dockworkers lifted her bodily up over their heads, snatching her away from her escort. Pride shrieked in surprised indignity. "Pass her up!" the dockworkers shouted as the crowd under the urging of the Firedrinkers kept on flowing up the road. "Miss Pain here, pass her up!" "Hey! Catch!"

They shoved her forward to more men, and some women, and they passed her on in turn. Hands kept buoying her up, tumbling her roughly forward borne on the surging mass of Lowtowners. Through the shadows of the gatehouse and past the Firedrinkers there. Pain didn't know the man finally who set her down. She hadn't known any of them, but they'd all known her. Pride stood and clung to the stranger for a moment to get her feet under herself.

The crowd's shouting and churning began to slow suddenly, an unnatural quiet spreading over them.

"The whore!" A shriek from the mob. "The witch! The

whore! It's her fault! Where is Oram! The witch has him! The bone witch!"

The man that Pain/Pride was leaning on stilled, face slackening. His eyes glazed.

Pride stumbled back from him, snatching her skirts up to her knees, sprinting up the hill in a fresh burst of terror. Two Firedrinkers lay collapsed by the back gate of Orchard House.

Behind her she could hear the mob coming. She staggered through the garden gate and slammed it closed. Pride could barely feel Pain anymore, knew she was present only because she could still see. Pride wove her way from tree to tree, using them for support. She staggered down the stairs of the lab, went to her knees beside the growth tank, and laid her hand on Oram's chest. *Oram, wake up*, Pride thought as loudly as she could.

Nothing. The garden gate groaned. Shouts, cries for the whore, the shrill scream of a woman. Like Inshil. The scent of the garden and dampness in the air, the screaming as Prince Aerleas's madness crept into the people, assaulted the psychics. Pride remembered how his hands had felt on her arms. They'd been smooth, cold, strong. He stank of smoke and sweat and exultation. "So much for your precious Luther taking the chancellorship of Inshil," he had hissed at her.

Pride could feel some of the attack on Pain, but Pain did not break. Could not break. Neither could she act. Pride could feel Pain, dug in around herself, defending Oram, hiding him.

Not again, thought Pride savagely. *Not again. I won't let it happen like this again!* She cupped Oram's face in her hand. *Oram! Oram, the Firedrinkers need you! Aerleas is in the city!*

Nothing. No mind stirred. Oram floated silently in the tank; only the faint flutter of his pulse under her fingers betrayed any life.

"Oram!" Pride screamed it at him.

Nothing.

He's gone, Pride realized in horror.

The garden gate boomed, and a mad bellow rose over the obscene cheer of the crowd. "GODDAMN YOU, WOMAN, WHERE IS MY SON!"

CHAPTER FORTY-TWO

Charm must be in the house. Pride stood. *The mob mustn't get in here. Oram is helpless.* She marched up the stairs and stepped out of the greenhouse. She closed the door hard behind herself, and heard the latch inside fall into place. Oram would be safe. For a while.

Aerleas stood surrounded by gibbering people who fell away from Pride/Pain as if she were poisonous. The way the guards in Inshil had fled. The Lady had sat in the gardens, hands folded in her lap, waiting for Boren's soldiers to reach her. She'd been so sure that it was Luther come for her at last.

Pride's memory flared. Pride remembered closing her eyes in her own mind. Remembered even before that, in the laboratories with the empaths sedated and the needles that dripped their precious spinal fluid into jars. It was all Inshil had judged them worthy to do, behind the walls where no one could see. Empaths. Empathy fluid. She remembered the world going dark because the Lady had refused to see it. Refused to know it. Spun off Pride to hold herself together. Then a flash of Aerleas's face, long and narrow as Luther's with the little muscles twitching around his eyes and mouth as he threatened to cut off her eyelids if she didn't watch. She remembered the screaming of the crucified and the impaled as he slaughtered everyone who had ever mattered to her, the horror of the laboratories where empaths didn't even scream anymore. Ruthlessly, Pride kept Pain's eyes open.

The years had savaged Aerleas into a gray-haired, narrow blade of a man in his battle-weathered brown uniform. Next to him, held by two men but definitely standing and alive, was Major Nathair, the Duchess of Madderley. Aerleas's eyes burned like the heart of a blacksmith's forge as he caught sight of Pain/Pride.

"HARLOT!"

In three strides he was to her, arm shooting out like a viper's strike. Aerleas took hold of the front of Pain/Pride's dress, whipped her around, and slammed her back against the bole of a bone tree. His mind dug into hers as his fingers strained the fabric of her gown. Pride looked into his eyes, cleared her throat, and spit in his face.

He snarled. "Ah, yes. I remember what you feel like. You're who she was hiding behind. Can you speak, now? Can you?" He gripped the front of her dress with one hand, drew the other back. His blow snapped Pain's head to one side, her cheek numb for an instant before a bloom of fire rose in it. He brought his hand back across. Left and right, in smooth, mechanical precision, jaw, cheekbone, temple.

The blows jarred her brain, blows and memories tangling together as Pain and Pride clung to each other in their shared mind to stay conscious. She was barely aware of the crowd in a semicircle around her. They whimpered and moaned.

"I know he's not dead. I can feel he isn't," Aerleas raved at her. "Where is he? My son a slave to that puling idiot, Strephon, when he should be emperor? Never! Eldest of eldest. Not me, no, Father was right; but I'm going to get my son back, you fish-bellied bitch. I'm going to get him back and I will make him the emperor he should be!"

Don't fight, Pain reminded herself. *It will be worse if you fight. He likes it when they fight.*

"Your Highness! Stop! It's not her fault he's dead!" screamed the Duchess, struggling in their bonds.

Sparks exploded behind her eyelids with each blow. His eyes gleamed, manic in the moonlight.

"Aerleas, please!" The desperation in the Duchess's voice rose to a shriek.

"Shut up, Aiglentine." Aerleas drew his revolver, and the shot boomed in the damp air.

The Duchess slammed back, and the gibbering guards dropped them in an unceremonious heap. A horrible burbling wheeze came out of their body. Aerleas had taken them through the lungs. He shot them again and shoved the revolver back into its holster.

"I'm going to like beating you to death," Aerleas told Pain/Pride with swelling excitement in his voice. "I'm going to beat your face soft enough, and then I'm going to peel the skin off it and keep it to remind me of you. And I'm going to do it while you're alive, so that my men can finish what they started with you." He was almost panting now. "They can have you the way you deserve, whore!" His blow set sparks dancing behind Pain/Pride's eyelids.

Pain and Pride scrambled at one another, a single thought blurring their edges together. The need to survive. Binding them. *I don't break*, Pain whispered.

I WON'T DIE, Pride howled. Her eyes flew open, hands coming up to grip the wrist holding her, clawing at Aerleas's glove and sleeve. His arm was longer than hers, and she could not reach his face. She kicked futilely at him through her skirts.

Aerleas watched her reaction and laughed, his fist falling without pause, without mercy. "Where . . . is . . . my . . . son!"

Her flailing hand rebounded off something hard and metal at Aerleas's waist. Agony squeezed her throat. *No. No, I won't die.* She put her hands up, trying to shield her face and head.

Aerleas gave a wild laugh and kept hitting her. All the time, his mind dug at her, cutting and slashing, trying to gouge out the single chunk of information.

Where is my son? he demanded in her mind, twisting and burning her brain.

Blood slid warm from her nose and down her lip. She couldn't see for the film of it in her eyes.

I will not let him kill me. I will not die, and I do not grovel! Pride sucked in a breath that felt like knives, and screamed. High and sharp as an eagle, full of defiance. She blinked and blinked, keeping their arms up, shielding their face as well as she could as the blows rained down.

"Your Highness, we have the women."

The blows stopped, and Pride collapsed to her hands and knees as Aerleas dropped her. Pain and Pride struggled together to blink and focus. The world began to resolve out of the bloody tears in their eyes.

A pair of Aerleas's men stood with Empress Ylsbeth and Countess Seabrough. The two women clung to one another physically, as Pride and Pain had mentally, and only the soldiers' grip kept them on their feet in the storm of Aerleas's rage.

Aerleas snatched Ylsbeth out of the Countess's arms. He shook her like a terrier with a rat and she screamed, fighting mindlessly, flailing. With a curse, Aerleas threw her to the ground, sucked in a deep breath. Around them all the madness of his mind pulled up and out. Not stopped, but excluding the orchard. "Where is my son?" he roared at the Empress.

Ylsbeth shook her head, weeping with her pale golden hair tumbled off to one side. "I don't know who you mean!" she screamed.

Aerleas rounded on Countess Seabrough, and the woman shrank back.

"Strephon was supposed to be here to talk to you! He said he would talk to you! He was going to explain everything!" she cried.

Aerleas stalked toward her.

"We let you in! Don't you see that?" the Countess reasoned desperately. "He sent Luther out with orders to pursue your ships specifically so that you could get in by land!"

"And why would Strephon let me into Borenguard?" Aerleas's eyes narrowed. "Of course. Father, however you did it, and . . . and then they'd have no obvious choice but go to Strephon. How very neatly packaged, Countess. Where is my son?" Aerleas smiled. Thin and humorless, it drew back his lips.

"Captain Oram is dead, Highness," said the Countess. "He killed himself. Mistress Charm buried him right here."

Aerleas slapped her casually. The Countess's head snapped to one side, but she didn't fall. "Useless, stupid woman . . ." He turned back toward Pride.

"I'll never tell you," hissed Pride through her swollen mouth. "Never."

The psychic stab into Pain went through her like a sword, and Pride screamed aloud.

"Oh no," Aerleas laughed. "No, you're supposed to be the silent one, remember?" He wrapped his hands around her throat. She struggled wildly, snarling and scratching. Her focus on the world began to blur around the edges and turn gray.

Pain fought to stay conscious, to hold against the gale force of Aerleas's mind. He forced a wedge into her brain, between herself and Pride. Pride stretched out into the grayness, gave a shriek and snapped away. Alone, Pain strove to keep her eyes open. Only one thing mattered. More than who she was, more than anything. As long as she lived, he wouldn't search for Oram. *I don't break. I won't die!* she screamed in silent, failing defiance. Her mouth worked above his hands, but a gurgle came out instead of the scream.

A figure rose up behind Aerleas, a long pale smudge as if the ground of the orchard had given rise to a phantom. Dimly, she heard a familiar voice.

"Hello, Father."

Aerleas's hands opened as he spun around. Pain slid to her knees, gulped in precious air. The pallid blur resolved itself into Oram, standing a trifle unsteadily, his pale nude body dripping with empathy fluid.

"You're alive!" Aerleas's cry was choked, full of joy.

Her diaphragm pushed out air, dragged in a breath. There was a bright oval on Aerleas's hip. His revolver butt, shod in silver. He'd slaughtered Inshil. He'd butchered Charm's child. He would kill Oram or else enslave him. On her knees, she jerked the pistol free, and raised it. Aerleas whirled back toward her.

Oram's voice was calm. "Good-bye, Father."

Aerleas's lips drew back in a savage snarl. She could see only his burning eyes and the tiny sighting pin. She squeezed the trigger. Aerleas's head exploded up and away from her, spraying Oram with blood and bone shards and globules of brain. Aerleas's body toppled away from her. Silence came suddenly, as if the gunshot had torn the possibility of sound from the air. Aerleas's men collapsed like abandoned toys, convulsed a moment, then lay still.

Oram crouched beside her. He touched her wrist and she jumped. Oram steadied the pistol and took it away from her, laying it in the grass. Shaking, she braced herself on Oram. The world seemed strange without so much crowding inside her skull.

"Who am I?" she asked him, the world shrinking around her.

"You are my lady," said Oram quietly, and he helped her to her feet.

She couldn't feel other selves. Only her own self. Just herself. Alone.

Oram's eyes focused on some distance that only he could see, and for a long moment he concentrated. He looked at her. "I need your help," he said. "The mindlock damaged me, or removing it did. Not as badly as it might've, but I need your mind to link me back to my Firedrinkers."

"I'm not psychic," she told him.

"You are enough," he assured her. "Your sympathy with them, the connections you've made over the years will be enough. You've felt my Firedrinkers' pain for decades. They're yours more honestly than they have ever been an emperor's. That's all you need."

She nodded, slid her fingers through his, and he put his other arm around her waist. He drew her in to his body, pressed his face against the side of her neck. Made not to break, made to ease pain, she absorbed the overflow of sensation that would have damaged him.

His touch on her battered mind made her flinch, but she swallowed hard and wrapped her arms around him, pressing her bare hands against the small of his back. Gently he teased open the connections in her mind, slid into her until she shivered, woke, and gasped. She arched in his hands as her mind seemed to expand.

All around them she could see a misty jumble of diffuse minds. The first in the misty confused people around them was Charm, a single ghostly scintillation now, with stray flecks flung through it, even those small flecks rapidly melting into the unity of her mindlock's shield. Charm stirred at their touch as they passed her by.

Oram went on, out and out, finding his Firedrinkers. Brighter, familiar to him, familiar to her. They searched until they had them all, and the Firedrinkers lay in her perception like an array of bright water drops suspended in a web. She could see other minds too, the soft glow of what Oram's perception termed civilian minds. Many of those were scarred and oozing like skin with burns made over and over in the same place.

"Aerleas's men," she realized aloud.

Oram's mind reached out, steering her to the nearest bright star of the Firedrinkers stirring at the orchard gate. He touched, and suddenly she was surrounded by a whirling rush of relief and renewal. Joy. Their captain was back. She was with them. Hundreds of minds surrounded her like old friends. Indeed, old friends. They had names, beings. John. Familiar faces. Annabelle with her red hair. She knew them. Every one of them, and they knew her, cared for her. There were gaps in the fabric of them, places where minds should be but weren't anymore. All over the city Firedrinkers began to stagger up to their feet.

Begin the cleanup, Oram told them. *The general is gone, they'll be off center. One pyro per squad to ensure they can't fire their guns. Engage them and drive them. Tell Uncle Luther we are retaking the city. Bring the right flank in against the army, sweep them up to the Lowtown gate. Accept any who surrender. Those who suicide against you, don't hesitate to grant their desire. I'm on my way.*

The bright minds at the palace reeled in dazed disarray. Oram sent, *Secure the palace. Let no one leave.* The Firedrinkers at the palace began to right themselves, moving to obey their captain.

The web of stars fell away, fading but not entirely gone. She could still feel them at the edges of her perception, now that she was aware of them. The other minds of the city, too. She kept herself gently around Oram's mind, like her arms around him, or her fingers combing his hair.

For a moment she and Oram were suspended in quiet. She and he simply together. His kiss caressed her mind instead of her battered lips, light as a butterfly's wing. He traced light hands up and down her back for a moment as his mind whispered across hers, exploring and caressing until she moaned, sagging against his support. He kissed her temple, but it touched her swelling bruises and she flinched. *I'm sorry I was so slow getting to you. It was harder than I expected to wake.*

I'll heal, she assured him. She didn't doubt it. She would recover.

What shall I call you? he asked gently.

She wasn't quite Pain. Pain was a fragment of Charm. An empty place. She'd outgrown it. *You called me Mercy, once. I like that better than Pain.*

My Lady Mercy. Oram breathed across a place in her brain that made her shiver, then drew back, leaving a lingering impression of his caress.

She laughed, low and shaky. "Are you teasing me?" she asked in a whisper.

"We will have our time," he promised her.

A Firedrinker pushed his way gently through the crowd to drape his cloak around his captain. Covered, Captain Oram stepped away from Mercy's concealing skirt.

Empress Ylsbeth was sitting on the bench by the laboratory. Outside the gate, people milled in confusion. Far away there was still screaming. The Firedrinkers outside the gate regained their feet.

"Should you go see how Charm is doing?" Oram asked Mercy.

"I'm quite well, Captain, thank you."

They turned to see Charm making her way through the orchard. She stopped, leaning on the slender swallow-bone tree. "You'll want to arrest Countess Seabrough," she told them serenely. "She killed our emperor."

Standing by the laboratory with Ylsbeth, the Countess froze. "What? How dare you accuse me, you gold-digging trollop!"

"I think that's the pot calling the kettle black, don't you?" asked Charm, raising one amused eyebrow. "I've known it was you since you shook my hand at the Empress's birthday masque. It took me a little while to figure out that you were in on the Aerleas scheme because Strephon called you 'Seabrough,' but Her Imperial Majesty referred to you that way the night of the ball. Strephon didn't mean Count Seabrough. He meant Countess Seabrough. You were in the palace all the time, with access to everything. Strephon couldn't possibly have had a better conspirator."

"Where is Emperor Strephon? What have you done to him?" demanded the Countess.

"I did nothing to him," said Charm with cool satisfaction. "He's dead upstairs in my bedroom chair from taking the Rejuv you so generously sent me. I grant you it's an indirect killing, more of an accidental homicide since he wasn't your actual target, but you have killed him very thoroughly. You did quite well blindsiding my emperor, and you almost succeeded in murdering your husband; but I'm disappointed, Countess, in your opinion of me. Did you really think I wouldn't detect the tampering with those capsules?"

"I have no motive for such a thing!" the Countess shouted.

"There is no woman who wants vengeance more than the one who's lost a child," said Charm softly. "Only two Firedrinkers ever came from Uptown. One is Captain Oram, son of Aerleas and grandson of my emperor . . . and the other is your son. John Seabrough. Because my emperor was only at Orchard House on Tuesdays, and even then he didn't want sex until he'd broken with you over his actual youngest son—John. That's why the Count was so well educated about mindlocks. Because he'd looked into it and judged it the better course. The Emperor took John away to save his sanity, and mindlocked him, and you never saw him again. He was, to some perceptions, as good as dead."

"Shut up, you, you . . ." the Countess spluttered in rage.

"Whore, strumpet, gold-digging trollop . . . you may be running out of vocabulary. All you have to do is say that you did not poison the Emperor," said Charm softly. "That's all, and Captain Oram or one of his people will know it for the truth."

"I told you she'd find out," Ylsbeth said from the bench, her voice full of chill satisfaction. She looked at Captain Oram. "I didn't realize what she'd done until after I was bullied into marrying Strephon."

Countess Seabrough stared at Ylsbeth openmouthed, and went a horrible shade of gray.

"The Empress is telling the truth," said one of the Firedrinkers.

"The Countess has already admitted to letting Prince Aerleas into the city," said Mercy.

The Firedrinkers at the gate moved toward the Countess. Countess Seabrough jerked a derringer out of the concealing ruffles in her bell-shaped sleeve and pointed it at the Empress. The Firedrinkers froze.

"Countess Seabrough, you can't hope to accomplish anything by this. Please give me your weapon," said Oram quietly, but it was only his clear, calm voice. There was no compulsion in the command.

"I want a boat to take me to Devarik," Countess Seabrough

said. "That is all I want. Come, Ylsbeth. I'll take you home," she coaxed, as if the Empress were a puppy or a child. "It's what you want, isn't it? To be able to go home?"

"Shoot me if you like, but I'm done being your hostage." Ylsbeth, tall and fine-spun as spiderwebs, pushed her pale hair back with one hand. Her lip curled in defiance. "You are the most evil woman in the world!"

Charm slid her hand into her pocket. Carefully, she drew out Nathair's revolver and kept it close in the folds of her skirt.

"Countess, please. You will have a trial to defend yourself." One of the Firedrinkers edged forward, hand out pleadingly.

The derringer rose as the Countess aimed. Without hesitation, the Firedrinker stepped between Ylsbeth and the Countess. Countess Seabrough fired. The Firedrinker staggered back into the Empress's arms as the other Firedrinker leaped forward. Charm squeezed the trigger of Nathair's revolver. It boomed through the derringer's smaller report and Countess Seabrough slammed sideways, weapon spinning out of her hand as she fell. Charm lowered the smoking revolver.

Ylsbeth eased the Firedrinker to the grass as their companion leaped to snatch up the derringer before Countess Seabrough could try to grasp for it.

"John!" Mercy ran to the injured Firedrinker.

"John?" Countess Seabrough coughed, tried to drag herself up, pressing her hand over the spreading stain on her side. Blood frothed on her lips. "Johnny?"

Empress Ylsbeth jerked open the Firedrinker's red coat as Mercy eased off his helmet. John Seabrough groaned softly, and Mercy gathered his head into her lap. Charm came to join them, tipping her head, gently pushing away Mercy's and Ylsbeth's hands to open his shirt. "There's no blood. The body armor held," she told them.

"Will he be all right?" asked Ylsbeth, coming to help

Charm. They eased John onto his side and unlatched the buckles of his armor. His breathing calmed as the dent stopped compressing his chest.

Charm probed carefully down his side. "Just cracked or broken ribs, I think," she said. "Stay still, John, until we can get them stabilized." She stood up and went to Countess Seabrough, who lay unmoving with her eyes fixed on her son. "You can put the gun away," Charm told the Firedrinker keeping the Countess covered. Gently, she closed the dead woman's eyes.

Lying in the grass, his head in Mercy's lap and Empress Ylsbeth tending him, tears slid down John Seabrough's temples.

CHAPTER FORTY-THREE

Mercy, who had been Pain, stroked John's forehead gently. She could feel him, one of the points in the misty web of Firedrinkers. She eased the pain in his ribs. His comrades, soft and warm and supporting around her mind, held him gently for the other pain.

"Your Imperial Majesty," said Captain Oram to the Empress, "with these walls and the gates, and the Firedrinkers here, Orchard House is a secure location. Would you be content to wait here until we have the situation at the palace and in the streets resolved?"

"Thank you, Captain, that would be quite acceptable," Ylsbeth said.

"Forgive me for commandeering your home, Lady Charm," Oram added.

"No apologies are needed. We'll get John plastered up, and figure out anything else when and as we need to," Charm assured Oram. "Do you happen to know if Prince Phelan is all right?"

Oram paused. Pain felt him reach, felt the answer before Oram spoke. "He was taken by the same madness as the rest of the city. He died of the injuries he inflicted on himself trying to bash down his cell door."

"I hope you won't think me rude when I say that is a great relief," said Charm.

Oram went to crouch by the Duchess of Madderley with

sadness on his long face. Before he could touch her there was a tremendous, wheezing gasp. He leaped back in surprise, then crouched again, cautiously. "Auntie A?"

A horrible metallic wheeze of a laugh came from the corpse. "Still here, apparently."

"Auntie A?" Charm echoed, smiling at the endearment he applied to the Duchess.

"She's not my actual aunt. She's a cousin."

"No, I'd realized that. John, please don't try to get up. I'll be right back with something to wrap your ribs." Charm gave the wounded man a smile and rose, dusting grass off her skirt as she hurried toward the greenhouse.

Aiglentine Nathair sat up, examined the hole in the front of their uniform, felt the back, and sighed. Oram offered a hand and pulled them to their feet. Nathair got a look at Mercy's face, made a wincing hiss of sympathy. They surveyed Empress Ylsbeth and John Seabrough on the ground, and took in the dented armor in the grass. "Well. Charm's gone for the bandages, I believe several of us can also use some ice." They strode away toward the kitchen.

"Until later," Oram told Mercy. He sketched a bow, and headed out the gate.

The Firedrinkers covered Countess Seabrough's body before taking up duty at the orchard gate, and Charm, Mercy, and Ylsbeth between them got John bandaged. The Duchess shooed them off John to help him through the orchard, up the back stairs, and into one of the second-floor beds. They followed along like anxious hens.

If Ylsbeth realized what sort of room she was in, she gave no sign. "If you'd like, I'll sit with Mr. Seabrough," she suggested. "I want to talk to him a little while . . ." She trailed off. "I'm sorry, I'm afraid we've not been introduced," she apologized to Charm's last ghost.

"I'm Mercy," the albino said.

"If Your Majesty needs anything, the bell pull will bring one of us. Or feel free to come downstairs when you're ready. We'll likely be in the kitchen," Charm told her. "Duchess, there's no hope at all that any female clothing in this house will fit you, but if you like there are some clothes in the closet next door. The Firedrinkers often leave us their laundry. What's there is waiting for its owners, so it's in all kind of sizes."

In the kitchen, Charm fetched a cup of spent empathy fluid from the laboratory. It would grow no more bodies, but it had saved Oram, and Charm saw no reason not to use it. Particularly knowing where it was from. It would be wrong to waste it. Charm carefully smoothed the fluid over Mercy's battered face.

"You're a mess, but I don't see anything too serious." Charm's smile wobbled a little, but she breathed and steadied. "Hopefully this will keep the swelling from getting worse."

"Thank you," murmured Mercy.

Charm attended to her own bruises and swollen mouth. Then, for a little while, they just sat by the table with the clock ticking, the kettle warming, and the empty trees in the orchard whispering to themselves outside. It felt to Charm as if eternity had passed in the last few hours. ". . . Mercy?" she asked finally.

"Yes?"

Charm chuckled. "No, I meant why 'Mercy'?"

"It's what he said I should have been named." And then, "I'm the last one. The only one who's still outside of you. I don't know where Pride went. She was just suddenly gone."

"She's here, or I'm here and Pride is a part of me, or I'm part of her . . ." Charm gave up. "I'm all the pieces of myself again, finally; except for you."

"What shall I call you?" asked Mercy.

Silence fell between them like the stillness of old bones. "Just Charm." Charm spoke carefully, afraid that somehow she'd slip, and something precious would be broken. "Pride wasn't meant for your body. When Aerleas split her off from you, she came back to this body the same as Shame, Justice, Desire, and the Lady. Pride was easier than some of me. We'd grown so much alike."

Mercy smiled a little at that. "You're you again." The smile fled again. "Except you don't have me with you, and I don't want to be you." She'd said the words before, but now she was sure in them. "And it isn't that I don't love you, or some parts of you, but I . . ."

"You are, as I told you when I was Pride, too much yourself," said Charm. A rueful quirk lifted the corner of her mouth. "You don't have any of my memories except the actually physical hurt, and you didn't even bear any of the guilt for those. You began as an emptiness, and all your experiences are only yours. I don't need an empty place now. It scares me to be without it," she admitted, "but I'm not going to let another person carry my hurt. You're a separate person now; so much so that you have your own name, and a rather lean, slightly sticky gentleman who loves you as you." She paused and tipped her head at the rosy blush that crept up Mercy's face.

Mercy clamped a hand over her mouth for a moment, giggling. Her scarlet eyes shone with tears.

Charm went on. "I wouldn't feel right taking your life away from you. So . . . welcome to the world." Charm smiled in spite of the pinch in her throat. Something that was hers, and not Pain's.

The fragility in the air seemed to fall away with Mercy's shaky smile. "Thank you."

A creak on the stairs and light footsteps announced Empress

Ylsbeth and the Duchess coming down. The Empress paused as she saw the two of them. "We're interrupting. Forgive me."

"Not at all. We'd just finished, I think. Come sit. Mercy was about to make tea, and I believe I want a sherry. What sort of beverage can I get for the two of you?" asked Charm, rising.

"Tea, please," said the Empress with gratitude in her tone. "Miss . . . ?"

"Mercy," said Charm firmly.

"Miss Mercy. Officer Seabrough has asked for you."

"I'll take him up some tea." Mercy assembled a pot to brew for the table, and then a second pot. She put it and two cups on a tray, taking it quietly away up the servants' stair.

Charm watched her go. Mercy would go on carrying pain for others. For Oram and for the Firedrinkers. But that was Mercy's choice and Charm could not make it for her. There were, of course, complications. Mercy was not quite human, for all she so clearly wanted to be. She could not have children. Charm would make sure the Assembly didn't weep about that or try to force some other bride on Oram. It would be easy to point out to Hanover that if the Assembly got into the habit of electing the emperors, they would retain a great deal of the Imperial power. It was the least Charm could do for her child.

The Duchess, still in guise as Major Nathair, was in a fresh shirt, with their own breeches and boots. They sat down and stretched out their long legs with a weary sigh. "If you're having something stronger than tea, and you have any, I'd have a brandy."

Charm brought the drinks to the table and sat down. "What will you do now, Majesty?" Charm asked the Empress.

"Stay, if I can. I'm not sure the Assembly will let me. Uptown all blamed me for the stupid tariff trade-offs with Devarik, the jewels, the expenses . . . I asked him not to do any of those things. He said I was reflecting badly on him, that I should be more grand," Ylsbeth said with frustration. She wrapped her hands around her teacup and smiled thanks.

"I think you'll find that the Assembly will change their minds now that Strephon's gone and be happy to blame him," said Charm. "Most of them aren't bad men. Just not very courageous. You won't go home, though, Your Majesty? Countess Seabrough seemed to think that was what you wanted—not that she seemed to really know."

Ylsbeth shrugged. "Our Emperor gave me a country house, which I'm told is rather nice. I've never been there, but I can fix a house if I don't like it. If I went back to Devarik I'd be . . . well. No matter what, I was a bed-tribute to someone who didn't quite conquer Devarik. I will never be able to repair my reputation, there. At least here I could try to just live quietly."

"Retire in shame at what's been done to you and never be seen again?" asked Charm, and regretted it instantly. "I'm sorry."

"No, no. You're right that it isn't admirable, but not everyone has your courage."

Charm choked on a laugh.

Major Nathair smiled at Charm across their brandy. "No," they said softly, "not everyone does."

"I'll tell you what not everyone does," said Charm, hastily diverting. "Not everyone is shot through the lungs and gets back up." She looked pointedly at the Duchess.

Nathair lifted their shoulders. "That's my gift. I am persistent. I bled out in childbirth when I was sixteen, and since then I've always reanimated. I've been shot, stabbed, burned, beheaded, disemboweled, and dismembered. None of it was pleasant, but more crucially none of it was permanent."

"Not poisoned?" asked Charm, teasing with some care.

"If anyone's tried it, it didn't do anything to me." They

lifted the brandy snifter in a toast and smiled before they sipped again.

"And what will you do now, Duchess?" The Empress seemed eager to get away from the ghoulish subject, and, as Charm had just done much the same thing, Charm couldn't really object.

"It will depend on what Emperor Oram . . . I presume they'll make him emperor. It's the obvious thing, and the Assembly does tend to leap to the obvious. What I will do depends what Oram decides to do with any of the army who are in Boren and who might have survived. They're welcome to execute me a few times if it makes anyone feel better, but if I can supply a sufficiently talented, low-power, high-manipulation telekinetic for Boren, I can probably do whatever I'd like. I know four, and surely one or two of them would be able to do the surgeries to implant mindlocks. The orders are a beargarden, I grant. I don't know how to guarantee someone is trustworthy to set the bloody things."

"Bern Ostander thinks he can make the mindlocks in such a way that they don't have a control portion," said Charm. "He told Mercy so. I assume it was you who blew up the Rejuv labs?"

"Being that I am not encumbered with any temptation attached to it, I decided I was best suited to decide how to proceed in the case. It was one of the more satisfying moments of my existence," they confirmed.

"Which still leaves the question open," said Ylsbeth, not to be diverted this time. "What will you do, Duchess? Captain Oram seemed to have a care for you. I doubt he'll imprison you. You could come with me, if you like. I very much enjoyed our short acquaintance."

"I have enjoyed spending time with Your Imperial Majesty,

and I would happily visit; but I confess I am tired of the country. I imagine there's going to be a lot of work to do, cleaning up the mess in Inshil. And I'm one of Aerleas's senior staff, after all. The ones remaining that I can't persuade back to sanity, I can get close enough to at least . . . give them a little mercy." Nathair was silent for a moment. Grim and hard. The sharpened, battle-tried sword. "I cannot deny having helped make the mess, and now that Aerleas is gone there's much I can do to clean it up. I suspect I'll be back and forth between here and Inshil for some time. It's your turn now," said Nathair to Charm. "What will you do?"

Charm blinked and laughed. "Me? Great heavens, you don't think I'd close this place? Unless you want your house back?"

Nathair shook their head, though there was a flash, for a moment, of something in their eyes. "It's much too thoroughly yours."

"Then let us decide that you are welcome at any time. We will make you up your own room on the third floor, a permanent apartment in case you tire of the palace or need another place. There's no reason it can't be just as grand as the rooms on the second floor." She smiled. "I'll even have a hot bath plumbed in, so you can warm up your cold hands."

"You'll have to hire more help," Nathair pointed out.

"There are always those who need work where they'll have hot meals, a roof, and their share of the earnings." Charm lifted her chin. "I shall not let our standards slip."

"Will you go on offering intimate services?" asked Nathair.

"Not personally, but I'm certainly going to take suggestions from my employees about what should be available on the second floor." She shrugged, smiling.

Nathair's thin lips lifted suddenly. "Are you going to let me keep coming to the card parlor to play? My secret seems likely to get out, after everything that's happened today."

"If it does not you can simply come down in trousers one day with your hair pinned on and we shall dare them to think what they may."

Nathair laughed. Their tinny amusement was at least, thought Charm, honest. "You'll make me scandalous."

"Will you mind that?" asked Charm. "The scandal of it won't last, you know. Everyone will get used to you after a while, but Mr. Anders would get a positive kick out of championing you in the meantime. Whether your scandalousness became fame or infamy would be entirely up to you."

"You make putting one's finger in the eye of polite society deeply tempting. What will Count Seabrough say about all your plans?"

"Whatever he wishes to, naturally; but I have no plans to change my independent state, if that's what you're asking. And I have reason to think he does not begrudge other people the same practicality he practices."

"And so you, Lady Charm, will go on exactly as you are, and sotto voce influence Boren's politics," said Ylsbeth softly.

Charm unlimbered her most sparkling and dimpled smile. "I don't know what you could possibly mean, Your Imperial Majesty. But please . . . I prefer to be simply Charm."

ACKNOWLEDGMENTS

I wrote this book over ten years, across four surgeries. The support I've had has been magnificent and humbling. My husband and my son had faith in my writing before I did. Fran Wilde refused to let me quit, and kept swinging for this book when I was too tired to lift my arms anymore. DongWon Song took up the banner and never let it fall. Miriam Weinberg, Devi Pillai, and a small army at Tor went into battle for this book in the midst of a pandemic.

I think I may've bribed or begged everyone I know into reading at least small chunks of this book. Those who didn't read it had to hear me talk about it. Some inspired me, some brought me food and ice packs, or watched my son, or otherwise kept me going. This is a very incomplete list—

David Tavakoli, Vrin Thomasino, Todd Worrell, Claire Eddy, Walter Jon Williams, Nancy Kress, Chris East, Lauren Teffeau, Chris Gerwel, Kelly Lagor, Sandra Wickham, Nicole Feldringer, Maura Glynn-Thami, Pat Scaramuzza, Corry Lee, Lia Bass, Rebecca Stevenson, Catherine Schaff-Stump, David D. Levine, Denny Bershaw, Jim Fiscus, John Bunnell, Gary Quay, Paul Schilling, M. K. Hobson, Robin Catesby, Kami Miller, Jeff Nicholas, Rhiannon Rasmussen, Tre Luna, Douglas Watson, Sandi Gray, Sonja Bolon, Corinna Bolon, George Walker, Jennifer McGinnis, Francine Taylor, Sarina Dorie, Phyl Radford, Simone Cooper, Amy Wood, Mickey Schultz, Kath Nyborg, Felicity Shoulders, Liz Argal, Jennifer Gibbons, Diane Nelson, Megan Cantras Lane, Julian Christopher Geritz, Holly Jarr, Kim Dewey, DeAnna

Riehl, Kris Fazzari, Michele Ray, Salli Ortiz, Julia Mueller Tayler, Carol Mueller, Cymry DeBoucher, Thornton Stone, Grace Poulsen.

And those who didn't live to see the day—Jon Elizabeth Frey, Alexander Forbes, and Gerald Warfield.

SARA A. MUELLER writes speculative fiction in the green and rainy Pacific Northwest, where she lives with her family, numerous recipe books, and a forest of fountain pens. In a nomadic youth, she trod the earth of every state but Alaska and lived in six of them. She's an amateur historical costumer, gamer, and cook. Mueller has spoken on panels at multiple Pacific NW cons on costume/clothing, horses, invisible disability, world-building, and aspects of literature and writing. *The Bone Orchard* is her debut novel from Tor Books.